ANOTHER

CU00829570

SHARI LOW lives in Glasgow and writes a weekly opinion column and Book Club page for a well known newspaper. She is married to a very laid-back guy and has two athletic teenage sons, who think she's fairly embarrassing, except when they need a lift.

ANOTHER DAY IN WINTER

SHARI LOW

www.ariafiction.com

First published in the United Kingdom in 2018 by Aria, an imprint of
Head of Zeus Ltd

9 7 5 3 1 2 4 6 8

A CIP catalogue record for this book is available from the British
Library.

ISBN 9781788541428

Aria, an imprint of Head of Zeus
First Floor East
5–8 Hardwick Street
London EC1R 4RG

Also by Shari Low

A Life Without You
With or Without You
The Other Wives Club

The Story of Our Life

<u>A Winter Day Trilogy</u>

One Day in December
Another Day in Winter

<u>Non-fiction</u>

Because Mummy Said So

About *Another Day in Winter*

On a chilly morning in December...

Forever friends Shauna and Lulu touch down at
Glasgow Airport on a quest to find answers
from the past.

George knows his time is nearing the end, but is it too
late to come to terms with his two greatest regrets?

His Grandson Tom uncovers a betrayal that rocks his
world as he finally tracks down the one that got away.

And single mum Chrissie is ready to force her love-life
out of hibernation, but can anyone compare to the
man who broke her heart?

Many of my past novels have been dedicated to Rosina Hill, my beloved aunt, god-mother, irrepressible cheerleader and unfailing friend. Now she is gone, far too soon, leaving a world that just doesn't seem right without her.

This book is for her.

Before she died, Rosina said that as one life ends, another one begins.

Welcome to the world, Aila Emma Murphy.

This is for you too.

And finally, to John, Callan & Brad.

Everything. Always.

Once Upon A Time There Was...

Shauna O'Flynn, 41 – widow of Colm O'Flynn, mum to Beth (8) and London-born granddaughter of Annie (Butler) Williams.

Lulu Channing, 41 – Shauna's lifelong friend, much loved despite being prone to barbed bitchiness and eternal cynicism.

Annie (Butler) Williams – deceased. Raucous, irreverent Glaswegian, granny to Shauna, sister of George and Flora.

Tom Butler, 31 – business partner of Davie Bailey in the marketing company, The B Agency, loving grandson of George Thomas Butler.

Davie Bailey, 30 – marketing guru; suave, successful and a serial shagger.

Zoe Danton, 32 – Tom's girlfriend and super-sharp sales director at The B Agency.

Norry Butler, 61 – Tom's father, self-made businessman, behind the door when the

universe was handing out family loyalty.

Rosemary Butler, 54 – Norry Butler's second wife.

George Thomas Butler, 85 – beloved grandfather, ignored father, brother to Annie and Flora.

Flora (Butler) McGinty, 82 – sister of George and Annie, wife to Arthur McGinty.

Chrissie Harrison, 31 – single mum of Ben, has finally decided to take her love life out of cold storage.

Ben Harrison, 12 – Chrissie's sometimes pragmatic, occasionally cool, always adorable son.

Val Murray, 60s – Chrissie's next door neighbour and all-round fairy godmother.

Josie Cairney, 70s – Val's straight talking best friend and partner in crime.

Friday 21 December

8 a.m. – 10 a.m.

One

Shauna

The flight attendant had one of those sing-song voices. 'Ladies and gentlemen, welcome to Glasgow. The weather outside is currently...'

'Raining,' Shauna said.

'...Raining, and the temperature is...'

'Bloody freezing,' Lulu added.

'Zero degrees. For those of you travelling onwards this morning...'

Shauna and Lulu zoned out of the rest of the announcement, gathering up their belongings and packing everything back into the handbags that had been obediently placed under the seat in front. Shauna glanced around at her fellow travellers, wondering how many of them were coming home to spend Christmas with the people they loved, to be with their families. It was the twenty-first of December, the last Friday before the crackers came out and, perhaps she was just being sentimental, but it felt like there was a buzz of happy

13

anticipation, despite the fact that the day had barely begun.

The seatbelt sign pinged off and almost all of the other passengers immediately jumped to their feet, ready for the exit scrum. Shauna and Lulu sat where they were. It would be at least ten minutes until the doors were opened so what was the point of jostling?

'Is it wrong that I want Scotland to live up to the stereotypes?' Lulu mused, while slipping her second bottle of on-board wine into the sumptuous red suede tote she brought out every year for the month of December. 'I want ten burly men in kilts clutching trays of shortbread and bottles of whisky to greet me as I disembark.'

Shauna nodded. 'Don't worry. They're sending them for me. Apparently it's all part of the service for Scottish descendants travelling here for the first time.'

The irony was that with her wild mane of red hair and creamy pale complexion, Lulu was the one who looked more likely to have Scottish heritage, despite the fact that she didn't have a relative north of Watford. Shauna's Glaswegian granny, Annie, had a glorious mane of auburn hair before the grey had set in, but those flame-haired follicles hadn't made it through the gene pool to Shauna, who'd been bestowed with a shade of mousy brown that had demanded blonde highlights every eight weeks since the beginning of time.

Shauna still found it bizarre that this was her first visit to Annie's homeland. She'd grown up not too far from her grandmother in Wimbledon, about half an hour south of where she lived now in the London borough of Richmond upon Thames, and – strange as it now seemed – Annie had very rarely mentioned her Scottish roots and her childhood in Glasgow. Only now, with the benefit of hindsight, did Shauna wish she'd asked why. As it was, there had been few details and any questions were met with hazy answers. Her granny was an only child, she'd said. Her parents had passed away years ago. Shauna hadn't realised it at the time, but looking back through a lens of maturity, she could see that Annie had kept that early chapter firmly closed, instead waxing lyrical about the next stage of her life. After a few festive Babychams, Annie would retell all her favourite stories of the trip to London on which she met Shauna's grandfather, Ernie, at a party, and within six months they'd married and set up home in Wimbledon. She said they chose to settle there so she could get in the queue early to watch the tennis every year. Annie was funny, she was fierce, she said exactly what she thought and she revelled in being absolutely outrageous, but she was also loyal to a fault and would fight any battle for the people she loved. That's what made it all the more incomprehensible that she'd had a family in Scotland that she'd walked away from and – worse – kept hidden for decades.

15

Annie had died back in 2009 but Shauna had only found the letters a few months ago, when she decided to take one of Annie's beautiful old handbags to a wedding. Inside, she'd found a slim sheaf of letters, bound with a red velvet ribbon, between Annie and her family members, her brother, George, and sister, Flora, in Scotland. Shauna had been truly shocked and intrigued. Why had Annie never mentioned them? Why had she spent a lifetime hiding her past? The mystery had given Shauna something to think about, to take her mind off... Colm.

She stopped, catching her breath. Two years, three months and twenty days. That's how long it had been since her beautiful, funny, intoxicating, Irish husband closed his eyes for the last time and her world had stopped. A brain tumour. One minute he was there and they had a family, a fifteen year marriage, endless love, naive hope that he would beat it... and then he was gone, taking a piece of her heart that had never returned.

In the first few months, she'd have stayed under the duvet from morning until night if it wasn't for Beth, their daughter, who was six when she lost her dad. Shauna had done everything she could to keep Colm alive in Beth's memory, and her girl had shown that childhood resilience and shrugged off the cloak of loss as the weeks moved on, finding happiness in everyday life.

Shauna had failed to find the same peace.

Only in the last few months could she think of him without a searing shock of pain gripping her heart. In truth, that was one of the reasons she'd been delighted when Lulu had volunteered to come with her this weekend, figuring her friend's predominant personality traits of cynicism, sarcasm, humour and flippancy would stop her sinking into sadness and sorrow. God knows, she'd had enough of that over the last few years.

It had almost been a relief when she'd closed the door on her flat overlooking Richmond Green this morning and drove the eight miles to London's Heathrow Airport. She'd moved to the flat from a house a few streets away after Colm passed away. It was upstairs from the duplex owned by Lulu and her husband Dan and it helped to have them in the same building, gave Beth a sense of family. Although, it would also have given her daughter a sense of a few great swear words if she'd been around to hear her mum rouse Auntie Lulu from her bed at 5.30 a.m. this morning, to head to Heathrow.

Today all sorrow was put to one side. She was going to a city that she'd never visited with Colm or anyone else. No memories here. No sentimental nostalgia. He'd never breathed Glaswegian air. This was somewhere new, where the only experiences would be the ones that Shauna and Lulu encountered before they flew back home tomorrow.

At the front of the plane, just beyond the flashing reindeer antlers propped on the grey haired bouffants of two elderly ladies in the front row, a stewardess was trying to suppress her understandable annoyance at the passengers who were already pushing their way forward, despite the fact that the doors were still not yet open.

Lulu leaned towards her. 'It must take every ounce of discipline and tact not to pick up that tannoy and make an announcement along the lines of, "Ladies and gentlemen, you may have noticed that there's nowhere to fucking go yet, so sit your impatient, unreasonable arses right back down in your seats."'

'There's a reason you don't have a job that involves dealing with the public,' Shauna replied, trying not to give in to laughter. It only encouraged Lulu to express more opinions.

There were several simultaneous beeps from nearby phones and they reminded Shauna to switch off airplane mode. As soon as she did, a picture message flashed up. Beth. At eight, she was already so tall, with Colm's dark hair and his green eyes. Colm, however, had never possessed a pair of Minnie Mouse ears, an Ariel costume, nor posed for a photo holding up a large, furry Daisy Duck.

Shauna immediately turned the phone to let Lulu see the picture.

'Aah, she's gorgeous,' Lulu said. 'And I'm not going to say that her Auntie Rosie is trying to buy your

18

daughter's affection. Nope, not saying that at all.'

'Good,' Shauna replied, with a raised eyebrow of scepticism. For over twenty years, Rosie had been the third friend in their trio. She'd slotted right into their group when Shauna and Lulu met her as teenagers, and their childhood duo became an adult trio. The three of them had developed a bond that was as close as sisters. Which was just as well, because like any family, they'd had a few dramatic ups and downs along the way. Somehow, though, their friendships always managed to get through everything life threw at them, and most importantly, Rosie and Lulu were incredible godmothers to Beth. Although, she couldn't remember it being in the christening vows that spiritual guidance included whisking your godchild off for a freebie weekend in Disneyland Paris, thanks to Rosie's new boyfriend being a travel writer who had received a personal invitation to an audience with a Mr M. Mouse. But hey, if a 1000 word article in an in-flight magazine got Beth the weekend of her dreams, it was worth it.

She texted back,

Gorgeous! Miss you so much! Hope you're having a fabulous time sweetheart. Love you!

and was rewarded with ten love hearts and a happy face emoji.

Shauna thought of a late comeback to Lulu's comment. 'Anyway, can I remind you that it was you who bought my daughter an iPhone for Christmas and then gave it to her early? Just saying…'

Lulu adopted her very best innocent face. 'That was purely for safety purposes. I was looking after her well being.'

'You were trying to be the super-cool, favourite auntie,' Shauna countered. She was touched that her friends were so kind to her daughter, and yes, they probably spoiled her more than a little, but Beth was a grounded, non-materialistic little kid who had been through so much when she lost her dad. A little bit of indulgence from her aunts wasn't going to ruin her.

'Absolutely not,' Lulu objected, before adding, 'but I'm way ahead of the competition. Even if they are bribing her with Minnie bloody Mouse ears.'

The doors finally opened at the front of the plane and the line of passengers slowly began to move forwards. Still, Shauna and Lulu sat. Another five minutes would clear the queues in front of them, and then they could disembark and head straight out of the airport, as they were travelling light with just hand luggage. Shauna's cabin bag was one she'd bought sometime back in the nineties, while Lulu's was brand new and came with Gucci tags. That pretty much summed up the difference between them.

Shauna slipped her phone into her bag, her fingers touching the letters as she did so. They were old, written back in the fifties, way before Shauna was born. She'd read them so often she knew them off by heart, but there was one that she thought of more than the others, one that had lingered in her mind long after she'd read it.

32 Parkland Street
Glasgow

Dear Annie,

Forgive me. I know that is more than I deserve, and that I have no right to ask... I have no defence for what I did to you, no excuses for my actions, for I always knew he was yours. I can only hope that in time the pain of my betrayal will lessen and you'll find a way to think of me fondly once again.

Sorry.

Your sister,

Flora

The first time Shauna had read it, she'd flinched as she got to the end. *Your sister.* How many times over the years had Annie made the comment that one of the things they had in common was that they had no siblings? And yet, there it was. *Your sister.*

And Flora wasn't the only one. In the letters, Shauna had discovered an entire family. As far as she could tell, there were three siblings in total – two sisters and one brother – her brother and sister both a similar age to

21

Annie. Parents were mentioned too. It was all there – Annie had a family, one that she had left and never went back to. And Shauna wanted to know why.

Actually, it was more than that. She wanted a connection to someone. Anyone. She wanted to give Beth relatives, history, a family tree, now that there was just the two of them. They travelled to Dublin to see Colm's family in Ireland once a year but they'd never been close and they rarely heard from them between visits. The only living relative Shauna now had was her mum, Debbie, and that paragon of self-centred shallowness was currently living in Marbella with a wealthy, paunchy, retired businessman who looked exactly like Shauna's late father and – like her dad – spent his days playing golf. Shauna received the occasional call from her in the rare moments her mother had free between shopping, spa days and throwing dinner parties for other expats who were exactly like them – wealthy, entitled, and totally self-indulgent. Debbie was no loss; Shauna had always fell somewhere below international travel, a daily blow-dry and early evening gin and tonics on her priority list. That's why Annie, her dad's mother, had stepped in and been more of a parent than the DNA donors that created her.

A surrogate parent who had, it now seemed, told her a pack of lies about her background. Disbelief had come first, then a flash of intrigue, with a topping of incredulity. Annie was the most forthright, honest,

22

loving and loyal person Shauna had ever known, so if she'd kept this a secret there must be a good reason why.

The mystery had nibbled at Shauna's curiosity, so when Rosie had scooped Beth away for a weekend of commercialised cartoon characters, she'd thought about coming here for the first time, but a booking by one of her regular clients to provide a Christmas lunch for thirty had stopped her. She'd scaled back her catering business after she became Beth's sole caretaker. Gone were the children's birthday parties, the weddings, christenings, soirees and dinner parties. Now, she only took on corporate clients and worked Monday to Friday. At first it had made a big dent in her income, but as word spread, she'd gained more and more professional business – functions, office lunches, board meetings. Her balance sheet was finally as healthy as her work-life balance, so she hadn't minded when today's lunch had been cancelled due to a flu epidemic at the client's offices earlier in the week.

On the night that the cancellation had come in, after a couple of glasses of wine, she'd re-read the letters and the next thing she knew, she was on the internet, on the British Airways website, and using the loyalty points she'd accumulated over the years to book a trip to visit her granny's homeland. A trip for two. Lulu worked part-time, or rather, whenever she felt like it, doing marketing for Dan's company, so she'd been delighted to have an excuse to bunk off. They'd hoped to do Friday to Sunday, but the pre-Christmas rush had squashed that plan. The only free seats were on the first flight up this morning, and then an early flight back tomorrow. They had twenty-four hours to learn something, *anything,* about Annie's life.

As yet, that was as far as the plan went. Shauna had the old letters with addresses and that was it. She'd tried social media, internet research, birth and death registers, and had ascertained that – as far as she could tell – Annie's two siblings were still alive. From the addresses on the letters, she'd located the houses on Google Maps, so they were still standing. It was somewhere to start. However, she had no idea if Annie's relatives were still there, so she was flying by the seat of her pants.

There was a ninety-five per cent chance this quest for living relatives was going to be a complete waste of time, but hey, it gave her something intriguing to do this weekend and took her mind off missing Beth, so how bad could it be?

Besides, it was ages since she'd had time away with Lulu and if all they did was explore a new city, do a bit of Christmas shopping and drink cocktails, well, that would be absolutely fine. It was better than the alternative, which would mostly involve doing anything at all to stop herself from rehashing memories of every Christmas she'd had with Colm.

The queue in the aisle had cleared, so Shauna and Lulu finally disembarked and made their way through

Glasgow Airport, stopping when they exited the glass sliding doors in front of the taxi rank. And yes, it was cold, and yes, it was raining, but it didn't dampen Shauna's excitement. Glasgow at Christmas. It was as unexpected as it was thrilling.

'So what's the plan?' Lulu asked, as they headed towards the car at the front of a line of white taxis.

'Let's go and drop these bags at the hotel. We're probably too early to check in, but I'm sure they'll let us store these,' she gestured to the small wheeled cabin bags they were both pulling. 'Then I'd like to go see where her sister sent the letters from because I think there's a good chance that was where Annie grew up. And then maybe go to the address on the other letters too.'

Lulu nodded in agreement. 'I'm down with all of that as long as we get a cocktail in between every step of the mission.'

'Wouldn't dream of doing it any other way,' Shauna replied, feeling a weird sensation of liberation. Back home, she rarely drank alcohol, as most nights were followed by early morning school or sports runs for Beth. It had been way too long since she'd relaxed and been an independent, commitment free grown-up for the day.

She followed Lulu into the taxi. 'The Blythswood Square Hotel, please.' She'd been intending to book a Premier Inn, but at the last moment had decided to treat them to a more luxurious experience – a twin room in one of the city's most lavish hotels. If it all proved to be a waste of time, at least they'd get a hot stone massage and a night in a comfy bed with Egyptian cotton high thread count sheets. Not that she was entirely sure what Egyptian cotton high thread count sheets actually felt like.

The taxi pulled away and Shauna looked towards the hills in the distance as the strangest feeling descended. She'd never been here and yet it all felt weirdly familiar. She half expected to turn a corner and see Annie standing there, waiting for her.

Shauna just hoped that today was the day that her grandmother was ready, finally, to share her secrets.

Two

Tom

Tom held the razor to the man's throat and inhaled deeply to steady his hand. The last thing he wanted to do was draw blood.

'Are you sure you don't want me to do that?' The voice from the doorway was soft, designed not to startle him into any sudden moves.

He pulled back the razor. 'Thanks, but I've got it. I prefer to do it when he's out for the count.'

The nurse, Liv – she insisted on first name terms – stepped forward with a gentle smile. 'He'll be exhausted, Tom. He had a restless night last night. A couple of periods of wakefulness though. Just fleeting, but he managed a few sips of fruit juice and to ask if it's Christmas yet.'

Tom smiled sadly as he foamed up a bit more shaving cream and applied it to his grandfather's face. The nurses took care of all his other needs – changing him, washing him, feeding him – but Tom liked to shave him and brush his silver hair every day. 'I hate this disease, Liv,' he said, stating the obvious.

George Thomas Butler had been diagnosed with bone cancer several years before. It had now spread throughout his body, and the last scan showed the presence of cancer cells in his brain. The combination of the disease and the medication was causing him to slip in and out of consciousness as he approached his final days in the palliative care ward run very efficiently by the charge nurse, Liv Campbell.

Tom had met her on the day that his grandad was transferred from the general ward three weeks ago and they'd struck up an easy friendship. 'A lovely lass, that,' George had stated firmly, after only a day in her care, when he was still well enough to sit and chat for a while. Born in 1933, his grandad was of the generation that didn't give out approvals easily, so Tom knew she had to be a very capable nurse. Liv's husband, Richard Campbell, occasionally popped down too. He was a consultant neurologist, one of the many specialists who had contributed to George's care, an easy going Mancunian who always made time to chat. They made a great couple, the doctor and Liv. It had been impossible to miss their easy going contentment, the instant smiles when they saw each other. Tom had had that once. Only once...

He ran his fingers through his dark hair, an automatic distraction to stop himself revisiting the past. In his head he could hear his grandad telling him to get a haircut, now that the waves were touching the back of his collar. He'd been way too busy with work and caring for George and hadn't been able to find time to get to the barber's for weeks. It wasn't a priority.

'Are your parents on their way?' Liv asked, keeping her voice steady as Tom was back at the job in hand, shaving his grandfather as he'd done every day for the last few weeks, since George had been unable to do it himself. Not an easy task for a thirty year old guy to master, but there had been no blood so far and it was taking less time every morning, so he must be getting the hang of it. Tom wasn't even sure that George was aware he'd been doing it, but it didn't matter. It had always been important to George to be smart, shaved, have a tie on and his shoes polished, so Tom wasn't going to let his grandad's standards slip on his watch.

'Yeah, my dad and stepmother. They're halfway here. They touched down in Dubai a couple of hours ago and their connecting flight took off on time. They should be here about three o'clock.'

He hoped his tone didn't give away the fact that he wasn't relishing the prospect of seeing his father, Norry, and his stepmother, Rosemary. Playing happy families was going to be a challenge. It had never come easily to them in the past and he'd no reason to think it would now. He wasn't even sure that George would want them here, and he'd been even less confident that they would want to come, but he'd decided to call them and let them know, then leave the decision up to them. To his surprise, they'd called back with their flight details.

An unexpected wave of anger got twisted in his gut. He wasn't one to bear grudges, to resort to rage and fury, but the thought of Norry and Rosemary threw up memories of the worst time of his life. On a day to day basis, he could let it be, keep it compartmentalised, act like he'd moved on, but he knew the scar was still there. So was the shame of what he'd done, what they'd persuaded him to do. He'd never forgiven them. Or himself. In a few hours he'd see them for the first time in ten years. He had no grand desire for a family reunion but he'd felt it was the right thing to do for his grandfather, to let them see him, thank him, say goodbye.

He finished off shaving, kissed his grandad's cheek, and spoke softly to him.

'I'll be back soon, Grandad. Just need to head into the office and take care of a few things.'

This had been his routine for the last few weeks. Gone were his evenings at the gym, his five-a-side football sessions with the guys, his nights with Zoe. Colleagues for years – she was the sales director at The B Agency – they'd started seeing each other a couple of months ago, just before George was admitted to the general ward. She was smart, funny, stunning, and she understood that this was where he needed to spend his time now. He owed her some serious attention to make up for being a mainly absent boyfriend.

Thankfully, they were flexible about visiting times on the palliative care ward and didn't mind family members coming and going. The lovely lady in the next room had four people round her bed all day long. Tom was all George had, so he did his best to be there as much as possible. He'd even helped the staff decorate the nurses' station for Christmas a couple of weeks before and he'd put a few of his grandad's favourite decorations in his room, the ones that had come out every year since he was a kid. It was a bittersweet moment, evoking memories of wonderful times in the past, while being a stark reminder that this was the last Christmas they would have together.

He didn't want to waste a moment of it. He'd come to the hospital first thing in the morning and sit with George for a couple of hours, shave him, and read him a few stories from the papers. He made sure he didn't miss any sports or politics stories. George prided himself on keeping up to date with the world around him. After the papers had been covered, Tom would head in to the office in the city centre, stopping on the way for a coffee and to recalibrate his mindset for the day ahead. Marketing was a world where he had to be on the ball and clear headed, keep the creativity sharp and the distractions to a minimum. Luckily, at The B Agency – the company he'd set up after University with his best mate Davie Bailey – they'd just put their biggest campaigns of the year to bed, and their major projects in the pipeline didn't kick off until January. It was an uncustomary lull, but one that was very welcome, because working the usual twelve hour days would be impossible right now. The slack allowed him to spend the morning in the office, sometimes making it back to the hospital for an hour at lunchtime if he could, then he'd work in the afternoon before heading straight there at around six and sitting with George until they switched off the ward lights. This daily schedule had become second nature to him now, and he'd only altered it over the last few nights, when he'd slept overnight in the chair beside his grandad's bed, because he knew they were getting closer to the end and although he was dreading the moment with every fibre of his being, he wasn't going to let George die alone.

Today would be different though. He was only heading to his desk for a few hours this morning, as it was the last day of work before the two week Christmas break. Before they swapped Secret Santa gifts and said goodbyes at the office, there were ties to be broken, truths to be delivered, questions to be answered... and that was before he even got around to dealing with his parents. Facilitating free time to spend with his father and stepmother had never proven to be a good idea. Still, this wasn't about him. It was about the man lying in the bed here and making his final days as comforting and comfortable as possible.

He squeezed George's hand as he said goodbye. It was strange how much easier it was to be affectionate and tender with George now. Before he'd got sick, his grandfather had been a kind, caring but emotionally distant figure, a man who never discussed his feelings or showed any kind of weakness. The only time Tom had ever seen his strength crack was when his wife, Betty, had died, and there was a moment at the funeral when Tom had held his arm, steadied him. Other than that, he'd been a loving but stoic man of pride and dignity, who rarely discussed his own life. In fact, Tom had realised only lately that he had known the man in front of him for all of his thirty years, yet he knew very little about him. He had no brothers, no sisters, no other family. Granny Betty had died when Tom was nineteen, and since then his grandfather had gone through the motions, made a life for himself at the lawn bowling club and the local social club. Tom had visited him at least once a week, but the conversations were always superficial: the football scores from the weekend before, the weather, the latest government screw up. There were certainly no hugs or kisses or displays of affection. It was a generational thing and Tom didn't take it personally. These were the strong, resilient wartime children who had battled hardship and impoverished childhoods. They didn't do weakness and dramatics. In fact, the only time he'd ever seen his grandad get emotional was when Granny Betty died and after the cancer diagnosis. There had been a glisten in his eyes on those days.

'Listen, son,' he'd said, after clearing his throat. 'The house is already in your name – I transferred it over years ago – and the life insurance will all go to you. Not that there's much, but what's there I want you to have. Just make sure that father of yours doesn't get his hands on it, because he doesn't deserve a bloody penny after what he did…'

It had taken Tom a moment to recover his voice. The subject of his father hadn't been raised in over a decade. That's why he'd hesitated to call him and let him know George was nearing the end, but perhaps there was still time for amends, for closure and for forgiveness.

Although, maybe forgiveness would be a step too far for him. His father, Norry, had pretty much ignored his grandad for all these years – no invitations to Australia, no phone calls, no visits, nothing. Seeing him today could either go very well or very badly – he just wasn't sure which one it would be.

He picked up his leather briefcase, then pulled on his Zegna coat over his Tom Ford suit. Appearances were important in his industry. On a day when there were no client meetings, he'd normally opt for smart trousers and an open neck shirt, but he'd felt the need to put on some armour this morning, to reinforce his confidence and add a metaphorical layer of protection for the battles ahead. He pulled his collar up around his neck as he stepped out into the freezing cold of the Glasgow morning, stopping to hold the door open for some incoming visitors, all of whom gave him the sad smile of empathy as they too faced the inevitable loss of their loved ones.

Out on the street, passers-by would see a well dressed, clearly successful, man in his early thirties heading to his car, the kind of guy who was cool and calm, was in control, who had life sorted. That morning, it couldn't be further from the truth. Not cool. Not calm. Struggling to maintain control.

He checked his watch. Just before nine a.m. He jumped into his white BMW, propelled by an excruciating mix of dread and fury. Yesterday, he'd stumbled across a message that was definitely not meant for his eyes. It was from his business partner, Davie, and the recipient was someone that was long gone from Tom's life, someone he'd searched for countless times over the years, someone he'd failed to find.

Now, he'd discovered that Davie was in contact with her, but he hadn't shared the information. Perhaps he intended to reveal all. Perhaps this was a plan to reunite Tom with the love of his life... Or maybe it was the worst kind of betrayal by someone he trusted.

It would take him a while longer to get to the office today because he was making a detour, stopping off somewhere. There was something he had to see with his own eyes, something that had the potential to change everything.

By the end of the day he'd either have nothing or everything that mattered... he just had no way of knowing which.

Three

Chrissie

Band Aid were belting out "Do They Know It's Christmas" on the radio as Chrissie stopped at the kitchen doorway and watched her twelve year old son, Ben, polish off the last of his Cheerios. He was eating while engrossed in a book that was balanced against the plastic semi-skimmed milk carton in the middle of the table. With his dark brown hair and huge hazel eyes, sometimes his resemblance to his father took her breath away and she had to pause, compose herself.

'Right, my love, come on. We've got ten minutes to get out of here.'

He reluctantly closed the book and slipped it into the backpack that was lying at his feet.

'Have you got your—'

'Homework, yes, PE kit, yes, packed lunch, yes, three bottles of bubble bath for the Christmas raffle and the Santa cupcakes that you bought but are pretending you baked...'

She smiled. 'And...'

'... And yes, I have the second backpack with pyjamas for tonight and clothes for tomorrow, because Josh's mum is picking me up from school and I'm staying over at their house tonight because you're deserting me.'

'Excellent,' Chrissie replied, laughing at his cheek and not rising to his jibe. Ben was the greatest and most important person in her life, and she adored him beyond measure. He wasn't the smartest kid in class, the sportiest or the girls' heart-throb, but he had an irrepressible knack for making people laugh that would get him a long way in life.

'And did you remember to pick up something to take to his house as a thank you?' she added.

'Yup, a bottle of vodka and twenty Benson & Hedges,' he replied, totally deadpan.

'Lovely,' she went along with it before lifting the carrier bag from the kitchen worktop to do her own investigation. She'd only given him a tenner to buy something from the corner shop last night, so she was fairly confident he was kidding. She opened the bag. A box of Quality Street and a yule log for Josh's mum, Karen, and a six pack of Freddos for the boys. 'Good work,' she told him, before enveloping him in a hug, which he succumbed to with a pre-teenage sigh, but little resistance. 'I'll miss you,' she told him. A few years ago, she would have kissed the top of his head, but now that he'd bypassed her 5'8", she had to settle for a kiss on the cheek instead. Again, he humoured her by not wiping it off with his sleeve. This was progress. 'I love you,' she said.

'I love you too, Mum.'

When he grinned he looked even more like his dad. Chrissie swallowed hard, banishing that thought and the pang of sadness that came with it. Was she really ready to open herself up to a situation that could end with the same world of pain as last time?

For a fleeting moment she considered cancelling tonight and just going to the cinema with Ben instead. For the purposes of this indulgent moment of weakness, she overlooked the fact that he'd rather be hanging out at his mate's house, destroying civilisations on the Xbox, than sitting in the multiplex on a Friday night eating popcorn with his mother.

Not that he'd admit that, of course. It had always been just the two of them, so they'd been a team for a long time, one that stuck together and looked out for each other. Ben's dad had left when she was pregnant and sometimes she felt guilty that she hadn't made a conscious effort to meet someone and give him a family unit, but she knew he'd had a happy childhood and he'd turned out to be as balanced and grounded as she could ever have hoped. Just as long as the vodka and Benson & Hedges comment was definitely a joke.

'Nip through and tell Val we're ready to go then,' she told him. 'I'll meet you at the car.'

Before he got to the back door, it opened and Val, their next door neighbour, poked her head around.

'Are you ready, love?' she asked breezily.

Chrissie smiled, delighted as always to see one of her very favourite people. 'We were just coming to get you.'

Val's gaze had already moved on to Ben. 'Morning, sweetheart. Did you get caught in a wind tunnel or have you not done your hair yet, son?'

Ben giggled at the familiar tease and headed to the door. Chrissie knew their relationship with Val and Donald next door was the biggest blessing of moving to this estate. When they'd first come here two and a half years ago, Val and Donald had been straight in to introduce themselves, and they'd looked out for her ever since, taking Ben under their wing, too. That was just Val's personality and their connection had been instant. Her heart was as big as the platinum blonde bob that was teased and sprayed to within an inch of its life, the perfect dressing for her blue eyeliner and baby pink lipstick. On anyone else, her look would be hopelessly outdated, but on Val it was the perfect reflection of her luminous, bright force of nature, one she managed to maintain despite suffering some real tragedies in her life.

Val's daughter, Dee, had been killed by a drugged-up driver almost three years before. It had taken Val a long time to come to terms with it and she still hadn't forgiven the junkie who was now in jail for causing Dee's death, but she had somehow managed to find a way to deal with the loss. Chrissie and Ben had moved in next door a few months after Dee passed, and despite her sorrow, or perhaps as a way of focusing on the positives, Val cared for people, helped others out. The last two years would have been a real struggle without her. Val and Don had looked after Ben more times than Chrissie could count, and they absolutely loved being his surrogate grandparents. The feeling was mutual. Ben adored them too.

'Did you hear from Mark?' Chrissie asked, while she grabbed her coat and bag.

Mark was Val's son, and he'd just left with his Australian wife Tara and daughter Claudie to spend Christmas with Tara's parents in Sydney.

'Landed safely a couple of hours ago. Only been gone a day and I miss them already. Might have to confiscate Ben to keep the house busy until they get back.'

'That's a contravention of my human rights,' Ben said, trying to act serious and suppress a giggle.

'I'll share the tin of Quality Street that's sitting under my tree,' Val bribed him.

Ben gave in to the giggles as he agreed to the deal. 'Done.'

Chrissie gave Val an impromptu hug.

'What was that for?'

'Just because we think you're fab,' Chrissie said, aware that while Val was the most loving, caring individual she'd ever known, she wasn't one for gushy sentimentality.

Right on cue, Val patted her hair, checking that the steel consistency of her coiffure hadn't been dented by Chrissie's embrace. 'Aye, well thanks, love, but careful you don't crack ma bob,' she said, feigning alarm.

A hug didn't even begin to cover everything Val had done for her. She had found Chrissie her first full-time job since Ben was born. And she was the one who had pushed her into agreeing to go out tonight, on her first date in twelve years.

Chrissie experienced a stomach lurch so violent she had to pause for breath. A date. With a real person. Who wasn't Channing Tatum and on screen in a movie where he took his top off.

Oh God.

What had she been thinking when she arranged this? A flood of anxiety made her throat tighten. Maybe she shouldn't be thanking Val after all. Why was she putting herself through this?

It wasn't too late to pull out.

'You're not pulling out,' Val said, as Chrissie reached her at the door.

'How...?'

'It's all over your face,' Val said, teasing her. 'You look like Bambi, in the presence of one of those twats that goes hunting for fun.'

'Yeah, you're not backing out, Mum,' Ben concurred, as the three of them made their way down the path in front of their row of terraced houses to the car park at the end. 'Just make sure he's not a serial killer. Or one of those blokes that goes out with ten women at a time and cons them out of all their money.' Chrissie wondered if she should be concerned that Ben was so relaxed about her entering the dating world, then decided instead to just be grateful that he was such a grounded, easy going guy. Serial killer comments aside.

'Thanks for the tip,' Chrissie replied, taking on board the first point and ignoring the second. If a man was after her for her money, he was going to be sorely disappointed. Although he was welcome to her overdraft, her credit card bill and her Tesco Clubcard points.

Chrissie's job had hugely improved their finances, but they still weren't splashing out on new cars and foreign holidays. After Ben had been born, and with his dad absent and no other family around, Chrissie had had no childcare, so she'd applied for a grant to cover the fees, and used the time to take an Open University degree in business management. As soon as he'd gone to school, she'd signed to a temp agency and spent the next few years working when she could, but had needed the flexibility to have school holidays off with her son. It was only when she'd moved in next door to Val, and her neighbour had offered to look after Ben for free whenever he was off school, that Chrissie had started looking for a full-time job. Initially she came up empty. Apparently no one wanted to hire someone in their late twenties with no comprehensive employment track record.

That's when Val had stepped in to help them yet again. When she'd recommended her for a job in Sun, Sea, Ski, the one stop holiday clothes and accessories shop her daughter Dee had owned with her best friend Jen, Chrissie had been beyond grateful. Two years later, she still loved every single day there.

Val helped out occasionally in the shop too, and was popping in to see Jen today, so had offered to give Chrissie a lift, dropping Ben at school on the way.

They chatted non-stop on the journey, laughing when they pulled into the kerb and he realised that they'd put him in a potentially life changing situation.

'I'll just stop here, Ben, right in front of all your friends,' Val chirped knowingly.

'No, it's OK. We can go on a bit further,' he said, his alarm obvious.

'Not at all,' she countered. 'They're right there. No point making you walk.'

A smile played at the corner of Chrissie's mouth. She knew exactly what Val was doing. How many times had Val dropped him off and then mortified him by shouting endearments as he raced into school?

Ben sat for a moment, contemplating his options before offering a deal. 'I'll give you my first selection box and I'll hoover for a week if neither of you kiss me or shout out the window that you love me,' he said, his face beginning to flush.

Val made eye contact with Chrissie. 'What do you reckon?'

'As long as I get the Curly Wurly, I'm in,' Chrissie agreed reluctantly.

'Och, you're spoiling all my fun,' Val moaned, with mock irritation.

His relief was all over his cheeky face. 'Thanks, Mum!'

'I do love you, son,' she added. 'So, so much.'

'Love you too. And you, Val,' Ben said with a grin, grabbed his bag and fled the car before she changed her mind.

Val dissolved into giggles. 'That's a special boy right there,' she said.

'Yep, I got lucky,' Chrissie agreed.

Val smiled at her. 'Don't think luck has anything to do with it, love.'

Chrissie smiled at the compliment and said yet another silent prayer of thanks that she'd met this woman sitting next to her... even if she did seem intent on pushing Chrissie right out of her comfort zone. Tonight being a case in point.

Her date this evening had started off as a Facebook connection. A guy from school who had sent her a friend request. Chrissie vaguely remembered him. Davie. Tall. Played football for the school team. May have snogged him once, very briefly, under mistletoe at the third year school disco. Hung around in the same extended group. Hadn't seen him since the last time she walked through the school gates about fourteen years ago.

They'd messaged each other on Facebook over the course of the last couple of months and that was as far as Chrissie had planned to take it. Things were getting good in her life. She and Ben were fine. Doing great. They didn't need anyone else. And if she introduced a guy into their lives, it would potentially open up a whole minefield of questions around Ben's absent father. No, that was the last thing they needed. Single life was just fine.

Unfortunately Val and her best friend Josie didn't agree. They'd badgered her into submission, until she'd finally agreed to Davie's suggestion that they meet up for dinner. Tonight was the night, a lovely little Italian restaurant just down the street from the shop, and every time she thought about it the butterflies in her stomach went on a spin cycle. She'd deliberately picked somewhere she was familiar with, figuring it was one less thing to be excruciatingly nervous about. With a bit of luck, it would be chock-full of Christmas parties and the melee would make it so difficult to hear each other that he wouldn't realise she had absolutely no dating game whatsoever. None.

Now she just had to get through the next eight hours or so without panicking, cancelling, or hyperventilating from the anxiety over having to make small talk in a potentially romantic situation with a bloke she barely knew and hadn't seen since she was carrying maths books and coming up with excuses to get out of PE.

Val's cheery chat made the rest of the journey fly by and as always, Chrissie's heart swelled a little when they climbed out of the car in front of the shop. Situated in the Merchant City, a lovely niche area of upmarket boutiques, bars and restaurants, the front windows were stunning. She'd spent a whole day on them last week, creating a spectacular Alpine winter scene, complete with fairy lights, fake snow, a mountainous backdrop and spotlighting their latest range of gorgeous skiwear. The benefit of stocking everything anyone could need for a summer or winter holiday – clothing, luggage, cosmetics, travel products – as well as maintaining an online store and a popular blog highlighting ideas for destinations and excursions, was that the shop was busy all year round. And Chrissie looked forward to every day.

The ding of the doorbell made the two people in the shop look up as Chrissie and Val entered. Jen, the shop owner, had her usual sunny smile, but it was the older woman, with the grey spiky hair, dressed in her trademark ninja black polo neck, trousers and leather stiletto boots that put Chrissie's senses on high alert. Val was around sixty, while her best friend, Josie, was in her mid-seventies, but it appeared that no one had informed her of this. She looked more than a decade younger, had the vocabulary of a thirty year old sailor and came with an incorrigible sense of mischief, daring and a fondness for the shocking. Chrissie adored her, but to see her here this early in the morning, with an expression of indisputable mischief, was definitely a cause for concern.

'Morning luvlies,' Josie greeted them. 'It's a fine day for an ambush.'

'What... ambush...?' Chrissie stuttered, a feeling of dread rising from her bright pink snow boots.

Val and Josie wore matching knowing smiles.

'Oh bugger, no. No way. I'm not for being ambushed today or any day by you two.'

'Ah, but you are,' Josie countered. 'Oh yes, the plans we have for you today. They're so exciting that if my nipples didn't point at the floor, they'd be on full beam right now.'

Chrissie turned to Val for help, but she was met with a cheeky smile.

'Better get started then. Right, love, you're coming with us. We are going to get you date ready and so entirely shaggable that this bloke will fall in love with you at first sight.'

'Jen, save me,' Chrissie begged.

Jen shook her head. 'There's a limit to my powers. I could maybe take one of them down, but I'll never defeat them both,' she said, laughing as she gestured to Josie and Val.

Chrissie wanted to turn around, to back out slowly, to flee the shop before she got roped into whatever madness the two women were planning.

Instead, she allowed them to take an arm each and march her right back outside. They turned right and headed towards the centre of the city, so quickly that Chrissie didn't even get a chance to survey the scene in front of her.

If she had, she might have spotted that the little café across the road had a customer sitting at a table next to the window. She might have seen that it was a guy with a familiar face. She might have seen that he was staring right at her. And she might have realised that today was going to be the day that every wall she'd built would come tumbling down.

<u>Four</u>

George

I'm dying. I just want to say that straight out. Or as the young ones would say, "put it out there". Bloody nonsense, some of the phrases that folk use nowadays. What's wrong with just plain speaking?

The boy thinks I don't know he's here, but I can hear and feel him fine. Tom. The boy. That's still how I think of him even though he's gone thirty now. Fine lad he's turned out to be. I couldn't be prouder. It's a bloody miracle when you consider his feckless father.

I can hear that lassie, the nurse, too. Liv, that's her name. Cheery thing. She's got one of those voices that reassures everyone who listens to her. Not that there's much reassurance to be had for me now. A painless exit is about as much as I can hope for, and these drugs that they're pumping into me are taking care of that. Don't half take the wind out of my sails though. Between the medicine and this damned disease, it's getting harder and harder to open my eyes.

That said, I'm not in any rush to leave this world. I've never been one for impatience. I've lost track of the days, and I hate to keep asking the nurse, but I'm fairly sure it's close to Christmas. The sound of festive songs has been drifting in from the corridor – Blue Christmas by Elvis was always my favourite – and on the few occasions I've managed to open my eyes, I've noticed people walking by the window with gift wrapped presents. It's always been my favourite time of the year, especially when our Tom was a boy. We would have Christmas morning at our house and my son Norry and his first wife, Catriona, would bring the boy round first thing. Catriona was a fine woman and so much more than that sour faced one Norry replaced her with. She was a smashing mother to Tom, too. It shames me to say it, but every bit of compassion and kindness in that boy came directly from her, not from that son of mine.

Anyway, where was I? Christmas. My darling Betty would cook and organise games and make it the perfect day for everyone. It was at times like that Betty and I wished there'd been more of us, a bigger family for the boy to share the day with, but Norry had been our only son, and then he'd repeated the pattern by only having Tom. Of course, there was more kin out there – I had two sisters, Annie and Flora, that I lost touch with long ago. Those memories pained me, and our Betty knew that, so we left them in the past and we never spoke of them, not to Norry, not to Tom, not to anyone. That doesn't mean I've forgotten them though. In fact, now I think of them more than ever.

Tom is shaving me now and I'm glad about that. No excuses for a shabby appearance, that's what my father drilled into us and I've always lived by it. I hope it's the only thing of that man's that I've taken to heart. By God, there was a father that ruled with an iron rod and wasn't one for sparing feelings. There were no tears shed when Billy Butler went to his maker, although it saddened me when my mother went only a few weeks after. Influenza afflicted the both of them. I wish she'd had a chance to live without him, even for a short while, to breathe without walking on eggshells, waiting for the next rage or rant. All of us kids – Annie, Flora and me – knew the feeling of fear and I vowed that I would never be that kind of father with Norry.

Instead, I tried to be the man who led by example and instilled decency and compassion in his offspring, but I'm sorry to say I failed. It's always been a great sadness that Norry was more of his grandad's ilk than of mine. A selfish boy, self-centred and prone to nastiness, who grew into an arrogant bugger of a man. It gives me no pleasure to say that of my own son, but one of the gifts of these last days is honesty. If I can't be truthful with myself, then what's the point? These are days of reckoning, of reminiscing, of looking back on eighty years that were well lived but not without mistakes.

The boy is mid-shave when the question the nurse asks him sinks in to my fuddled brain. 'Are your parents on the way?' she says.

I try to focus on the answer so I get it right. I hear him say, 'Yeah, my dad and stepmother. They're halfway here. They touched down in Dubai a couple of hours ago and their connecting flight took off on time. They should be here about three o'clock.'

Bloody hell. So Norry and that wife of his are coming. I must be close to dead if they're making the effort, because they didn't bloody come when I was alive and kicking, or when my darling Betty was sick and passed away.

And of course, it wouldn't be Tom's mother, Catriona, that would be with Norry. That poor lass was treated terribly by my son and he forced her out of their lives when Tom was sixteen. To be honest, for her sake I was glad she got out of that marriage. She had a lucky escape. I was only too glad to give her as much help as I could to start her new life down south. She kept in touch with me right up until she passed, a few years ago. Cancer. This bastard of a disease. I was only grateful that the lass found happiness with a man who treated her well. I never met him, but Tom would visit them and he told me he was a decent chap. That made me sleep a bit easier at night. I felt it was the least she deserved after being married to my son.

Norry had barely batted an eyelid when she left. He'd never admitted it to me, but I had a fair idea that he was already up to no good with the next one. Rosemary. She wasn't like Catriona. This time he'd met his match and someone who was as contemptible as he was. They'd tied the knot as soon as his divorce was final – went off to Bali or someplace like that. Didn't even invite us. Not that I'd have gone. Not after their antics. Next thing we knew, Norry sold up his business and off they went to Australia, taking our Tom with them. Norry said it was about work-life balance and enjoying the fruits of his labour, or some nonsense like that. The truth was, he'd made a killing and reckoned he could live like a king down under and he had so much in the bank that he got a visa to live there without a problem. That Rosemary one encouraged him every step of the way. Fancied herself living in a big house in the sunshine, with no ties or commitments, so off they went, and damn everyone else. Losing Tom near broke my Betty's heart. It was one of the happiest days of her life when the boy came back to live with us a year later. He'd never settled out there and we were glad of it.

Through the haze of the buggering pills, I can hear the beeping from the monitor beside me getting faster. That's what I get for thinking about those two. It wouldn't surprise me if the bloody thing exploded when they walk through the door. I can only hope their plane gets delayed and I get to spend another day without them here.

Days.

Hours maybe.

That's all I've got left. I've accepted it now, but that doesn't mean I don't have the odd moment of sadness.

What's that song? "My Way". Regrets. I've had a few. More than a few.

I don't trust anyone who says they've got no regrets. All that stuff about learning from mistakes is bollocks – far better not to make the damn mistake in the first place.

If I could change anything, it wouldn't be the life I lived with my Betty. No, that was as good as any man could wish for. I wouldn't even change the estrangement with Norry. In fact, I'd have told him to sling his hook long before he did and kept Tom with Betty and me, instead of letting them drag him to the other side of the world in the first place. But then…

The heartbeat monitor speeds up again and I can feel the tension across my chest. It's the shame that does it. Pure shame. You see, I did the boy a disservice. While he was away, I found something out that could have changed the whole course of his life, and yet I didn't tell him, not then, and not afterwards when he came back to us.

It's the biggest regret of my life. All these years, I still haven't told him the truth. And why? Because I was too bloody terrified that he would never forgive me and I'd lose him too. Selfish old bastard that I was. Maybe there was a bit of my father in me after all.

If there's such a thing as heaven, I'll have to account for what I did then. I'll have to explain why I didn't tell the truth, stand up and be counted.

It wasn't the first time either.

No, it was the second time in my life that I'd failed when I should have done the right thing for the folk I loved.

Years before, when I was younger than our Tom is now, my actions cost us all so much. None of it was my doing, but I should have stepped in, should have stopped life tearing us apart.

Us.

Annie. Flora. Me.

Strange that I still think of the three of us as a group, despite the fact that we were only together for the first twenty-odd years of our lives.

My thoughts are interrupted by Tom. I can feel that he's finished shaving me now, hear the clink of the glass as he shakes the razor in it to let the water clean the blade. He picks up the sponge that I know sits beside my bed and he dabs it on my lips to moisten them. My mouth is always so dry now.

I want to open my eyes and speak to him, but they're heavy.

Later. I'll talk to him later.

I can hear him moving around, following the same routine that he's kept to every morning without fail. He'll be getting his jacket now, and his bag, and then he'll...

'I'll be back soon, Grandad. I just need to go into the office and take care of a few things,' I hear him say. He's such a good man. More than I ever was. I just wish I'd told him more often how proud I am of him. I try to open my eyes, to speak to him, but the body isn't responding. Maybe later. I feel his breath as he leans down and kisses my cheek. It wasn't something he ever did before I was in this hospital bed, but he does it every time he leaves now. To my surprise, as I hear the door open, a single tear escapes from the corner of my left eye and drops on to my pillow.

Foolish old man I've become, bloody weeping for no good reason.

Liv, the nurse, comes into the room and as always she chats away. I've met her husband, he's a doctor here and he came to see me when I was first admitted. Showed me the scans that proved this bastard thing had spread to my brain. He seemed like a decent enough man. I just hoped he realises he's lucky to be married to this nurse. She reminds me of my Betty. Same calm manner. Same knack of caring for others. Same twinkle in her eye that suggests she doesn't mind a wee bit of mischief. For the second time in minutes I can feel a moistness under my eyelids. Jesus wept, what's happening to me? Must surely be whatever was in that drip that was connected to my arm.

At least, that's what I'm going to tell myself instead of admitting that I'm just getting soft in my fading days.

Enough of this.

I try to distract myself by rewinding my thoughts.

Where was I?

That's right. Annie. Flora. Me.

Today might be my last day on this earth, or it may not. But I'm going to spend as much of it as I can with people who have loved me.

Even if most of them are only alive in my memories...

10 a.m. – 12 noon

Five

Shauna

'Here's to Annie, to a weekend away, and to alcohol for breakfast,' Shauna toasted, laughing as she clinked her glass against Lulu's champagne flute. 'I feel completely rebellious drinking gin at ten in the morning,' she added, after she'd taken her first sip.

'Then you really need to get out more,' Lulu teased. 'Actually that's not exactly a newsflash. You really do need to drop the hermit status.'

'I have a social life,' she argued.

Lulu's comeback was swift. 'Taking Beth to Pizza Hut doesn't count.'

Shauna surrendered. There was no defence and arguing would only make Lulu more insistent that she was right. Which, of course, she was. The problem was there was no manual for losing your husband at the age of thirty-nine, no natty step-by-step guide to rebuilding your life and planning a new future that was very different to the one you had envisaged. All she could do was go with the old clichés, recognise that she'd have good days and bad days and just do the best she could. It was a process, she'd decided. The last two years had been about surviving, and she'd just about made it, so perhaps this was the first step to finding a way forward.

'Anyway, I'll resume nagging you about that on the plane home, but I'm suspending being critical of your life choices for the next twenty-four hours,' Lulu announced.

'Excellent. And I'll try to refrain from mentioning that you're way too old and way too married to have been flirting with that barman when you ordered our drinks,' Shauna countered, playfully.

'I'm just spreading festive joy,' Lulu said, grinning. 'It's a public service.'

Shauna was unable to suppress a chuckle. Lulu would never change. She'd been with Dan, Colm's best friend, for nearly twenty years, married for half of that, and yes, they had the most tumultuous relationship in the history of mankind, but somehow they were still together despite several break-ups, affairs on both sides, and Lulu's insatiable need to flirt with every good looking man she encountered. She claimed it was a genetic flaw. It was only since Colm had passed away that Lulu and Dan had finally put their energies into making their marriage work. Realising that life really could be too short had been a catalyst for them to get their act together. Although, Lulu had clearly decided that a bit of harmless flirting didn't compromise the marriage vows.

'To us. And to morning drinking!' Lulu said, holding up her glass for another toast, while making sure her back was straight, her porcelain white teeth were flashing and she was giving the barman her best nonchalant smile.

When they finished their drinks, Shauna pushed herself off the bar stool. This had to be one of the most beautifully decorated hotels she'd ever seen, from the lavish garlands that wound around the majestic front doors, to the grand tree in the foyer and the subtle silver and white lights in the bar. It would be impossible not to get into the festive spirit here. It would have been so easy to just stay in this haven of bliss and while the day away drinking cocktails, people watching and laughing with Lulu but there was a point to this trip and Shauna didn't want to lose sight of that.

As she stood up, her phone buzzed with an incoming text.

'Right, come on, that's the taxi outside.'

Lulu reluctantly slid off her chair, pulled on her hat and scarf, grabbed her gloves and bag and followed her.

'Morning, ladies,' the driver greeted them with a cheery grin. 'Where to, then?'

Shauna pulled out the first letter and read the address out to him. She'd looked it up on Google Maps and she knew it was in the south side of the city.

'No problem at all,' he announced, then proceeded to chat all the way there. By the time they arrived at the destination, they'd discussed the weather, Shauna's reason for being in Scotland and he'd revealed every detail of his family's plans for Christmas.

'Aye, fifteen of us for lunch, God help us. Ma Agnes makes Brussels sprouts that are so hard they could take a man out at fifty feet. Honestly, if we ever go to war and run out of bullets, I'll make a fortune as an arms dealer.'

Shauna was still laughing when they pulled to a stop.

'Do you want me to wait here?' he asked. 'I won't put the meter on. You two ladies are far better company than junkies needing a lift to their dealers.'

Shauna didn't need to think about it twice. 'That would be great, if you're sure?'

'No problem. You take your time and I'll just park up here.'

'In fact, could we hire you for the whole day? We're going to be going to loads of places and it would make life so much easier if you'd stay with us.'

He thought about it for a moment, making some calculations in his head. 'How about £150 for the day, until, say, seven o'clock, and £200 if you keep me until midnight?' he offered, almost apologetically. 'I know it's high, but it's the Friday before Christmas and that's always a good earner for me.'

'Done.' Yes, it was a lot of money, and she could have hired a car for less, but he knew the city, and Shauna had no time to waste looking for places or waiting on ten different cabs. 'I'm Shauna. And this is Lulu, by the way.'

'I'm John. Pleased to meet you, ladies. And did you say Lulu? Like the singer?' he asked, referring to the Scot who'd had a huge hit back in the sixties with her song, 'Shout'. It was one of those tunes that was ingrained in Scottish culture, up there with anything by the Proclaimers or played on bagpipes.

'That's the very one,' Lulu said, chuckling. 'Tell me, is everyone I meet today going to mention that?'

He nodded. 'I'd bet a week's wages on it.'

'Excellent,' Lulu grinned. 'Right, come on,' she said, opening the door.

Shauna got out the other side and gazed at the row of dark stone terraced houses in front of her. They were just off a main road in Shawlands, a suburb of Glasgow. This was the sender's address that had been on Flora's letters to Annie: 32 Parkland Street, Glasgow. And since Flora had been a young woman at the time, Shauna assumed that this had been their family home, where Annie had lived too.

There was a plaque, carved into the stone at the top of the end house's wall, that said 1904. Over a hundred years ago. The terrace had worn well. Some of the windows had been replaced by new ones, apart from one or two that still had the old wooden sash frames. There were Christmas trees in most of the large bottom windows, their lights waiting for darkness to twinkle. The gardens that were there were neat and tidy, but a couple of them had been taken away to make off-road parking spaces for cars.

Shauna stood, staring straight at the middle house, number 32, trying to imagine a young Annie opening the wrought iron gate, walking up the path to the heavy wooden door, opening it, calling out that she was home.

'Are you just going to stand there?' Lulu asked, fidgeting from foot to foot to keep out the cold. 'Only, I've just realised that I'm only wearing four pairs of socks and this is clearly sixteen sock weather. I'm pretty sure if I could feel my toes I'd realise that they were falling off.'

Shauna ignored her, suddenly falling into a deep well of emotion. She felt sure that Annie had lived here. Her Annie. The most precious person in her world, until she was joined on that podium by Colm and Beth. Someone who had given her a lifetime of love and whom she'd loved right back. Someone who had died in her arms, without warning, on the most traumatic night of her life. When Colm had passed it had been peaceful, and they'd known for almost two years that it was coming. Not that that made it any easier. But with Annie there were no red flags. They'd had a brilliant night, out with all Annie's pals at their line dancing session, showing off their talents to the soundtrack of "Achy Breaky Heart" and – much hilarity – "Honky Tonk Badonkadonk". They'd just got home and Shauna was making a cup of tea when there was a loud crash. One minute Annie was sitting in a chair, the next she was on the floor. A massive stroke. Shauna's heart was decimated.

'Oh Jesus, you're crying. Bugger. I didn't come prepared. Here, use this…'

Shauna glanced down to see that Lulu was holding up the edge of the cashmere scarf Shauna had bought her last Christmas. The laughter came as quickly as the tears.

'That's true devotion there, Lu,' Shauna said, wiping away the tears with her sleeve instead.

'Not really. I'd have charged you for the dry cleaning,' Lulu retorted, but softly, and Shauna knew she was kidding. Humour was Lulu's default position for dealing with all emotional situations – along with shopping and vodka. 'So what do you want to do now?' Lulu asked.

'I don't know. I hadn't really thought through a plan. I just wanted to see where Annie had lived. At least, I'm guessing it was their family home. It was the address Flora's letters were sent from.'

Shauna had done some basic searches on the Scottish ancestry website, Scotland's People. She'd found records that indicated that Flora Butler, George Thomas Butler and Bethany Butler had all been born in Glasgow, in the thirties: George in 1933, Bethany (Annie's full name, which had, according to her grandmother, been discarded in childhood in favour of "Annie") in 1934 and Flora in 1936. She'd planned to get copies of their birth certificates, but this trip had been such a spontaneous decision that she hadn't had a chance yet. What she did know was that, according to the ancestry website, neither George nor Flora had death certificates registered in Scotland. Of course, that meant that they could have moved abroad, or even like Annie, down to England, and passed away there, but it still gave Shauna a glimmer of hope that somewhere out there was a family. *Her* family.

'Right, no point standing here freezing our tits off...' Lulu declared.

'You're right,' Shauna said, suddenly feeling inexplicably anxious. She didn't want to lose the image of Annie being here by meeting the current owners and having reality get in the way of her imagination. 'But it doesn't look like anyone is home and there's no way Annie's family will still be there after all these years. I'm happy just to see it and picture her here. There was one other address on a later letter, so we'll just go there now.'

Lulu rolled her eyes. 'You'd be a crap private investigator. I'm coming over all Cagney and Lacey and you're giving up without even trying. I'm going to go and knock the door.'

'Lulu, you can't just...'

Too late. Lulu was up the path and banging on a heavy brass knocker on the front of the black door.

'Oh, bugger,' Shauna added, chasing after her.

Lulu banged again.

'Right, there's no one here,' Shauna pointed out the obvious. 'Let's go before we get arrested for casing the joint and harassing innocent householders.'

'Nope, not giving up yet,' Lulu said, before reaching over a waist high fence and banging on the door of the next house along.

An irrepressible fit of giggles consumed Shauna. 'Christ. This is like the million times we played "chap door, run away" when we were kids. And I was always the one that got caught. There's no one…'

Her words were halted by the opening of the neighbour's door.

A woman in her thirties, in jeans and Converse, with a toddler on her hip, pushed back some stray hairs into her ponytail as she spoke. 'Can I help you?'

'We're really sorry to bother you,' Shauna stepped in, 'and I know this is a long shot, but I think my grandmother and her family used to live in this house and I was just hoping that someone from the family still lived here?'

Shauna could hear how crazy that sounded. It was almost sixty years after the last letter was sent. The chances of the same people still living there were miniscule.

The woman shook her head, dislodging the stray hairs again. 'No, it's a family from down south that lives there. Been there a couple of years, same as me.'

Shauna's heart fell as she shrugged. 'Oh well, thanks anyway. And sorry again to have troubled you.'

'Hang on a minute there, Cagney,' Lulu said, digging her in the ribs, before addressing the woman again. 'Is there anyone in this terrace that has lived here forever? An elderly person maybe?'

The woman thought about it for a moment. 'I don't think so. These are four bedroom houses so they're probably too big for an old person to manage on their own. That's why my gran passed it down to me before she moved on.'

'Oh. Sorry to hear that,' Shauna said, desperate to get away before they upset this lovely lady by dragging up memories of her dearly departed granny.

'What?'

'Sorry to hear that your gran passed on,' Shauna repeated gently.

The woman laughed. 'She didn't. She's at the Sunnyvale Care Home. She's probably leading the bingo right now.'

Shauna sagged with relief. 'Thank God, I thought we'd just upset you there. Listen, thanks anyway. We appreciate your time. We'll get out of your way before we do say anything stupid.' She gave Lulu a pointed glare.

'Not at all. It was nice to meet you.'

Shauna gave her a smile of gratitude and was just about to turn away, when the neighbour spoke again.

'Was the person you were looking for called Mrs McGinty?'

Shauna and Lulu stopped in their tracks. Turned.

'I've no idea. I just knew her maiden name. Flora Butler.'

'Yes. I think that's her. Flora was Mrs McGinty's first name.'

Shauna's heart swelled. 'Do you know her?'

'I spent most of my childhood here. She was Gran's neighbour for decades.'

'Do you know where she is now?'

'No. I lived abroad for years and only came back when Gran gave me this house. The folk next door were already there by that time. But you should ask her.'

'Ask who?'

'My gran. Isa McNair. She loves a visitor. Sunnyvale Care Home on Clyde Street. She's sharp as a tack and as bolshy as they come, but I know she'll be happy to help if she can. Mrs McGinty was lovely.'

Shauna experienced a swell of... something. Happiness. Relief. Excitement.

She'd only ever been her parents' daughter, Annie's granddaughter, Colm's wife and Beth's mum. Now she could be Mrs McGinty's niece – if her aunt would have her.

<u>Six</u>

Tom

The office was unusually quiet, due to the fact that most people had opted to "work from home" today. Tom knew there would be little work actually getting done, but his team put in heavy hours all year round, so he was happy to cut them some slack. It was a fair assumption that they wouldn't be of much value today anyway, given that some of them were still tweeting this morning at 5 a.m. after the office Christmas party. Zoe had texted him at eight o'clock and he wasn't sure if she was just getting up or just going to bed.

For the first time, he hadn't attended the annual bash, worried about two devastating possibilities: the first being that his grandfather would slip away with no one at his bedside, the second being that he'd have a couple of drinks, his inhibitions would lower, and he'd punch his partner, Davie Bailey, in the face for being a duplicitous bastard.

Even thinking about it made his nerve endings pop to the outside of his skin and his fists clench. Tom had never punched anyone in his life. He wasn't prone to rages, didn't have a temper, but as he strode into the office, he never wanted to deck someone more.

Davie Bailey. A school acquaintance who'd become his best mate at uni, a brilliant creative mind, risk taker, the life and soul of every party. He was also a Porsche driving fast talker, up to his arse in debt, prone to competitive petulance and the most self-indulgent, egotistical twat Tom had ever known. Not to mention that he was on his third divorce, a serial womaniser who was currently seeing a woman that he'd had an affair with during his last marriage. Tom and Davie were yin and yang. Tom was the calm, steady, strategic thinker, and Davie was the wild chancer who forced them to aim high. It was the perfect partnership and Tom had loved him like a brother. Until yesterday, he'd thought that was reciprocated. How wrong he had been.

Davie wasn't in yet, so Tom went into the office to check yet again what he'd seen yesterday. He switched on Davie's computer, watched it fire up, clicked on the Facebook page, into the messages section and, yep, there it was.

Thank you. I'm looking forward to tonight too. Chrissie.

He'd first spotted it yesterday, when they'd been brainstorming ideas for the HoopSport campaign in

Davie's office. HoopSport were one of their biggest clients, a basketball kit supplier that was fast rising up the ranks of sportswear companies in the UK, thanks to their comprehensive, cutting edge range of designs and imports. Tom and Davie had been discussing the prep for the next pitch yesterday afternoon, when the ideas started flowing.

Davie, shirt sleeves rolled up, lying flat out on his sofa, had looked over to Tom, who was perched on the edge of Davie's desk. 'Can you type these up? You know I'll have forgotten them by tomorrow.'

'You're a lazy bastard,' Tom had teased, as he duly slipped into Davie's chair and clicked the mouse to wake his computer. They'd spent the next two hours pulling ideas and concepts together, before Dex Jones, the head of their art department, had put his head around the door.

'We're just heading out for some pre-party drinks, if you're interested.' It was enough to make Davie levitate off the sofa.

'Indeed I am. Hang on for me – I'll leave the car here and come with you guys.'

'Tom?' Dex had asked.

'Sorry, mate. Going back to the hospital tonight. Just do me a favour and try and keep this one out of trouble, out of jail, and out of the bed of someone he meets at the bar.'

'I create magic, not miracles,' Dex had drawled. In the office, Davie wasn't entirely popular with the staff – too quick to fly off the handle and too single minded. But Party Davie, the one with the company credit card, was always in demand for out of hours activities. Tom didn't mind. It kept morale high and he reasoned that was always good for creativity.

'You leaving now, too?' Davie had asked, picking up his jacket, raring to get the party started.

Tom shook his head. 'Soon. I'll just stay and format this lot into a game plan,' he'd said, pointing at the screen. 'Then I'll head off. Have a good night, mate.'

'Oh, I'm sure I'll manage that,' he said with a wink, before heading out of the door.

Zoe waved through his office window and blew him a kiss as she joined the mass exodus, and within ten minutes, the vibrant buzz of the office had fallen to nothing but the sound of Tom's fingers on the keyboard.

Until the ping.

One ping.

One life changing, friendship wrecking, fucking ping.

In the corner of the screen, up popped a notification from Facebook.

You have a new message from Chrissie Harrison.

Tom blinked. It couldn't be right. He looked again. Still there.

You have a new message from Chrissie Harrison.

A new sound now, a thunderous thudding in his head caused by a heart that was pounding out of his chest. How long since he'd seen that name? Not that he hadn't thought about her, because he had, every single bloody day since…

His breath was coming heavy and fast, like a sprinter after a ten second hundred metres.

Chrissie.

Surely it couldn't be his Chrissie? And if it was, why would she be messaging Davie? Was something wrong? Was she looking for him? Why hadn't Davie told him that she'd made contact?

He'd been unable to stop himself looking further. He'd opened up the message history, his hand trembling on the mouse as he read the chain of communication.

Davie had initially messaged her on Facebook two months ago. Two. Months.

At first it had been friendly chat.

> How are you? Good to hear from you. Do you still keep in touch with anyone from school?

Chrissie had asked that question and it left no doubt that this was the same Chrissie Harrison who'd filled his thoughts since the last day he set eyes on her. Tom's gaze had immediately jumped to Davie's answer.

> Not much. Bump into some of the guys every now and then. Don't really move in the same circles.

Why would he lie? Bastard.

Tom and Davie had known each other at school, but they'd only become friends when they'd found themselves in the same dorm room at University, shortly after Tom had returned from spending a year in Australia.

Even after all that time, he was still devastated about the break-up. Davie had been on the same side of the bar when Tom had talked about Chrissie over and over, he'd watched as Tom searched for her, saw his desolation when he'd drawn a blank again and again. He'd been there as the years passed and Tom had been totally disinterested in a long term relationship with anyone else, because, well, they weren't Chrissie.

Now Davie had been in touch with Chrissie for two months and he hadn't said a word. Tom read the rest of the messages. They'd gradually become more and more personal, culminating in Davie asking her to meet him for dinner. She'd resisted at first, but Davie had worn her down, using the same bullshit chat that Tom had heard him use on countless other women over the years.

An uncharacteristic tsunami of rage had consumed him then, but that had immediately dissipated when he'd clicked on to her Facebook page. He didn't use Facebook, or Twitter, or any other social media for personal use, but he'd googled her name and searched all the social media sites for her over the years. There had never been any mention of her. Now there was. Although he wasn't on Facebook, he was familiar enough with it to find his way around her profile and timeline. There was no personal information at all and very few posts, just a couple of photographs of her, one from school and one more recent, laughing as she stood in the window of a shop next to a bikini clad mannequin. She was clutching a surfboard and a beach bag, wearing huge sunglasses and a big floppy hat, clearly joking with the person taking the picture. Her hair was a bit longer, and he couldn't see her eyes behind the sunglasses, but even from that one photo he could see that she was exactly as he'd remembered her. Gorgeous, funny, always the first to joke, usually at her own expense. She'd also been self-conscious, self-deprecating, and totally unaware of how special she was.

How long had he searched for her after she fell off the face of the earth? And how long had he beat himself up about what he'd done to her? It was his fault. All of it. He'd broken Chrissie's heart because he'd been too weak, too young, too stupid to stand up for them against their parents and he'd spent the last twelve years paying for it.

He'd stared at the picture for so long, yet he'd almost missed the significance – the fact that she was in the window of a shop. It had finally dawned on him that there was a good possibility that she worked there.

He'd clicked on the image, blew it up, studied it, and there it was. The shop sign wasn't in the picture, but there was an advertising board in the background of the window display.

He'd looked it up and saw that it was an online store and travel blog, but based in a shop in Glasgow. He clicked another link, went on to Street View, and there it was – the window that Chrissie had been posing in.

So she was still in the city and that's where she worked. What was even crazier was that it was only a few streets away, in the Merchant City, in a row of shops he'd visited many times. In fact, he got most of his clothes from a men's store called Camden that was right next door to it. She was in touching distance. How long had she been there and he didn't know it?

He hadn't slept a wink last night. He'd sat by his grandad's bed, desperate to tell him what had happened, but George had looked so peaceful he had decided against it. Meanwhile, Davie bloody Bailey, serial shagger and man without a moral conscience, was partying the night away, before his date with Chrissie.

Chrissie. Just thinking her name made something ache in his gut.

What should he do now?

She wouldn't want to see him, he was sure of it, yet…

He'd gone there this morning. On the way from the hospital to the office, he'd stopped for his usual morning coffee at a new location – a little café directly across from Sun, Sea, Ski. He'd only been there a few minutes when he'd seen her arrive, watched her through the window, then, just as he'd stood up to pay, she was ushered out again and down the street by two other women. She was laughing and he could hear the sound in his head, despite the trio being far out of earshot. Chrissie. His Chrissie.

He'd loved her. The only woman he'd ever loved. No one else had ever come close. Yet, he'd left her. She was both a reminder of the best time of his life and the worst thing he'd ever done.

And that prick Davie was meeting her tonight and had told him nothing about it.

Eight p.m. An Italian restaurant.

How the hell could his so-called mate do this to him? And what could Tom do about it?

Rational thought was a struggle, but he knew he couldn't go barging into Chrissie's life, show up where she worked without any warning, but he could speak to Davie, find out what the fuck was going on.

He went into his own office, the one next to Davie's, and sat, seethed, waited, as the clock ticked. He tried to focus on other things, but nothing worked, all he could picture was Chrissie laughing in that shop window.

It was close to noon when the main door finally opened and his teeth instinctively clenched in fury until he realised it was Dex, not Davie, who had arrived.

He attempted to de-escalate his rage.

Dex came straight to his office and groaned as he opened the door. 'Never again. My head feels like it belongs to a middle-aged alcoholic who's been drinking paint stripper every day for a fortnight.' Political correctness wasn't Dex's strong point.

'Good night then?' Tom joked, using every ounce of discipline to appear as normal as possible.

'Great night. And morning. It's still going on over at Davie's flat. It's a mess. There was the added bonus of a 6 a.m. drama when Roxy came home and caught Davie in bed with Carina from accounts.'

Tom closed his eyes and tried to breathe. Davie's standard behaviour. And now he was planning on adding Chrissie to his list of conquests? Over his dead body.

Dex wittered on. 'I'm just grabbing some stuff from my desk – my laptop, my keys and my dignity would be a start – and heading back home. Merry Christmas, boss.'

'Merry Christmas, Dex,' Tom replied, trying to keep his frustration out of his voice.

There was no point waiting here any longer. His partner wouldn't be in today, and there was no way he was going to Davie's apartment to discuss this in front of an audience. Fuck.

He had three hours until he had to be at Glasgow Airport to pick up his parents. He should really go and do some Christmas shopping or get some work done, but he was in the mood for neither. He could send Chrissie a text. Or call her. She'd put her mobile number on one of the messages she'd sent Davie. But this wasn't the kind of thing that could be done without planning. Or perhaps at all. He was very aware that he was the last person she'd ever want to see again.

No, the only place he could bear to be right now was at the hospital with George.

He was on his way out of the door, when his plans were changed for him.

'Hi baby!'

The sound of Zoe's cheery greeting stopped him in his tracks.

'You look surprised to see me,' she said, laughing as she kissed him on the lips. 'Did you forget we were having lunch today?'

Yes.

'No. Sorry, I'm just...'

'It's fine. Let's go. I booked a table in Princess Square and I've got all the gossip from last night. It was a train wreck.'

He weighed up the options. He didn't want to go to lunch. He didn't want to hear the gossip. But he knew without a doubt that he had to have a difficult conversation with Zoe, so this was as good a time as any.

'Lead the way,' he said.

He had a sinking feeling that by the end of lunch, there would be another name to add to the list of women who considered him to be a complete arse.

Seven

Chrissie

'Absolutely not! No way! The world definitely does not need to see this much of my pasty flesh,' Chrissie argued, taking in the disgruntled faces of the two women in front of her.

'Och, for God's sake, lass. If I had a figure like yours I'd be coming to work in a bra and tea towel,' Josie said, clearly disgusted at Chrissie's modesty.

Chrissie's gaze went back to her reflection in the mirror. The dress was beautiful, but it was red, figure hugging, had shoestring straps, and stopped about six inches above the knee. In other words, there was more chance of finding Brad Pitt in her wardrobe than this frock.

'Right, you two, you've had your fun, but if I'm going to do this it has to be something I'll actually want to wear.'

'Okay, love. We understand and we'll absolutely abide by your wishes,' Val said.

'Really?'

'Nope, we're lying, but we're hoping we'll wear you down. What about the pink sparkly one?'

Chrissie's laughter could be heard throughout the whole of the womenswear department of House of Fraser. Despite being accompanied by two elderly Scottish versions of Gok Wan, and currently being dressed as a jalapeno pepper, this was the most fun she'd had in ages that didn't involve sport, pizza, or superhero movies.

Today had definitely been a surprise. She'd been expecting to head into work, to have a busy pre-Christmas rush of customers, and then to hastily change into jeans, her one sparkly top, and a black jacket that she'd packed in her bag this morning and go meet her date. Val and Josie had other ideas. They'd arranged with Jen for her to have time off because they were taking her shopping for a new outfit. It was the loveliest, sweetest most thoughtful thing anyone had done for her in a long, long time and she welled up every time she thought of it. For so many years it had been just her and Ben – it never stopped being a wonderful feeling that she'd been welcomed into this crazy extended family.

'What is it you'd actually like to wear?' the assistant asked, enjoying the camaraderie between the women, but conscious that this was one of the busiest shopping days of the year and they were blocking a changing room.

Chrissie shrugged her shoulders helplessly. 'I don't know. Something... classy.'

Josie, all seventy odd years of her, rolled her eyes. 'Dear God, I've taught her nothing.'

'Something elegant, that I'll be able to wear again. I prefer black. Maybe with just a little bit of sparkle. And something not too expensive.' Christmas had already wiped her out, but she'd managed to avoid putting anything on the credit card, so that was a huge bonus. Still, the last thing she needed to be doing was blowing what little she had left on a dress, especially one she'd never wear again.

Val stood up. 'Josie, come with me. You slip back into the changing rooms, love, and we'll go on the hunt. I'll supervise Josie, so hopefully we'll find something that doesn't make you look like you're auditioning for Little Mix.'

Josie's face was a picture of disgust. 'Girl's got to get out there,' she argued.

'Oh, sweet Jesus, you're channelling Beyoncé again, Josie,' Val chided. 'She does indeed need to get back out there, she just doesn't need to look like she's escaped from Santa's porn grotto.'

'Now there's somewhere I'd like to visit,' Josie admitted, grinning, while the assistant's jaw dropped lower than the cleavage on the last three navel exposing frocks.

Beyoncé and her sidekick were back in ten minutes with a new array of outfits. Chrissie discarded anything that had sequins – around ninety per cent of the options – finally coming to a beautiful black mid-calf crepe dress that was sleeveless, had a fairly modest thigh split, and was adorned only with a very simple diamanté studded strap draped diagonally across one shoulder. Chrissie had never come even close to wearing a dress this gorgeous.

'I picked that one,' Val told her proudly, while Josie muttered something about funerals and mourning.

In the changing room, Chrissie checked the size – Fourteen. Perfect. She slipped it on, pulled up the side zipper and felt a rush of… something. She wasn't sure what it was. Relief. Appreciation. Happiness. Freedom. Joy. And a tiny little bit of self-belief. She looked okay. She actually looked okay. It would need a nice shrug or shawl, because there was a fair chance it would freeze her bits off, but for the first time in forever she could see a glimmer of her former self in the mirror – the person she'd been before she'd slipped to the bottom of her own priority list.

Even if she bottled out of going tonight, which was still a very strong possibility, at least she'd have this stunning dress to wear in the future – even if it was only on the couch while binge watching the latest series of *Grey's Anatomy*.

She stepped out of the changing room and both Val and Josie gasped, then Val pulled a hankie out of her bag because she'd welled up and didn't want tears to make her eyeliner run.

'You are gorgeous, sweetheart, absolutely gorgeous,' she said, her voice wobbly. This was the woman who was strong as steel, with the most resolute game face, who endured every challenge and tragedy like a warrior, but who crumbled with happiness when something good happened to someone she loved.

Josie's heart was every bit as huge. 'Okay, I give in to your better judgement. You look gorgeous. But how about a wee red jacket to go over the top. Gold? Silver?'

Eventually they settled on a beautiful shrug made of a silver web that matched the dress perfectly, before detouring to the shoe department for a stunning pair of black velvet shoes, with skyscraper steel heels.

'The chances of ending up in A&E are high, but they're worth it,' Val told her.

She couldn't argue. 'Just promise me you'll visit when I'm in traction,' she said, with a grin, realising that resistance was futile. One new dress. One new pair of shoes. One gorgeous new shawl. One highly enjoyable morning.

At the till, she pulled out her purse, but Josie barged her out of the way and handed over a credit card. 'This is our treat...'

'No, Josie, you can't!' Chrissie objected.

'Indeed we can. It's a Christmas present from me, Val and Jen. It's that or a subscription to Match.com, your choice.'

Chrissie knew when she was beaten and flushed with yet another wave of gratitude. She hugged them both in turn. She really could not wish for better friends. 'Thank you, Josie. And you, Val. Suppose this means I actually have to go tonight. I'd pretty much talked myself out of it.'

She was just verbalising what she'd been thinking since last night. She didn't need to go. She could cancel. Why did she need this kind of stress in her life? They were doing just fine, her and Ben. Relationships just complicated things, sucked up time and emotional investment. The thoughts had been tumbling over in her mind since the moment she'd agreed to go.

The only reason she'd said yes in the first place was because she had a vague recollection of Davie Bailey from school. He'd been one of those guys that everyone knew because he played for the school football team and he had a good looking, confident, swagger thing going on. Half of the girls in Chrissie's year had been madly in love with him, but not Chrissie. She found that kind of popularity mildly terrifying. And besides, back then it was all about...

She blocked the thought. If she let herself go down that path she would cancel tonight and end up spending the whole weekend thinking about *him*, feeling that pain again. In the early years, self-preservation had forced her to develop tools and strategies to keep going – refusing to allow herself to wallow in the past was at the top of the list.

Now, she knew it was time she developed tools and strategies to open her life up to a romantic relationship again. Even that thought made her feel nauseous, but she had to get over it, embrace the fear. When Davie had suggested they meet, her first instinct was to refuse point blank, and she did, a couple of times, but he'd persuaded her in the end. What did she have to lose, other than a night of her life and a bit of her confidence, if it all went wrong? Well, hello again, nausea.

'Thank you very much,' Val said to the cashier, as she handed over a large bag containing their purchases. Let's go,' Val said, 'Lots more to get done today.'

'But I have to get back to work. Jen will be rushed off her feet...'

'Don't you worry about that. The Saturday staff are in working extra hours today so the shop will be absolutely fine,' Val told her. 'We have plans...'

'Oh God. Should I be worried?' Chrissie said, only half-joking.

'Absolutely,' Josie told her. 'If Liam Neeson was your dad, he'd be getting a message that you'd been kidnapped right about now.'

'But we're good to our hostages,' Val added. 'So, lunch first, then the next surprise of the day. We've booked a table over at the Italian restaurant in Princess Square.'

Chrissie felt yet another jolt of happiness. Princess Square was one of her favourite places in Glasgow. Built in the 1840s, it was originally a merchant square, but was now a huge shopping and dining centre that housed several stories of upmarket stores and restaurants, all situated around a glorious glass roofed atrium. Chrissie had never had the money to shop there, but every year at Christmas, she'd take Ben and they'd sit on the steps at the edge of the courtyard on the lower floor, eat ice cream and listen to the carol singers or watch the bands playing. It was the perfect way to top up their Christmas spirit.

They crossed over Buchanan Street and entered the centre, then headed for the escalators. 'We're going to the Third floor. Och, isn't this gorgeous,' Val said, as they stepped on to the moving stairway.

As they rose, Chrissie scanned the area. It was truly beautiful. The Christmas tree on the ground floor was a stunning masterpiece of white and gold. The cascades and spirals of lights hanging from the higher floors were magnificent. The festive music and the crowds of shoppers bustling along behind the glass balconies and brass railings only added to the Christmas spirit. And the...

Chrissie froze as her eyes caught sight of the curving, majestic stairway diagonally across the centre. The couple. He had jet black hair, wide shoulders emphasised by the impeccable cut of his suit. She had tumbling waves of brunette curls that fell almost to the point where his hand rested on the small of her back as they climbed the stairs. She could only see him from behind, but she knew. The way he moved. The way he walked. The gesture of protection…

She felt herself wobble, lose her grip on the top of the escalator, then the steadying pressure of Val, pushing against her to hold her upright.

'Chrissie, are you okay? Jesus, love, you look like you've seen a ghost.'

Chrissie couldn't find the words to tell her that she had.

Eight

George

She was a real looker, our Flora. My da was always saying he had to beat them off with a stick when it came to that lass, and he wasn't kidding. The cricket bat sat right inside the front door, where it had been since we were kids. He wasn't afraid to use it then when we stepped out of line, and he wasn't afraid to use it on any poor bugger who thought they could come calling for our Flora.

Flora had our father's dark hair and our mother's piercing blue eyes. Always thought she looked like that actress. What was her name now...? Bloody brain is so riddled with cancer it's deserting me.

Not Joan Crawford. Or Bette Davis. The other one. Ava Gardner! That was her. Stunning looking lassie. Aye, our Flora bore more than a little resemblance to her. Not that she was ever going to be an actress, mind. Our da would have gone to his grave before he allowed that. He made no secret of the fact that she was his favourite and he protected her at all costs.

Flora worked for my father in his bookkeeping business. I'm fairly sure he took her on to keep her out of harm's way, because she was never particularly good with numbers. She went along with it though, after my mother begged her to do as he wanted and keep the peace. That was my ma. Bloody terrified of upsetting him and triggering one of his rages. Anyway, Flora did as she was bid, took the job and even began courting the son of one of my father's business clients. Da was well pleased. They had a huge house in Newton Mearns and I think he could see himself up there, hobnobbing with the posh ones.

Our Annie, though? Well, she was a different case altogether. Her full name had been Bethany, but my parents had decided early on that Annie was more suited to her than her more formal given name. She was a wild one all her life, always the first to try new things and push boundaries. She even saved up her money from her job as a typist in an insurance company in the city centre and bought a record player. It seemed like every week, home she came with another single by Elvis or The Everly Brothers. I was more of a Frank Sinatra fan myself.

She was a case, our Annie. She didn't have the looks of Flora, but she was pretty enough, with her red hair and the freckles on her pale cheeks. But oh, she was quick with her mouth. She could make anyone laugh and she let no one get away with anything. Fearless, she was. My da… well, she was the bane of his life, quite frankly. The only one that had the nerve to stand up to him, until he was red in the face and my mother had to get between them and shoo Annie out of the door before my da lost his head and went for her.

We would hear Annie laughing as she jogged off down the path and that would just set my da off again. More than once he tore out there after her but she was too fast for him.

I actually think he was relieved when she got herself a boyfriend, because, unlike how he felt about Flora, he wanted Annie up the aisle and off his hands and didn't much care who took her.

Declan Docherty was an insurance broker at her firm, and by God, Annie was besotted. Never liked the look of him myself. Too cocky. Too sure of himself. Too fast with the chat. There was no use telling Annie that though, because that lassie didn't care what anyone else thought. She had a heart of gold but she was bold as brass and the only thing she'd inherited from our father was sheer bloody mindedness. Nothing could stop her when she set her mind to something.

Still, I did speak up when I found out she was sneaking Flora out at night to go dancing with her crowd from work. Annie would have been twenty-four then, and Flora twenty-two. They were grown women with their own minds, but I could see what was coming if my father found out what Annie was doing with his favourite child.

I waited in the kitchen after I'd come home from a date with Betty one Saturday night. I left the light on until I heard them coming down. They'd both been home at 11 p.m., as was the rule in my da's house, but now it was midnight and they were sneaking out again. I knew how it went. Declan Docherty had a car, the flash bastard, and he'd be waiting around the corner for them.

'Da'll not be pleased, Annie,' I said, as I switched on the light.

'Christ Almighty, George, you near gave me a heart attack there,' she hissed. Their outfits would have had my da reaching for the heart pills too. Both of them had on skirts so tight it was a wonder they could put one foot in front of the other. 'You'll not be telling him,' she said, her voice low, her hands on hips, challenging me, her face making it clear it wasn't up for discussion.

'No, I won't. But you shouldn't be dragging Flora into it, too.'

Annie laughed. 'Is that what you think?'

For the first time Flora stepped forward. 'She's not dragging me into anything, George. I begged her to take me. It's the only bloody time I can get away from him looking over me.'

I was as surprised by her language as by what she was saying.

'He's determined to get me married off and I'm not having it. I want to have some fun first, do a bit of living.'

Well, that had me stunned.

'Let her have her night out, George. I'll make sure I get her back in one piece.'

Annie was less than two years older than Flora but it could have been ten years in maturity.

I shrugged and went off to bed, tossing and turning until I heard them coming back in at 4 a.m., only an hour before my old man's alarm went off. Thank God he'd always been a heavy sleeper.

It went on for months, and I never spoke of it again. Betty and I got engaged and set to be wed, Flora seemed happy and Annie was full of the joys and the chat about how great her man was.

'He's going to propose, George, I know it. He says I'll always be the only one for him and we're made for each other,' she told me one night, just a week or so before her birthday.

That's when I knew they were sleeping together. There was something in the way she said it, an excitement, and let's face it, Annie had always been one for staring danger in the face and asking for more. I should have tracked him down then and leathered him. Or at least, given him a warning and told him to back off, but I didn't. I did nothing. Just kept to my own business and stayed out of it. I took the easy option. Shameful, when I look back on it.

I realised the following week that was a mistake. On Annie's birthday there was no engagement ring, just a bottle of cheap perfume and a Cliff Richard single. She didn't even like Cliff Richard. Always the tough one, she tried to act like she wasn't bothered, but I could see how hurt she was and I cursed Declan Docherty for messing with her feelings.

The next evening, I headed out late to my night shift at the factory, I turned the corner of our street and I started at what I saw.

Declan Docherty, up against a fence, kissing my sister.

But it wasn't Annie.

I pulled him off her and smacked him straight across the face, while Flora begged me to stop. I couldn't. Punch after punch I landed on his face, until I heard another voice.

'George, stop it. You'll kill him.' Annie. She'd heard the commotion and come out to see what was going on. She wasn't screaming hysterically like Flora. Her voice was deathly calm and controlled. 'You,' she said to Declan, who was scrambling to his feet. 'You can fuck off.'

He dragged himself back into his car, and only when he was inside with the doors locked did he wind down the window.

'You're a dead man,' he shouted at me.

'Aye, come ahead, ya prick,' I replied, angrier than I'd ever been in my life. I wasn't a fighter, but he'd deserved every bit of that.

He roared off in the car and I knew that was the last I'd see of him.

'And you,' Annie said, turning to face Flora. 'You can fuck off too, you treacherous bitch.' The hurt in her words was tangible and I ached for her, but I had sympathy for Flora too. She hadn't stood a chance against a fast talking scumbag like that.

Flora wailed and fell against the fence she'd been kissing that weasel against only moments before...

I hear the beep of the monitor next to my bed get louder, and Liv, that lovely nurse, is by my side just moments later.

'Are you all right there, George?' she says. I can tell she's just chatting to me, as she always does whether I'm asleep or awake, and she doesn't expect an answer. Just as well, because the memories are choking me and I couldn't speak if I'd tried. My eyes stay closed.

'Let me just check a few things here then,' I hear her say, as I feel her hand on my wrist, taking my pulse, and then feel the stethoscope on my chest. The sound of the monitor has slowed again now. She must be satisfied with whatever she's learned, because the next thing I hear is her voice, and there is no trace of alarm in it. 'Ah, you're okay there, George,' she says. 'I don't want you to worry about a thing. We're right outside and we're keeping an eye on you. Tom will be back in a wee while. I'm just going to leave this bell in your hand...' I feel her place a button attached to a wire in my palm, and know it is the one that I am supposed to use to call a nurse if I need anything. I haven't pressed it for days. There is nothing that anyone can get for me now. But it is kind that she is doing that for me and talking to me even though she has no idea whether or not I can hear her. '... And if you need anything, you just press it and we'll be right here.' As always, the reassurance in her voice means the world to me.

My mind goes back to Flora, sobbing that night, a sound that I never forgot.

I went on to my night shift at work, and when I got back the next morning, there was silence in the house, except for the noise of my mother crying. I knew my father and Flora would already be long gone and that Annie would be leaving in the next half an hour or so to get to work.

'What's happened?' I asked, knowing full well what was going on.

'Annie's taken leave of her senses,' she said, as she cleared away the breakfast plates. She's upstairs. Go on up, George, and see if you can talk some sense into her.'

I climbed the stairs and opened her door, not sure what I would find. Nine o'clock in the morning and she already had an Elvis song on the record player. "Hound Dog". I turned down the volume and she looked up from what she was doing – packing a suitcase on her bed.

'Where are you going?' I asked her.

'London.'

'With him?' I had to know.

Her face darkened. 'Not with him. He can rot in hell.'

I tried not to show the relief.

'So why then?' I asked, careful to keep my voice casual.

'I need to get away for a week. I've got some money saved so I'm going to use that.'

I knew that telling her she was wrong wouldn't work, so I settled for logic instead.

'Why are you wanting to spend all your savings in one week? Sure, you could just go down to Ayr or over to Edinburgh for a fraction of the cost.'

She put the last of her clothes in the suitcase and closed it.

'Tilly from our office transferred to London a couple of months ago, so I'm going to visit her. I'm not changing my mind, George, so there's no point in trying to make me. I'll be back for your wedding.' It was only two weeks until I was going to marry Betty and Flora and Annie were to be bridesmaids.

'You promise?'

'I promise,' she said. 'I just need to get away from Flora for a while. And I'm sorry that means leaving you too. God knows, there's nothing else about this place that I'll miss.'

There was a toot of a horn outside, and she peered out of the window.

'That's my taxi.'

There was no point trying to stop her leaving. When our Annie was settled on a course, she rarely veered from it.

I went over to the bed and picked up her case. 'I'll carry it down for you,' I told her.

Our mother gazed at her with tear filled eyes as we walked through the kitchen. 'Don't be crying, Ma,' Annie said.

My ma wiped away the tears with the hanky she always kept up her sleeve. 'What's he going to say, Annie?'

We all knew she was talking about my da. There would be hell to pay when he found out about this.

'I don't really care, Ma,' Annie replied.

'Annie Butler, don't you dare speak of your father that way.'

Annie would usually bite her lip where my mother was concerned, but not this morning. 'The way he treats you, the way he treats us, and you still defend him? Are you upset because I'm going or because you know he'll be furious?'

My mother didn't answer. She didn't have to. She'd lived by his rules since she was a teenager and she wasn't going to change now.

'Goodbye, Ma,' Annie said, kissing her on the cheek.

I followed her out to the taxi and put the case in the boot of the car, sad that she felt the need to get away.

'Bye, George,' she said, going up on her tiptoes to hug me.

'Take care of yourself, Annie,' I said.

'For God's sake, you'd think I was leaving forever. I'm only going to London for a week.'

Looking back, I think we both knew that wasn't true.

I never saw our Annie again.

<u>Noon – 2 p.m.</u>

Nine

Shauna

Have I ever told you that Mariah Carey song makes me want to gag her with tinsel?' Lulu asked, as she put two paninis and two highly decorated cocktails down on the table in front of them.

Shauna feigned gravity and sorrow. 'Many, many times. And it hurts my feelings, because all I want for Christmas is you.'

'Shut it and eat your turkey panini.'

John, the taxi driver, had chauffeured them to the Sunnyvale Care Home, and they'd been told at reception that the residents were having lunch until one o'clock. They'd left a message that they'd like to see Mrs McNair, then popped into a wine bar across the road for a quick sandwich and a drink, keeping to Lulu's pledge to have a cocktail between every stop. Shauna didn't even want to contemplate how she was going to feel tomorrow morning on the plane to Heathrow. In fact, there were a whole load of things that she didn't want to contemplate right now. Unfortunately, Lulu hadn't got that memo.

'What are you thinking about?' she asked, as she slipped into the chair across from Shauna, then grinned as Shauna picked up the bright red drink with the flashing cocktail stick.

'Nothing.' She didn't want to admit that all this festive stuff was giving her flashbacks to every Christmas she'd ever spent with Colm. He'd been like a big kid every year, even before they'd had Beth to make it a family event. He'd dragged huge trees into the house every December, the presents would pile up under them and everyone was invited to Christmas dinner with the obligatory board games afterwards. The year he bought a karaoke machine had damaged her eardrums for life. God, she missed every bit of him, but most of all she longed for his enthusiasm, his joy, his laughter.

'You're thinking something. You've got that sad expression going on and you're chewing your lip. You're going to look like a before advert for cold sore medication if you carry on doing that. So spill.'

Shauna attempted to rally. The one annoying thing about hanging out with a lifelong friend was the fact that they could read you far too well. 'It's nothing. I'm not going to be a downer today. I'm having too much fun.'

Lulu held up her wrist and pointed at her watch. 'Okay. You have sixty seconds to say sad things and then we're going to switch back to random musings and discussions about how you can coerce Dan into buying me a new Prada bag for Christmas. Right... go.'

'It's just...' She took a deep breath, then let it all tumble out. 'I want to call Colm and tell him about what we're doing this weekend. It's my first instinct. Whenever anything good happens, or anything bad too, I still reach for my phone to let him know, to hear his voice. This is our third Christmas without him and I still miss him so much. How am I doing for time?' she asked, trying to inject some levity into the moment.

'Thirty seconds.'

'Right. So what really worries me is that... okay, I'm just going to say it. I'm scared that Beth will stop remembering him. I want her to always have him somewhere in her memories. But what if she forgets? I show her videos when she wants to see him, but she's asking less and less and I don't want to push it. I just... I fecking hate that he's not here.' The last work got caught in the lump in her throat.

'Me too.' Lulu said sadly, before reverting to type. 'Okay, time's up. She won't forget, Shauna. She's got all of us, and he's part of us and he's part of her too, so even when she isn't talking about him, he's still there. Holy shit, did I sound wise and profound then?'

'You did.' Shauna couldn't help but smile.

'Bollocks. That will completely dent my shallow and superficial reputation. Talk to me about that new Prada bag until I feel myself again.'

It was impossible not to laugh. This was exactly why she'd brought Lulu along. No melancholy. No wallowing in the past.

'Okay, tell me about you and Dan.'

'We're okay. Great even. Probably the best we've ever been, at least since the early days, and that's pretty good because most of the time we were naked back then.'

'And he's over his wobble about the parenthood thing?'

Lulu had never wanted children. At school, when her friends were talking about dream weddings and future families, she was trying to work out ways to get on the Take That tour bus and shag Robbie Williams. Dan had been on the same parenting page until just after Colm died, when he started to wonder if perhaps they should consider starting a family. Shauna had thought it was a reaction to the grief of losing his best friend, and Dan had eventually come to the same conclusion.

'Yeah. Thanks be to the God of Stretch Marks. We've decided that being Beth's favourite aunt and uncle is more than enough responsibility for this lifetime.'

'Second favourite. I think Rosie has definitely swung it with Disneyland,' she teased.

'Bugger, I'm going to have to up my game. Think Justin Bieber's security is good enough to prevent a kidnapping attempt?'

'I think you could handle them,' Shauna retorted, finishing off her panini, just as Lulu gave her verdict on their lunch.

'Outlawed carbs and a drink that looks like it belongs on the top of a Christmas tree. I'm going to diet hell, but at least I'll be in the Christmas spirit when I get there,' she mused.

A huge wagon wheel clock on the wall made a dinging noise to announce the hour.

'Shall we go then?' Shauna suggested. 'I asked John to come back and get us at two, so that gives us an hour to chat to Mrs McNair if she'll see us. If not, we'll come back here and console ourselves with another one of these cocktails.'

'Santa's Little Helper,' Lulu said, standing up.

'Who is?'

'The cocktail. The girl behind the bar says that's what they're called. Santa's Little Helpers.'

'I bloody love Glasgow,' Shauna said, amused. 'The hotel is pure luxury, we've found the nicest taxi driver on the planet, a nice lady helped us out at Flora's old house, and now we're fuelled up on a cocktail called Santa's Little Helper. If I were home I'd be doing three rounds of laundry and speeding round packed stores doing Christmas shopping. This is much more fun.'

It was. In fact, maybe it was the change of scene, the company, the thrill of the quest, or the power of Santa's Little Helper, but other than her little outburst of melancholy, this was the lightest she'd felt since Colm had passed. For the last three years she'd been… heavy. That was it. Like her heart weighed a ton in her chest and she had to make a real effort to appear happy. She realised right then that, for once, she wasn't having to try too hard and it felt really good.

The same receptionist greeted them as they arrived back at the care home and asked them to sign in. 'Mrs McNair's granddaughter called and said you'd be coming. Carla here will take you through,' she said, gesturing to a nearby assistant, who then escorted them to the residents' lounge. The room was decorated in pale pink, with matching floral sofas and chairs, with a huge Christmas tree in the corner, piles of presents gathered around the bottom of it and strings of tinsel draped along every wall.

'This will do me fine when I'm old,' Lulu whispered as they sat down. 'Just make sure there's a bar in the corner and a nightly run to a good club, and I'll be happy in my dotage.'

Shauna playfully slapped her thigh. 'Behave yourself. And you're not coming here. We're going on a permanent cruise – all five star restaurants and sun decks. I read somewhere that it's actually cheaper than a home.'

'I'm in,' Lulu concurred, just as Carla, the assistant, returned holding the hand of an elderly lady, impeccably dressed in a red jumper and tartan skirt, her curly grey hair suggesting a very recent blow-dry.

Shauna and Lulu immediately stood up and shook her hand.

'Thank you so much for seeing us,' Shauna said gratefully.

'That's all right, dear. Who are you?'

'I'm Flora McGinty's niece, Shauna. And this is my friend Lulu,' she said.

'The singer?'

'No, not the singer,' Lulu said, amused. 'But I'm happy to give you a song.'

Shauna nudged her and carried on with the point of being there. 'Mrs McNair, I spoke to your granddaughter and she said you knew my aunt, Flora Butler – I think her married name was McGinty – and that you might be able to answer some questions for us.'

'Ah, lovely Flora. Yes, her maiden name was Butler right enough. Och, I do miss her.'

Shauna tried to hide her disappointment. She bit her bottom lip again, before deciding to address the pressing question. 'Is Flora... still alive?' she stuttered.

'I do hope so, dear. I got a Christmas card from her yesterday.'

'Yassssss!' Lulu exclaimed, making Shauna laugh.

'So tell me again, who are you, dear?'

'I'm her niece,' Shauna gushed, unable to hide her delight. This wasn't a wild goose chase. One of her family members was still alive. This was incredible! 'Or great-niece, I suppose. My father, Jeff, would have been her nephew.'

'Ah right. And was he George's or Annie's son?'

Hearing her grandmother's name said by someone else was like an electric jolt to the system.

'Annie's son. She was my grandmother. Did you know her?'

Mrs McNair shook her head. 'No. When I moved in next door, it was just Flora there and her husband Arthur. Flora became a great friend and she spoke about Annie many times, especially in the early days.' This surprised Shauna, as Annie had definitely never spoken of Flora.

'Did Flora and Arthur have children?' Shauna asked hopefully. Cousins! She might actually have cousins that she knew nothing about. Her hopes rose.

'I'm afraid not. Such a sadness it was for her.'

Hopes deflated.

She pressed on. 'Can you tell me where my aunt is now?'

Mrs McNair pursed her lips. 'How do I know you're genuine? I watch the news. Con artists everywhere. I'm not sending a couple of scammers over to wrestle Flora's pension from her.' Shauna smiled in admiration at the old lady's gumption.

'I promise I'm not a scammer, Mrs McNair.'

'I'll require proof,' she said, with total conviction.

111

'Tough crowd,' Lulu murmured.

Shauna reached into her bag and pulled out her trusty sheaf of documents – her own birth certificate, Annie's birth and marriage certificates, a couple of photographs of her with Annie, and finally the letters.

Shauna hadn't witnessed such thorough evidence scrutiny since the last episode of Line of Duty.

'Well, that all seems to be in order. But I'll be checking with Flora and if I find out her pension is gone...'

'I promise her pension is safe,' Shauna assured her.

'Right. Carla, can you fetch my address book for me, dear? It's on my dressing table next to that bottle of port I'm saving for Christmas Eve,' she asked the nursing assistant, who'd been by her side the whole time. As soon as she left the room, she turned back to Shauna and Lulu. 'Need a drop of port after dinner on Christmas Eve,' she said conspiratorially. 'It's the only way to survive all those bloody carol singers.'

They chatted for a few moments about her plans to spend Christmas Day with her granddaughter and her family, before Carla reappeared with a beautiful old book with an embroidered cover. Mrs McNair flicked through it until she found Flora's address and read it out to Shauna, who noted it down.

'Can I ask just one more thing? Do you know why my grandmother and Aunt Flora didn't keep in touch?'

Mrs McNair's face darkened. 'Well, I don't think that's my story to tell, dear, so I'll say no more.'

The elderly lady folded her hands on her lap and raised her chin in a gesture of defiance. Shauna could see that she wasn't going to be budged and wouldn't dream of pushing it. She had an address and another lead, and she knew for sure that Annie's sister was still alive. That was incredible. However, there was definitely something in Mrs McNair's response that was a little unsettling. Shauna hoped she was just being a bit dramatic.

'I understand, of course. Thank you so much. I can't tell you what it means to me.'

'That's quite all right, dear. If you see my friend Flora, please give her my love.' Despite her strong and capable veneer, Shauna was sure she spotted the glisten of tears in the old lady's eyes, and, on impulse, leaned over and gave her a hug.

'Thank you for the address,' she said again, thinking how heart-breaking it must be to leave friends behind. Mrs McNair and Flora had lived next door to each other for decades, and yet, here they were, keeping in touch by sending Christmas cards.

'I'll walk you out,' Carla said as Shauna and Lula went to leave.

Shauna had a sudden thought and stopped.

'Mrs McNair, you mentioned Flora and Annie's brother, George. Did you ever meet him?'

Mrs McNair's jaw clenched in what looked like fury, and it was a few moments before she answered.

'I did not. And let me tell you, I always wished I did, because I would have given that terrible man a piece of my mind. What he did to Flora was unforgivable. Unforgivable!' Agitation made her voice rise with the last word and Shauna decided that asking more wasn't an option, though the vehemence in Mrs McNair's voice made her desperate to know what George had done. Was that why Annie never mentioned her family?

'I'm sorry – I didn't mean to upset you. Thank you again, Mrs McNair. Have a lovely Christmas.'

'You too, dear,' she replied, her voice calmer again. 'It was lovely to meet you. I'm sure Flora will be thrilled to see you.'

After hearing the lady's verdict on George, Shauna wasn't so sure.

Another letter came to the forefront of Shauna's mind, one from George to Annie, and Shauna remembered every word.

> *Dear Annie,*
>
> *It gave me no pleasure, but I did as you asked. I told him. I hazard by now you will have heard that it did not draw the response that was hoped. I fear Flora will never forgive me and I'm destined to lose two sisters.*
>
> *Your brother,*

George

As far as Shauna could tell, George's fears of losing both sisters had been realised.

Address in hand, they headed back out into the crisp, cold afternoon and towards John's taxi, which was sitting parked and waiting as requested.

'Well, she's a feisty one,' Lulu said. 'Add a couple of mojitos and a *Best of the Nineties* soundtrack, and she's me in forty years' time.'

'Promise me you'll never do that to me,' Shauna blurted out.

'Do what?'

'Leave me in a home and just send me Christmas cards.'

'I'd never do that,' Lulu replied, consoling Shauna until she added, 'I'd at least break you out once a week to take you to the bingo.'

Shauna rolled her eyes. 'It's sad, though, isn't it…?'

'What is? That looked like a lovely place and Mrs McNair was clearly well cared for.'

'I know, but it's just…'

'Oh, arse, you're coming over all sentimental again,' Lulu groaned.

'I'm not. I've just got a tad more emotional depth than you – which wouldn't be difficult, because you're shallower than that cocktail we had at lunch.'

'I'm aware of my failings and fully embrace them,' Lulu said, chuckling. 'So tell me what's sad then.'

'The whole situation with Annie, Flora and George. Annie was never close to my parents, and she had tons of friends, but in terms of family, she only had me. At least, that's what she told me. All that time she could have had a brother and sister in her life, but some ancient rift tore them apart. They missed out on a whole lifetime of caring for each other.'

Lulu nodded thoughtfully. 'You could be right, but, Shauna, you know as well as I do that there are some people who you really are better off without, even if they're family.'

That was true. Shauna and Lulu had bonded as children over the fact that their parents were completely self-obsessed and treated their daughters as trifling inconveniences.

Their conversation was brought to a halt by John, who had stepped out of the cab.

'At your service, ladies,' he said, with a mock bow. 'Where are we off to now?'

Shauna gave him the address and he whistled.

'Newton Mearns. Very posh. Your aunt must be doing all right for herself.'

'How long will it take to get there?' Lulu asked.

'About twenty minutes.'

Shauna had spent a lifetime not knowing the truth about Annie's background. It was both nerve wracking

116

and thrilling to know that in less than an hour she could have the answers.

Ten

Chrissie

'Are you sure you're okay?' Val asked, as soon as they were seated in the restaurant. 'I thought you were going to keel over back there on the escalator.'

Josie lifted the carafe of water in the centre of the table and poured some water into the glass in front of her. 'Are you pregnant? I was forever fainting when I was up the duff with our Michael and Avril.'

'Josie, I haven't had sex since 2006. It would be a miracle.'

'Well, this is the time of year for an immaculate conception,' Josie joked, making Chrissie feel so much better in the space of seconds.

But still, she couldn't shake the image from her mind.

Was it him?

She wasn't going to tell Josie and Val because she knew exactly what they'd do – they'd spend the next hour commando-crawling through every restaurant searching for him and that was the last thing she wanted. Not long after they'd met, Chrissie had given in to their curiosity and told them the basics – that Ben's father was her childhood sweetheart, but he had left before he knew she was pregnant and cut off all contact. She knew their first instinct would be to confront him and make him face his responsibilities.

Besides, it couldn't have been him. He was long gone, and probably decorating a tree right now with his wife and three kids. Damn, that thought stung.

'I don't think I can go tonight.' It was out of her mouth before she even knew she'd said it. In fact, she was only sure the words had come out because Val and Josie had both stopped, mid-chuckle, and they were staring at her.

'Why, love?' Val asked, the furrow between her eyes, underneath her platinum blonde fringe, deepening.

'I just think… I'm not ready.' In truth, she would never be ready, because she'd never forget the pain of the last time she'd loved. And lost.

Josie leaned forward and placed her hand over Chrissie's. The younger woman braced herself for dark humour and a large dose of cajoling, but surprisingly, neither came.

'Look, ma darling, whatever you decide to do is fine with us. I know we're nudging you along with this, but if you don't want to do it, we'll go and grab a couple of bottles of wine and have a wee night in with the girls. But think about it. You deserve this. At your age, you should be out and about, meeting people and having a bit of love in your life because you're pretty bloody brilliant. Ben's getting older, and he's less reliant on you, so it's time to have a bit of fun, not be staying in with two pensioners.'

'Although we are pretty fabulous pensioners,' Val interjected.

Josie ignored her, but paused for a second as she spotted Chrissie's reaction. 'Oh, Jesus, there's tears. Val, give me one of those napkins, pronto.'

Chrissie took it gratefully and dabbed at her eyes.

'I thought I saw him,' she said, feeling a sudden need to explain after all.

'Who?' Val asked, confused.

'The last guy... my ex... Ben's dad. Tom,' she answered, the words choking her.

'Oh, dear God! When?' Val again.

'When I was on the escalator. I looked over and I thought I saw him on the stairs.'

As predicted, Josie immediately went into ninja mode. 'Let's go and find him then. Come on. Let's see what he's got to say for himself, the cowardly b—'

'Josie, no. It wasn't him. There's no way it could be. But it just... rattled me. And it's making me think... what's the point? Why put myself through that again? Ben and I are great. We're happy. We're on our feet. We've got you lot...'

'That's the best bit,' Josie interjected, earning a slap on the shoulder from Val.

Chrissie went on. 'We don't need anything else. We're good.' Chrissie knew that was the truth. She didn't need a man to complete her happiness. However, there was no denying that seeing someone who looked so like Tom had shaken her.

Val sighed as she took her large glass of vodka and cranberry from the waitress. 'You're right, Chrissie,' she said. 'You absolutely are. You've made a great life for you and the boy and we're all delighted to be part of it, but, love, you need some happiness for yourself too. I know that Ben's dad hurt you...'

'He really did,' Chrissie said, her voice just above a whisper. She'd only ever told Val the bare minimum, unwilling to dredge up the past or look back on the most painful time of her life. She'd been with someone she loved beyond words and he'd left her. That was it. In fact, he'd gone as far away as it was possible to go. That was all anyone needed to know. That whole chapter of her life was locked in a steel box and placed in the vault of her mind, never to be opened for fear of massive pain and regret.

Val nodded, then went on, 'But that doesn't mean you should go through life and not give anyone else a chance. For all you know, this guy you're meeting tonight could be the loveliest, sweetest, most caring man, and it could be the start of something great for both you and Ben.'

'Or just an almighty shag that will make you happy for a couple of hours,' Josie added.

'In the name of God, Josie, will you put something in your mouth to stop words coming out,' Val blurted.

Josie pursed her lips, unrepentant. However, the hilarity of the two women bickering made Chrissie's shoulders slide down from "high tension" to "slightly stressed".

'Okay,' Chrissie said, exhaling. 'I hear you. I know I need to get some courage and do this.'

'You've got more courage than anyone I know, pet,' Josie said, being unusually serious. 'So don't diminish what you've done or who you are. You're protecting yourself and Ben and that takes strength. We just don't want you to miss out on some joy along the way.' Chrissie felt yet another lump form in her throat at Josie's words until she added, 'Or some great sex.'

'Damn, Josie, you were doing well there right up until the end,' Val chuckled, echoing Chrissie's thoughts. 'She's right though. And we'll be here to support you if this date does go wrong tonight and the guy is a total knob.'

Josie nodded. 'And by "support you", we mean kidnap him and tie electric probes to his nipples until he says sorry.'

'Nothing to lose then, really,' Chrissie shrugged. She loved this, loved these women, even more so because they gave her the kind of support that her own mother never had.

Okay, she had it together again. She was going on this date. It was going to be fine and if it wasn't, well that was okay, too. It was time to move on. Take a few chances. Wasn't it?

The waitress took their order and left a basket of bread in the middle of the table.

'So, tell us about this guy you're meeting tonight then,' Val asked, picking up a piece of ciabatta and dipping it in the olive oil on the plate next to the basket.

'His name is Davie and I went to school with him,' Chrissie said. 'Actually, I didn't know him that well there, but I remember him because half of my pals had a crush on him, so they'd drag me to watch him playing football at lunchtime. I think I also kissed him under mistletoe at the third year Christmas disco. That's about it. I didn't see him again after he left, then he contacted me about a week after I put that Facebook page up a couple of months ago. I only joined because Ben will be thirteen in a few months and he'll be old enough to sign up. All of his school pals are already on there. I just wanted to make sure I knew what it was all about.'

'Just be careful,' Val warned. 'I've heard criminals search those sites for information about folk.'

'Don't worry, Miss Marple, I put absolutely nothing personal on it.' That was true, but not for the reasons Val mentioned. She didn't put anything personal on there because a long time ago she'd cut ties with everyone she knew and she didn't want them, or anyone else, finding out anything about her life, about the choices she'd made, about where she was now.

She still found it bizarre that Davie had tracked her down. The only group she'd joined on Facebook was for former pupils of her school, and only because she couldn't help an insatiable urge to check if Tom was there. He wasn't. But a couple of days later Davie had got in touch.

'So what does he do now, this Davie?' Val asked.

'Marketing. Started up his own company. He's got an office in the city centre. They do advertising and press campaigns for loads of different companies. Seems to be doing really well for himself.'

'Good looking? That's important. Never marry an ugly man,' Josie said with solemn sincerity.

Val was outraged. 'Josie! You can't say that!'

'It's true!' Josie argued. 'Because at least when you realise you're stuck for life, he's still good to look at.'

'Your values are despicable,' Val sighed.

'They are,' Josie agreed, but Chrissie got the impression she took that as a compliment.

'I'm not marrying him, Josie, I'm meeting him for dinner. But yes, he's good looking.' She pulled out her iPhone and loaded his Facebook page. It was work oriented, with no personal details, more of an advert for the campaigns his company had worked on, but his profile picture was at the top.

'Yup, if I was forty years younger I'd shag him,' Josie whistled, just as a startled waitress put down a large pizza and three plates on their table.

'Again, I'm meeting him for dinner, not shagging him,' Chrissie objected. It had taken twelve years to contemplate sharing a meal with a guy. There was every chance it would take another twelve years to get round to actually having sex with someone new.

Josie shook her head. 'I don't know what's happened to the younger generation. Wasn't like that in my day.' Josie had been married and widowed once, two decades ago, and had never married again, but she made no secret of the fact that she'd enjoyed many romances over the years. And still did.

Chrissie was still laughing as she glanced around the centre, at the restaurants over on the opposite balconies, at the shops up on the higher floors. Was he here? For a long time after he left, she would search for his face in crowds, knowing that he wouldn't be there but unable to stop herself.

No. She shook the thought away, berating herself for even thinking that way. He was off living another life in another world. And even if he wasn't, she didn't want him back. He'd burned that bridge and then torched the ashes just to make sure there was no going back.

They settled into idle chit-chat about their plans for Christmas (dinner at Val's house with the whole extended family) and New Year (party at Josie's house with everyone they'd ever known), until the waitress cleared their plates.

'I'd better be getting back to the shop now. Thank you for this. I've loved it,' Chrissie said gratefully.

'Ah, we're not done yet, lovely,' Val said. 'Come on, let's head to the next destination.'

Chrissie was about to question her, but then stopped, deciding this was a riptide situation and the best thing to do was float until she had a clear path to the shore.

The three of them linked arms as they walked to the escalator, gazed around in wonder at the decor as they descended to the ground floor, then joined the crowds heading for the row of gilt-edged doors.

Chrissie looked ahead as she pulled her collar up and scrunched her ancient but beloved red beret on to her head, ready for the assault of the cold as they stepped outside.

She had no idea what made her look back, but she turned her head, caught sight of the glass elevator descending on the other side of the centre and saw...

It was him again. The man she'd seen earlier.

Their eyes locked and she thought she saw a flare of recognition, one that was cut short when the woman

126

who was with him stepped forward and kissed him.

She had two choices. One: go over there, find out if it was really him. After all, the last time she'd seen him was twelve years ago. He probably looked completely different now.

Or two: go on with her life, and accept that the teenager who had loved and left her when she was eighteen, who'd ignored her calls, left her letters unanswered, left her without a backward glance, was someone who well and truly belonged in her past.

Chrissie kept on walking, hearing that vault door slam shut once again.

Eleven

Tom

Princess Square was packed with Christmas shoppers and office workers bunking off early on the last day of work before Christmas. Last year Tom had brought his grandad here and they'd sat on the outside patio of one of the courtyard level restaurants, underneath sparkling ice white snowflakes and galaxies of lights. The centrepiece of the atrium was a stunning cone shaped tree that soared from the lower ground floor to the third floor, visible to all on the layers of balconies that swirled around it. Tom and George had sat, soaking up the festive atmosphere while enjoying lunch and a pint. He'd had no idea that was the last Christmas they'd do that.

'What are you thinking, darling? You look so serious,' Zoe commented as they climbed the stairs. There were people jostling both upwards and downwards, so he instinctively put a protective hand on her back. They'd been dating now for a couple of months and on the rare occasions they'd actually managed to snatch a night together they'd had a good time. He'd been happy to see how it developed. He'd thought that perhaps he was ready. He knew now that he wasn't. The thought of Chrissie had changed that.

They were seated at a corner table in the restaurant on the top floor of the centre. It was one of their favourite spots. Zoe didn't like to sit out at the balcony tables – said it was too noisy and busy and she preferred the more intimate setting inside. Tom was always happy to go along with it. He realised with a jolt that he'd been doing exactly that since the start of this relationship – just going along with it. Another jolt, this time one of self-reproach. Zoe was everything most guys could want. She was smart and had one of the most incisive business minds he'd ever encountered. As head of sales, she was largely responsible for bringing on new clients and she'd exceeded every target over the last year. She was fun, she could hold her own in any company, she was gorgeous, she was… He could hear himself repeating all the things he'd first told himself when he started seeing her. It was a checklist of attributes. He'd never done that with Chrissie. Never had to. Maybe it was because they'd been so young, but he hadn't needed to list her qualities in his head, he'd just known he wanted to be with her every waking moment.

'Looking handsome today, Mr Butler,' Zoe told him as the waiter disappeared with their coats and their drinks order. Water for Tom, champagne for Zoe.

Normally, he'd compliment her right back, but... he couldn't go on with this. It wasn't fair. He'd honestly thought he was ready to have a real relationship when they started seeing each other, but there was no doubt now that he'd been mistaken.

She was still talking. 'I've said to my sister that you'll try to make it for Christmas dinner. I know it'll be difficult with your grandad being ill, and your family here, but I'm hoping you'll get a chance to slip away. Or maybe you could bring your parents? I'm dying to meet them and I'll have to do it at some point, so Christmas dinner is as good a time as any. She always does far too much food anyway – I think she's doing turkey, ham and steak pie this year – so there will be loads to go round. I was going to pick up a gift for your parents this afternoon, so they won't feel left out. I want to make a good impression on your mother...'

'Stepmother.' It was out before he realised it.

If Zoe registered the bitterness of the word, she didn't show it.

'Of course, stepmother. Anyway, I was thinking we could nip to Vivienne Westwood and pick up something nice, maybe earrings for her. And for your dad...'

'Zoe, we need to talk.'

There it was. The first line of almost every break-up speech in history.

Again, she didn't register. 'Yes, of course, darling. You don't think you'll make it for dinner. It's fine. I understand. I really do.'

'We need to talk about us.'

The other infamous line of the traditional break-up speech. He was so weary he'd lost all power to be original.

This time she paused, eyed him warily, reality registering.

'About?' Her tone was steady and she had a fixed smile on her face.

He'd seen her take this stance before, usually just as a potential client was about to raise an objection to something in her sales pitch. She invariably came back with something brilliant that won them over and persuaded them to sign on the dotted line. This wasn't going to be one of those times.

'I can't see you any more. I mean, outside work. In a relationship.' He was stumbling. 'I'm sorry. I hate to do this, I really do. I've had a great time with you but...'

'Who is she?'

'What?'

She took a slug of the champagne that had just been placed in front of her.

'Who is she? There's someone else.' Zoe was calm. Measured.

'I promise there isn't,' Tom vowed.

She thought about it for a few seconds, then, like the trained negotiator and communicator that she was, she came back from a different, incredibly perceptive angle.

'But there was?' she countered.

He didn't answer.

'An ex,' Zoe repeated, realising she'd hit bullseye. 'How long ago?'

Tom felt his shoulders sag with defeat. 'Twelve years ago.'

'Twelve years? But you must have been…'

'Eighteen,' he replied, saving her the mental arithmetic.

Zoe seemed to find this amusing. 'And you're seeing her again?'

'No. I haven't seen her since.' He wasn't going to tell her that wasn't true, that he'd seen her face, in full colour, on that bastard Davie's computer yesterday. Or that he'd stopped by a café across from her work this morning to catch a glimpse of her, like some weird stalker.

'For God's sake, Tom, you were a kid. You can't still have real feelings for her. You're seriously dumping me for the memory of some high school girlfriend?'

'I know it sounds crazy but—'

'There is no "but". It's completely bat shit crazy.'

It was probably time to cut his losses and leave, but there was a strange relief in talking about it, even if it was to a woman whom he was ending a relationship with.

A waiter arrived for their food order, but they asked for a few more minutes, then resumed their conversation as soon as he'd gone.

'So, did she break your heart and leave you scarred for life?'

'No. I broke hers.'

'Oh, for fuck's sake,' Zoe said, sighing. 'This is what I get for choosing a nice guy for once. I bloody knew it was a mistake. So, go on then, tell me. How did you break her heart and why did you not fix it?'

He paused, unsure as to whether he wanted to reveal all the gory details. 'It's all a bit tragic and pathetic.'

'I like tragic and pathetic,' she said, ruefully. 'I was supposed to be having lunch with my boyfriend but he just dumped me, four days before Christmas. Right now, I'm cornering the market in tragic and pathetic.'

Another quality on Zoe's plus side – she was great with a one liner.

Tom hesitated, then realised that he really wanted to tell someone. Wanted to hear the words. Needed some kind of outside perspective. Admittedly he wasn't sure this was the right outside perspective, but he didn't have much choice. He couldn't tell Davie for obvious reasons, his grandad could no longer give him words of wisdom, and hell would freeze over before he had such a conversation with his dad and stepmother. Zoe was his only option and besides, she deserved the truth.

'We were inseparable for years, best mates all through school, then we realised we loved each other, but our parents didn't approve.'

133

'Why?'

'It's a long story. Basically, they thought we were too young to be so serious.'

It wasn't the entire truth, in fact there was so much more, but now wasn't the time to be upending the family's dirty laundry basket.

'Anyway, my dad had an affair and my mum left when she found out. Then my dad remarried and decided to move to Australia, and I went with them. I didn't have enough bottle to refuse, so I left Chrissie.' He was omitting pertinent details, but the bullet points gave the gist of it.

'Chrissie,' Zoe repeated. 'That's her name?'

Tom nodded, wishing there was some cathartic effect of revealing the truth. There wasn't. Only guilt and pain. 'I never saw her again. I came back a year later, searched for her but never found her. I stayed, went to uni, met Davie again there – I'd known him in school too – and you know the rest.' At least, up to the point that Davie had tracked down Chrissie and decided to keep it to himself.

'And you're still beating yourself up about this all these years later?'

He shrugged. 'I know. Like you said, "bat shit crazy".' Even crazier, he could still remember every detail of the night they'd realised they were more than just friends. He'd been sitting on the back step of his house and Chrissie had jumped over from her garden next door.

'That doesn't look like the face of someone who snogged Carol Carter tonight,' she'd teased. She was right. He'd had a date with the most lusted after girl in the school, who was already doing part-time modelling at fifteen and tipped to be the next big thing. He should be elated. Over the moon. Instead, he felt... weird.

'What should my face look like?' he'd asked.

'Oh, I don't know, but I'd start with happy and pure gobsmacked that she lowered her standards to kiss a mere mortal like yourself.' She always took the piss out of him, and vice versa. They'd been best mates since first year, and now they were going into fourth year and mutual mocking was still the platform on which their relationship was built.

She was right though. She plonked down next to him on the step and as he turned to face her he knew the problem was sitting right in front of him. He'd tried to tell her dozens of times but backed out on every occasion. Chrissie was strong, she was determined, she made him laugh more than anyone he'd ever known and she was absolutely clear that she wasn't interested in boys because she had big plans for her life. She was going to go to university, then start her own business and...

'She's not you.' He'd said it so quietly that he wasn't sure she'd heard. Actually, now that his stomach was churning, he really hoped she hadn't heard.

'What do you mean by that?' She was looking at him now, their eyes locked, only inches apart.

Carried away with the moment, instead of answering he'd leaned over and kissed her and, to his complete shock, she didn't punch him in the throat. Instead, she'd kissed him back and by the time she stopped he couldn't even remember who Carol Carter was.

'I thought you weren't interested in boys,' he'd said, confused.

She'd laughed as she shook her head. 'God, you're a moron sometimes, Tommy Butler. I've never been interested in boys because I was only ever interested in you. You have so much to learn.' He'd only managed to stop her laughter by kissing her again. And again. And again. They'd stayed together for three years and he'd loved every single day of it. Until the end.

Zoe's voice brought him back to the present. 'So, are you going to try to track her down now?'

'Trust me, I'm the last person she'd want to see – but I found out yesterday where she is and it's just thrown me. Unfinished business.'

'Then I think you need to finish it, one way or another, otherwise you're going to live a lonely life, Tom,' she said, not unkindly. 'And if she's married, with sixteen kids, and has an arse the size of Govan, give me a shout. In the meantime, I'm going to go to Vivienne Westwood for some consolation retail therapy.'

'Before we eat?'

'I've lost my appetite,' she said, before signalling the waiter for the bill. 'And you're paying,' she said, handing it over when it arrived. He was happy to.

They pulled on their coats and headed to the glass lift in the corner of the centre. They were the first ones in, so ended up against the glass, watching the buzz of the centre as they descended. It stopped at the second floor, then slowed as they approached the first floor.

'I'm going to get out here,' Zoe said, before the usual scrimmage to enter and exit began. Just as it stopped, a sequence of events changed everything. His eyes caught a head in the distance, a bright red beret that he'd seen so many times before. Then he saw the face as the head turned round. Their eyes locked. It was her. It was definitely her. At that second, Zoe leaned over, kissed him. 'Merry Christmas, Mr Butler. I hope you stop being bat shit crazy sometime soon.' Then Zoe was gone and so was...

His eyes scanned the path to the door, but she was no longer there.

'Excuse me. Excuse me!' he said desperately as he barged his way out of the elevator.

A lift full of people watched as the guy dived out of the lift, ran down another flight of stairs and then started racing to the door.

Twelve

George

It was Betty who noticed it first. I think men, especially back in those days, don't notice these kinds of things in the early days.

It was a few weeks after our honeymoon and we'd settled into our new house over in the West End near Betty's family. She was about to start her training to be a nurse and it was closer to the college and to the hospital she would be working in at night. I'd managed to get a job as an engineer at Barr and Stroud, an optical engineering company in nearby Anniesland.

Flora was over at our house for her dinner. It was the only place that my da let her go to alone. She'd broken up with Arthur, the boy she'd been seeing from Newton Mearns, so she had barely any life now.

We'd had a smashing meal – my Betty was a cracking cook – but Flora hadn't eaten much and it was fair to say she didn't look herself. She was pale, drawn, and when Betty dished up the beef stew, Flora had to excuse herself from the table.

After my da had come in his car to pick her up, I could tell there was something on Betty's mind. Eventually, when we'd settled into bed, I got it out of her.

'I think your Flora is pregnant.'

'Don't be daft. She can't be...' I stopped. Realising. I'd thought that kissing that arse Declan had been a one-off, but what if it wasn't? I wasn't in the house any more, so I had no idea if she was still sneaking out at night to meet him. I'd assumed that after Annie had left, she'd stopped.

Annie. There was no denying the sadness when I thought of her. Of course, she hadn't come back. Deep down, I'd always known that she wouldn't. She'd written to me before the wedding and apologised, said that she'd decided to stay with her friend and work down in London, and she was sorry she wouldn't be bridesmaid. Her letter filled me with sadness, even more so when she said there was nothing in Glasgow to come back for. When the family realised she wasn't returning they made it very clear how they felt. Flora had been devastated, I'm guessing through guilt as much as the love she had for her sister. My dad had been thunderous, and declared that he didn't want her name mentioned and my mother had gone along with it, even though I knew she would miss her. It wasn't in her nature to disobey my da.

As soon as I realised Betty was right about Flora, I'll not lie, I had a fair notion to move to London myself. My da had never lost the rage about Annie leading Flora astray, and he'd been unbearable ever since. My mother teetered between eggshells and tears, trying desperately to cajole him back into some state of normality and recoiling like an injured deer every time he bit her head off.

Our Flora pregnant? I didn't even want to think about how he'd handle that.

I hoped our fears were wrong, but when Betty questioned Flora on her next visit she broke down and admitted it was true. Inconsolable, the poor lass was, and frankly I was at a loss as to how to help her.

Not that she wanted our interference. She made me promise not to tell Ma and Da, and I was only too happy to agree to that. I wanted to be nowhere near my father when he found out.

'Is it Arthur's baby or...' Betty trailed off, unwilling to say the name of that other cretin.

'No, Arthur and I have never...' she paused to swallow a sob. 'It's Declan's. I'm about three months along.'

'Jesus Christ!' I spat. 'You carried on seeing him?'

'Yes. But I'd been seeing him for a couple of months before you... saw us. I think that's when I fell pregnant.'

'Jesus Christ!' I repeated. So that night I'd given him a leathering wasn't the first night she'd been with him. And worse – I did the maths – she was already pregnant then.

Straight away my Betty gave me such a glare that I didn't speak again.

'I did. I know what you must think of me, but I... I... love him. And he loves me. I can only get to see him once a week or so, when Da is at the pub, but it's better than nothing.'

'So what are you going to do, pet?' Betty had asked her, while I kept my jaw clenched shut. I didn't trust myself to speak.

Flora revealed that she'd thought it all through and she had decided on a course of action. She was going to tell Declan when she was ready, and she was absolutely positive that he would do the right thing by her. They could then tell our parents that they were getting married and get a hoof on up to the registry office.

I didn't share her confidence on any of the details of that plan, not least telling Declan in the first place. I knew Flora. She didn't have the nerve to face difficult situations, nor was she worldly wise enough to realise that there were some people out there who were just bad bastards.

At a loss, I sought help from the only person who knew enough about the people involved to give advice on how to proceed.

141

I wrote to Annie. I'd heard from her only once since she moved away, and it was to tell me she wasn't coming back. My next two letters had gone unanswered, so I knew nothing of her new life down south.

I can't remember now what I wrote, but I broke the news to her that Flora was pregnant by Declan, and that I didn't know what to do. I didn't tell her that Flora had already been seeing him, or that she'd continued to court Declan after Annie had left Glasgow, fearing it would hurt her even more.

Her reply was swift. Only a few months ago, after this bastard disease was diagnosed, I came across her letter of reply when I was putting my affairs in order. I read it a dozen times and it still stung on every reading.

Dear George,

I wish I could tell you I was surprised to receive your letter, but I was not. He has no shame, that man. I was a fool to have trusted him, and I curse my stupidity for doing so every day. I can also say with some certainty that he will not stand by her. I also think, knowing Flora as I do, that she will delay telling him until the last possible moment, until she is showing and there is nothing to be done. Much as she has wounded me to the soul, I would not want to see that happen to her. I think the only way forward is for you to confront him, to tell him the truth, and to hope he does the right thing. They can be married, and Flora's life will not be tarnished. However, be prepared that he will want nothing to do with this. If he does not, then at least it is early enough in the pregnancy for Flora to make the best choice for her situation, perhaps to leave and go elsewhere until the baby is born, because you know that Da will surely intervene and no good will come of that.

I trust that you will do the right thing.

Annie x

Back then, I could see the sense in what she was saying, so I decided to carry out her suggestion. A few days later, I waited round the corner for Declan Docherty to leave his office, though once again I had to restrain myself from killing him when he emerged with his arm casually slung around another girl's shoulders. He didn't notice me at first, too caught up with his latest fling.

'A word,' I said as he reached me. I don't mind saying the look of fear on his face pleased me.

He told the girl to go on.

As soon as she was out of earshot, I interrupted his fidgeting.

'Our Flora's pregnant,' I told him, then watched as his face paled. Then – and God help me I wanted to kill him

– he laughed.

'Yeah, must be that rich git from Newton Mearns,' he said, but I could see he was bluffing, trying to bluster his way out of it. Once again, I had to restrain myself.

'The baby is yours,' I told him through gritted teeth, 'and the only reason I'm not pummelling your head with my bare hands is because I'm going to give you the chance to do right by her. I've no idea why she ever lowered her standards and got in with scum like you, but it is what it is. Go see her. Do right. Now I'm going to leave before I can no longer fight back the urge to splatter you all over this pavement.'

I strode away, realising that I'd meant every word I'd just said. Especially the bit about the pavement. Only twice in my life had I entertained violent thoughts or instincts and both times they'd involved this man.

Still, I hoped that there was some goodness in there somewhere that would force him to step up to his responsibilities.

Sadly, there was none.

A few days later, Flora appeared at our door, inconsolable once again. Declan had done a runner, taken off like the scumbag coward that he was. Worse, she'd had to find out in the most brutal way. He hadn't turned up when he'd been supposed to pick her up. She'd stood out in the cold around the corner from Ma and Da's house for an hour. She'd tried phoning him for days afterwards, but he didn't pick up or return the calls.

In the end, she'd snuck out from Da's office when he was away meeting a client and gone to Declan's office – the same place our Annie had worked too. She'd waited for him just as I'd done the week before, but he hadn't come out. Instead, Flora had spotted a woman that she knew he and Annie had worked with, and shouted her over.

She recounted every word of the conversation in painful detail to Betty and me.

'You're Annie's sister, aren't ya?' the woman had said.

'Yes. I'm looking for Declan,' Flora had replied, and she'd confessed she'd got teary at that point.

'Oh God,' the woman had responded. 'It's you he's knocked up. Well, hen, if I were you I'd get that seen to, because he'll not be back. He's taken off to his brother's in Aberdeen. Don't suppose we'll be seeing him again. Fucking chancer. He hadn't even cracked a light that he was winching you too. I believed all that shite about me being the only one.'

At that point, Flora had buckled at the knees and the woman had been kind enough to get her a cup of tea in a nearby café until she'd recovered enough to get the bus to our house.

'The thing I don't understand,' she'd sobbed, and the words cut me like a knife, 'is how did he know? How did he know I was pregnant?'

145

I thought about saying nothing, about letting it be, but I've never been one for keeping secrets and backing down from the truth. I also wanted her to know that I was on her side and that I'd only done it because I wanted to protect her.

'It was me, Flora,' I'd admitted, my heart pounding. 'I told him.'

2 p.m. – 4 p.m.

Thirteen

Shauna

'I should have known it was all going too easily,' Shauna said, as they pressed the buzzer for the third time, to no avail. The address Mrs McGinty had given them was of a very smart apartment block, overlooking a river in a beautiful grassy, tree lined street. She was fairly sure they were retirement flats.

'Okay, so what shall we do? We're not falling at the first roadblock. We're made of sterner stuff than that,' Lulu said, making Shauna laugh.

'I'd like to wait a while and try again,' Shauna said. 'There's no point in travelling back into the city centre, so why don't we find a pub and…'

'My God, it's like we're psychic,' Lulu gasped, pointing two fingers at her own eyes, then swivelling them round to Shauna's and back again.

'Not psychic – I just know how to keep you on side,' Shauna replied with a grin.

Lulu thrust her arm through her friend's. 'Well played. Doing a great job.'

They jumped back in the taxi and John, who was now heavily invested in their search, looked as disappointed as they were. 'Not in? Bugger. I was sure we were on a roll. Right. When we find a pub, I'll drop you two ladies off and then I'll come and sit here and keep an eye out.'

'No, John! Come into the pub with us,' Shauna pleaded.

'Absolutely not,' he objected. 'It'll only make me want to have a beer and I'm not one for denying myself life's pleasures. It's why I'm on my fourth wife,' he said, making them chuckle. 'Anyway, you're paying me for the whole day, so sitting here with a coffee and a sandwich is the least I can do.'

'Stop!' Lulu bellowed. They'd passed a row of little boutique shops and it activated her internal alarm, the one that prohibited her from passing any new and enticing shopping opportunities. In the middle of the row was a little coffee shop, the kind of upmarket bijou ones that peppered Richmond High Street.

'Okay, I know what you're going to say. You want to go shopping...' Shauna said.

Lulu eyed her knowingly. 'And you're going to say you'd rather have a smear test than join me,' she answered, making John choke on a gulp from a bottle of Irn Bru. Her point had merit though; Shauna hated shopping with a passion.

'I tell you what. I'll be in that coffee shop there, and you go shopping and come and join me when they block your credit card,' Shauna suggested, making Lulu's face light up.

'Excellent plan.' She was out of the taxi and in the first shop like a hare after a tinsel bejazzled rabbit, her long mane of red corkscrew curls waving in the wind as she ran.

As always, Lulu made a striking sight. She was wearing white jeans – yep, white in December – tucked into grey, over the knee suede boots, a long silver threaded chunky jumper, with a cream cashmere wrap and gloves. She belonged on the pages of a fashion magazine.

Shauna really needed to up her game, she decided. Her blonde hair was partially covered by her favourite black beanie hat, and she was in her standard outfit of black skinny jeans, an ebony V-neck jumper and a waist length leather jacket and matching boots. The only items of clothing that weren't black were the red scarf and gloves she'd pulled on in a bid to get into the Christmas spirit.

'John, are you sure you don't want to come in for a coffee?'

'Nope, I'll just grab one to take away and nip back round to that address and stake it out. Makes me feel like Colombo. Though you're way too young to remember who that is.'

'Nope, I remember just fine,' Shauna said. 'Many afternoons on the sofa with my granny during the school holidays.'

'Glad to see she taught you well,' he quipped, as she jumped out.

'Wait here and I'll get you that coffee,' Shauna said, grateful that they'd met this lovely man today.

She nipped into the coffee shop, ordered a take away latte and a carrot cake for John, and a sit-in Americano for herself. As soon as his was ready, she took it out to the car and handed it through the window.

'Let's give it an hour or so,' she suggested. 'If she's not there by then, come back and we'll come up with another plan – one which might involve setting off the fire alarms in those shops to get Lulu out,' she said, only half joking.

Back inside, she took her coffee over to a corner table, removed her scarf, hat, jacket and gloves, and pulled out her phone to text Beth. Her daughter was named after her great-grandmother. It had been a huge surprise when she'd found out after Annie passed away that her full name had been Bethany. She'd just always been Annie, her favourite woman on earth. The two of them had spoken most days and while Shauna would like to say it was for her wisdom and profound philosophies on life, the truth was that Annie delighted in being thoroughly irresponsible. She was the one who had told Shauna to punch a playground bully at school, then gave the teacher a piece of her mind when she got detention for it. She'd taught Shauna to cook, to change a plug, and how to make a decent pina colada. She'd also threatened Shauna's first boyfriend with kneecapping if he ever hurt her or let his hand wander under her jumper. He was never seen again.

As Shauna sat, lost in the past, another memory came flooding back. Her first date with Colm. The phone had rung just as she was about to meet him. 'I phoned your house first,' Annie had opened, her Scottish accent still detectable even after decades in London. 'And Lulu tells me your dress should be tighter and show more cleavage. Dear God, you'll be single forever.' Her woeful tone had made her words even funnier, especially because they were coming from a woman who resolutely refused to even entertain the idea of a relationship. Widowed over twenty years earlier, she regularly declared herself an "independent woman who had no desire to wash a pair of men's socks ever again". She went on, 'Now have you given Lulu the address so that if you don't come home we can storm the building?' she'd asked.

'I have.'

'Right then. Better to be safe than sorry. Have a lovely time though. I'm fairly sure it won't be a situation that'll end up on *Crimewatch*. Right, I'm off to bingo. Love you, lass.'

'Love you too, Gran.'

But Shauna's most prevailing thought? The fact that Annie had been in her corner on every occasion, happy to challenge anyone who slighted or insulted her, especially if it was someone who should know better. Annie had never had a close relationship with Shauna's mother, due to the fact that, in her informed opinion, Debbie was a fake, self-indulgent snob. She wasn't wrong. At Shauna's parents' twenty-fifth wedding anniversary, Shauna's offer to do the catering had been rejected by her mother, with Debbie saying they wanted to go "a bit more upmarket". Shauna had tried not to be offended at the slight. It was just one in a long line of many, so they tended to bounce right off her mother-proof vest. However, at the party, Annie had pulled her aside when she was barely in the door.

'Don't eat the food,' she'd hissed, gesturing to the buffet table. 'Your mother got some fancy caterer to do it instead of you, so we're protesting with a hunger strike.'

Shauna had found it both touching and hilarious that Annie was, as always, outraged on her behalf and prepared to engage in battle to avenge her honour. Or at least, avoid the chicken and sweetcorn vol-au-vents.

Shauna closed her eyes as another playback flipped to the front of her mind. The one that she tried her very best to keep locked away because the night Annie died broke something inside her that was never healed.

Annie left them in 2009, and Colm followed in the September of 2016. The two people Shauna loved more than life, both gone.

That's why this trip was important to her. Maybe she'd never grieved properly. Perhaps she hadn't yet healed. But, whatever the reason, she had a burning need to find a connection, to find a piece of her that was still here, that she could hold on to.

'Aw God, you look upset again. Have they run out of strawberry tarts? I'm going to raise holy hell if they have.' Lulu put her handbag down on the seat, then tucked half a dozen carrier bags under the table.

'Holy crap, did you do a trolley dash? How is it even possible to buy that much stuff in such a short period of time?'

'It's a special gift, only given to the few who won't waste it,' she said solemnly. 'So you still haven't told me why you look sad. What's happened?'

Shauna shrugged, forcing a smile. 'Nothing at all. Just thinking about Annie. I miss her.'

'Me too.' Lulu had known Annie all her life and she had been a surrogate grandmother to her – one that gave her cast off mini-skirts and provided an alibi when Lulu and Shauna were seventeen and wanted to go clubbing. They told their parents they were at Annie's house every weekend for about two years, and she went along with it every time. Her only condition was that she took them to whatever club or party they were going to. She'd then wait outside with her flask, her sandwiches and a good crime novel, until 3 a.m. when the club closed or the party emptied, and she'd drive them back to her place, hooting with laughter at the tales of their night.

That's who Annie Williams was.

Before Lulu could order a drink and enquire as to the status of the strawberry tart situation, the door opened again and John rushed back in. 'I think your aunt might have returned. An elderly lady went in the main door, then I saw a light go on in the flat on the second floor. The left one. That's it, isn't it?'

Shauna's excitement surged. 'I think so. It's definitely the second floor, so even if it's not the right one, it must be her neighbour.' She said a silent prayer of thanks for the lack of Scottish December daylight. It wasn't even four o'clock yet and already it was dark. If Flora hadn't put a light on, John would never have realised the newcomer was on the second floor.

They ran out of the café, jumped in the car and raced to the flats. On the way, she texted Beth.

Hi babe, hope you're still having a fab time. Remember to hold Auntie Rosie's hand on roller coasters because she's really scared of them. Love you. xx

The reply was instant.

Don't worry, Mum, she hasn't fallen out of one yet. I'm taking good care of her. Love you back.

155

Then twenty hearts and kiss face emojis. Shauna would never admit it, but she was so pleased Lulu had bought Beth that phone.

She'd barely slipped her phone back into her bag when they arrived at the flats.

'My heart is racing,' Shauna told Lulu, as they walked up the path.

'For God's sake don't faint. You know I'm crap in an emergency. I'm far too self-centred to get involved in other people's health dramas,' she said. It was funnier because it was absolutely true.

'Okay, here goes... please be her,' Shauna whispered as she pressed the button.

Nothing. No reply.

She pressed it again.

Nothing.

Crestfallen, she was getting ready to scoop her hopes off the floor, when a voice crackled through the speaker.

'Yes?'

'Hi. Er, hello. Good afternoon,' Shauna stuttered. 'I'm really sorry to bother you, but I'm looking for Flora McGinty.'

'She doesn't live here,' the voice said. 'You've got the wrong house.'

'Oh.' Hopes. Floor. Scoop. 'Do you think you can pass a message on to her please?'

'I'm not promising anything,' said the voice, a little hostile now.

'That's okay. Can you just tell her that I'm looking for her, please? My name is Shauna O'Flynn. I'm her sister Annie's granddaughter.'

Before she could say anything else, or leave a contact number, there was an audible gasp, then the voice was back, different now. Stunned. Breathless.

'I don't give my name to cold callers,' she said. 'But I'm Flora McGinty. You'd better come on up.'

Fourteen

George

I try to keep my breathing steady as the memory of Flora's reaction to my confession that I'd told Declan about her pregnancy makes my gut ache. I don't want to be setting off the machines again and have that poor lass Liv running in here like I'm about to pop my clogs. That'll come soon enough. Right now, I don't want to be a bother to her.

The scream had come first, so loud I'm sure the neighbours must have thought someone was being murdered. Then the shouting. And, dear God, she gave me my character, called me words I'd never heard come out of her mouth in our lifetime.

Thing is, I can see that I deserved it. I was trying to help, but it was a foolish notion and anyone with an ounce of sense would have known he would flee.

The only consolation was that she didn't have to see his bastard face when he told her that he wouldn't be standing by her. This way he was gone, and she didn't have to witness his cruelty first hand.

That's not how she saw it at the time, mind, and I don't blame her.

I reckon she would have gone for me if our Betty hadn't put her arms around her to calm her down, then caught her when she fainted.

We'd just got her on to the couch and revived her with a cup of tea when there was a thump on the back door. We all knew it could only be one person. In he came, letting himself in, just as he always did. Nobody locked their back doors in those days – but we did after that night. He had my mother with him, too. Turns out he'd stopped to pick her up on the way over, after Flora hadn't come home for her tea. Well, as soon as Ma spotted Flora, she rushed to her side, convinced she was ill.

I don't know what came over my sister. Maybe it was exhaustion. Or grief. Or she was just overcome with the nerves. But she just said it, right there, like it was nothing important. 'I'm not sick, Ma, I'm pregnant.'

If the neighbours didn't already think there was a murder taking place in our house, they did now. My da yelled, a guttural, wounded, animal scream, then lost his head completely. Flora sat, like she was in a trance, as she answered his questions and they got the whole story out of her. No, it wasn't Arthur, that boy from Newton

Mearns. No, the father wouldn't be standing by her. It was my ma who asked first.

'Who is he, Flora?'

My sister didn't even flinch, just told her in a matter-of-fact way, as if she was rhyming off the shopping. 'Declan.'

'Declan who?' my ma asked, clearly confused. It took her a while, but then you could see by her face that the horrible truth was dawning. 'That boy Annie was seeing?' she prompted, and my dad's head whipped around. He had no idea Annie was seeing anyone, because she told him nothing, but she'd confided in our mother. Of course, my ma had kept it to herself for fear of sending the old man into a rage.

Too late for that now.

My da punched the wall so hard he broke two bones in his fingers.

The rest of the night passed in a riot of recriminations and threats and tears. Eventually they left, taking Flora with them, and I slumped in the chair.

'It was a mistake to tell him,' I said, my voice heavy with sorrow.

'Aye, it was, but you meant well, George. It's a lesson. We'll not be interfering in other people's lives again. No good ever comes of it.'

She was only saying what I already knew.

Poor Flora's troubles were far from over. It was a different time back then. It wasn't right, but there was a stigma to being an unwed mother, and my da wasn't having his daughter's reputation ruined by a child out of wedlock. He took her to see another one of his clients, a doctor who ran one of those posh clinics in the city centre, and he arranged for Flora to terminate the pregnancy. Betty and I begged my mother and father not to make her do it, said we would raise the child as our own, but my da wouldn't hear of it and Flora had no strength left to fight him. In the end, his wishes were carried out, as always, and Flora had the operation. The problem was, it didn't go as it was supposed to. Something went wrong afterwards, some kind of infection, my ma said, and Flora ended up in the hospital for weeks. For a while it was touch and go, but she survived, though I wasn't sure that she was happy about that. The doctors told her she would no longer be able to have her own children and it just about broke her.

I've no idea how long it took her to get over it, because it broke us, our family, too. I never forgave my father for not allowing us to adopt the child, and as always my ma took his side. Flora never forgave me for my part in it all and never spoke to me again, just as I remembered predicting in a letter I sent to Annie letting her know that I'd done as she suggested.

And Annie, she never came back. Too many wounds, too many lies. I didn't blame her. Her letters stopped coming and mine were returned, saying not known at that address. I knew why. She was proud and she was embarrassed, and she'd decided to close the door on a father who disliked her, a mother who didn't understand her and a sister who'd betrayed her. And me? Well, I figured I was a connection to that world that she didn't want to think about. That was Annie. Uncompromising. Resolute. Stubborn. She'd rather forge a new life than deal with the disappointment of the one she left behind. I missed her terribly, but I understood her wanting to start over. I hope the new path she chose brought her happiness. She'd be eighty-four now, our Annie, a year younger than me, and Flora would be eighty-two. I'd give anything to see either of their faces again and I know there's a good chance that they'll already be on the other side. If they are, I just hope they're waiting for me, with new found forgiveness for the mistakes that were made a lifetime ago.

The family rift left Betty and I on our own, and we made a different life for ourselves. Our Norry was born, and then later, he gave us Tom and my word, that boy was a blessing.

Sometimes I wish he could have known my sisters, but it wasn't to be, and for what time I've got left on this earth, I'll regret that.

I feel a touch to my cheek and I realise someone is there. A couple of seconds later, I hear Liv's voice and realise it's Tom who is by my side.

'Tom, I thought I saw you come in. Everything okay?'

'It's fine,' I hear him say. 'His eyes were watering, so I was just drying his face.'

Silly old fool that I am, crying over ancient history at this time of my life. Nothing that can be done about it now.

'If you need anything, just press your grandad's buzzer. I put it in his hand earlier,' Liv says, then I hear her soft steps as she leaves the room.

The boy is sitting next to me and I can tell from his breathing that he's agitated. I wish so much that I could open my eyes, talk to him, but this damn body isn't responding much any more. So tired. Just want to keep my eyes closed all the time.

'Grandad...' I can hear him though. Even that one word sounds stressed. 'You'll never believe who I just saw. At least, I think it was her. She had on that hat she used to wear before... before... It was Chrissie, Grandad. I'm sure it was her.'

A sound gets stuck in my throat and I wonder if he realises that my hand is suddenly clammy. A shroud of shame consumes me for the second time today.

Tom is still talking. 'And the weird thing is, I just found out yesterday that my partner Davie – I know you never liked him – has arranged to meet her tonight. He found her. I never told you this, but I spent years looking for her, and he found her first. I want to kill him for not telling me. He once admitted he'd had a crush on her at school, but I thought he was joking, just trying to

163

wind me up. I guess not. Thing is, I've seen him do stuff like this before, just get consumed with the thrill of the chase and go after someone and screw everyone else. Other guys' wives and girlfriends. Married women. He can't help himself. It's like some kind of game with him. I just never thought he'd do it to me. Eight years we've been partners, since right out of university. I went all in with him in the business, risked everything – even your and Gran's savings – and now he does this?'

I've never heard him speak so freely like this before. I guess confiding in someone who can't answer is a lot easier than baring your soul to someone who can talk back. He is right about our savings though. What he didn't say was that Betty and I had been happy to give him our nest egg because we had faith in him. And we were right. He paid back every penny with interest as soon as he started bringing in clients. And as for that arse Davie, if I were fit for it I'd quite happily wring his neck myself. What a scumbag to do that to his pal. Tom was right when he said I never did bloody like him. Just like that Declan one. Too smooth by half.

'I just don't understand and I don't really know what to do for the best. I've found out where she works, so I'm thinking I'll go there tomorrow. Or maybe wait until the shop closes and wait outside for her? She always hated a scene, so maybe that would be the best bet. Every chance I'll get arrested for acting suspicious if I did that though.' He is trying to joke but I can hear the strain in his voice. Oh son. I'm so sorry.

'Thing is, Grandad, she probably won't want to see me again and I wouldn't blame her if she hates me. I just left her. She never wrote, never called, just cut off all contact and I deserved it. By the time I came back to find her, it was too late – she'd disappeared.'

I feel a cloth return to press against my face.

'Your eyes are watering again, Grandad. Listen, I'll tell you more about it later, but I need to shoot off to the airport to pick up Dad and Rosemary. Not looking forward to it, I don't mind telling you. I really hope you're not furious with me, Grandad. I know how you feel about them, but I felt I had to give them their place and the opportunity to make things right with you. That's as far as it goes though. I'll be civil, but I'm not interested in anything they've got to say. Christ, what a day, Grandad. Parents arriving. Davie going behind my back. Seeing Chrissie again. Strange thing is, that's the only thing I really care about. I know it sounds crazy, but she's the only person I ever loved. Aaargh, sorry, I'm rambling again. Right, I'm away.' He leans over and kisses me on the cheek, as he always does now, and his affection warms me. 'See you soon, Grandad. Have a good rest. I love you.'

I love you too, son, I think to myself. My heart breaks in two, both for the person he is now and the boy he was back then. I desperately want to tell him what I know. You see, I have two big regrets in my life. Interfering with our Flora's situation, and then sitting back when I should have interfered in Tom's life many years later.

It had been a freezing cold winter night, two or three months after Norry, Rosemary and Tom had left for Australia. Betty and I had just sat down to watch Morse when the doorbell rang.

No one ever visited at that time of night, so I got up to get it, figuring it was some of the neighbourhood kids playing chap door run away.

It was the red hat I recognised first. She'd worn it for years and it fair suited her.

'Chrissie! Come on in, lass,' I said.

Fifteen

Tom

If Tom was hoping that the drive out to the airport would clear his head, he was wrong. He was replaying that moment in the shopping centre over and over again. It was her. He was sure of it. Okay, he was perhaps ninety per cent sure. It was from a distance and there were dozens of people in between them. But that moment when their eyes met, he was certain he saw something. Recognition. Or maybe she was just some random stranger and he was hallucinating because seeing her on Davie's computer was messing with his sleep deprived, stressed out mind.

This wasn't how life was supposed to be. The mistakes that you made when you were eighteen weren't supposed to change the whole course of your life. At that age, the biggest screw-ups he should have been making were drinking until he puked and developing a poker habit, not losing the love of his life and rendering himself incapable of holding down a decent relationship ever since.

Now he was the one cornering the market in tragic and pathetic.

The M8 motorway was fairly clear and he made good time all the way out of Glasgow, heading west to the airport junction. It was 3 p.m. now. Most people would be leaving their offices for the last time before Christmas, shift workers would be flying around picking up last minute presents, students would be travelling home to their families. Here he was, deliberating life changing decisions while on the way to pick up a father he hadn't seen in over a decade, and a stepmother he vehemently disliked, while mourning the imminent loss of the man he loved more than any other. This Christmas definitely rated at the bottom of the festive scale.

His phone lit up and he checked the screen. Incoming call. Davie Bailey. The vein on the side of his clenched jaw began to thud. Yeah, definitely the worst Christmas ever.

His first instinct was to reject the call, but he wanted to give Davie the chance to come clean. Perhaps that was what he was calling about. Maybe there was some bigger plan in play here. For all he knew, Davie could be meeting with her to tell her about Tom. Yep, that could be it.

Tom pressed the green telephone button on the steering wheel to accept the call and immediately heard a groaning sound.

'Christ, tell me this headache isn't going to kill me,' Davie moaned.

Fighting back fury, Tom tried to act normal. 'I think there's every chance that it will. Good night last night?'

'Ah, mate, it was brutal. In a good way.'

'So I heard. Carina from accounts? Think that's you hooked up with someone in every department now.' Tom couldn't keep the irritation out of his voice. Some could look at Davie's behaviour and say that it was a misconduct in the workplace lawsuit waiting to happen, but the thing was, he rarely made the first move. Nine times out of ten, it was one of the sharp suited, smart women that worked in the office who set their sights on a boss that aced charm school and looked like he'd wandered off the front cover of *GQ*. If only they realised sooner what a dick he actually was.

'Eh, pot, kettle.' Davie retorted. 'Last time I checked, you were dating our head of sales.'

It was a struggle, but Tom tried not to get combative.

'Past tense,' Tom replied. 'We decided to call it a day. And I'd just like to point out that Zoe is the only woman I've ever dated who works in the office and even then she made the first move.'

It was true. She'd cornered him after a late night strategy session back in the autumn and told him it was time he realised how much he liked her and took her out for a drink. They'd been together ever since. Until today.

Tom heard himself getting another dig in. 'And I wasn't seeing someone else at the time.'

'Okay, okay. Man, this is like talking to my mother. Anyway, where are you? Wanna come by for a beer?'

'Why. Something wrong?'

This was Davie's chance to come clean.

He didn't.

'Nah, nothing at all. Just got nothing on this afternoon and gonna watch a bit of sport on the telly.'

Bastard. Tom struggled to keep the anger out of his voice. 'Can't. Picking up my dad at the airport. His flight's due in any minute. Then we'll head back over to the hospital so they can see Grandad.'

'How's the old man doing?'

That threw Tom, reminding him that there was a good guy in there somewhere, far beneath the insatiable libido and arteries that were undoubtedly sixty per cent vodka.

'He's holding on, but he's not in good shape. I haven't seen him awake for a couple of days now, though the nurses say he woke up for a few minutes last night. You should stop by and see him.' He knew there was no way in hell Davie would agree to this, but he just wanted to hear him squirm his way out of it.

'Think I'll pass on that. Not because I'm a thoughtless dick, but because the old man always hated me. I didn't take it personally but I don't want mine to be the last voice he hears.'

'Fair point,' Tom agreed, ruefully. George had never taken to Davie. Always said he was too flash, and not to be trusted. Turns out he was right. Or maybe not. Tom still held out a glimmer of hope that he had this all wrong. He had to know. 'So, what are you up to tonight then? You got another night on the town with a hot date?'

Only someone who knew Davie as well as Tom did would register the hesitation in his voice before he spoke. 'Nah, having a quiet one in front of the telly tonight. Need to recover from last night and get my energy levels back up. Too old to be doing two in a row now.'

Tom felt his hands tighten around the wheel. The bastard. He wasn't going to tell him.

Tom gave him one more chance. 'That's not like you. Friday night before Christmas and you're staying in? What happened to the party animal?'

Tell me. Tell me. Tom willed him to do the right thing.

'Party animal is having a night in with a few bottles of Bud and Sky Sports.'

Fucker. He wasn't going to come clean.

Tom knew he had to get off the phone before he blurted out something he'd regret. 'Okay, mate, you have a good one. I'll speak to you later,' he said through gritted teeth, before disconnecting the call.

Part of him already regretted not saying anything, but bringing it up on a phone call to a hungover man wasn't the right time. This had to be done properly for two reasons – first, and it was only a tiny possibility, but perhaps Davie did have some ulterior motive and was planning to tell Chrissie that Tom was his partner and help bring them back together. And second, if that wasn't the case, then this was a partnership ending betrayal and Tom would walk away from everything they'd built in a heartbeat. There was no way he could look at Davie's smug, crowing face in the office every day if he was dating Chrissie. It was way beyond the realms of his tolerance. Also, stopping himself from killing him would be a new challenge to his days that he wasn't sure he could conquer.

No, this had to be done with a cool, clear head, and in the right way. Today was already shaping up to be the most emotionally draining of the year, and that was before he picked up the new arrivals at the airport.

Davie's voice echoed in his head. *'Party animal is having a night in with a few bottles of Bud and Sky Sports.'*

A lie. A blatant lie. Of course, there was another, very obvious course of action. He could go to the restaurant and confront them, just show up, give them a wave, say hi and see what happened. It would remove all possibilities of Davie denying or squirming out of what he'd done.

However, the last thing he needed today was Chrissie seeing him and telling him all the reasons she hated him. There was too much water under that bridge and it had to be navigated safely, with proper planning, caution and at exactly the right moment. Friday night in an Italian restaurant wasn't it. If he was going to be ritually humiliated and shamed for the actions of his past, he at least wanted it to be in a private environment with the fewest number of spectators possible.

He realised that he'd already come off the slip road and was on the one way system around the airport. He'd been on autopilot for the last twenty minutes. He pulled into the segregated lane for the car park and followed the signs all the way up until he found a space on the third floor.

He sat in the car for a moment, composing himself after what he'd just heard, and gathering the strength for the next challenge of the day: seeing his dad and stepmother.

When he finally felt his blood pressure was somewhere near normal, he walked over to the terminal building and bought a Starbucks latte, before making his way to international arrivals. It was like the opening scene from *Love Actually*, with a sparkly tree, festive music, and the waiting area packed with people looking happy as they waited in anticipation of their loved ones coming home for Christmas. He didn't share their excitement. Instead, he checked the board and saw their flight had landed twenty minutes ago, but it would take them a while to get through customs and baggage reclaim. It was another ten minutes, during which he stood and silently seethed at the duplicity of his partner, before he spotted his dad's face in the crowd coming through the doors.

His first reaction was that Norry didn't look much older than when he'd seen him last. Maybe it was the dark tan, or the yellow polo shirt, or the baseball cap, but he gave off an air of health that probably came with living in a sunny environment, where his main focus in life was to play golf and keep himself fit, with no time for worrying about his son or his aging father. Australia clearly suited him. Tom's gaze flicked left, to Rosemary, who was, as always, welded to his father's side. Life in Oz was obviously treating her well too. Her ash blonde hair was pulled up into a sleek ponytail, her skin was tanned to a perfect shade of caramel, and despite the fact that it was December and she was indoors, she sported huge oversized sunglasses.

Tom stepped forward, trying to dislodge the lump of dread that had settled in the pit of his stomach. The last time he'd seen these two, they were raging in fury at the fact he'd decided to return to Scotland after only a year in Brisbane. There was nothing they could do about it. He'd saved up money from his weekend and holiday job on a local farm, and he had enough for the ticket and to help him get by at his grandad's house back in Scotland. He'd known that George would welcome him back, no questions asked, and he'd been right.

He'd come back, gone to university, worked in McDonald's at nights to pay his way and met Davie Bailey. The bastard. He couldn't get the lying, scheming prick out of his mind.

'Son,' Norry greeted him with open arms. To any onlooker, they'd be just another family reunited for Christmas. How appearances could be deceiving. They would see nothing of the undercurrents, the grudges, the past hurts and resentments.

'Hey Dad,' Tom said, returning the embrace, because he couldn't be rude and refuse. He turned to Rosemary, who automatically leaned in to do the whole "two cheek kiss" thing. He felt the vein on the side of his face pop again. He wondered how long it would take her to ask the big question, the one that any other mother would ask in the first few seconds of seeing him. But then she wasn't just any other mother, was she?

Norry and Rosemary had pulled thick jackets – his a padded North Face parka, and hers a silver fur coat – from their hand luggage and they headed out of the airport, into the car park, and unloaded the suitcases into the back of the car.

'You're looking well, son,' Norry said, jovially.

Tom marvelled at his father's ability to act like absolutely nothing had happened. Their contact in the last twelve years had been minimal. Birthday and Christmas cards. That was what happened when you crossed Norry Butler. Yet, here he was, acting like the big shot father, happy to see his boy. But then, that had always been the way. Norry Butler was big on three things: charisma, charm and control. It was a pretty toxic combination.

They were back on the motorway when Norry asked about George. 'So how is he?'

Tom shook his head. 'Not good. They say he has a few days left. Maybe a week. No one really knows for sure. He wakens every now and then, but just for a few minutes. They've got him on pretty heavy meds to help with the pain. I thought we'd go by there first and see him.'

'Sounds like a plan,' Norry said. Tom couldn't guess what was in his dad's head. You never knew with Norry. Maybe he was here to make amends, to lay old ghosts to rest. Or perhaps he was already adding up what he thought he was due when the old man passed, and he wanted to make sure he didn't miss out on anything.

Still Rosemary said nothing, just sat in the back, staring out of the window.

They'd taken the slip road off to the West End of the city before that changed.

'Weather hasn't improved any,' she said with a sigh. Tom had never been great at reading her, but he'd bet a month's salary that she'd rather be anywhere else but here. 'So...' She paused, pursing her lips, as if it was just too great an effort to ask the question. Finally there it was: 'Have you seen my daughter?' Fifteen minutes, that's how long it had taken her, and only then after she'd commented on the weather first. Rosemary had never been big on priorities.

There was a silence that was colder than the temperature outside, so she repeated the question, with just one variation.

'Have you seen Chrissie?'

'No,' Tom bit back. Yep, there was the truth of it. Tom's dad had an affair with Chrissie's mother, then the two of them fucked off to Australia. Tom had gone along with them, Chrissie had refused to go. Not only had he left his girlfriend, but he'd done it when her mother had deserted her too. She'd been left with no one.

Maybe she was better off with Davie, because no matter what that duplicitous dickhead did, it couldn't be worse that what he had done to her all those years ago.

Sixteen

Chrissie

'Are you sure you're okay?' Val asked. 'You look paler than Josie after half a dozen tequilas and a go on those dodgy cigarettes she brought back from Morocco. Herbal, my arse. If there had been sniffer dogs at Glasgow airport, she'd be doing six months in the slammer right now.'

The pendulum on Chrissie's emotional state swung back to amusement. 'I promise I'm good. And, Val, I can't thank you two enough for all this. I really can't.'

The pendulum swung from amusement back to confusion. It had looked so like him. The bloke in the lift. Although, she didn't have her glasses on and she couldn't be sure. God, she really was losing the plot today. She was seeing him everywhere. There must be a name for this. ExBoyfriendus Bastardous Hallucinatitus. If that wasn't already a thing, then she was inventing it now.

They'd left Princess Square, crossed over the pedestrian precinct on Buchanan Street, then nipped straight back into House of Fraser to pick up a pair of furry gloves Val had seen earlier. 'I think our Liv would love these. I've already got her a new soup flask for when she's on double shifts – the hours they put in at that hospital are brutal – but these will be good for when she's trudging in and out in all weathers. The staff car park is bloody miles away from the ward.'

'She will love them,' Chrissie assured her. Liv was Val's niece – Val's husband Donald was brother to Liv's mum, Ida – and Val had a particularly soft spot for her. She was just one of the many people Val had the capacity to love. Chrissie felt lucky to be one of them.

They left the shop by the Argyle Street exit and Josie immediately hailed a taxi. As they jumped in, manhandling their bags through the door, Josie gave the address of Sun, Sea, Ski.

Chrissie's first reaction was relief. No more surprises. She was hugely grateful, and it had been a wonderful day, but she wasn't sure her heart could take much more.

Ten minutes later, they pulled up outside the window with the gorgeous Alpine village display and climbed out.

'Thank you so much, I've had a brilliant time. And I'm so grateful for everything you've...'

'Stop! It's not over yet, my love,' Val proclaimed.

Chrissie was puzzled, but that was soon remedied when Val and Josie slipped their arms through hers and marched her twenty feet further along the street, to the front door of Pluckers, the beauty and hair salon owned by their friend Suze.

'Oh, no. Don't make me,' Chrissie begged as they ushered her through the door. 'I'll come out with eyebrows like caterpillars and lips like a sink plunger.'

From her vantage point in Sun, Sea, Ski, Chrissie had a daily view of the women who came in and out of here and some of them were impossibly glamorous and seriously high maintenance. She knew Val and Josie were in every week and Suze regularly popped in to Sun, Sea, Ski to have lunch with them in the staffroom. She'd been badgering Chrissie to come in for a bit of pampering for the two years she'd worked there, but Chrissie had other things to spend her money on. Even if Suze did give them a forty per cent discount. Besides, she could dab on a bit of nail varnish and slap on a facemask by herself and it would cost her almost nothing.

Val and Josie ignored her objections, nudging her through the door where they were immediately assaulted by a riot of activity. Pluckers was one of the most popular salons in the area, and today was one of the busiest days of the year, with clients lining up to get their pre-Christmas treatments and pampers. Chrissie felt a twinge of relief when she saw that it wasn't wall to wall model types. There was a whole section of hairdressers, working on the crowning manes of a range of women, from teenagers to ladies of Josie's generation. At the nail bar and make-up section, every seat was taken, and there were several people sitting in the reception area, flicking through magazines, waiting their turn. Chrissie had a tiny hope that she was going to escape the onslaught, because perhaps the salon would be too busy for Suze to fit her in.

Josie took charge. 'Look, we know you hate all this stuff, so we we've just booked you in for some make-up and a manicure and a bit of—'

'A bit of what?' Chrissie asked, fearing the answer. So they'd made an appointment. Bang went the hope of escaping.

Suze, one of Chrissie's favourite people, opened her arms to welcome them. 'Josie, for a woman with a big mouth, you don't half keep it quiet when it suits you.' She turned to Chrissie. 'She's trying to avoid telling you that these two...' she pointed to Josie and Val, 'have booked you in for make-up, manicure and a leg and bikini wax. Apparently they're concerned you'll get lucky tonight and the bloke will need the assistance of garden shears.'

Chrissie turned to a shamefaced Josie and Val. Actually just Val. Josie was trying to supress a smile. 'Is nothing sacred with you two? You've seriously been in here discussing my sex life and my nether regions?'

181

'It was her,' Val said, pointing at Josie. 'And you're right. It's unforgivable. To be honest, I've never liked her. If you no longer want to be her friend, I'll take your side.'

The two of them crumbled into peals of laughter, leaving Chrissie to throw her hands up. 'What can you do with these two?' she asked Suze with mock outrage. Although, that might turn to genuine outrage by the end of the waxing session.

'Don't do anything this week,' Suze said. 'Because Val's cooking Christmas dinner and I'm really looking forward to it. After that, I say we sell them on eBay.'

'Done. I'll split the proceeds with you,' Chrissie said, not quite sure how to feel about this. For a moment she considered resisting, but then she folded. She'd never had her make-up done by a professional before, a manicure would look lovely for Christmas, and they probably had a point about the excess hair situation. Not because she had any intention of having sex – because she didn't at all – but because her plastic razor had been lying unused on her bath top since she pulled out her stash of opaque tights in September. 'Okay, I surrender. Do whatever you have to,' she said, conceding defeat.

'Ah, another excited customer,' Suze said, smiling despite the sarcasm. 'We love all our clients to have that positive, can-do attitude.'

Chrissie was still grinning when she was led through to a large treatment room, with two beds and couple of comfy chairs in the corners.

'You're getting the VIP room today,' Suze told her. 'Mostly because I can't leave Josie out in the salon. She always feels compelled to speak to every customer and tell them exactly what she thinks of their treatments. She told someone the other day that her hair looked like she'd been in contact with a live electrical cable.'

'It did,' Josie interjected. 'Although the sooner huge perms come back, the better. I couldn't get through a doorway without turning sideways from 1980 to 1985.'

Val and Josie plonked themselves down on the two armchairs, Suze paused at the door. 'Help yourself to drinks and if you'd like snacks brought in, give me a shout. I'm sending Kylie in. She's young but she's lovely, and she's less likely to sue if these two say anything that constitutes a hostile working environment.'

Right on cue, Kylie sprang in, a ball of energy and enthusiasm, channelling a young Gwen Stefani with her shock of platinum blonde hair and deep red lips. She wore the salon's uniform of black trousers and a shirt with her name embroidered in gold on the left shoulder and was pulling a trolley loaded with products.

'Val!' she exclaimed, deserting the trolley to give Val and hug. 'And Josie!' Another hug. 'That's made my day, you two being here.'

'Lovely to see you too, pet.'

She turned to Chrissie and held out her hand. 'I'm Kylie. I think I've seen you before, when I came in for all my holiday products before I went to Magaluf in the summer. Don't ever go. I came home with a wonky tattoo and an aversion to vodka.'

Chrissie laughed. 'Thanks for the advice.'

Kylie leaned over and flicked on a switch that was attached to a pot-like container on the nearby counter. Chrissie momentarily wondered if she could get to the door before one of them caught her.

'Okay, so here's the plan,' Kylie announced. 'Let's get the least enjoyable things out of the way first. We'll do the waxing, then you can relax and enjoy the make-up and manicure. How does that sound?'

'Erm, great. Yes,' Chrissie replied. 'Happy to go with whatever you think.' And by happy, she meant "prepared to be tortured in the name of friendship."

'Great,' she said. 'Okay, if you can remove your trousers, but leave your knickers on...'

'Josie, let's go and give the lass some privacy,' Val suggested.

'No, it's fine,' Chrissie countered, which was just as well, because Josie was already fishing refreshments out of the under counter wine fridge. She unscrewed the top of a bottle of rosé and poured it into three glasses that were among many on a silver tray on the countertop. 'I've long accepted that there's no such thing as privacy when it comes to you two,' Chrissie teased.

'Amen to that,' Kylie echoed. 'It's like they've got some cosmic force that just makes you tell them stuff.'

'Ah, but your secrets are always safe with us,' Val said, winking at the young woman.

Kylie got a fit of the giggles, then reached down and pulled something from the bottom shelf of the trolley she'd brought in with her. 'Right, ladies, here's the swear box.'

'What's that for?' Chrissie asked.

'When we do waxing the language can get a bit… interesting. So we have a swear box that we donate to a children's charity every Christmas. Josie has almost single-handedly bought them a new bus.'

'I love that idea,' Chrissie said, trousers off, and now taking up a comfortable position on the bed. She wasn't looking forward to this at all, but it was too late to get out of it.

Kylie got to work and the swear box was owed at least a fiver by the time she was done. She did, however, keep Chrissie's mind off it by chatting the whole way through.

Balm on, she stepped back and surveyed her work. 'Perfect. Okay, let's do nails next.' She pulled her trolley over and offered Chrissie a selection of colours. 'Let's go for bright red, since it's Christmas,' she suggested. Chrissie went along with it.

Again, Kylie got on with the job, chatting as she went. Almost an hour later, as she put the finishing touches to one gorgeous smoky eye in shades of browns and golds, she returned to the subject of Chrissie's plans for the night ahead.

'So, let me get this straight. This is your first date for twelve years?'

Chrissie nodded. 'I know, pathetic. The last one didn't turn out well and it put me off for a bit.'

'A bit?' Val said, eyebrow raised. 'Folk get less than that for murder.'

Chrissie nodded. 'It's true. But I'm getting back out there now. This is a start.' She realised that she was actually feeling quite emotional. It had been a tumultuous day and she felt loved, cared for, and terrified all in the same breath. More than that, no matter how much she tried to suppress it, the prospect of going out with another man and the scare she'd had earlier when she thought she saw Tom, was dredging up those feelings again.

'Are you okay?' Kylie asked, realising that her client was suddenly misty eyed.

'Oh love, not again,' Val said to Chrissie, her voice thick with sympathy as she reached over and took her hand. Then to Kylie, 'She's been doing this all day.' She turned to Chrissie. 'Chrissie, I need to say this… I think you need to tell us what happened. We won't judge. And I'll gaffer tape Josie's gob up so there will be no comments either. I think it's only if you get it off your chest that you'll be ready to move on.'

Silent tears were running down Chrissie's face now.

'Oh, fuck, the make-up. The make-up!' Josie wailed, rushing towards her with a packet of tissues.

'Swear box!' Kylie exclaimed.

Chrissie took a tissue gratefully, realising she'd cried more today than she had in years.

'You're right, Val,' she said, when the mascara had been saved. 'It's time I stopped bottling everything up. Okay, here goes...' she took a deep breath. 'Josie, you might want to keep the swear box handy.'

4 p.m. – 6 p.m.

Seventeen

Tom

'No, I haven't seen Chrissie,' Tom responded, grinding the gears as his fury affected his driving. Not that either of those two would notice.

Norry sat in the front, facing forward. 'Just as well. It's terrible what she did to her mother. Don't I always say, Rosemary? You gave that girl a great upbringing and then she turned her back on you. It's a crying shame what she did to you.'

Tom had promised himself that he'd make this amicable, that he'd avoid confrontation, play nice, but it seemed that no one had informed his mouth of this decision. He hadn't stood by Chrissie when he was eighteen years old, but that was a painful lesson well learned. 'What Chrissie did to you? Are you joking me?' he blurted out. 'Do you mean, what you did to her? You left her when she was barely eighteen and never looked back. You two are unbelievable. What makes it worse is that you feed each other's deluded points of view.'

'Don't you dare speak to us like that,' Norry growled.

'Or what? You're going to ground me? You've got nothing to hold over me any more.'

His frustration was palpable, but he knew that this wasn't going to help anything. The whole point of them being here was to mend fences, to build bridges before it was too late. And he knew if that was going to happen, he had to be the bigger person.

'Look, I don't want to fight. God knows, this time is hard enough. But, for what it's worth, don't criticise Chrissie around me. In fact, don't even mention her, unless it's to say that you want to see her and beg for forgiveness…'

'Indeed I will not,' Rosemary spat.

Tom ignored her, just kept on talking. '… For what you two did to her. What I did too. I'm not denying my responsibility in this either.'

Norry's expression was one of inner seething, but at least he kept his mouth shut. And so he should.

Once again guilt tugged at the memories Tom had spent the last twelve years trying to forget. Chrissie. They'd started seeing each other after that night on the step, been a couple in every way, but there was a complication. Norry and Chrissie's mother, neighbours for over ten years, had started an affair. Chrissie's father had never been in the picture, but Tom's mother Catriona definitely was. In fact, Catriona and Rosemary had been friends. Unfortunately, that wasn't enough to stop Chrissie's mother from getting intimate with Catriona's husband. Tom and Chrissie had discovered what was going on at right around the same time as Catriona realised her husband was shagging their neighbour. It had been – to put it mildly – a clusterfuck. Catriona had eventually packed up and left but taking Tom had never been an option. He was sixteen by then, and Norry wouldn't hear of it. He called the shots, always did. The thing was, Tom could see he hadn't kept him through love, but through some spiteful, twisted power play. He couldn't bear to be beaten, even in battles that meant nothing to him.

At first, Catriona lived in a flat in Glasgow, but she was miserable and the only way to make a new life was to move back to Leeds, where she was originally from, but Norry manipulated her into believing that Tom would be better off staying with him to finish his schooling. Eventually, Catriona conceded defeat and left, on the promise that Tom would join her after sixth year. They didn't know then that Norry would make sure that would never happen. In the meantime, Rosemary was obsessed with her new boyfriend, worshipping the ground he walked on, the adoring partner his gargantuan ego needed.

For Tom and Chrissie it had been horrible to watch, but rather than drive a wedge between them it had merely pushed them closer together.

'We've got to tell them eventually,' Tom said to Chrissie, as they sat in the local cinema waiting for the start of *The Notebook*. It had been Chrissie's turn to choose. He'd already dragged her to *Shaun of the Dead* and *Hellboy*.

'No way. My mother won't approve. I'm telling you, she'll go ape shit.'

'But why?'

'In case it interferes with her precious new romance.' She'd leaned over and scooped up a handful of Tom's popcorn. 'You really don't understand such devious minds, do you?'

'Nope,' Tom replied honestly. 'If we just all became zombies that mutated into killing machines, life would be so much easier.'

She'd laughed and then reached over for his hand. 'Shut up and be romantic, otherwise I'm leaving you for Ryan Gosling.'

Tom couldn't remember much about the movie, but he did remember that Chrissie was absolutely spot on with her prediction. The night Rosemary found out had set everything in motion for what would happen later.

Rosemary and Norry were out at some posh dinner, socialising with the companies Norry dealt with in his engineering company. He was a self-made man, as he never stopped reminding everyone.

Tom had bought Chrissie a bangle for her seventeenth birthday the month before, and had it engraved on the inside, where only the two of them would see it.

Chrissie, I love you now and always. T. xx

Okay, so it wasn't exactly Ryan Gosling level romance, he decided, but he was doing his best. He'd given it to her at the beginning of the night, and she'd loved it. She'd clipped it on, promised never to take it off. He should have held her to that.

They'd been hanging out in his bedroom all night, making love, watching TV, eating pizza, when they'd heard Norry and Rosemary come in the front door.

'Shit! I didn't think they'd be back this early,' Chrissie had wailed, running around the room, picking up her clothes and throwing them on. She'd kissed Tom, before, shoes in hand, she'd jumped out of his window – thankfully his bedroom was on the ground floor – and climbed over the fence that separated their houses.

His dad and Rosemary would never have known... if Rosemary hadn't gone to the bathroom and found the bangle lying by the sink. Chrissie had taken it off while she'd had a shower earlier.

The slamming of the door as Rosemary charged out had reverberated throughout the house.

Two hours later, Tom's mobile phone rang. 'So I was right about my mother's reaction then,' Chrissie had whispered, in the voice she used when her mum was in a nearby room. 'She threw a complete berzy. Says I'm a selfish cow and I could fuck everything up for her. Apparently, I'm stealing her moment.'

It was difficult to follow Rosemary's logic, but basically she took the view that a relationship between Chrissie and Tom could threaten her romance with his father. Nope, didn't make sense to him either, but there was no arguing with Rosemary.

There was nothing Rosemary could do about it though, no matter how hard she tried to persuade Chrissie she should end it. They continued seeing each other for another year, until the day that Norry came home and made an announcement that would change everything.

Tom's thoughts were broken by a car horn, as he crawled around the hospital car park looking for a space. It wasn't directed at him, but at someone who had given up hope and stopped their vehicle right in the middle of one of the access rows, deciding to just wait for a space to open up. It was the same every time he came here, but he'd learned to be patient.

He did a couple more circuits of every floor of the multistorey and eventually snatched a space left by a departing Range Rover.

Not a word was spoken as Tom guided them through the maze of corridors and lifts at Glasgow Central Hospital, until they reached the calm of the palliative care ward.

The first person they met when they went through the double doors was his grandad's favourite nurse. And his.

'You still here, Liv?' he said, as she looked up from her monitor and smiled.

'I'm doing a double shift today. I'll stop now for a couple of hours and be back later. Flu always hits staffing levels at this time of year, so we all pitch in.'

'George will be glad,' Tom said, smiling. His grandad had really taken to this nurse and Tom could see the feeling was reciprocated.

'Liv, this is my dad, Norry, and his wife, Rosemary,' Tom said, stepping to the side as he made the introductions.

Liv stood up and shook their hands in turn. Rosemary managed the not insignificant feat of smiling while looking like she'd rather be absolutely anywhere else in the world except right there.

'Lovely to meet you both. Your father…' she said to Norry '… is a remarkable man. It's been a privilege to care for him. Shall I bring you up to speed on his condition and care?'

Norry frowned, then switched on the charm. 'No, no, that's not necessary. Tom here has it all in hand and he's already filled us in with the important stuff.'

It was all Tom could do not to roll his eyes as he saw any hope of a new, caring, sharing, Norry slip right down the sluice drain. The truth was, he just wasn't interested. George was dying, and that's all he needed to know. He wasn't to be bothered with pesky details about George's care, far less take on any responsibility.

Nope, he just wanted to waltz in and be the prodigal son who had travelled back from Australia to see his old man, then he'd waltz right back off again.

It had been a mistake bringing him here. Tom could see it now, but it was a bit bloody late.

'Oh. Okay then.' Liv tried to hide the fact that she was a bit startled by Norry's reply. 'Well... yes, Tom has taken wonderful care of his grandfather.' She turned to Tom. 'It's beautiful to see the bond that you have.'

'Thanks. He's a special man,' Tom said, feeling a twinge of sadness that she hadn't known him when he was younger and vibrant. 'I'll take them through to see him,' he added.

'Of course,' Liv replied, kindly. 'We'll be right here if you need us.'

Tom led them down the corridor, through two sets of double doors, to his grandad's room. As soon as he opened the door, he saw that a flurry of snow was now falling outside and some of it sticking to the window. His grandad would have loved that.

George was lying in the same position that he'd left him, still hooked up to an array of drips and monitors.

'Hey, Grandad, it's me,' he said, crossing the room to take his grandfather's hand. He was glad that he'd shaved him this morning. Grandad always liked to be smart for visitors, even if it was two people he probably didn't want there. 'And Dad and Rosemary are here, too.' It was only then that he looked behind him and realised that Norry and Rosemary were still standing in the doorway, just staring at George, their faces both masks of shock. Tom immediately felt a twinge of remorse. Had he not prepared them enough for the change in George's appearance? The last time they'd seen him he was still a strapping man, but he'd been fighting cancer for years now and it had taken its toll. The weight loss was the most startling thing. He doubted if George made it past ten stone now, at least three stone lighter than he'd been for most of his life.

No matter how he looked though, he was still his grandfather, and he didn't need two onlookers standing gaping at the door.

'Dad? Are you coming over?'

The pointedness of Tom's words flipped Norry into action and he crossed over to the bed, leaving Rosemary still standing in the doorway, clearly undecided whether to stay or flee.

It was the first time Tom could ever remember seeing his father looking like he didn't know how to act, like he wasn't in control.

'So how long do you stay here for?' he asked Tom.

Tom shrugged, addressing his response to his grandfather. 'A while, don't I, Grandad? I come in the morning for an hour, then pop back at lunchtime if I can, then I come back at six and stay until late. This week I've been staying overnight too. It's peaceful. And I think you like knowing someone's here, Grandad, don't you?'

There was no answer from the man in the bed, but Tom didn't mind. The truth was, he came because he didn't want George to be on his own. George had been there for him his whole life and now it was Tom's turn to be there for his grandad.

'And what do you do when you're here?'

'I talk to him. Read the papers or a book.'

Norry still wasn't comprehending the situation. 'What's the point of just sitting here?'

Tom sighed. 'Because he knows. And even if he doesn't, there's nowhere more important to me than this. I don't get why you can't see that.'

'There's a weight of evidence to suggest that even when someone is in this end of life period, they can still hear you.' That came from Liv, who had entered the room and was now noting down readings on the chart at the side of George's bed. 'Isn't that true, George?' she said, smiling.

'Do you believe that?' Norry asked, his scepticism obvious.

'I do,' she said, simply.

Rosemary still hadn't said a word, or moved from the doorway.

'I'll bring another chair in so that you can sit by George's bed too,' Liv offered, leaving and then reappearing a couple of minutes later with another chair.

Rosemary, somewhat reluctantly, took up a position to George's left.

'It's snowing, Grandad,' Tom said, taking a cloth from the side and patting George's face dry. His eyes had been watering all day today. 'You'd love it. Not heavy enough to get the snow shovels out, but just enough to make everything look Christmassy.'

Norry still wasn't saying anything and Tom was starting to feel really uncomfortable. He racked his brain for something to say to Rosemary, some way to break the ice, to engage her in conversation.

'I just realised I never asked you the same thing,' he blurted to her.

'What?'

'You asked me if I'd seen Chrissie. Have you seen her or heard from her?'

Eighteen

Shauna

Shauna's hands were shaking as they climbed the stairs to the second floor. They could have taken the lift but she didn't have the patience to wait. Her whole life, she didn't even know that she had family in Scotland and now she was about to meet her aunt. Or rather, great-aunt. Annie's sister.

'I may pee myself with excitement,' Lulu whispered as they got to the second floor landing.

'Just don't do it on her couch,' Shauna replied. 'Not a great first impression.'

They turned a corner, went through a heavy door, looked left to see closed apartment doors, looked right to see…

Shauna stopped. She didn't know what she expected, but this lady wasn't it. She'd had an image in her mind, a version of Annie, with the flame red hair she'd had in Shauna's youth, or maybe the salt and pepper grey of her adult years. She'd expected a short woman – Annie was only five foot two – and the pale skin, green eyes and freckles that she'd assumed Flora would share with her sibling.

This lady had none of those things. She was taller for a start, maybe five foot six, slender, with a sallow complexion and piercing blue eyes, made all the more striking by her bold red lipstick. Her hair was a stunning tone of steel grey, a shade that suggested it had been dark in her younger days. She was wearing a gorgeous claret wool skirt, with a cashmere jumper in a lighter shade, and a long string of pearls hung from her neck.

She was… elegant, Shauna decided. Elegant, chic with an air of serenity – not adjectives that would be top of the list when she thought of her outrageous, cheeky, hilarious granny.

'Hi, I'm…' Shauna started to say, holding her hand out to the woman in the doorway.

'You are Annie's granddaughter,' she said, staring at Shauna's face, scrutinising it closely. She paused then, taking a few seconds to gather herself before she went on, 'Oh, you certainly are!'

'And this is my friend Lulu,' she added.

Lulu shook her hand warmly. 'Lovely to meet you.'

'Lulu?'

'Yes. Not the singer, though.' She got in there first.

There was another pause, and it took Shauna a moment to realise that Flora's eyes had gone to the stairway door, then flicked to the lift, then back to the door, and she realised, with a wrenching pain, who Flora was looking for.

'I'm… I'm so sorry, Annie isn't with us,' she said, her voice thick with sorrow. 'I'm afraid she passed away many years ago.'

There was a flash of sadness across her aunt's face, before she stood to the side of the doorway. 'Come in, come in,' she ushered. 'Well, this is certainly unexpected. How in goodness' name did you find me?'

'Ah, it's a long story,' Shauna replied, as she passed her.

'Well, I can't wait to hear it. Oh my. Just as well this old ticker is strong enough to handle surprises.'

Shauna warmed to her immediately, despite the fact that she couldn't yet spot a single similarity between Flora and Annie. Even their accents were slightly different. Annie never lost her Scottish brogue in all her years down south, and it was a more guttural sound, occasionally peppered with profanities if she was riled. Flora's was a softer, gentler version.

'The lounge is through there, but why don't we have a seat at the kitchen table and I'll make a cup of tea.'

There it was. The first resemblance. All her life, whether with friends or family, Annie had dispensed with formality, preferring to sit at the kitchen table for a good gossip. Just hearing Flora say that made Shauna smile.

'That's exactly what Annie loved to do,' she said.

Flora looked pleased to hear that as she guided them through to an immaculate kitchen with cream units, a deep oak floor and a cream quartz worktop. No old fashioned influences here. Auntie Flora was bang up to date.

'That doesn't surprise me.' There was a wistfulness in her voice. 'When we were growing up, our father and mother would sit in the front room, listening to the radio, and woe betide anyone who distracted them. Annie and I would sit at the kitchen table, sometimes for hours, and while the night away. I've always been more comfortable there.'

As she spoke, Flora flipped on the kettle, and then pulled three beautiful art deco mugs from the cupboard, all of them etched with Charles Rennie Mackintosh's Glasgow rose.

'Me too,' Shauna agreed. 'I have to ask, you seemed so sure when you saw me that I was Annie's granddaughter, yet I wouldn't have said I looked very much like her?'

Flora placed the mugs, sugar and milk on the table, then took a glass dome off a plate of mince pies that were on the counter and brought them over, too.

'You don't, dear, but you are the spitting image of my mother.'

A lump suddenly formed in Shauna's throat. 'Really? I've never been told I look like anyone, not ever. I feel quite... quite...' she struggled for the words.

'Overwhelmed. In a great way!' she added, just to be clear.

Flora brought a teapot over and let it sit for a moment.

'I have some photographs in my sideboard. I'll get them after tea. The resemblance really is uncanny.'

Tears welled up in Shauna's eyes and Lulu pulled a tissue from her bag and handed it over. 'I brought supplies, just in case.'

'Thank you,' Shauna said. 'Sorry, Mrs McGinty...'

'Flora,' the older woman corrected her.

'Flora,' Shauna smiled through the tears. 'I'm not usually one for crying, but this is... amazing. I was sure we were on a wild goose chase this weekend and all we'd go home with were memories of Glasgow in winter. I don't think I actually believed we would find you.'

Flora put her hand over hers, and Shauna could see her eyes were glistening. 'I feel quite emotional myself. And I'm so glad you did find me. So tell me everything,' she said, brightening as she broke off to pour the tea.

'I don't know where to start,' Shauna said, before giving it a go. She pulled out the photos she'd brought with her and handed them over. There was one of Annie on her wedding day, then two more with Shauna, one when she was a teenager and another when she walked up the aisle with Colm.

Flora studied them for a long time, before asking gently, 'Was she happy? Did she have a good life?'

'She did. She was married to my grandad, Ernie, for over thirty years and they adored each other. They lived in Wimbledon, near the common, and that's where they brought my father up. His name was Jeff and he was married to my mum, Debbie. He died a few years ago too, unfortunately, although we weren't particularly close. I was far closer to my grandmother. I was always at her house when we were growing up, lived there at weekends and school holidays, and she was the person I loved more than anyone...'

'Even me, but I don't bear a grudge,' Lulu interjected, making Flora laugh.

'She was bold, and fierce, and wise, and I adored every single thing about her.'

'She always was,' Flora said quietly. 'Although, maybe not so much the wise part. She always had a tendency to think and act first and ask questions later.'

'Ah, yes, well she did that too. She once tried to punch a bloke that was harassing me outside a nightclub. Came flying out of the car like some kind of granny warrior.'

The memory sent the tears back up to Shauna's lower lids.

'So tell me, how did you come to be here?' Flora asked.

Shauna took a sip from her mug. 'I recently found some old letters and there was an address on one of them. We went to that house this morning, and one of the neighbours, Mrs McNair's granddaughter, sent us to speak to her gran, and then she gave us your address. She told us to give you her love.'

'Lovely Isa. I do miss her. She was a great neighbour for many years in that house. So you say you found letters…'

There was a flinch of something that looked like worry across Flora's brow, but Shauna went on. 'Yes. Until then, I had no idea that she had family up here. I really don't want to upset you or make you sad, but she never mentioned any siblings. She always said she had no relatives left when she came down to England, and then she married my grandfather and created her own family. I was stunned when I found out the truth. When was the last time that you saw her?'

Flora sat back, crossed her hands on her skirt, and Shauna could see that some element of this was paining her.

'1959,' Flora said. 'About a year after she left Glasgow. I travelled to London to see her.'

'Why did she leave?' Shauna asked. She had a glimmer of an idea from the letters, but they were too vague to piece together the whole story.

Flora started to speak a couple of times, but couldn't quite get the words out. 'Oh dear. I haven't talked about this for many years and I'm afraid it's not something I'm proud of.'

'Then please, you don't need to tell us. It's fine. I'm just happy to have found you,' Shauna said truthfully. If all she got out of this trip was a lovely new aunt that she could keep in touch with and visit with Beth, then she'd be happy with that. She didn't want to reopen old wounds.

'No, I made my peace with it a long time ago. The foolishness of youth. And I think we all paid in the end, me included. Although, in my case, it was deserved.'

Shauna wanted to stop her, to tell her it wasn't necessary to dredge up the past. She couldn't imagine this very measured woman doing anything that warranted recriminations or retribution, but as she was about to say that, Flora stepped back in time.

'I always wanted to be Annie,' she began. 'She was just under two years older than me, but she was wild as could be. Nothing stopped her when she set her mind to something. Our parents... well, they were old school. Our father considered himself the head of a dictatorship, and my mother, like so many wives of that generation, acquiesced to his every word and want. Some would say she was a weak woman, but I always thought it took a certain strength not to let a man like that break you.'

Shauna felt a moment of sympathy for a woman she never knew.

Flora went on, 'Annie never bowed down to him and she paid the price. She was defiant and bold and more than once she had to flee the house and his rage.' There

207

was an overtone of pride in her voice as she said that, and Shauna could image Annie standing up to her bullying father

'My father was overbearingly protective with us, me especially. So when Annie started sneaking out of the house at night, I was desperate to join her. She tried to talk me out of it, but I wouldn't listen, so she took me with her. I dare say she always regretted it.'

Shauna could feel the anxiety rising in her chest. It was crazy – all this happened decades ago, but hearing Flora tell the story was giving it a reality that was wrapping around her heart, especially as she knew there had been no happy ending.

'She had a boyfriend,' Flora's voice hardened as she said that. 'Declan. Looking back, I can see him for the lying, cheating, despicable man that he was, but back then I fell completely under his spell. I was infatuated, completely seduced by his flattery and declarations of love. I'm ashamed to say I began seeing him, too.'

Shauna tried to hide her surprise that the classy woman in front of her could have it off with her sister's boyfriend. Lulu didn't even make an effort to disguise her reaction – chin dropped, eyes wide.

'I was incredibly naïve and young for my years, but that was no excuse. It was the most shameful thing I've ever done. Annie found out and... well, she left the following day. Tenth of June, 1958. I'll never forget the day. It was a torrid episode, and I've regretted it all of my days.'

There was a silence as the two younger women sat in stunned silence, unsure what to say to console Flora, while feeling deep sadness for the young Annie.

Shauna was so immersed in Flora's words that she almost missed a pertinent point. Almost.

'So Annie left in 1958? But didn't you say you last saw her in 1959?'

'I did,' Flora nodded. 'And that was another torrid episode altogether.'

Nineteen

Chrissie

'Hang on,' Val said, her brow frowning in puzzlement. 'So you and this boy...'

'Tom,' Chrissie clarified. She'd filled them in on the saga of her relationship with Tom, and now she'd got to the crunch bit.

Val took that on board. 'Yep, Tom... you were going out together and your mother and his father were a thing, too?'

'I know – we were a talk show waiting to happen,' Chrissie mused. 'Thing is, my dad had buggered off when I was six, and my mum had had a trail of deadbeat relationships afterwards, so Norry was a major catch for her – if you like wealthy, megalomaniac control freaks.'

'Can I ask the obvious question?' Josie pondered.

'Shoot.'

'You say he was wealthy, but he lived next door?'

Chrissie nodded. 'Yeah, they hadn't always been loaded. A couple of years earlier, Tom's dad sold a patent for some kind of engineering part that was used for drilling. Made a killing. None of that surfaced until afterwards though. I think he was waiting to divorce Tom's mum before he let the deal go through and got the dosh. Instead, he promised her a monthly payment and basically pushed her out. She went back to live in Leeds because that's where her family were from. Norry and my mother married as soon as the divorce was finalised. She moved in next door with him and I stayed on my own.'

'Bastard,' Josie spat.

'Swear box!' exclaimed Kylie. She was on the contouring now so Chrissie was having to speak with minimal cheek movement.

'Anyway, my mother wasn't happy about Tom and me. To be honest, we were never close. She's not like you two... I think she was lost in a well of bitterness about how her life had turned out. Although, at the time, I just thought she didn't like me very much.'

Val tutted and pursed her lips.

'Anyway, with Norry she got everything she'd ever wanted and she was delighted, but she was worried that any problems between Tom and I could rub off on her relationship. Think she felt it was just an extra complication.' Chrissie could see that Val just could not fathom that kind of thinking from a mother.

'What a shocker she is,' Val snorted. 'I mean, surely you'd just want your kids to be happy? So did she stop you from seeing each other?'

'Yes, but not for the reasons you think. Norry decided to take early retirement now that he'd made a fortune and announced he'd always wanted to live on the Gold Coast. They decided they were going, and Norry insisted that Tom go too. You have to understand, Norry was a tough guy to say no to. He basically threatened Tom that he would cut him off and promised him this great life abroad. But he also said that if Tom didn't go, Norry would stop all payments to his mother. She was finding it tough to get back on her feet at that point, so he felt responsible and agreed to go.'

'Poor boy,' Val said. 'But what about you?'

'I refused. And I was furious with him for going. I thought he should have stood up to him, fought harder, forced him to do the decent thing.'

'Good girl,' Josie contributed.

'I'd just been offered a place at university – studying business at Strathclyde – and I wanted to stay here. My mother made no secret of the fact that she didn't want me there, wanted a fresh start with her new man, so off they went.'

'They left you?' Val gasped.

'Bastards!' Josie proclaimed.

'Swear box!' added Kylie.

Chrissie shrugged. 'They didn't have a choice. I wouldn't go. It killed me to watch him leave, even though, in hindsight, the truth is that he didn't really have an option.'

Val still wasn't impressed. 'I can't get over your mother, though. Richard bloody Gere could try sweeping me off to a life of luxury and I wouldn't leave my kids.'

'My mum paid the rent on our house for three more months, told me I'd need to get a job, and off she went. To be honest, that bit didn't sting – it was the fact that Tom left that hurt me. And then what hurt even more was that it all turned into a complete nightmare.'

'You were pregnant.' Josie this time.

'Yes,' Chrissie said, welling up again but fighting back the tears. The smoky eyes got a stay of execution. 'Found out a month after they'd gone.'

'So what did you do?' Kylie – who'd been engrossed in the story from the start – chimed in.

'I knocked back the university offer, found a job, worked crazy long hours for two months and saved up a rental deposit for a flat. Then I carried on working as many hours as I could until Ben was born, then I had to give up for a while and live on benefits. It was rough making ends meet, and don't even get me started on the stigma I felt being a teenage single mum. But I managed to do my Open University degree and as soon as Ben was entitled to free childcare, I went back to work, temping in part-time jobs for years and just juggling things and scraping by. I was on the waiting list for a council house the whole time but didn't get one until Ben was ten – when I became your next door neighbour,' she finished, smiling at Val. 'Best thing ever. I feel like in some ways it was all meant to happen the way it did.'

'Do you really believe that?' Val asked, touched.

Chrissie shrugged, smiling ruefully. 'Sometimes.'

'Hang on, hang on,' Josie interrupted again. 'Go back a bit. What about your mother? About Tom? Did you tell them about the baby?'

'Of course. I called my mother and asked her to tell Tom. I also wrote to her, telling her I'd moved to a different flat. And I tried to speak to him, but his mobile phone didn't work over there and when I called the house he was never there. She didn't renew my mobile phone contract because she'd been paying for it and I didn't have the money to keep calling Australia on the landline. In those days, it cost a fortune., so I wrote to him, too. I had an old email account but it was on my mum's computer and she cancelled it, so I just sent letters. Anyway, I never heard from any of them again.' Even saying that caused a physical pain. She'd expected nothing of her mother, but she'd thought Tom was better than that. She'd hit an all time low, but it had made her even more determined to make a life for herself and her son – a thought that was reinforced by the fact that she'd heard nothing from her mother since a few weeks after they left and Tom had abandoned her all together.

'Bastards,' Kylie sighed.

'Swear box,' Josie took great delight in saying.

Kylie changed position slightly. 'Okay, I'm going to do your lips now, so try not to move them.'

'Wait a minute though. How do you know that your mother told Tom you were trying to get hold of him? She sounds like a right devious cow... sorry for saying that,' Val apologised.

'No worries,' Chrissie said, bearing a very close resemblance to a ventriloquist's dummy because she was trying desperately not to move her lips. 'I did think of that, but it's not the case. He knew,' she said sadly.

'How can you be so sure?'

'Because the one person Tom loved more than anyone else on earth was his grandfather, George. So when I didn't hear from Tom, I went to George's house with a letter for Tom. George promised to pass it on. So even if Tom wasn't getting the letters I sent to him directly, and even if my mother wasn't telling him that I'd called, then he would definitely have got the letter from his grandad with mine inside.'

'Och, love. My heart breaks for you, it really does.' Val's voice wobbled a little.

Kylie sat back, finished work on the lips and picked up a piece of blotting paper, ready to dry them.

Chrissie took the opportunity to speak with free facial movements. 'Thanks Val, but honestly, it's fine. Ben and I have done great on our own. I've just always told myself that it's their loss, because they've missed out on this amazing kid. And when you think about it, Tom, his dad, was only a few years older than Ben is now when he left. What kind of age is that to be making huge decisions? The poor guy was probably absolutely terrified of coming back here and being stuck with a partner and a baby and no way to support us. He was a smart guy. He had a bright future ahead of him. Much as it hurt, I can absolutely see why he wouldn't want to be tied down at such a young age.'

'True,' Josie nodded, 'but that's no excuse to not make sure that you were cared for. He could have spoken to his dad, asked him to help...'

'Believe me, Norry Butler wouldn't help his granny if she needed a loaf, never mind helping a teenage girl his son had knocked up – even if she was his wife's daughter. I don't even know if they're still together. She might have met an even richer surf dude and buggered off with him,' Chrissie tried to inject a light-heartedness that she didn't feel. But then, it was true. She knew absolutely nothing about her mother or Tom. Until a couple of hours ago, she'd believed he was still in Australia. He probably still was, and just had a lookalike wandering around Glasgow. That thought made her tremble. She briefly wondered if perhaps she should have gone after that guy in the shopping centre, but she knew it would have been foolish. Even if it was him, he'd clearly made a new life for himself and a second rejection wasn't something she wanted to expose herself to. It was the past. Bygones.

'Okay, let me look at you,' Kylie said, admiring her work. 'You. Are. Beautiful.'

'You. Are. Biased,' Chrissie responded, making Kylie gasp in mock outrage.

'I am not! I swear you look amazing. Go look for yourself,' she said, gesturing to the huge mirror on the wall behind where Chrissie was sitting.

'Ouch,' she yelped, as she shuffled forward on the bed. 'My bits may never be the same again.'

Her mind was distracted from the stinging pain as soon as she saw herself in the mirror. Her smoky eyes had survived the turmoil, he skin was radiant, and now that her hair had been released from the hairband that was holding it back while Kylie worked, it was falling in waves around her shoulders. 'Kylie, you can work miracles,' she told the young beaming girl. Gone was the knackered mum and here was someone who looked alive, who definitely didn't look like she hadn't been on a date for twelve years.

The thought sent the butterflies soaring skywards in her stomach. Her first date, well, *ever* really. When she'd got together with Tom, it had been a natural progression from neighbours to friends to lovers. But it was time to move forwards now, much as it terrified her. Val was right – talking about it was another step in letting it go.

She'd been devastated by the way everyone had acted. In a fit of temper, when she'd moved into her own little flat, she'd destroyed their addresses and phone numbers in Australia, decided to cut off all contact with them. There was no point doing otherwise. When she'd told her mother she was pregnant, Rosemary had told her she could handle it on her own. She'd offered to send a bit of money, but Chrissie had told her to go to hell. She didn't want money, she wanted support... she wanted Tom. He hadn't come.

Tom Butler had deserted her when she needed him, when she was young, vulnerable and pregnant with his child. And despite the reasons behind what he'd done, that said everything about how he'd felt about her.

She'd given birth on her own, she'd raised Ben on her own, and they were happy. And if she had to go through every bit of that pain again, then she would, because it had given her Ben.

'Come on then, I just want to give your hair a curl and then we'll be done.' Kylie added.

While the young girl attacked her mane with curling tongs, Chrissie looked at her reflection in the mirror again. The woman looking back at her had been through the wars. She'd been down as far as she could be, and she'd fought her way back, built a life that she loved. It was time to move on to the next chapter of her life.

Chrissie and Ben had survived the last twelve years and they'd made it – she finally had a life that she loved and was ready for where it was going to take her. So sod Tom Butler. He was in the past. Perhaps Davie Bailey would be her future.

Twenty

George

Here they are then, like the bad bloody pennies. Vultures back to feed on the carcass.

I don't know what I expected, but nothing has changed. Not a damn thing. If this body of mine was working, it would be showing all the signs of mighty irritation just now, but of course it isn't. I can't even open my eyes and right now I'm fairly convinced that's not a bad thing, because I don't have to look at those smug faces.

It's not a kind thing to think about your own son. I know that and I'll have to be judged on it when I move on to the next life. But just to hear Norry there, asking, 'What's the point of just sitting here?' breaks my heart. I tried my best with him, I really did. My Betty was the most kind and caring woman, but he got none of that. Maybe we spoiled him. Or maybe there's no outrunning genes and they catch up sooner or later, because that boy is my da all over.

I can sense that Tom is struggling, finding it difficult to deal with him. I still don't understand why they've come. It has to be for the money. Of course, Norry's ego will have stopped him considering the possibility that it won't go to him. He'll be thinking they'll get the house, and they can flog it and add another few quid to their stash, but they'll be sorely disappointed when they find out it's all going to Tom. He's been more of a son to me than Norry ever was and it's only what he deserves after what I did to him.

'It's snowing, Grandad,' I hear Tom say and, my God, my heart breaks. The memories of sledging, of snowballs fights, of Tom's excitement every time flakes fell. Out we'd go, desperate not to miss a moment of it. Betty loved it too – except when she was having to trudge through it on the way to work. Oh Betty.

That's what I'm looking forward to most about getting to the other side. I'm not scared, because I know Betty will be there waiting for me. Living without her these last few years hasn't been easy and, I'll not lie, there have been many times when I wished I'd been taken at the same time. I'm glad now that I've had the extra years to spend with Tom, though. It would have been great to see him married, with children of his own, but it's not to be and I accept that. Wherever I go, I just hope I'll be able to watch over him every day of his life.

I hear Tom speaking to Rosemary and the tension in his voice is palpable. 'I just realised I never asked you the same thing,' he says. They must be going back to a conversation they had in the car on the way here.

'What?' she says. The voice hasn't changed. It almost amuses me that she's been forced to come, because God knows, it's not as if she's here out of love. She's barely spoken a word to me in ten years. Not that I minded. To be honest, I had no desire to keep in touch with her anyway.

The boy speaks again, trying to get some information out of her. 'You asked me if I'd seen Chrissie,' he says. 'Have you seen or heard from her?'

The nerves on the outside of my skin begin to tingle as I wait to hear her answer. That poor girl.

'No,' Rosemary replies, as if she is being asked if she has a bloody umbrella on a rainy day. 'We lost touch when we moved away. Her choice. She decided to stop writing and, last time I spoke to her, she said she wouldn't be back in touch.'

Norry's voice butts in. 'Terrible, the way she spoke to you.'

Our Tom is right in there. 'You two are...'

I can feel my heart speed up again, and it only takes a few seconds before Liv pops in, calm as ever. 'How are we all doing in here?' she asks, her voice steady, but it gets louder as she speaks, so I know she's coming closer to me. I feel her hand on my wrist as she checks my pulse, then she listens to my chest.

'What's wrong? Is something happening?' Norry asks. It isn't concern I hear in his voice though. More like anticipation.

'Everything is fine,' Liv answers, as I take deep breaths to slow my heart back down.

I wish I could tell them that it isn't a physical problem that's causing this. It's guilt. Pure and simple.

I'm right back there again, with my other regret in life.

That young lass was standing at our door.

'Chrissie! Come on in, lass,' I said. I could see that she was chilly and I wanted her in out of the cold. It was only September, but someone forgot to tell the weather gods. It was bloody freezing that week – some cold snap from the East, the weatherman on the six o'clock news said. We had the central heating back on and the winter coats out.

'No, it's... er... fine. I... I... won't thanks, Mr Butler.' Back then, I knew Tom and Chrissie had been courting of course, but I'd no idea how close they'd been or how broken-hearted Tom was to leave her.

My Betty came at my back and peered over my shoulder. 'Nonsense, Chrissie. Come on in. You'll catch your death out there.'

Betty shooed her on in to the kitchen and put the kettle on. 'Sit yourself down, pet, and I'll make you a cup of tea. My goodness, your lips are near blue,' she said.

'Thanks, Mrs Butler. That would be nice.'

'So tell me,' Betty asked, 'have you heard from your mum? Ah, you'll be missing her.'

You have to understand, we had no idea of the extent of the problem between the lass and her mother. We knew they didn't always get on, but then, that's not an unusual thing at that age. We only found that out much later, when Tom came back after a year over there, and told us all about it, that the mother hadn't even wanted the girl to go to Australia. That's when we realised what the poor soul had been going through when she came to us that night.

'Yes... I've spoken to her on the phone once and I've been writing,' she said. 'It's too expensive to call regularly. Costs a fortune.'

'It's an outrage,' Betty agreed. 'I've told my George, once a month. That's it. Otherwise he'd be on the phone to Tom once a week, wouldn't you, you soppy old bugger?' I can hear her laugh now. There was no other sound like it. It soothes my soul that I'll be hearing it again soon enough.

Betty continued to chat as she poured the drinks and put out a plate of biscuits.

'Such a shame you didn't want to go over too,' I said. 'Are you still staying at your mum's house?'

The girl was a bit awkward as she answered, but I assumed that was because this was the first time she'd been here without Tom. Teenagers could be that way – a bit daunted and shy when they were with folk they didn't know so well.

'I couldn't go because I've...' I definitely remember her pausing, being a bit stuck for words. 'I've been accepted for university. I'll be starting next week.'

'Oh, that's smashing,' Betty said. 'What'll you be studying?'

'Business,' Chrissie replied. 'And yes, I'm still staying at my mum's, but I'll be moving out of there in a couple of months. I'm not sure where I'll be going to yet, though.'

'Well, you know our Tom's always had a bedroom in this house and you'd be very welcome to stay here.'

The lass looked like she could have a good weep when Betty said that.

'Thanks, Mrs Butler. That's so kind of you.'

'It's no bother at all, pet. You'd be most welcome.' Everything sorted, Betty had finally sat down at the kitchen table and was sipping at her tea. 'So, what brings you here tonight, then?'

The lass fished into her bag and pulled out a letter, then placed it on the table. It was in one of those airmail envelopes and already addressed.

'I just wanted to ask... I've got a letter here for Tom. I wonder if you could make sure it gets to him? I need to get in touch with him. I've written, but I'm not sure my letters are getting through. My mother didn't really approve of me and Tom going out together, so I don't think she's giving him my mail.'

'Och, I'm sure that's not the case,' I said, puzzled as to why Rosemary would do such a thing. I'd never liked the woman, but surely no one would be so duplicitous as to do something that went against their own daughter.

'Perhaps I'm wrong. I hope I am,' Chrissie said. 'But I thought, maybe if you sent it to him? Or if you told him on the phone that I need to speak to him?' I could see she was holding back the tears now and I felt right sorry for her. Even though she hadn't been for going along with them, it must be hard being on her own. I really hoped she took us up on Betty's offer to come and stay here. Would be good for us, too, to have another teenager around the house again. It was way too quiet without our Tom popping in every day. Monthly calls just weren't enough.

'Of course we will,' Betty said, 'Don't you worry, pet, I'm sure it's just a misunderstanding. Or maybe a problem with the mail. It'll all get sorted out in no time.'

'Thanks, Mrs Butler. And thanks very much for the tea.' She took her bag strap and put it over her shoulder, then stood up. 'I'd better be off now before it gets dark.'

Betty and I saw her to the door and Betty gave her a hug. 'Don't you be a stranger now,' she said.

'I won't, Mrs Butler. Thanks again.'

We stood at the doorway for a few moments, until she'd walked on down to the end of the street and turned the corner, then went back into the kitchen.

Betty sat at the table and picked her mug of tea back up. 'Well, what do you make of that then?' she asked, frowning.

'Aye, these postal services can be right unreliable. Terrible that the lass's letters aren't reaching them,' I said.

'Och, George, what are you like? It's not what the girl said, you have to read between the lines. I think something's far wrong there.'

Betty was so much better than me at sensing undertones and emotional stuff. As always, I'd just taken everything at face value.

'Oh, aye, Betty Poirot,' I'd jested with her. 'And what exactly do you think is going on then?'

She was pensive for a moment. 'I'm not sure. I just hope it's nothing that will cause problems for our Tom. I know we didn't want him to leave, but it's a smashing opportunity he's got to go over there and make a great life for himself.'

'I'm sure it won't be anything dramatic. I'll send the letter on and...' I caught the expression on her face. 'What?' I asked.

She shrugged. 'You've got to wonder what the problem is. I don't think for a minute that her mother isn't passing her letters on unless there's good reason. I just get the feeling that we don't understand what's going on here, George. And much as I feel heart-sorry

227

for the girl, and you know we'll help her in any way we can, I just think we need to be careful about interfering. You know as well as I do the consequences that can bring.'

How could I forget? The one time I'd interfered in my kinfolk's lives had brought the sky falling down on us. I'd never seen our Flora or Annie again, never spoke to my ma and da before they were taken from us in 1960 by an outbreak of influenza. The thing that haunted me most though, was that bairn. If I hadn't got involved, hadn't scared that scum Declan off, would Flora have managed to persuade him to stay, even long enough to marry her and let her have the baby? Was I the reason that child never made it into this world and the reason that Flora wasn't able to have children afterwards? I'd do anything to go back and change what happened and I'd have kept my nose well out of their business.

I picked up the letter and went through into the living room, where I sat in my chair and thought about it for a while longer. I'd no way of telling what was in it, without invading the lass's privacy, and that was something that went against every ounce of decency I possessed. However that also meant I had no way to know if interfering in this would have consequences for my boy. And, God knows, that was something I'd go to the ends of the earth to avoid.

I sat there, troubled, thinking about the options, until my Betty appeared in the doorway some time later.

'Tell me your thoughts, my love,' she said.

'I just can't shake what you said earlier. I interfered once and look where that got us. Who's to know what is in this and whether Norry and that woman are keeping the two kids apart for a good reason. I just don't know.'

'Would it make you feel better if you knew what was in the letter?' she asked, her voice as understanding and gentle as ever.

'Aye,' I said honestly.

She sighed, knowing how much I wouldn't want to do what she was about to suggest.

'Then maybe you need to open it, my love.'

6 p.m. – 8 p.m.

Twenty-one

Shauna

Flora wiped some imaginary crumbs from her chic claret skirt. 'Before I tell you that story, I'll just get those photographs,' she said, and Shauna had a real sense that Flora needed a break from recounting her history.

As soon as she was out of the room, Lulu leaned in. 'Is it wrong that I love her, even with the whole "shagging her sister's boyfriend thing"?'

Shauna shook her head. 'No. I'm having the same thoughts. It was one mistake and it defined her whole life. Although, if I were you, I'd sit a bit further away from me because you know Annie could bear a grudge forever and there's every chance a bolt of lightning will come through that roof any second.'

'Good point,' Lulu agreed, leaning the other way.

Flora returned with a dark wood chest about the size of a large shoebox, and opened it on the table, before taking out an old black and white photograph and holding it up. 'This was my mother.'

'Oh my effing God,' Lulu exclaimed, then, 'Excuse my language,' to Flora, who laughed heartily. 'That could be you!' she said to Shauna.

'This is making me an emotional wreck,' Shauna sniffed, taking in the image. Lulu was right. The young woman staring back at her, wearing a crisp lemon shift dress, her hair in a conservative bun, was her double.

Flora removed a pile of photographs and passed them to Shauna and Lulu one by one. At one point, Shauna pulled a picture of Beth out of her bag to compare it to one of a young Annie. The resemblance in their eyes was uncanny.

'She's called Beth. For Bethany,' Shauna said, quoting her grandmother's full name.

Flora's eyes glistened as she put her hand over Shauna's and squeezed. 'I think Annie would have liked that very much.'

They had to stop for another emotionally stabilising cup of tea before they went on. Photo after photo, the images followed the lives of Annie, Flora and...

'And this is your brother, George?'

Flora looked startled. 'Ah, so you've met George?' Flora asked.

The question took Shauna aback. 'No, but I found a letter from him, too.' Shauna was very aware of the correspondence in her handbag, but the time didn't seem right to share it with Flora. If there was some secret between Annie and George, as the letter suggested, then she didn't want to cause Flora more upset when she was clearly feeling nostalgic about the photographs.

'Is he still alive?' Flora asked.

'I don't know. All I had to go on were the two addresses – one was on your letter and the other was on a note from George. They were both from back in the late fifties. You lost contact with him, too?'

'It all seems so silly now. So unnecessary.' Flora's voice broke and she was still for a moment, before going on. 'You see, George told Declan that I was pregnant, probably threatened him or battered him senseless, and he disappeared off the face of the earth. When my parents found out I was pregnant with Declan's child, they forced me to… to… terminate the pregnancy. That caused a complication that left me unable to have children. I never forgave any of them. I stayed until I found somewhere else to go, then I broke off all contact with them, got a new job and a room in a bedsit. I started seeing Arthur again, the lovely man I'd been seeing before the affair, and he was gracious enough to overlook my transgression. I only went back to live in the house you visited earlier when my parents passed. They didn't make it past fifty. Both died of influenza at the end of 1960. George had already moved out and cut off all contact with my parents. He was so furious with them for what they'd put me through. Didn't come to the funeral. I suppose I could have tried to make amends, but you have to understand I was so hurt and

233

so angry for a long, long time. And then, it seemed like too much time had passed, so I just… moved on. Arthur and I married, just the two of us in a registry office, and we've been together for almost sixty years now. We've had a good life and he accepted that I couldn't have children right from the start.'

'I think Annie would have been glad about that,' Shauna said. 'She could be stubborn as a mule and, yes, she could hold a grudge, but she wouldn't wish unhappiness on anyone. Except that bloke that harassed me outside the nightclub.' That made Flora and Lulu laugh.

'I'm sorry Arthur's not here to meet you. He's in hospital at the moment. He had a fall at the weekend and broke his hip. Old age. That's what happens to us. I'd only just got back from visiting him when you buzzed my door.'

'I'm sorry to hear that. We're only here for one night and head back home tomorrow, but perhaps when we come back again we'll meet him then.'

Flora's face brightened. 'I'm sure he'd like that.'

Shauna took a deep breath and went on, as gently as possible. 'So, you said that you saw my gran in 1959?'

Flora nodded. 'Yes. It was after I left hospital where I'd been treated for complications arising from the termination, and before I moved into my little bedsit and began to see Arthur again. I felt so ashamed about what I'd done to Annie, and so suffocated by life up here. She wouldn't return my letters and no one had heard from her. I knew that she'd gone to stay with a work friend who'd moved to London, so I got the address from another of her friends at work and got the bus down there myself. Didn't tell my parents I was going, of course, but by that time we weren't on speaking terms. Living at home with them was intolerable. They were so disgusted by me. Anyway, I left them a note and got the bus down to London, planning to beg Annie to forgive me and let me stay with her. It was the most excited I'd ever been. The people. The crowds. The sheer size of it. I found my way to the flat she was living in near Earl's Court – bit of a dump if I'm being honest – and she nearly died when she opened the door and saw me.'

'I can imagine,' Lulu said, entranced by the story. 'Was she furious?'

'Absolutely. I begged her for forgiveness, pleaded with her to let me stay, but she wouldn't have it. Took me back to Victoria Station and didn't leave the platform until my bus had left with me on it. I was heartbroken.'

'And what did she say?' Shauna asked, very aware that she'd only known Annie as a warm-hearted, loving adult, not a hurt, scorned, inexperienced twenty-five year old.

Flora's face was a mass of contradictions. Sorrow. Sadness. Reflection. Understanding.

'She told me that I had no place in London, that she didn't want to live with me again and that the best thing

I could do was turn my skinny arse around and go right back to where I'd come from. Those were her actual words, I believe.'

'Sounds like her,' Shauna agreed, consumed by sadness for her aunt and for Annie.

'I sobbed all the way back to Glasgow. I was devastated and hurt. I'm not sure what crushed me most –that she hadn't forgiven me or that I was returning with my tail between my legs. Looking back now, I think perhaps I see it a little differently. She'd taken me under her wing once before and it had been catastrophic. I think perhaps she didn't want the responsibility of looking after me again and thought I'd be safer back home. At least, I hope that's what it was.'

'I do too,' Shauna agreed.

'You said you had letters?' Flora said questioningly.

Shauna's heart plummeted. It felt so intrusive, like such a breach of privacy to have read the letters that this woman sent at the worst time of her life, when she was in the midst of heartbreak and turmoil.

'I do.'

An internal mantra kicked off in her head. *Please don't ask to see them. Please don't ask to see them. Please don't…*

'Can I see them?' Flora asked, with some hesitancy.

Despite her better judgement, Shauna realised it would be rude of her not to show them, when her aunt had been so kind and open in sharing her past.

She dug into her handbag and pulled out the two that she had reread so many times. She handed over the first one, the one from Flora to Annie.

Dear Annie,

Forgive me. I know that is more than I deserve, and that I have no right to ask... I have no defence for what I did to you, no excuses for my actions, for I always knew he was yours. I can only hope that in time the pain of my betrayal will lessen, and you'll find a way to think of me fondly once again.

Sorry.

Your sister,

Flora

A single teardrop fell on to the paper as Flora read it, then she was still for a few moments. 'I wrote that after she left, but before I found out I was pregnant. I thought if she would just come back, then we could make it right again. I had no idea it would never be so.'

'I'm sorry,' Shauna said, rising from her chair to hug Flora. They held each other for a couple of minutes, both lost in their memories. It was hard to believe that only a couple of hours ago they'd never met. The connection had been instant, the bond weaving them together like vines on a tree. A family tree.

The eventually let each other go. Shauna sat back down and Flora blew her nose, then patted the tear stains from her face, composing herself again.

'My goodness, it's strange seeing those words on paper after all these years.'

'It must be. And I think it says something that Annie kept your letter all that time. She wasn't the sentimental type, so it must have meant something very special to her, must have been important.'

'Thank you for saying that.'

'I promise it's true.'

The three of them sat with their thoughts for a few minutes, Flora re-reading the letter while Lulu and Shauna continued to scan the photographs. The resemblance to Flora's mother really was uncanny, as was the fact that Annie had changed so little as she progressed through her life. She'd kept the same hairstyle, a bob that fell to halfway between her chin and her shoulders, until the day she died. The cheeky smile and the twinkle in the eyes that were so like Beth's remained. Shauna touched her face in one of the images, the pain of missing her sharpening its claws.

It was Flora who broke the silence first.

'You said that you had a letter George sent to Annie, too?'

'Yes. Here it is.' Shauna handed it over tentatively, knowing that, though brief, it would provide a new piece in the jigsaw of Flora's life. She recited it in her mind at the same time as Flora read it.

Dear Annie,

It gave me no pleasure, but I did as you asked. I told him. I hazard by now you will have heard that it did not draw the response that was hoped. I fear Flora will never forgive me and I'm destined to lose two sisters.

Your brother,

George

Flora's gasp was deep, as she raised her head.

'It was Annie? This can only mean that it was Annie who asked George to tell Declan I was pregnant. But why?'

'I have no answers,' Shauna replied, wishing so much that she did, that she could redeem the past once and for all. 'But he says it didn't get the response that they hoped for and you said that Declan disappeared when he found out you were pregnant. She must have wanted him to stick by you.'

'But why? After what we'd done to her?'

'Like I said, Annie had a huge heart,' Shauna said softly. 'She didn't always go about things the right way, but she took care of people she loved.'

Whatever had passed between the sisters, Annie had been thinking of Flora all along, trying to make things right for her. The realisation made Shauna ache for her even more.

'What fools we all were,' Flora mused again, sadness in every word.

'All those years I hated George, because I thought he'd interfered out of some macho pride, or disapproval, but actually he was trying to do the right thing. And Annie had encouraged him, tried to make things right. It swells my heart that she had been trying to help me after all.'

Her eyes went back to the page, to the top of it this time, to the address that was written with a flourish in deep blue pen.

'That was the address he lived at when I last saw him,' she said, and Shauna noticed that she was beginning to look weary, whether from the emotion or the shock. 'Did you say you were returning home tomorrow?' she asked.

'Yes. We're on an early flight.'

'So when were you planning to visit this house?'

Shauna shrugged. 'Erm, tonight.' She checked her watch. Almost 8 p.m.. She couldn't believe how quickly the time had flown by. 'Hopefully it's not too late in the day to go there. We didn't have a set plan, as such. We just thought that we would try the addresses and hope for the best. I'm just beyond grateful that we've found you.'

'As am I,' Flora responded. 'I can't tell you how much this has meant to me. However, I've no idea if my brother is alive or...' She couldn't say the alternative.

'Don't worry, I promise that I'll call you and let you know if we find anything out about him.'

'Oh, I can't have that,' Flora said, and for a minute, Shauna was saddened. Couldn't her aunt find it in her heart to forgive him? 'I've wasted all these years living on past hurts and misconceptions,' Flora continued. 'It's time that stopped. So, if there's any chance that you may find my brother this evening, then I'd very much like to join you.'

At that, she got up, picked up a thick, red coat from the back of the one empty chair, pulled it on, then lifted her handbag.

'Shall we go?'

Shauna didn't hesitate, accepting her aunt's arm as the three of them marched out of the flat.

'John, this is my Auntie Flora,' Shauna explained as the three women climbed into the car, Lulu in the front, Shauna and Flora in the back.

'Well, well, well, you found her! Ach, that's great news. You've fair made my day.'

'Made my day, too,' Shauna admitted, reaching out for Flora's hand and relishing the soft touch of her aunt's fingers. This was more than she could ever have hoped for. She was beyond thrilled to have met Flora because this meant she belonged to someone. She had family and her aunt was fast shaping up to be fascinating and delightful company. But it was more than that. Flora bore absolutely no physical resemblance to her gran, but the more time Shauna spent with her, the more she realised that they definitely shared some subtle mannerisms. The way they moved their hands when they spoke. The way their voices lilted when they asked a question. The expression on their faces when they were contemplating something important. This was more than just gaining an aunt, it was recapturing a bit of Annie, and Shauna couldn't believe she could have got this lucky.

She glanced upwards, and said a silent prayer of thanks. She wasn't religious. She didn't particularly believe in the afterlife or the paranormal, but there was a comfort in believing that Annie was up there somewhere. That's why Shauna spoke to her every day, just general chat as she was going about her life. There was only one person who could have engineered this, who would know how much Shauna needed to find someone, and Shauna was fairly sure that person would be looking down on them now.

'Where are we off to now then?' John asked, then reached back for the piece of paper Shauna was holding out to him. A letter. He checked the address on the top. 'No problem at all. It'll take about half an hour to get there, so you ladies just sit back and relax.'

Shauna pinged off another text to Beth, and immediately received a photo of a huge burger and fries in return. They'd clearly had a lovely dinner.

Love you,

she replied.

Love you too mum.

Shauna couldn't wait to tell her all about today, but now wasn't the time. Let her concentrate on Disney and she'd tell her about her new family when she saw her on Sunday.

John turned a dial on the dashboard and an advert announced that they were listening to Smooth Radio. Blue Christmas by Elvis was the first song to come on.

Flora smiled, 'Annie loved Elvis.'

'She sure did,' Shauna agreed. 'And she loved the Beatles and the Rolling Stones too. She told me she once bought Keith Richards a drink in a bar, but I don't know if that was true.'

Lulu turned around. 'I so hope it was. Could you imagine Annie and Keith Richards out on the town? I'd have loved to have seen that.'

Shauna's jaw was beginning to ache with smiling. 'You've got to understand,' she explained, 'that Annie wasn't the conventional grandmother. She would be disappointed in me if I was home before midnight and it broke her heart that I didn't grow up to be a backing singer for Jon Bon Jovi.'

The expression on Flora's face was an exquisite combination of delight and pain. 'I just wish...' she started, then stumbled for a few seconds. 'I just wish I hadn't lived all these years without her. She was a very special girl. And it sounds like she definitely became a very special woman, too.'

'She did,' Shauna replied, understanding her aunt's feelings of loss. She just hoped that for Flora, the joys of today would be some compensation for the pain of realising what she'd missed and lost.

They listened to the hits of the last few decades all the way to the other side of the city, singing along when it was a song they knew, telling Flora stories of Annie's escapades when it wasn't.

Eventually they pulled off the motorway and began to navigate the beautiful Victorian streets and crescents of Glasgow's West End, house after house illuminated with fairy lights and Christmas trees in the windows. Shauna thought of all the families in those houses and a bubble of joy rose from her heart. She had a family now, too.

'Coming here brings back so many memories,' Flora said. 'I used to visit George and Betty here, before...' her voice trailed off.

Shauna squeezed her hand again, feeling nothing but compassion for a woman who'd made a mistake and paid a terrible price.

John's voice was chirpy as he updated them. 'The satnav says it's just around...' The car swerved slightly, then John righted it again. 'God Almighty, I thought that car was going to pull right out on us there,' he said, gesturing back to a white Audi that was edging out from the side of the road behind them.

A few moments later, they drew up outside a beautiful old Victorian semi-detached house, with an impeccably tended garden.

'Oh no.' It was Lulu who vocalised everyone's thoughts. The house was in complete darkness. 'Hang on, I'll just go check, in case they're in a back room or something.' Lulu jumped out of the car, went up the path, and pressed on the doorbell, while Shauna and Flora watched, almost unable to breathe as every cell in their body willed someone to open the door.

No one did.

Despondent, Lulu returned to her seat in the taxi. 'I'm so sorry,' she said to the women in the back.

Shauna squeezed Flora's hand. 'I hope you're not too disappointed,' she said to her aunt.

Flora shook her head. 'No, dear. I've already had the most wonderful gift today. You found me, and I'll treasure this always.'

'As will I,' Shauna agreed. 'And it's only the start. I'll bring Beth to visit too, and make it a regular trip.'

Flora's eyes were glistening. 'That would mean the world to me. And to Arthur too. We'll come back here when Arthur gets out of hospital and hopefully George and Betty will be here. It's time to make amends. I hope they've been blessed with a family and a happy life because they're good people. I think I lost sight of that.'

'Let's get you home then,' Shauna suggested gently, so pleased that Flora was going to make the first step. She just prayed George would be there and he'd welcome her. Right now, though, she wasn't ready for the reunion to be over. 'And if it's okay with you, Lulu and I would love to come in and drink coffee and swap stories for a while longer.'

Flora hesitated, and Shauna immediately felt guilty that she was asking too much. She'd absolutely shocked this woman today and now she was asking for more. Just as with Annie, it was easy to forget that she was in her later years.

'But of course, if you're too tired...' she blurted out.

Flora cut her off. 'Pet, I am not tired in the least. In fact, I don't quite remember when I last felt this sprightly. I was just thinking that perhaps, if it wasn't too much of an inconvenience, we could pop along to Glasgow Central Hospital. It's very near here and it's where Arthur is being treated. A bit of a distance from our home, but we were over this way at the Botanic Gardens when he had his fall. He would so love to meet you and visiting finishes in...' she checked her watch. 'Just over an hour.'

'We'd love that,' Lulu got in first.

'We absolutely would,' Shauna agreed, laughing. A hospital, late at night, in a city she was visiting for the first time, with an auntie she'd only just found. Today just couldn't get any crazier.

Twenty-two

George

I hear Liv's voice cut through the silence that has been consuming the room for the last hour or so. It is difficult for me to keep track of time now. 'You know if you want to pop on down to the hospital restaurant, I'm very happy to sit here with George,' she says. 'I'm just about to go on a break anyway, so it's no bother at all to bring my baked potato in here and have this lovely man keep me company.' God bless her, she's a gem, that girl.

'There's a restaurant here?' I hear Norry ask.

Tom answers before Liv. 'Yes, down on the first floor. Sorry, didn't even think to ask if you were hungry, but —'

'I'm ravenous,' Norry blurts out. 'Rosemary, what about you?'

'I could definitely eat something,' she says, sounding lively for the first time since she arrived today. What a couple of wallopers these two are. They are obviously looking for any excuse whatsoever to get out of this room. If this bloody cancer doesn't take me soon, then the reality of being stuck in a room with these two definitely will.

'It's fine, Liv,' Tom says. 'I'll grab dinner later so I'll stay with Grandad.'

'Are you sure?'

'Absolutely,' he says.

I hear her footsteps disappearing as she leaves.

'Dad, you and Rosemary go get something to eat and then I'll go when you get back.'

They don't need to be asked twice. They are off like rabbits out of a trap. Surprised they'd lower themselves to eat hospital food and not swan off to some fancy restaurant.

They've barely gone when I hear Liv has returned. 'Tom, here's your grandad's laundry.' It was one of the things I insisted on when I came in here. I wasn't going to be a bother to anyone, but I wanted to wear my own pyjamas, my own robe, and slippers when I could still get about. I'd bought three of everything, except the slippers, and Tom takes them home for me and washes them as they are rotated.

'Thanks, Liv,' I hear him say. 'He's out of that shaving foam he likes too, and I know there's another bottle in his house, so I'm going to pop over there in a while and I'll pick up fresh pyjamas while I'm there.'

'That would be great, thank you,' she says.

'Then I'll be back. I'm going to take my parents to my place to sleep, and I'll stay here with Grandad again.'

There is silence for a few moments, and I can feel the movement of Tom's thumb, up and down my forearm, as if he is lost in thought and almost doing it subconsciously. I can sense he is troubled and I'd give anything – my last breath on earth – to be able to lean over and hug him, to let him know that I'm with him in thought, if not in this failing body.

'I'm really sorry, Grandad,' he says, with sorrow in his voice. 'It was a mistake telling them and letting them come. I really hope you're not hearing how much of an idiot he's being. Jesus, I hope I'm nothing like him.'

You aren't, son, I want to say it, but I can't. I just hope he trusts himself enough to know.

'Like I said to Liv, when they come back, I'll nip over to your house and get your shaving stuff, but I'll be back. I'm not letting them stay at your house, just so you know that. They can stay at my flat. I've got a feeling that you wouldn't want them at your place, raking through your stuff, and I suspect that's exactly what they would do. What does that say about me? Not great on trust, am I?'

Naw, but he is great on common sense and decency – and pretty perceptive because he is absolutely right on how I feel about them staying in my house when I'm not there. Over my dead body.

Tom's sigh snapped me out of my rage.

'I can't stop thinking about her, Grandad. I just can't. The thought that Davie, that smug prick, is going to be seeing her tonight makes me want to punch something. Preferably his leering face. He's a player, a top-class player, and the Chrissie I knew would have seen right through him, but how can I know what she's like now?'

I can feel the tentacles of regret moving under my skin again. I'd been wrong. I know now that Betty and I were wrong.

'You know,' he carries on. 'I always thought she would change her mind and come to Australia. Every day I would wake up and hope that was the day that she would arrive to surprise me, despite what Rosemary and my dad thought. And I know that's a cop out, because the truth is, I should never have left her in the first place, but it took me a while to realise that she wasn't coming. I think that's why I had to come back. Rosemary told me that Chrissie had phoned to say she'd met someone else, but I didn't care – I needed to see for myself.'

Christ, he's never mentioned that before. I don't know when the lass had found herself another boyfriend, but she was certainly still hankering after Tom on that night she'd come to my house.

I feel another wave of shame as it dawns on me that Rosemary had probably lied. She hadn't passed on the letters. She'd lied about the calls. That woman had been determined to keep them apart and would sink to any level to do so. Not that I had the moral high ground here.

I feel my throat tighten as I try to speak, but nothing will come out. This damn body.

Instead, I listen as Tom goes on, 'Then I couldn't find her. I came to terms with the fact that she was probably married, had kids, and now... now she's meeting Davie fucking Bailey. Sorry for swearing.'

I want to smile at that. He'd have got a severe talking to if my Betty had heard him use that kind of language. Considering the circumstances though, I'm all for letting it go this time.

'There's part of me that wants to just charge on in there, but that would be stupid, I know that. I'll just go see her tomorrow. But what if she doesn't make it to work tomorrow because she's off somewhere with Davie? That's the kind of thing he does – convinces people that the party should never end. Man, I'm torturing myself here.'

The rubbing of his finger up and down my arm is still going on and I can almost feel his tension seeping into me, meeting the wave of regret that I'm already feeling. I dearly wish I could take this sorrow away from him, make it right.

I should have sent the letter. I know that now. Instead, I'd opened it. The words are imprinted on my brain.

Tom, I need to speak to you. Not sure how I can tell you why in a letter, but trust me, I need you to call me. Actually, it's more than that. I need you to come back. I'll explain why when you phone me. I'll be at my mum's house until the end of October, and then I need to find somewhere else to live. I so hope you're back with me by then.

Please, please call.

I love you,

Chrissie xxx

She wanted the boy to come back. And I knew what he was like – if he read this he'd be back in a second, because he had a big heart that didn't always do what was best for him. Over there, he would be going to university, then our Norry had told me that he'd set him up in business. He had a great life all mapped out for him, and if I sent this I could take it all away from him, and for what? A teenage romance that probably wouldn't have lasted the year anyway. Young ones didn't marry in their teens and stay that way these days. They were waiting longer and longer to settle down, and although I'd been lucky with my Betty and wouldn't have changed it for the world, I didn't want Tom settling down too young and regretting it later. I felt like I had the boy's entire future in my hands right there and I didn't know what I should do with it.

I feel a gentle pressure on my arm as Tom begins to speak again. 'I just wish I'd never left. Or that I'd come back straight away, before she disappeared. Before I lost her.'

Christ, the grief in the boy's voice is killing me. This is on me. It is all on me.

I hear our Betty's voice again.

'What are you going to do?' she asked, when I put the letter down on my lap after I'd read it.

I took my spectacles off and looked up at her. Over in the doorway, with only the light of the floor lamp and the coal fire illuminating her face, she looked more beautiful than I'd ever seen her. Even now, I can still picture every curve and crevice of her face and I long to see it again.

I passed the letter over and watched as she read it. She handed it back with a sigh and, I knew, a heavy heart.

Tom is speaking again. 'The thing is, Grandad, there's only ever been her. I wanted to meet someone else, wanted to fall in love, but no one compared to her. And the stupid thing is, that girl probably doesn't even exist any more. I mean, who still loves the same person that they loved at eighteen? If you were awake, I'm pretty sure you'd be telling me I was being ridiculous. Shit, I wish you could talk to me.'

For once, I didn't want his wish to come true, because then I'd need to tell him. I'd need to confess the truth.

Back on that night, I'd needed to know what Betty was thinking.

'Well?' I asked her, fearful of her answer because I knew what was going through my mind and I didn't want to admit it to myself.

'You know I'll stand by whatever you decide,' she told me, unnecessary as it was, because even when we disagreed, we still stuck by each other, for good or bad, right or wrong. 'But this is another one of those situations that could completely alter a life. God help us, we've already done wrong by reading that poor lass's letter, but I hope God knows we were doing it to protect Tom and we'll have to live with that. If we send it, he'll come back, no doubt about it. I'm not sure we can put that kind of pressure on him. Maybe it's better to let people figure out their future for themselves.'

With that, she got up and went to the kitchen, touching my shoulder tenderly as she passed. I gazed at the letter on my lap once again and thought about it. I thought about Flora. I thought about Annie. I thought about all that I'd lost by interfering in other people's lives.

I had lost Tom to the other side of the world, but he was still in our lives and I knew we'd see him again. This letter would bring him back, but at what cost to him? His future? I had no way of knowing. But it wasn't a risk I was about to take.

Betty never asked me about it again and I was glad, because it would have pained me to admit that I did something that I know now was so wrong.

I scrunched that letter up and I threw it on the fire.

Now, over twelve years later, I realise that it wasn't just the letter that I destroyed. My Tom's chance of happiness with a woman he loved went up in flames that evening too.

Twenty-three

Chrissie

'I can't do it. Let's just do what you suggested earlier and have a couple of bottles of wine and a girls' night in,' Chrissie implored, her voice wobbling. How many times was she going to go back and forward on this today? She'd suddenly morphed into an emotional bloody pendulum.

'Sorry,' Josie answered. 'That was a time limited offer and you're way past the deadline. You really need to woman up.'

The seriousness of Josie's face made Chrissie giggle. Or that might have been the glass of rosé she'd already had. She wasn't a huge drinker, so she felt the effects pretty swiftly.

'Another terrific motivational speech there, Josie,' Jen said, from her vantage point behind the desk, where she was cashing up the days takings from Sun, Sea, Ski. They'd come back here straight after the make-over at the salon, closed the blinds, and convened a pre-date

256

preparation session. Jen was the owner of the shop, Chrissie's boss and Val's adopted daughter. She had a smile that was as huge as her heart and Chrissie had clicked with her the moment they'd met, right after Val had marched her in and strongly suggested that Jen interview her for the assistant manager's job. Chrissie got both the job and a new friend who complemented her perfectly. Jen handled the accounts, the business side of things and social media, while Chrissie was the creative one, who looked after marketing material, advertising and the company blog. And, of course, they both worked in the shop, selling merchandise and helping the clients plan and book the perfect holiday.

Not that there was much work getting done right now. The shop had closed at 6 p.m. after a monster day at the tills. Most of the other staff had headed out for the night, while Jen, on a post-busy high, was starting to wind down by counting the takings armed with a large glass of vino. Val and Josie, both sitting in bucket chairs in the middle of the shop, hadn't taken much persuasion to join her, whereas Chrissie had knocked back one glass, then gone to get changed into her new purchases.

She was worried that she'd imagined it, but no, the dress still fitted her perfectly, the shrug was stunning, and her make-up was flawless. In fact, everything was on point, except for her courage, which appeared to have temporarily deserted her.

'Wow, you look incredible,' Jen had whistled when she'd finally emerged from the fitting room where she'd been getting changed.

'Are you sure?' Chrissie asked, needing the reassurance.

'I'm positive.'

'Okay,' Chrissie said firmly. 'I can do this. Although, this is the only time I have ever, ever hoped that Ben calls me from a sleepover and announces that he ate something dodgy, isn't feeling well and wants to come home. I'm a terrible mother.'

Jen found this hilarious. 'You are not a terrible mother! You're just slightly terrified. Okay, massively terrified.'

Chrissie perched on the edge of one of the free seats so that she wouldn't crease her dress, and fretted a bit more. 'I really hope this guy is not a dick.'

'Or a mass murderer,' Val added. 'But if he is, don't worry – I'll adopt Ben and make him mine. We'll give you a lovely send-off.'

'Great!' Chrissie grinned. 'That's a huge weight off my mind. Huge. I've got absolutely nothing to worry about then. Apart from the bit where he slaughters me over pudding with an ice cream wafer.'

She needed this. Needed to be having a laugh that would take her mind off the dual pain of her first date in a decade and having her intimate follicles ripped out by lashings of hot wax. Her eyes watered every time she moved, peed or thought about it.

'Okay, rules,' Val said, in all seriousness. 'You must text us every hour and tell us that you're safe and enjoying yourself. If you don't contact us, Josie will enter the building in a covert manner and you just know that won't end well.'

Josie nodded the affirmative.

'No problem,' Chrissie concurred.

'You must also text us when you're leaving, and let us know where you're going,' Josie added. It was becoming like an episode of *Criminal Minds*, where each of the BAU team gave separate elements of their serial killer profile.

'DO NOT GO TO HIS HOUSE,' Val emphasised. 'Because we don't know where he lives and then anything could happen and we wouldn't be able to get there to break you out.'

'If you intend to have sex, and God help us, I hope you do—'

'Josie!' the others exclaimed at exactly the same time.

She ignored them and just kept on going. 'Then use protection and keep the light on, otherwise you don't know what he could surprise you with. I say that from experience.'

'I don't want to know,' Val drawled, trying to keep a straight face. 'But was it the time with the rubber sex toys?'

'I can't possibly say,' Josie replied, feigning distress. 'But I've never been able to change a tyre since.'

When the laughter subsided, Chrissie started to fidget. 'Aaargh, I'm getting more nervous by the minute. I think I'm just going to go now.'

'It's only 7.30,' Jen pointed out.

'I know, but by the time I get there...'

'It's a three minute walk.' That was Val.

'... And get organised...'

'Organised for what? You're having dinner, not planning a fortnight in Benidorm.' Val again.

'I'd much prefer that,' Chrissie countered. She picked up her phone and texted Ben for the tenth time that day.

I'm just off out now. Remember to call me if you need me. Or if you're missing me. Or for any reason at all

she typed, then pressed send.

The response was almost instant.

Sorry, who is this?

The boy would go far with that sense of humour.

'Ok, I'm going to go,' Chrissie said, with finality this time.

Sighing, Val and Josie both got up.

'We'll walk you there,' Val said.

'No, it's fine. Honestly. I'll be okay...'

'We're not worried about that,' Josie said. 'We're more concerned that you'll bottle out, jump in a taxi and you'll be home with a tub of ice cream, watching *The Greatest Showman* before the poor guy even knows you've stood him up.'

'You probably have a good point,' Chrissie conceded, thinking that she would indeed love to be home in her jammies right now having a musical interlude with Hugh Jackman. She picked up her bag – a beautiful berry coloured Mulberry clutch borrowed from Jen for the night – and gave her friend a hug.

Jen squeezed her back. 'Good luck. I'm sure you'll have a brilliant night. Phone me tomorrow and tell me how it goes, but I'll be here for the next hour or so in case you need me,' Jen promised. 'And I'll make sure these two come back and don't just press their faces against the restaurant window for the rest of the night.'

Chrissie grinned. 'Thank you. But I think there's probably a limit to your superpowers.'

'Right, come on then,' Josie beckoned, holding out her arm. Chrissie took it, and as soon as they were outside, Val joined in. The three of them walked, arm in arm, down the street.

They were just passing CAMDEN, the gents' boutique on the other side of Sun, Sea, Ski, when the owner, Cammy, another long time member of this extended group of friends, and his wife, Caro, emerged from the doorway. There was a round of hugs and kisses between them all.

Val was first to find out what was happening. 'Caro, you look beautiful as always. Cammy, son, you're definitely punching above your weight there. You off out somewhere nice?'

'Anniversary dinner. Kind of. Tomorrow is a year since the day we met.'

'And that was one helluva day last December,' Josie said, grinning. Cammy had been planning to marry someone else, but it hadn't worked out, which was just as well because he'd met Caro and she was oh so right for him.

'Have a fabulous time, you two. You know we're all so happy for you,' Val said, hugging them again.

'Where are you three off to? Is there a girls' night I'm missing, because, you know, I could stand this guy up,' Caro asked, laughing.

Josie got in there first. 'Nope, we're pimping Chrissie out. First date. We're just walking her to the restaurant to make sure she doesn't flee the country.'

'Do you want me to create a diversion and see if you can outrun them?' Caro asked, gesturing to the older women.

Val interrupted. 'Don't even think about it. With my new knee, I'm practically bionic.'

With another flurry of kisses and good luck wishes, they said their goodbyes, and the three women carried on down the street.

'You're going to be great,' Val promised Chrissie. 'Just be your normal, chilled out self and he'll realise how incredibly amazing you are. I'm proud of you, love. I really am.'

'Oh, Val, don't make my mascara run again,' she wailed.

A huge chunk of Chrissie's nerves were melted by the warmth of Val's words. She really was so lucky to have found this group, this extended family. Her life would be so much less without them in it. They made her laugh, made her feel loved, safe… she'd always be grateful. And despite the protestations, she was thankful, too, that they were encouraging her to do this. It was time. After seeing Tom's doppleganger today, she knew that more than ever. And there was definitely a little chink of excitement in there amongst the nerves.

As they got to the front door of the restaurant, Chrissie adopted a demeanour of positivity and resolve. 'Right, I'm going in. Thank you so much for everything you two have done for me today. I love you both,' she said, kissing each woman in turn.

'Back at you, love,' Josie responded, hugging her. 'Sure you don't want us to wait here and vet him?'

'I'm sure.' She broke the news as gently as possible. She knew how much they would relish the opportunity to meet, interrogate and judge this poor guy.

'Okay. Hourly texts or we'll be back.'

'Done,' Chrissie said, as she stepped back, pivoted and stood for a moment to gather herself. Deep breath. Head up. Walk in.

The restaurant manager was standing by the door. 'Sun, Sea, Ski!' he bellowed, making Chrissie laugh. The staff from the shop came here at least once every couple of weeks or so after work, and Gino, the manager, was always an exuberant host.

'Gino, I'm so glad you're here tonight. I'm on a date. If I look like I'm having a terrible time, please rescue me.'

'Ah, lucky, lucky, man. You look very beautiful tonight.' Gino crooned. 'Not a worry, I will keep my eyes peeled and I will throw him out immediately if I do not see you smile,' he assured her, feigning seriousness. 'Okay, table five, please come right this way.'

She followed him as they crossed the room. It was a small bistro, maybe twenty tables in total, but it was the perfect example of an authentic Italian restaurant. The aromas were breath-taking, the decor a combination of deep wood panels and exposed brick walls, one of them almost entirely covered in a wine rack containing hundreds of bottles. The ceiling was draped in Christmas fairy lights and the tables were thick mahogany slabs, surrounded by beautifully carved wooden chairs, upholstered in red leather. At least half of the tables on the other side had been pushed together to accommodate a party of about twenty, all wearing festive hats and draped in tinsel. A few of them already looked like they'd been over-indulging in the mulled wine. Chrissie was glad. If they broke into an impromptu medley of Christmas songs, it would be a great ice-breaker with Davie.

'What can I get you to drink?' Gino asked as she took a seat.

'A rosé please.'

'Uno momento,' he said with a smile, before turning and heading in the direction of the bar.

Chrissie felt herself exhale. She was on home territory and she loved this place. This was going to be okay. And if it wasn't? Well, that was fine too. The important thing was that she was finally moving on, opening herself up to new possibilities and to having new people in her life. Leaving Tom Butler in the past.

She nibbled on one of the breadsticks from the pot in the middle of the table, as she ran through everything Davie Bailey had told her about himself. He ran his own marketing agency. He lived in Glasgow. He was single, obviously, and loved to travel and try out new things. That was about as far as it went, but then, when you met any new guy you didn't have their résumé beforehand, unless it was a dating app set-up and she hadn't tried those... yet.

Besides, she already knew more about him than vice versa.

She hadn't told him yet about Ben, mostly because she made it a rule not to discuss her personal life and family situation with people online. If he had a problem with the fact that she was a single mum, and that ruled out any potential romance, that was just fine with her – it would mean he obviously wasn't the kind of guy she wanted to date.

It was time to just go with the flow... to roll with the punches... to do all those clichéd things she'd been avoiding for so long.

She checked her watch. 7.55 p.m.

Gino returned to her table, delivered her glass of wine, then gestured to the doorway, where a tall man with dark hair had just entered. 'Is that the gentleman the signora is waiting for?'

Twenty-four

Tom

Tom's glance went to his watch when he heard Norry and Rosemary's unmistakable chatter as they approached the room. Norry always had been too bloody loud for his own good.

Seven o'clock. They'd not been away long – barely an hour. Maybe he had them all wrong. He'd been sure they would have strung this out for at least a couple of hours, given how uncomfortable they'd seemed when they were here.

He felt a twinge of guilt for misjudging them. He picked up the damp sponge and was moistening his grandad's lips when back they came, although Rosemary hovered at the door again.

He bit his tongue. He had to be civil if there was any hope of getting some kind of peace and reconciliation in George's last days.

'Rosemary and I were just talking,' Norry said, 'and we're exhausted. This jetlag is a bloody nightmare.'

Tom just stared at Norry's face, thinking that he didn't look jet lagged in the least. Neither did Rosemary. Although, he had a growing sense of impending doom about what was coming next.

'So we're just going to go jump in a cab and head on over to Dad's place. If you can give me your car keys, we'll get our luggage out of the boot. Oh, and I'll need a set of Dad's keys, too.'

Tom had to take his hand off George's arm, for fear his clenching fists would squeeze his skin. But he couldn't hold his tongue.

'Well done, Dad. You haven't seen Grandad in twelve years and you didn't even manage a couple of hours with him before you felt the need to bail out,' he said, his voice softer than his words suggested.

'Don't you dare—' Norry started.

No. Not this time. Norry didn't get to dictate what happened here. Tom cut him right off. 'No, don't *you* dare. Don't you dare waltz back in here and treat Grandad as if he doesn't matter. Don't you dare deprive him of the respect he deserves. This is your father and all he gets is a brief appearance from you? You really are despicable. And, just so you know, you're not staying at Grandad's house, you're staying at my flat. Grandad wouldn't have wanted you there. I'll take you to my place and then I'll come back and sleep here.'

Norry's caramel tan was fast turning a shade of pink. Thankfully he lowered his voice, but Tom knew that meant nothing because he was still speaking through clenched teeth and looked ready to explode at any second. It was a familiar sight from when he was a kid. Norry would pass the shouting stage and go deadly quiet as he issued a warning that inevitably ended in punishment for Tom. 'We. Will. Stay. At. My. Father's. House,' Norry said, with absolute menace.

Tom decided to take a completely different route and went for flippant. He lightened his voice, carefree and blasé. 'You know, this is just awkward, Dad. Do you mind if I call you that?'

Stony silence.

'I'll take that as a no. Great. So. This is awkward because you seem to think I'm still a young kid that you can intimidate and push around, but those days are long gone. Grandad and I talked about this before he got sick and I know exactly what he did and didn't want to happen. He didn't want you in his house. Period. Do you know how gutted he was that you never bothered to check in on him, never gave him the time of day? It was actually me who decided to tell you he was sick because I wanted you to be able to make your peace with him after pretty much ignoring him for all these years. Do you know what hurt him the most? That you didn't bother coming back for your mum's funeral. That cut him to the quick. The only family there were me and Grandad because her son was too busy to show.'

'We were on a cruise—' Rosemary started to object.

Tom just cut her dead with a glare.

Norry started to speak, but Tom just talked right over him. 'You probably didn't know he was upset because you wouldn't have given it much thought. And I'm guessing you didn't spend the money coming home because there was nothing to be gained that time. We all know this time it's different. What is it you want? The house? The life insurance?' He knew he was being seriously cruel now, but he didn't seem to be able to stop himself. He sighed, exhausted, the fight sliding right out of him, before he went on in a calmer voice, 'Make your peace. Grovel. Apologise for everything you've failed to do to repay this man for being your father. I'm going to go now. I need to take Grandad's washing home and I need to pick up some things from his house. I'll be back in an hour or so to collect you and take you back to my place. If that isn't agreeable, you can stay in a hotel. Your choice. In the meantime, you can sit here and find a way to make things right and to compensate for being an absolute dick.' At that he stood up, lifted his jacket from the back of his chair, and headed to the door. When he passed Norry, he patted him on the shoulder. 'Good luck with that.'

Rosemary stood to one side to let him exit and, as he did, he saw Liv standing just to the right of the doorway, her expression suggesting that she'd heard some or all of what had just been said.

'That you away now?' she asked, with a loaded grin.

'I am,' he replied. 'Like I said, I'll be back in a little while to pick them up and take them to my place. Thanks for putting up with all the toing and froing today.'

Liv smiled. 'No problem at all, Tom. See you soon.'

Most of the visitors started to leave around this time, and the ward would begin winding down for the night. Sometimes, when it got to ten or eleven o'clock, it was just Tom and George, with the bedside light on and the rest of the ward – apart from the nursing station – would be in silent darkness. It reminded him of the nights he'd spent by his mum's bed before she passed too. Not a day went by that he didn't wish Catriona was still here to speak to him, to give him advice, to share the life he'd built for himself. He knew she'd be proud. Throughout his childhood she never missed a school show or a sports day, always cheering him on, making excuses for Norry's absence. How was it right that she was taken, that George would soon be gone too, and yet those two cretins he'd just left up there would probably bloody live forever?

He realised his fists were still clenched. It took until he'd descended in the lift, walked to the car park and got into his car before his fury dissipated. All these years and his father and stepmother could still have that effect on him. He was only happy that his mother had a chance to leave and find happiness for the last few years of her too short life. Catriona put up with far too much for far too long, and it was a blessing for her when Norry finally cut her free. God, he missed her. He missed Catriona and he missed Chrissie.

As he pulled on his seat belt, he tasted the saltiness of a tear. He hadn't even realised that one had fallen. Frustration, that's what this was. Added to devastation over George, disappointment about Davie, and the sheer emotional turmoil of finding Chrissie. He couldn't get her out of his mind.

The snow had stopped now, leaving only a layer of slush on the streets. Fireworks were going off somewhere in the distance as Tom flicked on the sound system and set off for his grandad's house. It was only fifteen minutes away and he could be there, find George's things, and be back in the hospital in under an hour.

As soon as he switched on the engine, the sound of Smooth Radio playing 'Blue Christmas', by Elvis filled the car. It was George's top choice of radio station, and Tom had switched it on for him when they were on their way into the hospital a few weeks ago for what would turn out to be the last time. George would love this moment, right here right now. Blue Christmas was his favourite.

Just thinking about the things George loved and would no longer do broke a piece off Tom's heart. George would never sit in this car again. His grandad had loved the BMW from the moment he'd spotted it on one of their afternoons out together browsing in car showrooms. It was the reason Tom had bought it. They'd never do that again. They'd never drive down to Largs on a sunny evening to have ice cream at Nardini's café. They wouldn't nip through to Edinburgh to have a wander around the Christmas markets. They wouldn't go to a football match in Glasgow or a rugby game in Edinburgh. Tom always made sure they went to the hospitality suite and he'd tell his grandad that he got the tickets for free, even though they'd cost him full price. He knew George was proud and he'd insist on paying. He wouldn't do that any more. They wouldn't do anything any more. They were done.

Several old songs later, he was almost at George's street when the pain in his chest became so sudden and strong that he had to pull over and stop at the side of the road.

They were done. That thought was going over and over again in his head, as he rested his forehead on the steering wheel, gasping for breath as he tried to force his body to breathe. In the end, the suffocation broke in a gut wrenching sob and more tears, bloody rivers of tears, slid down his face.

They were done. His life was never going to be the same again. The most important person, by far, in his world would be gone and all he'd be left with were memories and the lessons that George Thomas Butler had taught him.

And they were many.

He sat for a while, through several old songs, until there was a change of tempo, and Tom's anguish turned to an almost incredulous laughter. Frank Sinatra. "That's Life". Another of George's favourite songs of all time, the one he sang to his granny, Betty, when he'd had a couple of whiskies at New Year. She would pretend to be embarrassed and implore him to stop, but then he'd win her over and pull her up to dance, and they'd waltz around the kitchen, both of their faces beaming. Tom would watch them and think they were hilarious. Nothing was funny any more.

That's life. He listened to the song, silent tears falling with every line, hearing George's voice singing every word.

That was who his grandad was. Someone who lived life. Someone who loved. Someone who never, ever let him down.

And how had he lived up to George's legacy? He hadn't. He'd bailed on the one important relationship he'd ever had, and then been unable or unwilling to find another one.

'You'll know it's right when you meet her,' George would say, but Tom couldn't even face trying. Every romance he'd had in the last decade had fallen in his lap, because he just didn't have the motivation to go looking for that woman who was out there. Probably because he knew he'd already met her.

'Fuck it.' It was out of his mouth before he even realised what was happening. His indicator went on, and thankfully he checked his wing mirror before he pulled out, because otherwise he'd have careered right into the taxi that was passing by and turning into George's street.

As soon as it was safely by, he pulled out, did a U-turn and headed along the expressway towards the city centre. His eyes flicked to the clock on the dashboard. 7.55 p.m.

In five minutes, Davie Bailey would be meeting Chrissie. *His* Chrissie.

He put his foot down on the accelerator and hoped that there were no speed cops in his future. He'd planned to go and see her tomorrow at her shop, but he couldn't wait. This was Chrissie, and he wasn't going to let that lying, cheating scumbag anywhere near her. If she didn't want Tom, that was fine. He wouldn't blame her if she couldn't forgive him for leaving. But at least he would know that he tried. Years ago, he'd let Norry and Rosemary dictate what happened in his relationship with Chrissie, and it had cost him everything.

He damn well wasn't going to let Davie Bailey do the same.

8 p.m. – 10 p.m.

Twenty-five

Shauna

'Oh I do like the songs on this radio station, John,' Flora said, swaying in time to "White Christmas" by Bing Crosby. 'Arthur and I have always liked a bit of a song and dance. Isn't it amazing? Sometimes I couldn't tell you what I did yesterday yet I can remember every word of all these songs from years ago.' She demonstrated this by singing along, and Shauna, Lulu and John joined in on the chorus. Shauna scrapped her earlier assertion that today couldn't get any crazier. She was now having a sing song in the back of a Glasgow taxi.

After belting out two more choruses and the big finishing line, John laughed. 'Have I mentioned I'm fair enjoying myself today?'

Lulu nudged him. 'You have. And if there's a café in the hospital, I'll bring you a wee coffee and cake to make it even better.'

'Aye, you're a grand one,' he told her, winking.

Ten minutes later, they pulled up outside the entrance to Glasgow Central Hospital and Flora led the way through the foyer to an elevator on the back wall. Inside, she pressed the button for the second floor.

'Arthur will be quite overjoyed. I usually come over once a day and now he's getting an extra visit from all three of us,' Flora chirped, delighted.

The elevator pinged open, and as Shauna stepped out, she checked the signs hanging from the ceiling above. General Surgical and Paediatrics to the left, Palliative Care and Cardiac Care to the right.

They turned left. She didn't even want to think about all those poor patients and families in the palliative care ward, preparing to say goodbye. Just heartbreaking. A sudden picture of Annie on that last night flashed into her mind again. If Annie had chosen a way to go, that was it – after a great night of dancing and laughing. Shauna was grateful she hadn't suffered.

Arthur's room was halfway along the corridor and his face lit up with surprise when Flora entered the room. 'Sweetheart!' he said, and Shauna suddenly felt quite overcome with emotion. He still called her sweetheart and was thrilled to see her, even after all these years. This was exactly how she'd imagined she and Colm would be when they got to that age, and it was a constant source of sorrow that she would never find out. Her throat tightened as she swallowed back a large lump that had lodged there. This was a happy time, not one for "could have beens".

'Darling,' she said, crossing the room to kiss him. He was a slender, smiling chap, who still had a full head of grey hair and wore pristine blue striped pyjamas. Shauna recognised them from Marks and Spencer adverts. 'You'll never guess who I've brought to meet you.'

Arthur's glance went first to Lulu and you could see by his penetrative expression he was searching for a clue. Finding none, he turned his gaze to Shauna and the reaction was instant. 'Dear God, I've no idea, but you're definitely related to Agnes Butler. You're her spitting image!'

Shauna felt a completely irrepressible burst of happiness.

'You're right! This is Shauna,' Flora announced triumphantly. 'She's Annie's granddaughter.'

'Well, my dear, I would have picked you out as a Butler in a crowd, that's for sure – you're Flora's mother Agnes right over the back!'

'I can't tell you how happy it makes me to hear that,' Shauna grinned, stepping forward to shake his hand. 'Please to meet you, Uncle Arthur,' she said.

'Oh my, I like the sound of that,' he said, smiling. 'Now, I cannot wait to hear how this happened between my Flora leaving here today and now,' he said, and Shauna could immediately see why Flora adored him.

He had the kindest face and a gentle way about him that was endearing.

Flora sat on the end of the bed, leaving Shauna and Lulu to pull over chairs from the wall under the window.

'We've got just over half an hour, so we'll have to make this quick,' Flora said, before going on to recount, with much happiness, the events of the last few hours. 'Oh, Arthur, it's been such a joy,' she finished, beaming.

Between the three of them, they just about had the full story told when the bell rang to signal nine o'clock, the end of visiting hours.

Arthur reached over and took Flora's hand. 'Darling, now that all this has happened, I promise you that as soon as I'm back on my feet, we will find out what happened to George. One way or another, you'll have all your answers.' He switched to Shauna. 'As for you, dear, please do come back, and often. And you too, Lulu.'

'I would love to,' she assured him, and Shauna could see that she meant it. Lulu was woefully short on family, too. They'd been like sisters since they were infants, brought up together thanks to the incredibly close relationship between their parents, so any gain for Shauna was a gain for her, too.

Arthur went on, 'Do you know there was a Scottish singer—'

'I do,' Lulu said, giggling. 'I think someone may have mentioned it.'

He nodded. 'Excellent. Well, thank you for helping to track down Flora. I haven't seen my sweetheart looking so overjoyed in years!'

All three women kissed him goodbye and then waved at the door.

'You know, I should be exhausted after all this excitement today, but I'm brimming with energy!' Flora announced as they entered the elevator. A middle-aged couple got in at the same time, both of them with dark, caramel tans and wearing bright clothes that were definitely not the typical attire of the Scottish winter.

'Told you it was a waste of time,' the woman was saying. 'I can't believe you dragged me all the way here to just sit in this hospital.'

The man didn't look pleased at all. 'Shut up, Rosemary. Just let me think, okay.'

Lulu's right eyebrow immediately raised in irritation, then she caught sight of Shauna's displeased expression too. They weren't ones for allowing any man to speak to a woman in that way.

Shauna gave Lulu a 'don't interfere' stare, just as the woman, who didn't seem concerned in the least about how he'd addressed her, bit back, 'Well, hurry up and think of something, because I just want a ciggie and a large drink and I'm only going to get the ciggie here. That son of yours has got way too big for his fucking boots. Who does he think he is? What the hell are we supposed to do now? I'm not bloody staying at his house. Are you sure we can't just go check into a hotel?'

Shauna noticed that the veins in the side of the man's neck had begun to throb. 'Don't you ever listen? I just told you upstairs that we couldn't,' he hissed. 'Or have you got some miracle bloody money tree that will cough up the dough for hotels and fine fucking dining?'

Shauna and Lulu both confirmed their dickhead judgements, then disengaged from the strangers, the comment reminding Lulu of another matter.

'Let's stop by the café on the way out. I promised John I'd pick him up a coffee and a cake. He's been an absolute star today.'

Shauna nodded as the doors pinged open and they alighted. 'He really has.'

The other couple stormed past them and out of the front doors. Lulu was about to comment when Flora spoke.

'I've been thinking, could I ask something of you?'

'Anything,' Shauna replied, deciding there was nothing Flora could ask that she wouldn't do.

'Could we just stop by George's house again on the way home? I keep pondering how I almost missed you today, and if you hadn't come back, then we wouldn't be here now. Let's give finding my brother one more try.'

'Great idea,' Lulu agreed. 'Let me just nip in for John's coffee and I'll be right with you.'

She was back in five minutes, carrying a tray with four drinks and a large brown paper bag.

'Snacks for the car,' she grinned.

Shauna laughed. 'This is what I'm up against, Flora. She does this all the time with Beth. I make her fruit bags, then Auntie Lulu shows up with a selection of treats and my bananas get tossed to the side.'

'I'm trying to buy her affection,' Lulu told Flora.

'Whatever works for you, pet,' Flora said, coming in on the joke. 'Nothing wrong with a bit of bribery in the right circumstances.'

They were still chuckling when they got back to John's taxi and handed out the supplies. Four rolls with chips, four carrot cakes and four hot drinks.

'Oh my God, that's so Annie! She loved a roll with chips,' Shauna said, revelling in the nostalgia of the moment.

What a day.

She'd met her aunt and her lovely husband. She'd gained two relatives.

As they set off for George's house again, she knew that there was every possibility that he wouldn't be in, or no longer lived there, or had sadly passed away.

She popped a chip in her mouth and glanced skywards once again, sending a silent thought to Annie. *You're doing a great job up there, Gran. But if you could just help us out with George, you'd be totally rocking this day.*

Twenty-six

George

They're still here. I can sense them, just sitting there, saying nothing. Every now and then, one of them will sigh and that's as close as they get to communication.

I've never been prouder of Tom than when he stood up to them and put them right in their place. But then, I shouldn't be smug about that because he's got more right to be furious with me than with them. You see, they were always useless, but he counted on me to have his back, to look out for his interests and what did I do?

I burned the letter from that lass.

One of the two biggest regrets of my life.

Couldn't do right for doing wrong. This time, I hadn't interfered, and I damn well should have.

What was even worse, God forgive me, was that I never admitted it to him. He came back from Australia a year later, a bit broken, a shadow of the bright, positive guy that he'd been. Of course, all Norry's promises had come to nothing and he'd basically been an extra pair of hands on the decorating and landscaping of their fancy big house. No university. No training. Nothing.

That wasn't the biggest problem though.

'I really thought she'd join us out there, Grandad,' he said. 'I thought she was just digging her heels in and she'd change her mind. I wrote to her time and time again and she just ignored me. The emails I sent got bounced back. Her mobile phone was disconnected. She just moved on.' The boy had been so stricken, so bereft that the pain of regret near cut me in two.

'How do you know she got your letters?' I asked, shamefully desperate for evidence that I was off the hook, that someone else had committed a worse crime in stopping them being together.

'Because I gave every one of them to Dad's housekeeper and she posted them,' he replied.

I should have said something then, voiced my suspicions that Rosemary and Norry were deliberately keeping them apart, but I didn't. Because I was no better.

Instead, I kept quiet, and watched as he searched for her. He went to the university she'd been due to attend and discovered that she'd never gone. She'd left the house a couple of months after the family had moved down under. She'd cut ties with everyone he could think of to ask where she was. And she'd left no forwarding address, no contact details, no trail of breadcrumbs... nothing. She'd simply vanished.

What a sorry state he was in. He only really picked himself up when he went to university to study marketing and started getting a bit of a life. Although, I was never keen on that Davie one he became friends with. Too slick for my liking. All mouth and no substance, I'd say to Betty.

University was the making of him though and when he left we were happy to support him until he got the business up and running. Later, he paid every penny back.

It should have been the happy ending. The triumph. But every single day I thought about that letter, and I'd kid myself that it didn't matter, that they were too young, that it wouldn't have worked out anyway... but the truth was that I'd taken the one person from him that he ever loved.

If I wasn't such a coward, and wasn't so scared that he wouldn't forgive me, then I would have confessed all, but I couldn't stand the thought of not having him in our lives, so I kept my mouth shut.

For the umpteenth time in the last few days, I'm wishing I could go back and change my two biggest regrets – interfering in Flora's life and keeping secrets from Tom.

Soon enough, our Tom is going to find out what I did. He's found that lass again, and whether he goes to see her tomorrow, or the next day, or the next, she'll tell him that she came to see me, that she begged me for help, that she entrusted me with her letter and he'll know that I didn't pass it on to him. It'll eat away at him, as he mulls that over and realises that I didn't even tell him when he came home looking for her. He'll be crushed. Devastated. And he'll look at me in a whole new light. The memory of his grandfather, of the man who he looked up to his whole life, will be tarnished by the stain of betrayal.

'His eyes are watering,' I hear Rosemary saying, with utter disdain.

A weeping old fool is more like it, I think to myself.

My lips are dry, but I wouldn't want either of these two to tend to me. Not that it would even cross their minds to help.

Norry does nothing. I can hear him breathing in the chair beside the bed, so I know he's there. Maybe he's sleeping. He still hasn't said a civil word to me since he got here. What was the bloody point of coming?

'Look,' Rosemary starts again. 'I've no intention of staying at Tom's place and having his disapproval follow every bloody thing that I do. He definitely takes after his mother, with his bloody judgement and holier-than-thou attitude. Why don't we just go book into a hotel and then we can get out of here?'

Norry's breathing changes and I have a sense of foreboding. 'We can't afford a bloody hotel?' he hisses. 'When are you going to get your head round this? We can't afford to be wining and dining, and you can forget about buying anything while you're here. And we definitely won't be paying for the funeral out of this old bugger's life insurance. Saint bloody Tom can cough up for that.'

Never had I prayed more that by some miracle I could rise from this bed, drag that sorry excuse of a son out of this room, and boot his arse all the way back to the airport.

'Do we have to stay for the funeral? I didn't bring anything black.' Rosemary again.

'We might have to. Depends how long it takes the lawyers to sort out the will and release the cash to me.'

So that is it. Money. I have no idea why or how, but somehow it seems they've managed to blow his earnings from the engineering patent. They aren't here to pay their respects, they are here to feed like scavengers on everything I've worked for.

Well, they'll be disappointed.

I desperately want to laugh, to roar with hilarity and watch their faces as they realise this meal ticket isn't meant for them. Uncharitable, I know. In Scottish law, the child of a deceased person is entitled to a percentage of their parent's estate, no matter whether a will states wishes to the contrary, but I've taken care of that by transferring everything I own over to Tom a long time ago. Norry will be lucky if he gets enough for a flight back to Oz. Although, in truth, I'd pay for that my bloody self.

'Christ, it's barely past nine o'clock. Today feels like the longest day of my life. Sod this,' Rosemary says. 'I'm going out for a fag.'

'I'm coming. Can't sit here a minute longer or I'll go fucking mad,' Norry spits.

Off they go. And to tell you the truth, I'm relieved.

Silence.

I didn't like it much when I was in the land of the living, but I don't mind it now. It's time for a bit of peace.

I doze for a while, maybe minutes, maybe hours, it's hard to keep track, until Liv's footsteps bring me out of it.

'How are you doing there, George?' she asks and I wonder if it's day or night. The hours that lass works are ridiculous. It must still be night, because she told me she was on a double shift today, and then off tomorrow. 'All your visitors are gone for now then. Tom said he'll be back though, and it's almost ten o'clock, so I don't think he'll be long. He was just going to stop by your house for some things. And your son... don't actually know where he's gone to. Perhaps just popped downstairs for a cuppa.'

I have only been asleep for a few minutes then. Like I said, hard to tell sometimes.

I feel her put the buzzer back in my hand. 'I know you're not likely to be using it, George, but just in case...

I'm right outside and I'll keep popping my head in until Tom comes back.'

If that lass wasn't married I'd be praying that my Tom would realise what a gem she is.

Tom. Just the thought of him is making me feel sick to my stomach. What's he going to think of me?

Another thought hits me then. Tom is taking his time in coming back. I know he was mighty irate with his father and wouldn't be in a rush to get back here to see him, but still. What if...

The dread begins to ooze from every pore of my skin. What if he's away seeing Chrissie now? Didn't he say she was meeting Davie tonight? He gave half a dozen reasons that it wouldn't be a good idea to go along there, but I know my Tom – he's got more passion than patience.

The dread is now burrowing into my bones, as I realise that's exactly where he is now. Of course he is. He'll have gone charging in there like a raging bull and tried desperately to make it right with her. More than likely he'll have punched that Davie one by now too.

And if Tom's with her right now... well, soon he'll know what I did, and I have to face the fact that I might not see him again. Why would he want to come back to this old fool after I've let him down so badly?

So this is how it will end then. My last hours in a hospital, with only my money grabbing son and his wife. In fact, I doubt they'll be back either, so it'll be me.

Just me.

It's time. There's no point in dragging this out, of worrying and fretting, of hoping every set of footsteps coming this way are his and then being disappointed that they're not.

I made a mistake.

I failed him.

I try to summon up an image of Betty in my mind, to send her a message.

I'm ready, love.

I'm ready to come to you.

Twenty-seven

Chrissie

It wasn't him. It was some other bloke, and his wife/ girlfriend/ sister came right in behind him.

Chrissie took another sip of her wine, struck by a thought. She'd been so busy contemplating bailing out of tonight that she'd hadn't given any real consideration to what would happen if he didn't show. It restored her equilibrium when she realised that the answer was fairly straightforward – she'd call Josie, Val and Jen, they'd come racing over, and the four of them would have a fabulous meal, loads of wine, and some great chat.

'Chrissie?' The shock almost made her topple her glass. Thankfully it wobbled but remained upright. Bugger. She hadn't even noticed him arriving and now he was... bloody hell, he was handsome. He didn't look like that when they were at school. And his Facebook photo didn't do him justice. He was one of those guys coming out of an exclusive hotel with his jacket slung over his shoulder in an aftershave advert. His dark blonde hair was swept off his face, and he had that male model jawline, the kind of male models that were in their late thirties and still got work because they rocked a great suit.

She sent out a psychic vibe of thanks to Val and Josie for upping her game today. If they hadn't intervened, she'd be here wearing her interviews/ funerals/ any formal occasion jacket and make-up that was purchased somewhere around the dawn of the millennium.

'Davie, hi!' she said, going for "sexy grin" and worrying that she'd ended up somewhere closer to "is my last snack stuck in my teeth?"

He half leant down, and she half stood up, and they met in the middle for a hug, the awkwardness covered by an anxious laugh.

This was why she'd avoided doing this for twelve years.

Thankfully, he didn't seem to notice her nervousness, or to be in any way uncomfortable. Instead, he summoned a waiter and ordered a Jack Daniels and Coke. Chrissie decided to overlook the fact that he didn't ask her if she'd like another wine. Maybe he was nervous, too.

'Wow, you're even hotter than I remember,' he crowed. Cancel the "nervous" theory. This guy was totally at ease.

Gino came right over with the menus. 'Good evening, sir,' he chirped, with his usual exuberance. Can I get you a drink?'

'Jack Daniels and coke.'

'Certainly. Here is tonight's menu and I'm sure the lady can suggest something delicious for you this evening.'

Chrissie had to stop herself from groaning. She knew Gino meant the comment in all innocence, but Davie's expression told her that he was interpreting an innuendo in there.

'I come here a lot,' Chrissie clarified after Gino bustled off. 'I don't think there's much on the menu that I haven't tried.' Contrary to earlier protestations, she'd give her last bowl of tagliatelle for Josie and Val to come storming in right now and break her free of this anxiety and awkwardness

The waiter delivered Davie's drink and he took a slug.

'So...' he said, when suitably refreshed, 'you haven't changed a bit since school.'

Chrissie smiled, hopefully not inanely this time. 'I've lost the backpack. And the devotion to Westlife. Actually, maybe just the backpack.'

That made the subtle lines on his face crease and Chrissie began to relax. She had this. It was going to be okay.

'It was a bit of a surprise when I heard from you,' she said. 'Joining the former pupil page on Facebook is the only thing I've ever done on social media. You said you didn't keep in touch with anyone from school?'

He shrugged. 'Occasionally see a few of the guys. We play five-a-side football once in a blue moon when we've convinced ourselves we're still fit enough to do it. Then we get on the pitch and remember why we're not. What about you?'

'No one at all. Life changed for me when we left school,' she decided to go with full disclosure straight away and tell him about Ben. His reaction would tell her everything she needed to know about him. 'I have a—'

'Are you ready to order?' Gino swept in.

'I'll have the veal Milanese,' Davie said. 'And a bottle of house red.'

'Penne arrabbiata please, Gino,' Chrissie ordered, realising she'd had to stop herself from correcting his manners by pointing out to Davie that he hadn't let her order first or said 'please' or 'thank you'. Hanging out with twelve year olds did that to you. Though she couldn't help thinking that Ben had a better grasp of politeness than this guy.

'I'm really glad you came tonight.' Davie commandeered the conversation before she could deliver the news she'd been working up to. 'You know, I always had a thing for you back in school.'

'Really?' she was genuinely surprised. 'I had absolutely no idea. We never really hung out in the same group, did we?'

'No,' he admitted, with a sexy smile. 'It was more of a "lust from afar" thing. Apart from that one night at the school disco. I'll always be thankful for mistletoe.'

Cute, but Chrissie could sense that charm came pretty easy to this one. She wasn't sure how she felt about that. On one hand, it was flattering; on the other, it made her wonder how much of a player Davie was. The overly confident type had never been her thing. Actually, she didn't have enough experience to even know what her "thing" was.

'Indeed,' she said. 'Anyway, Davie—'

'I don't know whether to be insulted that you didn't want to jump my bones back then,' he said, with a wide, cheeky grin that told her he was joking.

Only… it wasn't funny.

'Well, back then I was in a relationship with someone else and I was never the unfaithful type,' she said, hoping her attempt at a jocular tone masked the fact that she was starting to feel more than a little defensive.

He leant towards her, that grin still there, his whole demeanour screaming 'suggestive and sexy'. 'You just didn't see a good thing when it was in front of you. I'm sure we can make up for that now.'

Something inside her snapped.

'I have a son. His name is Ben.'

Every single thing about his demeanour changed. 'You didn't mention that before,' he said, his tone cold.

'I don't discuss my family on social media. Is it a problem?' Chrissie was already sensing that it most definitely was, but strangely, she wasn't in the least bit upset. Her "he's a dick" radar was flashing like a strobe light and her libido had already decided that she wouldn't touch this guy with Josie's bargepole, so she really did not give a flying toss what he thought of her. Too smug. Too smarmy. Too overly suggestive. And he didn't fucking say 'please' or 'thank you'.

'No, it's not a problem…' Now he was the defensive one and Chrissie wasn't proud to admit she was glad she'd made him squirm just a bit. Arse. 'I mean, if you're just into something casual.'

Wow. Just wow. He clearly wasn't in the least bit interested in Ben and didn't even have the decency to act like he was. Not a single question about the most important part of her life, just straight on to what it meant for him.

Chrissie required clarification. 'By "something casual" do you mean just sex?'

The suggestive grin was back. It took every ounce of Chrissie's restraint not to slap it with a breadstick.

'Well, if that's what you're thinking, I'd be good with that.'

Chrissie barely stopped herself from rolling her eyes. Did anyone actually fall for this crap? Or was this what dating was like these days? Had she missed a whole decade where stuff like… oh, say, getting to know each other, having lunch, going to the cinema, had all been circumvented and it now just went straight to "get them off and climb on"? If so, she was going to be single forever. Right now, that didn't seem like such a bad thing.

She'd been here barely fifteen minutes with this bloke and already she was calculating that if she left right now, she could be home and in her pyjamas watching this week's episode of *Chicago Fire* by nine o'clock. And at that moment, she fancied a night of escapist drama much more than she fancied a night with Davie Bailey.

So what to do? Stay or cut and run? It would be polite to stay. Of course it would. And Val and Josie had put so much effort into supporting her tonight. Yes, of course, she should stay.

Unfortunately, no one notified her left hand of this, because it was currently creeping across the table. He took this as a sign, put his hand on top of hers.

'Shall we just get the bill?' he asked, obviously getting completely the wrong impression.

'Not quite yet,' she said, and as she slipped her hand out from under his, she just happened to collide with his drink, send it tipping into his lap. Oh dear. Sorry, not sorry. 'But if you want to send me the bill for your dry cleaning, that would be fine,' she said, matching his sexy tone.

It took him a moment to realise what was happening, and his reaction was instant. His drink had been finished, but there were still ice cubes in the glass, four of them, all of which were now sitting in his crotch.

'What the f—?' he gasped, as he scooped them up and deposited them on the table.

Chrissie picked up her bag from the chair next to her and stood up. 'I don't think this is working for me. You have a lovely evening.'

With that, she strode across the room, passing Gino on the way out.

'If he doesn't pay the bill, I'll settle it tomorrow,' she promised.

'I promise you, that won't be necessary,' Gino replied pointedly, and Chrissie made an educated guess that he'd seen everything that just happened. 'Why don't you wait in the staffroom and I'll call you a taxi?' he suggested kindly. She was sure now that he'd seen what she'd done.

'Thank you, Gino, but I'm just going to go back along to Sun, Sea, Ski. The rest of the girls are still there. I'm sorry if our order goes to waste.'

'Do not dare apologise,' he countered. 'It is no problem at all.'

'Thank you,' she said again, making a mental note to double his tip next time they were in here.

She slipped out of the door, just as a white car screeched to a halt in front of her. Breathing in the cold air, she felt an irrepressible urge to laugh. What. A. Dick. She hadn't even lasted twenty minutes. And oh, his face when the ice fell in his crotch. Just as well she didn't actually mind being single. If this was the modern dating game, she was bailing out and sticking to nights out with the girls.

'Chrissie?' Oh, for fuck's sake, he'd come out behind her, and now he was…

She stopped. Froze. It had taken a second to register, but now she knew that wasn't his voice. It was…

Slowly, really, really, slowly, she turned round.

Tom. Standing there, about fifteen feet away, was the man she'd thought about every single day for over half of her life.

In all the eventualities she had planned for, this had never come up. An explosion of feelings consumed her. Fury that he'd left. Devastation that he hadn't come back. Resentment that she'd been alone for all these years. Heartbreak that her son had never known his father. And all of that translated into a stunned, shocked paralysis.

'Chrissie, I…'

He started to walk towards her, slowly, as if she could bolt if startled. He had no idea that her mind was too busy imploding to send out any signals to the rest of her body. Nothing could make her legs move right now as she stared at him, took it all in. It was him. The guy from the shopping centre today. Now he was up close, she could see he'd barely changed. The same dark wavy hair, more groomed now but still verging on chaotic. Those brown eyes. The lips that she had kissed so many times.

'Can we talk? I just need to exp—'

'Mate! What are you doing here?' Not her. Davie had come out of the restaurant door and was addressing Tom like he was his best buddy.

'Not doing the beers and the Sky Sports after all then?' Tom sneered.

'Nah, mate, change of plan. Fancied a bit of dinner.'

When Tom didn't reply, Davie's gaze went to the side until he saw that Chrissie was still standing there, further along the pavement.

'Shit,' he sighed. Hand. Cookie jar.

'Mate?' Chrissie this time. Her brain now starting to form connections. 'Is this some messed-up game? You set your pal up to date me?' her voice was barely above a whisper and dripping in both fury and disbelief.

She watched as Tom turned to face Davie. 'Seriously? You honestly didn't think I'd find out?' Back to Chrissie, 'He didn't tell me he was seeing you. I only discovered that yesterday. I promise I had nothing to do with it.' He turned back to Davie, 'All these years you knew I was looking for her and you never told me this?'

Davie looked shamefaced for about two seconds, before he reverted to type and tried to bluster his way out of it. 'Come on, man. What's the big deal? You haven't seen the chick since school. Anyway, you're welcome to her, she's—'

No one would ever know what he was about to say because at that point Tom stepped forward and punched

301

him in the face. Chrissie gasped, her hand flying to her mouth, while Davie yelped, then bent over and spat a mixture of blood and saliva on the ground.

'Fuck! What the...'

No one listened or cared.

One line was replaying itself over and over in her mind: *All these years you knew I was looking for her...*

He'd been looking for her? And he'd been back for years? None of this was computing.

He held out his hand to her. 'Please, come with me, I'll explain everything.'

She was still stuck to the ground.

All these years you knew I was looking for her...

She had questions. And she couldn't just stand here all night or she'd freeze to death.

Before her conscious brain had even given the instruction, she walked towards him.

He immediately flushed with relief, opened the car door to allow her to climb in, then raced around the other side.

'And you...' he said to Davie, who was still standing against the wall, rubbing the side of his face. 'Start looking for a new partner, because we're done.'

He jumped into the car, and before she had time to speak, to ask questions, to say anything, they roared off from the kerb, turned left at the end of the road, and then...

He pulled in and stopped.

'Sorry, but I'm going to kill us if I keep driving while my hands and legs are shaking like this,' he said, turning to face her.

Tom. Right there. His face only an arm's length away from hers. Her heart was beating like a train and she could not find words, except...

'You've been looking for me for years?' she asked, barely able to get the words out.

'Oh God, I've got so much to say,' he replied, his voice almost desperate. 'Yes. I came back when I was nineteen. I searched everywhere, but I couldn't find you.'

'But... I had no idea. Why didn't you return my calls and letters?'

'What calls and letters?' he asked, and she could see his reaction was absolutely genuine. None of this was making sense.

'When you left, I called and wrote a dozen times, asking you to get in touch.'

'I had no idea. I thought you didn't want anything to do with me after I left, and I wouldn't have blamed you. I'm so, so sorry I went with them. I know Norry told me he'd cut off all payments to my mother if I didn't go, that he'd drag out the divorce settlement and give her nothing, but I should still have stood up to him. I should have stayed here with you, called Norry's bluff, done the right thing. I knew I'd screwed up, so I came back after a year to find you and beg you to forgive me and...'

'I can't believe this,' Chrissie whispered, tears falling down her face now.

'Please don't cry. Please. I'm so sorry. I know you must hate me but—'

'I thought you'd cut me off because you couldn't forgive me for not coming with you,' she blurted out.

That stunned both of them into silence for a moment.

'Listen, I want to sit and talk to you all night, but I need to get back to the hospital.'

'You're a doctor?'

'No, I'm Davie's partner in a marketing company.' That triggered a vague recollection of him shouting something about finding a new partner at Davie. 'I met him again at uni and… Christ, I'm rambling. I'll tell you about that later. I need to get back to the hospital because my grandad, George, he's… dying.' The word stuck in his throat. 'He doesn't have long. I sit with him during the night because I don't want him to be alone. Would you come with me? I know it sounds like the worst idea ever, but it's quiet there, we can talk. Problem is, our parents are there.'

'My mother is back here?' Tonight just could not get any stranger.

'She flew in today with my dad. It's not gone well. Oh God, I need to tell you about that, too.'

She watched as he stared forward, biting his bottom lip. He always did that when he was thinking. Just like Ben.

'Thing is, I've got all their luggage in my boot, so I have to take it back to them. How about if we go back to the hospital, and I'll give them my car keys and they can go back to my house. You can stay downstairs for five minutes and then come up if you don't want to see them...'

'I don't,' she said fiercely.

'I get that, completely. Shit, this is all crazy. All I want to do is go somewhere with you and talk all night, but I can't leave him alone. Not now.'

'No, it's okay. I understand.' His love for George, his complete decency took a wrecking ball to her emotional wall.

'Is that a no or a yes?'

'A yes. I'll come with you.' She should have said that to him twelve years ago. He'd been taking all the blame so far tonight, but the truth was, she had been the one who had refused to go to Australia. No matter what her reasons, she shouldered some of the blame for this, too. If she'd gone, perhaps none of this would have happened.

'Okay, let's go,' he said, pulling out and driving in the direction of the hospital. 'I just need to stop at my grandad's house and grab some things for him. It's only ten minutes from the hospital and we pass it on the way. I'll be two seconds,' he said.

'That's okay.'

She had so much to say. He had so much to say. And yet, there was a few seconds of silence.

'I went to his house after you left,' Chrissie said.

His surprise was genuine. 'What?'

'After you left. I had a feeling that my mum and your dad weren't passing on my letters or phone messages. So I took a letter to your grandad. He told me he would pass it on.'

'He didn't,' Tom said, and there was no mistaking the frown of confusion or the desperation in his voice. He slouched, crestfallen. 'I swear I never got it. It must have gone missing in the post or... but why didn't he tell me that when I came back? He knew I was searching for you. Why didn't he say?'

Chrissie instinctively knew he was telling the truth.

'Perhaps our parents asked him not to,' she said, wishing she'd thought of that possibility before now. She'd always been so sure George would have passed on the letter and told Tom she needed to speak to him. He was such a lovely and trustworthy man that she hadn't even contemplated that he wouldn't do that. 'I think we need to start at the beginning,' she said, desperate to blurt out the most significant fact of all, but deeply aware that doing it when they were driving could cause a ten car pile up and leave Ben orphaned. Ben. She was completely overwhelmed by the thought that the situation was going to change his life and she wasn't sure whether that was a positive thing, or completely terrifying.

'We will,' he said. 'Let's just get to the hospital, and then we'll have all night to talk and to figure stuff out. Chrissie, I'm trying desperately not to say the wrong thing here, but I can't tell you how happy I am to see you again. You've no idea how much I've wanted this.'

Chrissie took a wrecking ball to her defences. 'Me too,' she said, realising that despite years of telling herself she didn't need him, there was nothing she wanted more right now than to be sitting here right next to him. It just felt so… right.

He asked her why she was storming out of the restaurant and she gave him the bullet points, before blurting out, 'I would sometimes imagine that I saw you,' she said. 'It happened today, in fact. I was in Princess Square—'

'I was there,' he gasped. 'I thought I saw you. I chased you but couldn't find you and figured I was mistaken.'

Another explosion of feelings. Incredulity that she had been right and…

'You were kissing someone.'

'Zoe.'

'Your wife?'

'My girlfriend.'

Chrissie felt something deflate inside her, but then, what did she expect? Of course he would have moved on and met someone else. She was the sad, pathetic one that had stayed off the dating scene for twelve years. Although, there had been extenuating circumstances…

'Ex-girlfriend,' he clarified. 'We broke up today. I was on Davie's computer yesterday, saw your messages to each other, and as soon as I saw your name… Oh God, Chrissie, I can't even explain it. That's how I found out he was meeting you tonight. And Zoe… I was already meeting her for lunch today, but all I could think about was you, so I told her I couldn't keep seeing her. Not that I'm expecting anything from you, I promise, but it would have been unfair to keep seeing her when all I cared about was seeing you again.'

Before she could answer, her phone beeped with an incoming text.

Hourly update? You're late. Josie currently suiting up in SWAT gear.

'Sorry, I need to answer this,' she said. 'It's my friends. I was supposed to text them every hour to let them know I was safe.'

'They sound like good friends,' he said, and she could tell he was happy she had them.

'They're wonderful,' she admitted, then went back to deliberating her reply. If she told the truth, there would be a huge drama. Val would be on the phone in seconds looking for explanations and reassurances that she was okay. How could she explain any of this when she didn't

308

actually understand it herself? She sent up a silent prayer for forgiveness as she typed a blatant lie.

> All fine. Will text again in an hour. Tell Josie to stand down.
> Xx

Chrissie slipped her phone back into her bag. She had no idea where to start, and she wanted to speak to him properly, so that they both understood everything that had happened, so that there could be – for good or bad – no more confusion. She shook off what he'd told her about splitting with his girlfriend. This wasn't the time for those conversations yet. There were way too many other things to deal with.

'So how is Rosemary?'

Tom sighed. 'Truth?'

'Yes.'

'Still exactly the same. So is my dad. Both self-centred, shallow cretins who wouldn't do anything for anyone unless there was something in it for themselves. I'm pretty sure they only came back to see what they could get when Grandad dies.'

He went on to explain how they'd had little contact over the years, how he'd only contacted them to tell them about George, how unbearable they'd been since they arrived. There was so much to say that it seemed like only a moment later, she glanced out of the window and realised they were pulling into George's street.

'Do you want to come in?' Tom asked. 'I just need to grab a few things.'

Chrissie hesitated, then a sudden feeling of wanting a connection to the past, to that teenage life, controlled her decision.

'Sure,' she said, opening the door.

They'd only got as far as the gate, when they heard another car door open.

'Excuse me,' shouted a voice.

They both turned round and Chrissie saw that it came from a woman who had jumped out of a taxi. Opening the door had illuminated the inside of the car, and she could also see a driver and two other women.

A mane of red curls ran towards them. 'Sorry. I know this is weird. But by any chance, do you know if George Butler still lives here?'

Twenty-eight

Tom

'Yes, he's my grandfather,' Tom answered, surprised. He was fairly sure he had never met this woman before and he had no idea why she would be looking for his grandad at 9.30 on a Friday night. Besides, all he wanted to do was get in, get out, and get to the hospital so he could finally spend time alone with Chrissie. He still couldn't believe he'd found her. The last hour had been the best and most surreal of his life.

'Yassssss!' she yelped, as she punched the air. At that, two other women, one about the same age as the first, the other maybe in her seventies, got out of the car and walked swiftly towards them.

'Okay, so this is going to be a bit of a surprise and I know you'll probably think we're scammers after your grandad's worldly goods,' the red-haired woman went on, 'but I'm Lulu. This is Shauna,' she added, pointing to the woman who'd arrived beside her, 'who is the granddaughter of your grandfather's sister, Annie. Jesus,

311

I feel like Davina McCall, reuniting families here,' she quipped. 'And this is Flora McGinty. Who used to be called Flora Butler. Your grandfather's other sister.'

Tom stared, trying to process what was going on. This couldn't be happening. Not tonight. Not now. Not ever. Heart racing, he searched his memory for a reference point. He was aware George grew up with two sisters but he knew absolutely nothing about them. His grandad would only ever say that there was a family rift many years ago, before Tom was even born.

His gaze went to the older woman, who was speaking to him now as she held out her hand. 'I'm sorry. I know this must be a shock, but it's lovely to meet you.'

Tom shook it with trembling hands, adrenalin once again in control.

'Definitely a shock,' he said, staring at her face. At first glance, with only the illumination of the streetlights, there was no immediate resemblance there, but when she spoke, he saw it. She had the same piercing blue eyes, same height and bearing as George. This woman could absolutely be his sister.

The other younger woman held out her hand. He hadn't caught her name so he was thankful she repeated it. 'I'm Shauna,' she said.

'Tom,' he replied. 'And sorry, I didn't introduce Chrissie,' he said. His stomach flipped. He was introducing Chrissie. His Chrissie. He'd found her. It was almost impossible to think of anything but that, but he could hear his grandad's voice telling him he was being bloody rude. 'I'm so sorry, please, come in. I was just stopping by to…' He let his voice drift off as another crushing wave of agony came crashing in. He was going to have to tell this poor woman that George was in hospital. 'I'm afraid my grandfather isn't here, but please come in.'

He walked up the path, the four women following behind him, and never had he felt the loss of George more. How badly he wanted him to be here for this. His sister. And Chrissie. He would give anything to see George's face as he opened that door and saw them all. But of course, that wouldn't happen.

He showed them straight into the kitchen and invited them to sit. Despite being in a dress and heels, Chrissie sat in the little window seat that had been his gran's favourite spot, while the three strangers sat at the table, leaving one empty chair for him.

'I brought my grandmother's birth certificate, and Flora brought hers, just in case you wanted to check we weren't fraudsters or anything like that,' Shauna said.

'That's okay,' Tom answered, already sure they were telling the truth. In the kitchen light he could see even more of a resemblance between Flora and George.

Chrissie was obviously thinking the same thing. 'Mrs McGinty, there's a definite likeness between you and your brother,' she said, making Flora beam.

'People always said that about us.'

Tom interjected, 'I can definitely see it too. Can I ask how you found him?'

Shauna pulled out a letter. 'I'm really sorry to say that my grandmother Annie, your aunt, passed away a few years ago. This letter was from your grandfather, written back in the fifties. It has his address on it...'

'Yes, he's lived here since he got married to my gran in 1958,' Tom confirmed, as he noticed that Shauna was beaming from ear to ear.

'I'm sorry,' she said, 'but I'm just so happy to have a cousin. Second cousin, but it's practically the same thing. I have no family to speak of, so Lulu and I came up here from London for the day in the hope of finding some relatives. There was another letter with Aunt Flora's address – an old one as it turns out – but we managed to track her down.'

'So you all only met today?' Tom asked, incredulous.

'Yes, pet,' Flora responded, then a shadow crossed her face. 'Although I'm afraid I knew all along where George lived, but there was a fall-out, you see... And we've discovered today that it was all based on a misunderstanding.'

Her dismay was palpable and Tom knew he couldn't keep putting off the inevitable. 'Mrs McGinty...'

'Please, call me Flora...'

'Flora,' he repeated. 'I'm so sorry to tell you this, but I'm afraid my grandad is in Glasgow Central Hospital...'

'My goodness, we've just come from there,' she exclaimed.

'… In the palliative care ward. Sadly, he's very ill – bone cancer – and doesn't have long left. We really don't know if he'll make it from one day to the next.'

Shauna gasped, while Flora's eyes misted with tears.

'What fools we've been,' she said quietly and Tom could see that her heart was breaking.

'Could I go tomorrow and see him?' Flora asked.

'Of course,' Tom said, then another thought. 'But Mrs… Flora… I do have to say that he might not make it through the night. I'm actually just here to pick up some things for him and then I'm going back to sleep at his bedside. The nurses in palliative care are amazing, and they're very accommodating at this… stage.'

He heard a sniff and realised it came from Shauna, who he could see was fighting back tears.

'I'm sorry,' she said, 'I'm just so sad to hear that. We leave first thing in the morning, so… Flora, will you tell him about us? About Annie?'

'I'm afraid he's not been conscious at all today,' Tom said, with palpable sadness.

'That's okay,' she said, oozing sorrow. 'Flora, will you tell him anyway?'

Tom made a split decision. His head was spinning from the chaos and turmoil of today's events, but strangely he was feeling such clarity. He glanced at Chrissie. He had no idea if she could still guess

315

everything he was thinking, but as she caught his eye, she nodded, so he was sure they were having the same thought. He turned back to the others.

'Look, do you want to come there with us now? It's only ten minutes away, and that way, you'll all get to see him. I know it's late, but the charge nurse is great and I'm sure she'll allow it.'

The three women made eye contact before Flora spoke for them. 'That would be wonderful,' she said. 'I've been apart from my brother for all these years and I don't want to risk never meeting him again.' The tremble in her voice as she said that tugged at Tom's heart.

'I understand that,' he said, his eyes flicking to Chrissie again. That was how he'd felt for twelve years – terrified that he wouldn't see her again. And now she was finally here, but he'd have to wait a little longer to talk to her. He just hoped she'd give him a chance.

'If you want to follow me, then. My father and stepmother are there at the moment...'

'More relatives,' Shauna said, grinning. Tom didn't like to say that those ones might not be such a joyful addition to the family.

The women had just stood up, when, over at the window, Chrissie's phone rang. She checked the screen and Tom watched as her whole demeanour changed.

'I just need to take this,' she said, awkwardly. 'I'll catch you up.'

So she didn't want him there to hear the call. Perhaps there was a boyfriend after all, or someone in the wings.

Tom walked the women back to their taxi, where he was surprised to see the driver greeted them like friends.

Shauna was the last to climb in. 'The smell of vinegar in here would knock you out,' she said to the others. 'We were eating chips,' she explained to Tom.

The absurdity of it all made Tom laugh. This was the strangest day of his life and it wasn't over yet.

'I'll just go back for Chrissie, I'll be two minutes.'

'No worries, we'll wait until you're ready.'

As soon as he saw Chrissie standing at the door, he knew something was wrong. 'I'm s... s... sorry. I need to go,' she stammered.

'No, you can't. Please,' he begged her. Not now. Not when he'd finally found her. 'We need to talk and whatever it is—'

'It's my son,' she said, cutting him dead.

'You have a son?' Just when he thought nothing else could surprise him tonight. He realised he'd asked the wrong question, and immediately rectified that. 'Is he okay? Is something wrong?'

'Yes. No. He's having a sleepover at a friend's house, but the friend has just become unwell so I need to go and pick Ben up.'

'I'll take you!'

'No, it's fine. I'll call a taxi. You go on with your aunt...'

'No. Chrissie, I can't. I honestly can't let you out of my sight yet. But...' Oh, shit, so many other things in the way. 'Hang on a minute, I'll sort this,' he promised.

He dashed back inside, running upstairs to his grandad's room as he dialled a number on his phone.

'Liv? It's Tom. I'm so sorry to ask, but I need your help...'

As he grabbed the things he needed for his grandad, he explained everything that had happened with his aunt – how she desperately wanted to see George, but he couldn't come back with her right now because a friend needed him for an emergency situation.

Liv listened to it all, including the issue with his parents, then together they solved every element of the problem. He was going to take that woman the biggest bouquet of flowers tomorrow.

He galloped back downstairs, 'All sorted,' he told Chrissie, as they stepped outside and he locked the door behind him.

At the car, he opened the passenger door for Chrissie, but she objected again. 'Tom, I really think it's better if I go myself and...'

'Please let me take you,' he said, willing her to agree, terrified that if he let her walk away he might never see her again.

It must have been the anguish in his voice, but after another pause, she finally acquiesced and climbed in. He darted to the boot and took out two cases, then wheeled them to the other women's taxi.

'Sorry, but we need to make a slight change of plan. Chrissie has an emergency with her son and he needs to be picked up from his sleepover.' He saw Flora's immediate disappointment and went on to remedy that. 'But I've spoken with the nurse in charge, her name is Liv, and she's agreed to let you come over for half an hour. Would that be okay?' he asked.

'We'll take any time we can get,' Shauna replied gratefully. 'Thank you so much.'

'I'm glad to do it. George would have loved to have met you all,' he answered, an unexpected choke of emotion catching the last few words. He cleared his throat. 'But can I ask a favour? My parents are at the hospital and the nurse tells me they're keen to get away, but I have their luggage. Could you take it with you please? I'm sure my dad will come down and collect it from you, so I'm not asking you to carry it up or anything.'

'Aye, no worries, son,' the taxi driver answered, popping the boot and climbing out.

Tom then handed a key over to Shauna. 'And could you give them this please? It's the key to my house. I assume they'll have the address on their phones, but if not, they can call me. Thanks so much.'

'No, it's us who want to thank you. I'm looking forward to having a cousin, Tom,' she said.

'I am, too,' he grinned, meaning it. If first impressions went for anything, he was going to enjoy having Shauna in his life. 'I'm just sorry you caught us on such a chaotic night.' He pulled a card out of his jacket pocket. 'Here's my card and number. I'll try to get to the hospital as quickly as possible tonight, but if I miss you, perhaps we can meet early in the morning before your flight? My number is on there. Please text me your flight details, and I'll be in touch. And Aunt Flora...'

'Oh my, no one has ever called me that before tonight and now both of you have done so,' she gasped delightedly.

'Please take my phone number from that card, so that you'll always have it. I hope I'll see you tomorrow, too.'

'You definitely will, pet.'

With that he waved them off, then climbed back into the car and saw that Chrissie was already speaking on her phone.

'Are you sure you don't mind, Val? No, honestly, that's not a problem, I'm on my way there now. No, not Davie. I'll explain when I see you. No, I promise I haven't been kidnapped. You don't need to call the police. It's a long story. Well, a lot can happen in two hours. Seriously, this will keep you and Josie talking for weeks. Okay, thank you. I love you. I'll see you soon.' She ended the call. 'That was my friend Val – who is also my next door neighbour. She's going to pop in and look after Ben tonight once we've collected him. I don't relish the thought of seeing my mother, but I'd like to come to the hospital with you. There's so much…'

She didn't have to finish the sentence because he was feeling exactly the same way. So much to say. So many years to catch up on. He realised that she was still speaking, but her voice had lowered and she sounded uncertain, nervous.

'… And I don't want to drop a bombshell and then leave you.'

He laughed, flicking a button to switch on his satnav. 'This isn't a bombshell, Chrissie. Finding you tonight has been the best thing that's ever happened. No matter what. Okay, so what is the address for Ben's friend?'

Her brow furrowed in confusion and he had a horrible feeling that they weren't on the same page here.

'The bombshell isn't us meeting again,' she clarified, and he stopped, turning so that their eyes locked.

Oh crap. This wasn't good. She looked absolutely torn up about something and unless she'd changed drastically in the last decade or so, he knew she wasn't prone to overdramatising things.

'So what is it?' he asked, heart thudding with trepidation, desperate to rewind to five minutes ago when he thought everything was going to be okay.

'It's about my son, Ben,' she began.

10 p.m. – Midnight

Twenty-nine

Chrissie

Chrissie couldn't say it. How did you just spring this on someone? It was inhumane. Shocking. All the times that she'd thought about this moment, and never once had it played out like this. In her imagination, it had always been a confrontation that was teeming with recriminations about the fact that he'd waltzed off to a new life and never looked back. Now she could see that wasn't the case.

Sure, he'd left, but he'd come back. This wasn't a desertion, it was a cruel hand of fate, one in which everyone paid a price.

Tom had lost out on his son, and Ben had lost out on his father.

Chrissie only had to watch the way Tom had handled his aunt's arrival to see that he was still the kind, caring guy she'd loved so, so much. She should have had more faith in him. In them. And now, she was crushed by regret that she didn't try harder to reach him, didn't have belief that he'd return, didn't leave a trail for him to find her. It had been so easy to stay off the radar. No social networking back in 2006, no Twitter, she'd got a new mobile phone when Rosemary cancelled her old one, and when she finally managed to buy a computer she set up a new email address. Just a single mum and her boy, starting over, living their lives.

He'd said finding her was the best thing that had ever happened to him, but she was about to wipe that right out by delivering the biggest blow of his life. And she had to do it now because she couldn't do it when he was driving, or risk him setting eyes on Ben and realising the truth.

'What about him?' Tom prompted.

Say it. Say it. Say…

'He's twelve years old, Tom,' she said softly. 'He's not my son. He's *our* son.'

Nothing. A void. A vacuum. For about three seconds. His eyes were locked on hers, his mouth slightly open, his whole face one of disbelief.

And then, 'I have a son? You had our son?' She heard the words but his shock was so all-consuming that she couldn't tell how he felt about this.

She nodded, tears prickling her lower lids but she fought them back. This wasn't a time for her to crumble. She had to be strong, for her, for Ben, for all of them.

'Oh my God, Chrissie,' he gasped, 'I left you and you were pregnant? I'm so sorry. Oh fuck, I'm so sorry. You must hate me.'

'You didn't know,' she said, trying to be calm. 'But yes, you weren't my favourite person for a long time, but only because I thought you knew and you were refusing to return my calls and letters.'

'I didn't... I would never... I have a son,' he spluttered. 'A son. I'm a dad.'

Chrissie watched as slowly the shock wore off and the contours of his face changed and then he was smiling and...

'Holy fuck, I'm a dad,' he said, laughing now, obviously ecstatic. Once again, in all the times that she'd thought about this moment, never once had it played out like this. In her version, he'd been shocked, angry, upset, in denial...

At no point had his eyes filled with tears of joy or had he leaned over and hugged her so tightly she thought her ribs would crack, like he was doing now.

'I don't even know how to say how happy I am. I swear there are no words. Does he know?' he asked finally.

'He knows your name and I was honest with him. I told him you moved away and we lost contact before I knew I was pregnant. He's a pretty grounded kid. He's also smart, and really funny. And kind.' Like you, she thought, but didn't say.

'Do you have a picture of him?'

Chrissie pulled her phone back out of Jen's bag and pressed the home button. An image of Ben immediately filled the screen and she heard Tom gasp again.

'He looks so like me when I was that age.'

'He does,' Chrissie said, smiling, although she could not have pinned down exactly what emotion she was feeling from one second to the next.

Tom was still staring at the photo.

He exhaled deeply. 'We have so much more to talk about than I could ever have imagined, but I don't want Ben wondering what's taking you so long...'

'I was about to say the same thing.' Chrissie clipped her seat belt on and gave Tom the address of Ben's friend so he could punch it into the satnav. Her home in Weirbridge was about twenty minutes away and Ben's pal lived on the way there. That gave them about fifteen minutes to work out how to deal with this. She had to be fair here. She had to give him the benefit of the doubt. 'Thank you for not freaking out.'

She almost jumped when she felt his hand reach over and take hers. She didn't move it away. 'Chrissie, no matter what's happened, and what happens from here on in, I have a son. It doesn't get any better than this.'

'You mean that?' She didn't even have to ask, now that she could see the delight in every contour of his face.

'I do. Tell me about him. From the start...'

The next fifteen minutes flew by in seconds, as she gave him bullet points about Ben as a baby, his nursery years, starting school, moving to the house they lived in now, the milestones of his life, and Tom took it all in, asking questions, desperate to know more.

'Who was with you when he was born?' he asked, and Chrissie could hear the pain in his voice.

'No one,' she answered honestly. 'I was on my own.'

'I'm…' He paused. 'It's so fucking inadequate just to say sorry, but please believe me.'

'I do,' she said truthfully.

They were about a minute away, when he asked, 'Are you going to tell him tonight? If you want to talk to him alone, to prepare him, I totally understand.'

She nodded. 'I think that would be best. Tonight, let's just act like this is no big deal, I'll just say you're a friend who gave me a lift home. I'll talk to him tomorrow, and maybe then you could come by tomorrow night and meet him properly?'

'Of course. I'll do whatever you want me to. It's enough that I'm meeting him tonight. Oh God, Chrissie, I have a son.'

She chuckled. 'You may have mentioned that already.'

'A son, though.'

She could see that he couldn't stop grinning and knew she was responding in the same way. Her happiness was all for Ben. They'd been great on their own and would have continued to live happy lives in the world that she'd built for them, but here was his father, a man who wanted him desperately and who would love him fiercely. That was a pretty good starting place for a relationship between them.

'Okay,' she said as they pulled up outside the house and beeped the horn. 'Be cool.'

'I don't have an ounce of coolness in me,' he said, like a runner loosening up for the race of his life. 'But I'll fake it, don't worry.'

The door opened and Ben came strolling out, past an inflatable snowman and two flashing reindeer in the garden, followed by Karen, his pal Josh's mum. Chrissie rolled down the window.

'I'm so sorry if I spoiled your date,' Karen said. 'But it's like a scene from *The Exorcist* in there. I'm not sure if it's food poisoning or a bug, so I didn't want Ben catching it.'

'Ouch, poor Josh. Give him a hug from us when it's safe to go near him again,' Chrissie said, using every ounce of acting chops she never knew she had to behave normally. Ben was about to get into the back of the car his father was driving. There was an irony in the fact that she'd told Tom to stay calm. Her hands were trembling and her heart was beating so fast she was sure she sounded like the thud of the music coming from the cars of the young racers that roared up and down their estate.

'Will do. See you later, Ben,' Karen said. 'Sorry about tonight.'

'No worries,' Ben said. 'Thanks very much for having me over.' Ben climbed into the car, barely giving a typically teenage "Hey," to Tom as he did so. Chrissie could see Tom desperately trying to keep his cool and his eyes on the road.

They waved as they pulled away and Chrissie told Tom her own address so he could use the satnav and save her having to give directions. She then switched her best acting skills back on as she turned round to face Ben.

'How're you doing, my love?'

Her son grinned. 'Traumatised that so much fluid can come out of one body. I thought he was never going to stop puking.'

'Gross,' she said.

'Totally,' Ben concurred. 'Think we can rule out me ever deciding to become a doctor.'

He was joking again, so Chrissie knew he was absolutely unscathed by the experience.

Out of the corner of her eye, she could see Tom giving her questioning looks, and she realised she needed to introduce them. If Tom was anyone else, she'd have done it as soon as Ben had got in the car, but her nerves were outweighing her manners here.

'Ben, this is Tom. Tom, meet Ben.' She couldn't believe she was actually saying those words.

'Good to meet you,' Tom said, and she could hear he was suddenly hoarse with emotion.

Not that Ben would know that, thankfully. He'd just assume his mum's friend had a slightly unusual voice.

'You too,' Ben replied casually. 'So am I like your least favourite guy on the planet right now because I blew your date with my mum?'

'I reckon you're my favourite guy on the planet right now because you've made it last longer,' Tom joked, and Chrissie wanted to punch the air.

'Smooth,' Ben said, laughing. 'Mum, he's got good lines,' he added, giving her a thumbs up. 'All we need is for him to have season tickets for the Glasgow Rocks games and he's a keeper.'

Going along to watch Glasgow's professional basketball team, the Rocks, was one of their favourite things to do together, often with Val and her husband Don in tow.

'Funny you should say that...' Tom said.

'Seriously? You have season tickets for the Rocks?' Ben's voice gushed with enthusiasm.

'No, but I was thinking about getting one. I became a bit addicted to watching basketball during the Commonwealth Games. Scotland were brilliant.'

'I know!' Ben agreed. 'Mum let me stay up so late to watch the games, but she told me if I grassed her to my teachers, I was grounded. She's pretty irresponsible like that.'

'Ben Harrison, you're are so grounded now,' Chrissie giggled, before a bittersweet aftertaste soured the moment. Ben had missed out on Tom for all these years. She just hoped it wasn't too late to make up for it.

The car began to slow down and she realised they were at the parking area at the end of her terrace.

'Okay, come on, love. Val is going to come over and watch a movie with you, and I'm going to head back out with Tom for a little while.'

Ben turned to Tom. 'Do you want to come in and meet my Auntie Val? She'll want to meet you.'

Chrissie tried to mask her panic with nonchalance. 'Ben, it's fine. Tom, just wait there, I'll be two minutes.'

'Aw, come on. It's just over there and if you're with us, then Auntie Val won't grill Mum for details. If she does that, Mum will be stuck for hours and you'll never get her back out.'

Chrissie was cringing now. Actually experiencing curling of the toes. Tom glanced at her, eyebrows raised, questioning.

Bollocks. If she protested any further, Ben would think it was weird. If she didn't, she would have to explain the change of her date's name to Val and she was sure to twig as to who he was. No contest. She was just going to have to disappoint Ben, because she wasn't ready to give a chapter and verse explanation to...

A spanner, wearing pink furry mules, just dropped into the works.

Chrissie saw that Val had come out of her front door and was about to head their way. She was going to have to introduce Tom out here, in front of Ben, and there was no way she could warn Val not to react if she realised who he was. And, let's face it, Val wasn't one for curtailing her emotions. There was every chance her friend would blurt something that would give the game away. She was going to have to take him in and hope she got a minute to prepare Val for who this man was.

'Okay then. Go run ahead and tell Auntie Val we're coming in for a minute, save her walking all the way up here.'

He was out of the car and away like a shot.

'Okay, I'm going to have to try to tell Val who you are and warn her not to say anything because she's sure to suss it. She's got serious detective skills.' She realised he wasn't responding to her. Instead, he was watching as Ben jogged ahead to Val, and then hugged her when he reached her. 'You okay?' She realised it was a stupid question. Neither of them were ok. Shocked. Stunned. Bewildered. In a complete state of flux. That was closer than 'ok'.

'Chrissie, he's incredible. Even if he wasn't mine, I'd love him.' The emotion in his words almost floored her.

'Please stop, because I'll be in floods of tears if you carry on, and then Val will kill you before she asks any questions. Let's go.'

She paused for a second, gathered herself, then got out the car. Tom followed her, past a row of houses that were bedecked with at least half of the Christmas decorations in the free world. They liked to brighten things up around here. Of course, the most elaborate of all was Val's house, because yes, every home should have a life size, neon Santa skiing on their roof.

By the time they got to Chrissie's house, Ben had used his own key to get in.

'What's this I hear about Rocks tickets?' Val asked jovially, the minute they walked in the door.

Chrissie went straight into action. 'Ben, why don't you go show Tom your room.' That would work, get Tom out of the way until she'd explained to Val, except...

'Tom?' Val asked, puzzled. 'Oh, love, I must have got mixed up. I thought it was someone called Davie you were meeting. I'm Val, pleased to meet you.' They shook hands, just as Ben suddenly twigged.

'Yeah, it *was* Davie you were meeting,' he said. 'I remember now, too.'

'Erm, that didn't work out,' Chrissie blustered. 'And then I met Tom, who is an old friend and he gave me a lift home.'

Val's gaze at Tom's face turned into a gasp that was so loud that it silenced the room. So much for warning her. Okay, plan B. Swift exit. She raised her eyebrows as she directed her words at Val.

'Actually, Tom is in a bit of a hurry, so we'll just shoot off.'

Ben would totally notice that she was behaving a bit strangely, but hopefully he'd put it down to date-night jitters. Her eyes flicked to him and she realised with a sinking heart, that might not be the case. Ben's gaze went from Val, to her, to Tom, and now he was just staring at him, unable to drag his eyes away.

Eventually he spoke. 'My dad was called Tom,' he said, still staring directly at him.

Tom looked to her for guidance and she felt herself twist into a frozen state of dread inside.

No. No. No. No. No.

There was no point keeping up the charade. Ben was already one step ahead of them.

'Ben?' she began. He finally broke the stare and looked at her instead. 'We were going to wait and tell you properly tomorrow, once we'd had a chance to talk it all through, but...' She paused, steeling herself for whatever reaction she might get. 'This is your dad.'

Ben's eyes widened to the size of side plates. 'Seriously?'

'Seriously,' Chrissie confirmed, unsure whether that was seriously good or seriously bad.

Val was watching this from the back of the room, with a concerned expression and her arms folded under her chest. Val was never this restrained or quiet. It was a worry.

Ben was back to staring at Tom again. 'You are actually my dad?' He still wasn't giving anything away, and Chrissie was beginning to feel physically sick.

'Yes. Although, I didn't know until tonight, so please don't think I was some terrible guy who abandoned you. I promise I didn't. Your mum says she told you that I'd moved away before we knew she was pregnant and that's true. I'm so, so sorry I missed you growing up. I'd never have left if I'd known anything about you. I hope you'll give me a chance to put that right.'

Before Ben answered, he turned back to Chrissie.

'Mum, what do you think? Are you okay, because you look just like Josh right before he puked his guts out?'

Chrissie crossed to him and hugged him. 'I'm fine, babe. Just as long as you're okay with this. That's all that matters to me. I'm so sorry we've sprung it on you. I had no idea I was going to bump into your dad tonight, and then you called to say you needed picking up and... I'm sorry. I'm rambling because it's not all really sunk in yet. Are you okay? Because it's totally fine if you're feeling unsure. It's a shocker.'

'It's definitely a shocker,' Ben answered. 'But if you're okay, then I think I am, too,' he said, finally smiling. 'Although I might be swayed by the Rocks tickets,' he said, laughing now.

The relief in the room bounced off the walls.

'Oh my word, that nearly ended me,' Val said, as she crossed to Tom and hugged him. Chrissie could see it was a little uncharacteristically stilted, but she knew it would be because Val was feeling protective of her. Tom would have to earn her trust. Still, she was friendly and even added a bit of humour to lighten the atmosphere. 'It's a pleasure to meet you. You're a lucky man to have this boy,' she cooed. 'And I'm swayed by gin, just so you know.' At which point, she cackled with laughter that was swiftly contagious. 'Josie will be spitting that she's not here,' she told Chrissie.

'Josie is Val's best friend. She loves a bit of drama. She'll be gutted she missed this,' Chrissie explained to Tom.

A thought struck her and she realised they needed a change of plan. There was no way she was leaving Ben tonight, not now that he'd had this news. She wanted to stay with him, talk it out, help him process it. She turned to Tom, still struggling to believe he was actually here, in her home. Not in a million years had she expected today to turn out this way.

'You should go on to the hospital. I'm going to stay here with Ben,' she said. Before he answered, she explained the situation to her son and Val. 'Tom's grandfather is in the hospital and he hasn't got long left, sadly. Tom has been sitting with him through the days and nights this week, because he doesn't want him to be alone.' She turned back to Tom, already guessing what he was thinking. 'I know you'll be feeling torn, but Ben and me, well, you know where we are now and we'll have our whole future to catch up with lost time. You don't have the luxury of time with George.'

He nodded slowly. 'You're right. It just kills me to leave you right now. To leave *you*,' he said, directing the repetition at Ben.

Ben looked at Chrissie. 'Do I have a grandfather too?'

'You do. And I promise we'll explain all that to you when the three of us can sit down and talk properly tomorrow. For now though, we have to let Tom, your dad...' her heart almost exploded as she said those words, '... go and be with his grandad.'

Ben was pensive for a second. 'Can we go with him?'

Chrissie shook her head. 'No, son. It's late, and it's bedtime, and a palliative care ward is no place for a child.'

'A teenager,' Ben countered.

'Not for another month,' Chrissie reminded him.

'Which palliative care ward is he in?' Val asked.

'Glasgow Central,' Tom replied.

'That's our Liv's ward,' Val exclaimed.

Tom was stunned. 'You know Liv?'

'She's my niece. Her mum, Ida, is my man's sister. She'll take good care of him. She's always been a natural nurse, our Liv. She's got a heart of gold.'

'She does,' Tom agreed. 'I don't know that I'd have got through the last month without her. She's been amazing. It's such a small world.'

'I didn't even put two and two together,' Chrissie said. She'd met Liv a few times and knew she was a nurse, but it was always in a party situation and they'd never discussed her job. She knew that Ben had spent much more time with her though, because he was often in Val's house when Liv was there. He'd mentioned many times that he liked her.

'Mum,' Ben spoke. 'I'd really like to go. If it's Tom's... I mean, *my dad's* grandad...'

Chrissie melted and she heard Tom clear his throat when Ben said that, but she didn't interrupt him.

He went on, '... That means he's my great-grandad, and I've never had a great-grandad. I'd like to meet him before he dies. I know it'll be sad, but I'll be fine.'

'Maybe we could go tomorrow?' Chrissie tried to placate him.

'What if he dies before I get there?' Ben pressed, then realised that might be a bit insensitive and immediately apologised to Tom. 'Really sorry, I shouldn't have said that.'

Tom smiled. 'That's okay. I'm sorry to say that could happen. Right now though, my grandad is mostly unconscious. He doesn't speak, it's just like he's in a deep sleep. So it's not like you'd be able to talk to him.'

'I know, but I'll see him. Then all my life I can say I met my great-grandad.'

Chrissie had to concede that in some ways it was difficult to fault his logic.

'Do you want me to call our Liv and see what she thinks? Whether it would be... appropriate?'

Chrissie and Tom shared a glance, then Chrissie spoke, 'Would you, Val?'

Tom speed dialled the number. 'Hi Liv, it's Tom again. Have the visitors arrived? Ah, that's good. And the first lot have gone? Even better. Listen, I have someone who knows you here and she'd like a word, can I put you on? Great, thanks.' He handed the phone over and Val disappeared into the kitchen.

Chrissie had listened with interest to Tom's side of the call. So Norry and Rosemary had left for the night. It was a relief that she didn't have to explain them to Ben just yet. One step at a time...

Val came back. 'Liv thinks it would be okay if Ben came with you now, just for a little while, though,' she said. 'If he doesn't feel comfortable, he can sit with her at the nurses' station. She's working until midnight and then she said she'll drop Ben, or both of you, back here. Whatever you think best. If you want to stay longer, he can just stay in our spare room.'

'What do you think?' Tom asked Chrissie.

'Please, Mum,' Ben implored.

She was torn, but Ben's point about missing out on meeting his great-grandfather had struck home. He had a family now. Norry and Rosemary would undoubtedly be a major disappointment, but Tom and George were the good ones – it would be nice for Ben to have his own memory of his great-grandfather.

'Okay then, but if you change your mind when we get there that's absolutely fine,' she assured him.

He hugged her – not too much of an occurrence since he became a pre-teen – and she savoured every second of it.

'Thanks, Val. I'll call you later. Can you take care of the other thing?' Chrissie asked with a smile.

'Oh yes,' she replied, relishing the thought. 'I'll go call Josie right now and tell her what she missed.'

'Right, Ben, let's go.'

'Mum?' he asked, and her stomach flipped yet again. What now? She still wasn't sure she was doing the right thing here, but she didn't want him to hold something so important against her when he got older. 'Can I sit in the front with my dad?'

Thirty

Shauna

'Are you sure you want to do this, Aunt Flora?' Shauna asked, as they drew up outside the hospital. It had been a lot for the elderly lady today, and seeing your brother in his last breaths of life, after an estrangement of over five decades, would be more than most people could bear.

'I'm absolutely positive, pet. Although I do wish I didn't smell of chips.'

Shauna leaned over and hugged her aunt. It was incredible to her that they'd only met a few hours ago and she already felt an inextricable bond.

'Hang on a minute. Here you go,' Lulu said, pulling a bottle of perfume out of her bag and spraying it on all of them. 'According to the advert, this makes you all powerful and men will view you as a goddess, so use that power wisely, Flora.'

'Aye, but you might want to use that power to come to my house and restrain my missus when I go home smelling like I've been up to no good,' John said. 'I think I preferred the vinegar.'

'We'll write you a note of explanation,' Lulu promised, laughing, as she climbed out of the car.

Shauna leaned down to John's open window. 'John, are you sure you still want to stay? You've been with us for so long, you must be knackered. I'm more than happy to pay you the full fare now and let you get home.'

John wasn't having it. 'Not at all. I've not felt like I've been at work all day today. I've had a smashing time.' He lowered his voice, 'And I won't be leaving in case this upsets Flora and she wants to get straight home afterwards.'

Shauna smiled gratefully. 'You're a smasher, you know that?'

'Aye, I get told that every day,' he joked.

Shauna caught up with the other two at the lifts they'd been in only an hour or so before, and ascended to the second floor. This time they turned right and went through the double doors, to see three nurses sitting behind the nurses' station, with a small white twinkling tree on the counter. Two of them went off, leaving the other to greet the new arrivals. She spoke in a quiet but friendly tone.

'Hi, can I help you?'

Shauna spoke for them. 'I'm Shauna, and this is Flora and Lulu. We're here to see George Butler.'

'Ah, yes. I'm Liv. Tom called and said you'd be coming.'

'Thank you so much,' Flora said. 'I can't tell you what this means to me.'

Shauna swallowed. Dear God, today had been an emotional roller coaster that showed no signs of stopping.

'Tom's father and stepmother are in the TV room at the moment, so I thought you might want to meet them first? I haven't had a chance to tell them you were on your way, so I'm afraid they might be a bit surprised. Shall I take you through there?'

Shauna nodded, excited at the prospect of notching up two more relatives. 'Please. That would be great.'

The TV room was over to the right of reception, across from the corridor that housed the patients' rooms.

Liv went in first, and the couple in the chairs barely registered her presence.

'Norry, Rosemary, these ladies are also here to see Mr Butler.'

Only Flora and Lulu heard Shauna's quiet gasp of recognition. Only Shauna heard Lulu's hiss of "Holy fuck". And only Flora handled herself with perfect decorum and class when she realised they were being introduced to the couple they'd shared a lift with earlier that evening.

She headed directly for them, her hand held out to Norry, who was now rising from his chair. Rosemary just sat, watching them approach, not so much as a smile. 'I'm Flora McGinty,' she said, shaking his hand.

The man was amiable enough. 'I'm Norry Butler, and this is my wife Rosemary.'

Shauna stepped forward and added herself and Lulu to the introductions. Throughout them all, Rosemary stayed in her seat, barely concealing her irritation at the new arrivals. Shauna decided to give her the benefit of the doubt. Maybe she was distraught, overwrought given the circumstances.

Neither Norry nor Rosemary showed any signs that they recognised the three women from the lift earlier in the evening – not a big surprise, as they hadn't taken any notice of them at the time.

'You're friends of my father?' Norry asked.

'Actually, I'm more than that. Do you mind if I sit?' Flora asked, gesturing to the seat next beside him.

'Of course,' Norry agreed.

Flora sat down in the blue padded chair next to him while Shauna and Lulu took the next two along so that they were all sitting in a semicircle around a low coffee table.

'I don't know if your father ever told you about his own family...' Flora began.

'Only that there was some kind of rift back in the late fifties. I believe his parents died soon after.'

'Yes. They succumbed to the flu in 1960. It was a terribly sad time. Did he mention his siblings?'

Norry shrugged. 'Two sisters, I think.'

'That's right. I'm sincerely sorry if this comes as a bit of a shock to you, but I'm one of your father's sisters. And this young lady here,' she smiled at Shauna, 'is the granddaughter of Annie, his other sister.'

Norry sat, mouth agape, for several seconds. 'He never told me you were back in touch.'

'We weren't,' Shauna spoke. 'We've only just discovered that your father is here.' She went on to explain the letters, and the trip north, and the meeting with Flora.

'Not being funny,' Rosemary said, with a distinct overtone of bitchiness, 'but how do we know all this is true? I mean, I don't want to be negative, but I've heard about people who find out about folk who are at death's door and show up claiming all sorts.'

'Let me...' Lulu hissed to Shauna, who put her hand on her friend's arm as a sign of restraint. 'That's okay, Lulu,' she said in her best sing-song voice, 'I'm happy to provide evidence.'

Shauna was seething inside. This woman was the rudest cow she'd encountered in a long time. Annie would have decimated her by now and she could see Flora's eyes narrowing. Her aunt may be a paragon of serenity, but Shauna could also sense that she didn't suffer fools and would only be pushed so far.

Endeavouring to keep things polite, she delved into her bag and pulled out the letters and Annie's birth certificate. Flora produced hers, too.

'And I can answer any question about your father's younger days that you may wish to know,' she said, admirably maintaining her poise.

Norry studied all the documents, then handed them back.

'Well, this all looks very straightforward. I'm afraid my father is unconscious though, so visiting him is a waste of time.' Shauna was so incensed she realised she was digging her fingers into Lulu's arm. Lulu was so incensed she didn't notice.

'Oh, my dear,' Flora said, her voice strong and unwavering. 'Visiting the sick can never be a waste of time.'

Norry shrugged. 'Well, you're welcome to it. We're actually just waiting for my son...'

'Oh, sorry!' Shauna replied, forcing herself to be civil. If Flora could do it, she could follow suit. 'We should have led with that. We've already met your son and we have your luggage downstairs in a taxi.'

'He just gave our luggage to complete strangers?' Rosemary blurted out, clearly outraged by this.

'Well, not complete strangers, but I can assure you we didn't ransack it or plant cocaine. At least, not enough for sniffer dogs to notice,' Lulu said, her tone jocular, but Shauna knew all too well that this level of sarcasm was the bit that came right before Lulu unleashed a tirade of merciless vitriol on her target. Rosemary was on her last warning, and she deserved it, especially for the way she was speaking to Flora, but this wasn't the time or place for disagreements. It was safe to say these two wouldn't be on any Christmas card list and they wouldn't be meeting up for chummy family reunions. Tom had seemed so nice as well. She decided to look at it as a numbers game. She'd met three lovely relatives so far – it was probably time for one or two dodgy ones.

'And here's the key, he asked me to give it to you – it's for his flat,' Shauna said.

'Okay, let's get off then,' Norry said to his wife, jumping up as if under starter's orders.

'You're not staying with your father? I believe Tom's coming back shortly,' Flora told him and Shauna could see she was finding this to be incomprehensible.

'No, we've been here all day,' Norry said. 'We'll get off and come back tomorrow.'

The others knew it wasn't their place to argue and, well, there was a silent consensus that they'd be happy to see the back of this pair.

They all walked out to the reception area together and Norry pressed the button for the lift.

'The taxi is right downstairs and the driver is happy to take you to Tom's home and then come back for us,' Shauna said.

'Right. Okay then. Well, we'll be off,' Norry said, as the lift pinged open and then they were gone, leaving the three women staring after them, open mouthed.

Lulu was the first to speak. 'What a pair of crackers those two are.'

At the desk, Liv smiled. 'I couldn't possibly comment. Shall I take you to meet your brother now, Mrs McGinty?'

'That would be most kind of you,' Flora replied.

Liv chatted quietly as they walked down the corridor. 'Tom explained the situation to me. I'm so glad you're getting this chance to meet George again.'

Flora's smile was layered with sadness. 'I am, too. You must see so many people in here with regrets and my biggest one is losing touch with my brother George and my sister Annie. If I could turn back time...'

'That's a phrase I hear often, too,' Liv replied kindly, as she stopped in front of a heavy wooden door with a small pane of glass above the handle. 'It's just in here.'

She pushed open the door and Shauna stepped in behind them to a pristine room with white walls and pale blue blinds. There was a drape of tinsel along the top of the window, and on a corner table sat some beautiful Christmas ornaments – a row of little drummers, a nest of robins, a collection of exquisite baubles – that looked like they belonged to a long gone era. George's bed was in the centre of the room, with a dozen or so Christmas cards taped to the wall above it and bank of machines and monitors to his right.

The four of them approached the bed, Shauna and Lulu walking round to the plastic seats on the opposite side, leaving Flora to sit in the more comfortable armchair beside her brother. Shauna hadn't known what to expect, but now, seeing George, she was so grateful that they'd come. He looked so peaceful, like an elderly man having a deep sleep after a long day. His hair was silver, but still surprisingly thick. He was slender, his face almost gaunt, as if he'd lost a lot of weight very quickly, but there was no sign that he was in pain, and for that, Shauna was grateful.

A sob interrupted her thoughts and she realised it came from Flora, who was weeping as she held George's hand. Shauna felt the hot sting of tears running down her face. An arm came around her, Lulu's, and the two of them wept in silence for this man they had never met but whom they felt they knew.

Shauna hadn't even realised that Liv was still there until she spoke. 'George, Tom called and said he'll be back soon, but there are some new visitors here to see you. I'll let them explain. Ladies, please just press that button lying next to George's hand if you need anything,' she said, pointing to the orange wire with the call button at the end.

There was a silence in the room for a few moments, before Flora reached over and slowly, gently, cradled his face. 'George, this is Flora.'

Shauna and Lulu were silent, both of them instinctively knowing that they were bystanders in one of the most heartbreaking moments of Flora's life.

'Oh, George, I have so much to say and I don't know where to start. I'm so sorry. I really am. You see, I thought... Oh dear, I've forgotten my manners. I need to introduce you to two very special women who travelled up from London today to find us. They're the reason I'm here now because they led me to you. One is Lulu, not the singer, and the other is Shauna. And George, you'll never believe who Shauna is.'

Flora raised her eyes and gestured to Shauna to take over the conversation. Shauna took a second to compose herself before she spoke.

'George, I'm your sister Annie's granddaughter. I'm really sorry to say that Annie passed away a few years ago, but she left some letters from you and from Flora. I found Flora today, and now, together, we've tracked you down.'

Flora spoke again. 'And the letters... Oh, George, one of them was from you to Annie and I know now why you told Declan and I've come to see that it was with good intentions. I should never have doubted you, George. I've realised today that we've wasted so much time. The years, they have just drifted past and I suppose I was too proud, too stubborn, to make the first move. I regret that more than I can say, and I'd give anything to make it different, to live my life with you, to be part of your family. I met your grandson, Tom, tonight and he is a remarkable chap. He's a credit to you, George.'

Shauna wondered if she would mention that she'd just met Norry, but sensed she was omitting that out of diplomacy.

'And I wished I'd met Annie's family, too. I'd love to have seen this young woman grow up,' she beamed at Shauna. 'It sounds like Annie had a happy life.'

Shauna sat forward, determined to hold it together despite the sadness of the occasion. 'She did, Uncle George. Annie's son, Jeff, was my dad, but I spent most of my life with Annie. She was wild and crazy and so funny. She may have been small, but she was mighty. My daughter Beth is eight and she's exactly the same. She definitely got Annie's genes.' Shauna held on to that thought for a moment before going on. 'My gran didn't let anyone get away with anything. I absolutely adored her and she was fiercely protective of me. She adored my grandfather, but sadly she was widowed and that broke her heart, but she never let it show. She just got on with it. She used to say that to me all the time. You just have to get on with it. It was like her motto for life. I'm so sad that she never came back to visit you and Flora. I think if she's up there watching this, she'll be so happy that I'm here now. I'm so grateful that I got the chance to meet you both,' Shauna said, holding in more tears. It felt self-indulgent to fall apart when the people in the room who had lost the most were the brother and sister holding hands on the bed.

Flora reached over again and ran her fingers through his hair, then gently stroked the side of his face, wiping away a single teardrop that was resting on his cheek. 'I still see the same man I knew back then, George Butler. You always were a handsome man. And a good man. I'm so sorry I forgot that for a while there.' She was weeping again now. 'Oh, look at the state of me. If this was our younger days, you'd be rolling your eyes and Annie would be telling me to get a grip of myself. I am so grateful we had this evening, George. I'm going to believe that you can hear every word of this. I do hope so. If you can, please know that I love you. I always did.'

The door opened and Liv popped her head around, smiled. 'Just checking everything is okay?'

'It is, thank you,' Shauna replied, before speaking to her aunt. Flora looked exhausted now, almost overcome by weariness. Shauna was starting to worry that Flora had done too much and it was her fault for springing all this on her. 'Are you okay, Aunt Flora? Shall we get you home?' she offered. 'I'm sure John will be back downstairs by now. It's up to you though – we will stay here for as long as you want to.'

Flora was still stroking George's face, staring at it like she was trying to memorise every curve and crevice.

'I'm going to go now, George,' she said tenderly. 'It's late and you need your rest. I shall come back tomorrow. My husband Arthur, I'm sure you remember that young man I was seeing before...' She trailed off, then regrouped. 'Anyway, Arthur is recovering in another ward after a fall and I visit him every day, so I'll come spend time with you, too. I hope you'll like that. We've had a happy life, Arthur and me. I hope you and Betty did, too. Sleep tight, my darling George.'

Shauna came round and took her aunt's hand to steady her as she stood.

'Goodnight, Uncle George,' she said. 'I so wish I'd known you. Tom and I are going to keep in touch, so at least I feel like I'll get to know you through him. And I'm hoping to come back in to see you tomorrow before I leave.'

'Goodnight, Mr Butler,' Lulu said, as she came round to join the others.

The three women took another moment to be with George, before slowly and silently leaving the room.

Liv was working on the computer at the nurses' station when they got there.

'I'll never be able to thank you enough,' Flora said.

'I was happy to help. George is such a lovely man. I'm just sorry you didn't get to spend more time with him.'

Flora explained that she'd be back tomorrow, then the three women held hands as they went down in the lift and out to the waiting taxi. As soon as they climbed in, Flora sank against the seat.

'Are you okay?' Shauna asked her again. 'I feel like we've exhausted you.'

Flora reached over and touched her cheek. 'I am as bone weary as I've ever been,' Flora admitted. 'But there are no words to describe how grateful I am for what you've brought to my life. I promise you this – I would not change a single moment of this day.'

'Me neither,' Lulu said, her voice thick with tiredness. 'But do you think there's any chance that tomorrow could be completely uneventful?'

Shauna thought about it. She was going to meet Tom in the morning before the flight and she was hoping he'd fill her in on a few loose ends about her Scottish family's lives.

'I hope so,' Shauna answered. 'However, I think we've got a few more surprises to come.'

Thirty-one

Tom

Tom struggled to keep his eyes on the road all the way to the hospital, but he forced himself to. In fact, he'd never driven more carefully or had such a precious cargo.

His boy. Chrissie. He just wanted to stare at them both.

'What happened to your knuckles?' Ben asked, putting him on the spot. This kid missed nothing. 'You look like you've been in a fight.'

Tom flicked his eyes to the rear view mirror. Chrissie was in the back seat as promised and he needed to gauge her reaction.

She shrugged. 'It's okay to be honest. We have a pact that we don't tell lies. And you can also explain all the reasons it's wrong to use violence,' she said, a challenge in her voice.

Tom decided to just go with the facts. On the car journey to George's house, Chrissie had told him briefly

355

about the conversation with Davie in the restaurant and why she'd walked out. He had always known Davie was a player, but now he could see his partner was nothing more than a sleazy prick. Tom now wished he'd punched him harder.

'The guy your mum was meeting tonight was my business partner. He knew I'd been searching for your mum for years and he didn't tell me he was seeing her because, well, he's not a very nice person. I found out and went to where they were meeting, but your mum was already on her way out because he'd been rude to her. He said some nasty things, so I punched him. And I can honestly say it's the first time in my life I've ever punched anyone. Please don't do it.'

Ben found this amusing. 'Violence is never the answer,' he said, aping Chrissie. Then to Tom, 'But he does sound like a tosser.' Chrissie ignored the fact that Tom grinned when he heard Ben's conclusion.

'Ben!' Chrissie chided him, then swiftly de-escalated as reality kicked in. 'Ah, what the hell – he was a tosser.'

For once, there was a parking space near the entrance, probably because many of the staff went off shift at eleven o'clock and had only just left for the night. Whatever the reason, he was grateful as he slid the car into the space.

In the lift, Tom got his first chance to just stare at Ben in the mirror of the doors. The boy was already close to six feet tall, just a couple of inches shorter than Tom, but already taller than Chrissie.

He marvelled once more at how much his son looked like him. The same wavy, dark brown hair. Tom's was pushed back from his face, but it fell forward like Ben's when he hadn't styled it. Identical hazel eyes. Matching shades of skin tone. There was no question they shared the same genes, but Ben also had Chrissie's smile. He was a beautiful combination of them both, and Tom felt a wave of sorrow for every single day he'd missed of his son's life. He pushed the feelings down. He'd found him now, found *them*, and that was all that mattered. This was the best Christmas present he could ever have. He was devastated that his grandad wouldn't be able to share it.

Liv was the first person they saw as they opened the door. She came round the desk, and hugged Chrissie, speaking in whispers, 'Hello, you,' and then to Ben, 'All right, squirt?' Ben clearly found this amusing and Tom thought again how comfortable the boy was communicating and interacting with adults. He was confident and so much more mature than he remembered being at that age. He could never repay Chrissie for bringing him up on her own.

'Tom, I can't believe this! This boy is my second favourite twelve year old ever,' Liv said, teasing Ben, who reacted by rolling his eyes.

'I keep telling her that Harry Potter doesn't count and, besides, he's an adult now.'

'Can you do magic?' Liv asked, tartly. This was obviously a discussion they'd had many times before. 'No? Then keep your comments to yourself.' She was still chuckling when she switched her focus to Tom. 'Your aunt and her friends have left now. They were so lovely and your aunt said that she would like to return tomorrow. Your cousin...'

'Shauna,' he said.

'Yes, Shauna, was telling me all about it. They've had quite a day.'

'I know the feeling,' he said, with a twinkle in his eye.

'And your other visitors have left, too,' she said tactfully, 'I've no idea when they'll be back.'

Tom could sense there was a story there, but he thought it best to discuss it later and could sense that Liv thought so too.

'Okay, have a seat here, so I can talk to you,' she said to Ben, as she pulled a chair over next to hers at the nurses' station. Ben did as he was told, while Tom and Chrissie listened in from their position across the desk. 'I just want to tell you what to expect,' she said, kindly. 'This is a palliative care ward, so do you remember what I told you before about what that means?'

Ben nodded. 'It's where you look after people right before they die and give them a peaceful and dignified death.'

'That's right. Now, in all these rooms,' she gestured to the long line of closed doors, 'there are people who are very ill and in many of the rooms their families are with them, even at this time of night. That's what makes this very different from a normal hospital ward, where you're only allowed to visit for a few hours a day.'

Ben was still listening intently.

'Now, Mr Butler...'

'My great-grandad,' Ben added solemnly, and Tom wanted to weep with pride.

'Yes, your great-grandad, is very ill, but he's not in any pain, so I don't want you to be worried or scared. When you see him, it will just look like he is sleeping, but he does have some wires connected to his arm, and those are linked up to machines that monitor things like his blood pressure and heart rate.'

'I had those when I was in hospital,' he said.

'Appendix,' Chrissie added. Tom was grateful for the reassurance.

Liv carried on with her pep talk. 'Although the patients seem like they're sleeping, many doctors think they can still hear you, so it's fine if you'd like to chat or say something.'

'What kind of things can I chat about?' he asked. Again, Tom was bowled over by how sincere and thoughtful Ben was.

'Anything at all. What you did today. What kind of things you like. I always just think it's best to say whatever is on your mind. It can be serious or not serious, or anything at all. Remember though, if you change your mind about visiting, that's absolutely fine too. You can go in with your mum and...' She paused, unsure how to address Tom.

Ben helped her out. 'He's my dad.'

Another piece of Tom's heart crumbled, even more so when he saw that a tear was falling down Chrissie's cheek.

'Exactly,' Liv agreed. 'So you can go in with your mum and dad, or you can chill here with me and keep me company. This is all up to you and you don't have to do anything that makes you feel uncomfortable.'

'I know,' Ben said. 'But I would like to see my great-grandad. Even just for a minute, so I can remember his face.'

'Okay then,' Liv said, then looked at Chrissie and Tom for a final agreement. Chrissie nodded. 'Let's go through then. I'll be right here if you want to come back out any time, though, okay?'

'Okay.'

They walked down the corridor, their footsteps making barely a sound on the floor, until they reached George's room. Liv opened the door and went in first, checking by the light of the bedside lamp that all was okay. As soon as she was satisfied, she gestured to them to follow and then touched Chrissie's arm in reassurance as she passed her on the way out of the door.

Tom had never been as stuck for words in his life as he'd been at some points today, but this wasn't one of them.

'Grandad, it's been a busy old day in here today and I've brought some more people along to see you tonight,' he said lovingly. 'You remember Chrissie,' he said, then watched as Chrissie walked round to the other side of the bed and sat down in a chair. She automatically put her hand on George's arm.

'Hello, Mr Butler. It's been a long, long time,' she said fondly.

'And, Grandad, this young man,' he said, putting his arm around Ben's shoulders, 'is Chrissie's son, Ben. And wait until you hear this – he's my son, too. We have a boy, Grandad, I just met him for the first time tonight. He wanted to come and meet you.'

Ben followed his mum's lead, slipping into the seat on the near side of George's bed. 'Hello Great-Grandad. I hope it was okay that I came. I was at my pal Josh's house, but he had a mad puking attack – seriously, it was everywhere – so I had to get picked up and then I talked my mum and...' there was barely a hesitation, '... dad into letting me come here with them. They weren't up for it at all, but my Auntie Val phoned Liv, she's Auntie Val's niece and everyone keeps saying things about it being a small world, whatever that means. Anyway, Liv said it was okay for me to come in here just for a little while, so I can't stay long.'

Tom knew, right there, that this was the proudest moment of his life and if he never experienced another high like this, it wouldn't matter. This was everything. He wheeled over the adjustable stool, the one he sat on when he was shaving George, and took up a position beside Ben.

'I wish you could see him, Grandad, he looks so like I did at that age. Maybe not quite as good looking,' he teased, earning an indignant nudge from his son.

'Don't listen to him, Mr Butler.' It sounded strange to hear Chrissie being so formal, but that was the way they'd been brought up to address that generation. Habit, too. She'd only ever called him by that name when she was a young girl speaking to her boyfriend's grandfather, so it would have been odd to change now. 'Ben is way better looking than Tom ever was. Smarter, too,' she said, winking at her son. 'But he does have his cheekiness.'

Tom wanted to freeze this moment in time. There was so much to discuss, to learn, to make amends for, to explain, but right now he was in a room with the three people in the whole world that he loved and he wanted to keep a snapshot of this moment in his mind.

'So we gave Tom a bit of a shock tonight,' Chrissie continued. 'But I think it was a good one.'

'The best one ever,' Tom heard himself saying.

'Yeah, and I'm not mad about my dad not coming to see me before now, because he didn't know about me,'

Ben added.

Chrissie stepped in to explain. 'I don't know if you remember that I came to see you years and years ago, just after Tom left,' she said. 'Well, I was pregnant then. I didn't want to say at the time. I wish now that I had because I think maybe things would have worked out differently. Anyway, I just wanted to say that I'm sorry if I put you in a tough position. I know my mother was keeping us apart...' She paused and smiled at Ben. 'If there's any of this stuff you don't understand, I'll explain it all later, I promise.' She went back to speaking to George. 'And I shouldn't have asked you to interfere, Mr Butler. I don't know what I'd have done in your position, but I do know that I would do anything if I thought I was protecting my son.'

'You're an amazing woman, do you know that?' Tom said gently. He knew exactly what Chrissie was doing. She had realised that his grandfather hadn't sent that letter or told Tom anything about her visit back then, and she had two choices – she could hate him for the damage that he had done to their lives, or she could choose to forgive him while he was still here to hear it.

Tom felt exactly the same. George had given him a lifetime of love, he had nurtured him, supported him, picked him up and cared for him. If he hadn't passed the letter on, it would have been out of a desire to protect him. Besides, George hadn't known about the baby, so he wouldn't have realised what was at stake. It was a mistake, and he wished it hadn't happened, but it didn't wipe out thirty years of unconditional devotion. He loved his grandad. That hadn't changed now and it never would.

Besides, right now he was praying for forgiveness for a huge mistake too, and he could only hope Chrissie found it in her heart to grant it.

Chrissie matched his gaze. 'Thank you,' she said. He'd always wondered if he would feel that same if he met her again after all this time, if he would feel that immediate connection and if the love would instantly reignite. After all, it was a teenage romance. A first love. Surely that would diminish over time? He realised now that the opposite was true. He loved her. He always had, and he still did now, more than ever.

What he found inexplicable though was his instant connection with, and the colossal strength of his feelings for, Ben. Zero to love in a split second, like lighting a fire and watching the flames explode into something ferocious.

'They're getting soppy, Grandad. They're totally staring into each other's eyes, and my mum looks the way she does every Christmas when we watch *Love Actually*.'

'Ben Harrison!' Chrissie chided him.

'Shouldn't it be Ben Butler?' he replied flippantly, in the way of a child who absolutely doesn't realise the emotional weight of what he just said.

'Yes, I suppose it should.'

Tom couldn't even take in what had just happened. Ben Butler. That sounded, oh, so right.

'They're staring into each other's eyes again, Grandad,' Ben drolled. 'Oh, and I need to tell you, my dad's hand is all bust up because he punched a guy in the face. I know I'm being a grass, but he wasn't a nice man so it wasn't a bad thing. Anyway, I need to go soon because Liv is going off shift and she's taking me home. I hope you've heard all of this, Grandad. It was really nice to meet you. I'll always remember tonight.'

If Tom had any doubts about bringing Ben here this evening, that wiped them out.

'Mum, I think you should stay, though.'

'No, I'll come home in case you want to talk...'

'I'll talk to Liv, and then Val and Don. Or I'll talk to you tomorrow. I promise I'm good. If you come with me, then you're leaving Dad here alone. Well, not alone because he can talk to Grandad, but he'll have no one talking to him.'

'How did you get so wise?' Chrissie asked him, her love for him written all over her face.

'Val. Definitely listening to Val,' he joked.

Liv knocked at the door. 'Just about ready?' she asked.

Ben looked questioningly at Chrissie, and she surrendered.

'Liv, would you mind just taking Ben back to Val's house please? I'll call her and tell her you're on the way.'

'No problem at all,' Liv agreed. 'I still can't get over the fact that you lovely people are a family – and that I knew you all individually. I couldn't be happier for you,' she beamed. 'Right, young man, let's move it. And I absolutely will not stop at the McDonald's twenty-four hour drive through on the way home. Absolutely not. I won't. No matter how much you beg.'

'I'll buy you a McFlurry,' he said.

'Done,' she agreed, chuckling.

Ben hugged Chrissie and for a moment Tom thought that would be it, but just as he was passing him, he leaned in and hugged him too.

Tom returned the embrace, desperately trying to stop tears of utter joy drop on his son's head. He blinked them back, and cleared his throat. 'See you tomorrow, son. I'll be bringing your mum home and I'll come in and see if you're awake.'

'If I'm not, will you wait until I wake up?' he asked, his enthusiasm for this idea obvious.

'Sure.' He'd promised to see Shauna before she left. He wanted to stay with George. There was the irritation of Norry and Rosemary. No doubt Davie would rear his head at some point. But the most important part of the day just became the time he would spend with his son.

'Cool,' Ben replied. 'Bye, Grandad,' he said again. 'See you later, I hope.'

Tom moved to the chair Ben had been sitting in and automatically slipped his hand under George's.

Only when the door finally closed behind Ben and Liv did Tom speak to Chrissie.

'I'll never be able to thank you for him. Grandad would have loved him, too.'

'I know,' Chrissie replied.

For just a fraction of a heartbeat, Tom thought he felt his grandad's hand tightening on his.

Thirty-two

George

I thought I was dead. It was the only explanation. I had been in a deep sleep and was stirred by hands on my face, stroking it, and I was sure it was my Betty. I knew she'd be the one to come for me when it was time.

But then I heard her voice.

'George, this is Flora.'

She didn't have to say her name. Her voice was still exactly the same as I remembered. I tried to make my way through the fog in my head. Flora had come for me? She was taking me to the other side? Was that how this worked?

Or was this a hallucination, a trick of the mind, some stage between heaven and earth, where you made peace with the ones that you've loved and lost?

Perhaps it was a rite of passage and, if it was, I was grateful, because Flora was saying things I'd waited a lifetime to hear.

She forgave me. She understood. She knew the truth.

If this was the first stage of death, I was happy to embrace it. I felt my heart soar, my soul lift, every part of me infuse with happiness and a peace that I hadn't known for the longest time, since we were back in the days when my sisters still stood by my side.

I surrendered to it. To death. To the process. To Flora.

To peace.

It was the sounds that made my thoughts clear. The creaking of chairs, the rustle of sheets, the sense of feeling someone next to me moving and breathing and weeping. It slowly came to me that I was still alive. Still in that hospital bed.

Flora was real, not a spirit sent to guide me to the next life. I got the shock of my fading life and I tried – you've no idea how hard I tried – to open my eyes, to see her face. Flora. My sister.

I pushed my mind to wake properly, to work, to explain to me how this could be, but it was beyond me. Then Flora explained, and there was another voice, a younger one, talking about Annie.

Annie was her grandmother.

It was hard to imagine that. I still pictured Annie as she was on the last day that I saw her, a young woman, furious, stubborn as a mule, defying those who had wronged her. Her hair was red, her cheeks freckled, her brow a furious frown.

And yet, she'd become a grandmother, and now her kin was here, saying that Annie had passed away many years ago. Selfish that I am, and it gives me no pride to admit it, I felt a measure of joy in the hope that I would soon see her in the next destination for my imperfect soul.

I listened to every word they both said, my strength returning by the minute and I shrugged off the sleep that was trying to claim me again.

It's impossible to measure the gratitude I felt that they were there, and for the things they were saying. It's also hard to express the regret I felt that this conversation hadn't happened back in 1958, or in the years soon after, when we could have made amends for the wrongs, real or perceived, that we had suffered and inflicted. Flora was right. What fools we had been. And while that thought pained me, it was numbed by the soothing anaesthetic of Flora's words of forgiveness, of love.

They didn't stay long, but I heard Flora say that she would be back, that Arthur was here, too, that they'd had a happy life together. The comfort that gave me. For so long I'd been anguished that my actions had condemned her to a life in which she'd never find contentment and now I knew that was not the case.

I wanted to thank her for what she'd given me, for removing that stain of regret from my soul, but my body would not let me. I hope she knew.

When they left, I felt no sadness, only relief.

If my life were taken from me right then, I would have gone to Betty and Annie willingly.

It was not to be.

And I will forever be grateful that it was not.

Another touch, another voice and, again, I recognised it straight away. The tone was slightly different, matured with age, but by God, I had replayed our last conversation in my mind countless times over the last twelve years and I knew every lift and inflection in that lass's words.

Chrissie.

She spoke kindly, she spoke of the past, and she spoke about understanding. It was more than I could ever have hoped for. The other person I had wronged in my life, relieving me of the burden of guilt that I had carried.

There could be nothing more blessed or wonderful.

At least that's what I thought.

And then Tom spoke too, and he told me about...

Words fail me. If only my Betty were here with me to see this now.

We have a great-grandson. Ben. He spoke and I only wish I could have shown him the wonder and happiness I was feeling, I wish I could have opened my arms and hugged the boy and told him how incredibly ecstatic I was that he was there. Even in his voice, I could hear our Tom when he was that age, and I can't tell you the pride I felt.

And the sorrow.

That poor lass. She had been pregnant and I hadn't helped her, yet she was here to tell me that she bore me no malice. That is a woman to be admired, a woman with compassion and I am overjoyed that she will be in Tom's life again.

None of this is the way I would have planned it. I wouldn't have seen my Tom go through years aching for Chrissie. I wouldn't have had him miss all those years with his bairn. But I am beyond grateful that I have lived to see him find them. And aye, I'm delighted that he punched that bastard, Davie, too.

My biggest fear, my greatest sadness, was that I was leaving our Tom alone in this world, without love to surround him and carry him forward. Now I can sleep, knowing that he has a family, a world without me.

They're still here now, Tom and Chrissie. I can feel a fear in the room, a heartbreak, an uncertainty. Right now, they have no words for each other, but I hope that will soon change, and it will be like a river bursting through a dam, finding its way home.

Midnight – 8 a.m.

Thirty-three

Chrissie

Chrissie opened her eyes and raised her head from the back of the chair as soon as she heard the door open. Tom came in with two cups of coffee. She should be hungry, given that she'd left before her meal was even served at the restaurant, but right now her body needed nothing other than to be here.

Tom had insisted they swap seats, so that she was in the armchair by George's bed, the one Tom had dozed in overnight for the last few nights. He had pulled the plastic chair from the other side round, so they were sitting next to each other now, chairs angled so she could watch him as he talked.

There was so much to say, and yet, before he had gone for the drinks, they had both fallen into silence as they tried to absorb the magnitude of the day.

Val had texted to say that Ben was asleep, that he was fine, that he was full of stories of his great-grandfather and that he said he was 'buzzing' to have met him and

Tom. That made Chrissie smile. He never stopped surprising her.

She took the coffee from Tom's hand and smiled. 'Thank you. Not just for the coffee, but for tonight. You were great with Ben.'

To her surprise, his eyes filled with tears. 'I know this sounds crazy, but, Chrissie, I feel such love for him already. It's like my heart is going to explode in my chest. Does that even make sense?'

'It does,' she said, emotion choking the words. 'Sometimes now, even at his age, I will go into his room to say goodnight and he'll be sleeping and I'll sit on the edge of his bed, just watching him, and think I couldn't love him any more. That's that feeling you're talking about. Unconditional, unequivocal love for your child. I felt it the minute he was born and it's why I moved away, left no forwarding address, cut all ties with everyone. I didn't want Rosemary and Norry in his life. I knew they would only let him down, disappoint him, walk away from him, and I couldn't bear the thought of him realising that two people who should love him didn't even want to give him the time of day. Perhaps that was wrong, but I didn't want him to feel a single shred of the devastation I felt every time Rosemary blocked my call, or rejected me, or made it clear she didn't give a toss whether or not I was in her life. I didn't want him to know that I'd told her I was pregnant and that she said it was my own fault and she wasn't sorting out my mess. That's what she called it. My mess. I didn't want him anywhere near grandparents who wouldn't love him more than life.'

It was only now, vocalising it, that she realised how that sounded to him.

He said it first, 'And you thought I wouldn't want him either.'

She took a moment to answer. 'I really thought you knew. Even if Rosemary hadn't told you, I thought...'

She didn't want to say it out loud, but her eyes flicked to George, lying there, a shadow of the man he'd once been, and she hoped Tom would know the words she didn't want to say.

She really thought George would have got her letter to Tom, but he hadn't. However, recriminations were pointless, so there was nothing to do but let it go.

'I'm sorry I didn't get it,' he said softly. Of course he'd known what she was thinking. 'I would have done anything to be with you.'

'Thing is,' Chrissie went on, 'perhaps in some way it was for the best. We were so young back then, so naïve. Maybe if you'd come back and we'd given it a go, tried to bring up Ben together, then it would have been too much and we wouldn't have made it. Perhaps we'd have been one of those couples that give it everything but eventually concede defeat, and then spend the rest of their lives driving the kids back and forward for alternate weekends of shared custody. I know you've missed so much, but Ben has only known happiness, only known love. He's never heard his parents fighting or had to live through the pain of watching them walk away from each other. I think we have to stop with regrets, with wishing that this had gone another way, because, believe me, I never want to feel another moment of resentment or sorrow.' As she said it, she knew every word was absolutely true.

Tom was staring at her now, watching every movement of her face. No man had looked at her that way in so, so long, and yet she didn't feel in the least bit self-conscious. 'I don't want you to feel that either. I know I don't deserve you to trust me—'

'That's the crazy thing,' Chrissie interrupted him. 'I do trust you. The moment I saw you again, I realised that. I knew instantly, and I still do now. I see who you are, Tom. I always have. For a long time, I thought I'd been wrong, but I know now I wasn't. I see you.'

He leant forward, wrapped his arms around her, hugged her tightly for the longest time, and she could feel his shoulders shaking with emotion.

Eventually, they released their embrace, leaving just their hands locked together.

'I've got no right to ask anything of you,' he said. 'But where do we go from here?'

Chrissie didn't trust herself to answer for a minute or two.

Where did they go from here?

There was an instant reaction, but she bit it back. She wasn't some young teenager now who could be impulsive and make spontaneous decisions. There was far too much at stake here.

'I think we just take it day by day. Ben will be desperate to spend as much time with you as he can...'

'Which is just as well, because I think I'll be sitting on your doorstep waiting for him to wake up every morning.'

A burst of pure delight made goosebumps pop out all over her body when he said that. 'I think that's called stalking,' she said, happy to tease him and release some of the tension of the night.

'I might be able to calm it down to every second day,' he joked. 'I'll try to determine the level that crosses from "yay, he's here" to "Oh God, it's him again".'

It seemed so strange to be sitting here, in a palliative care ward, with a dying man by their side, and yet they were laughing. Was that wrong? Her thought must have shown on her face, because Tom immediately countered it.

'I've no idea if my grandad can hear this, but if he can, he'll be so happy, I promise you. He said to me once that his biggest sadness was leaving me on my own, but now he'll know that's not the case and, I promise you, inside he'll be singing "That's Life" and snapping his fingers.'

'I hope so,' she said, before another thought crossed her mind. 'I know you said that you broke things off with your girlfriend today, but you never married before that? Never had children?'

He shook his head. 'Barely had a relationship,' he conceded. 'A few casual things, but nothing…'

'You never fell in love again?' she pushed, desperate to know. She'd kicked off her shoes now and pulled her feet up so that they were curled under her on the chair.

'Sad and pathetic, Zoe called me today,' he laughed. 'Nope, never fell in love, never even came close.'

She was sure the emotion she was feeling right now was surprise. Yes, that was it. Okay, maybe a little bit of relief, too.

'What about you?' he asked.

'Married three times,' she said solemnly, before the aghast look on his face made her feel like a terrible person. 'I'm kidding!'

'Oh, thank God,' he gushed. 'I promise I wasn't going to judge you.'

'You totally were,' she said, trying not to laugh.

'Okay, I might have been a little bit, but only because it's been a crazy day and I might not be my usual stoic, non-judgemental self at the moment.'

'You were jealous,' she said, giving in to amusement.

'Maybe. I can't possibly say,' he countered, feigning innocence.

This was without doubt the most bizarre experience of her life. She hadn't seen him for twelve years and yet it felt like they were right back there on his doorstep, mocking each other, joking around, falling in...

She stopped herself. That wasn't what this was. That was the teenage Chrissie, not the "jaded by heartbreak" Chrissie. This adult version was far more cautious with her heart.

'Well, there's not much to be jealous about. Unless you count a passing crush on The Rock. My date with Davie was my first one in twelve years.'

His jaw dropped. 'You're kidding.'

'Again with the judging,' she reprimanded him, with mock exasperation.

'Honestly? But... but... Sorry, I'm just really surprised.'

Chrissie shrugged. 'Truth?'

'Always,' he answered.

'I was pretty beat up about us for a long time. I also had absolutely no money, every penny I earned went towards the bills, with nothing left over for babysitters. Ben and I were fine though. It was just the two of us, and we got by. I made friends with the other mums at his school, he found a great little group of pals, and we lived this lovely little, skint but happy, life. The last thing on my mind was hooking up with someone. I didn't have the time or the energy for it.'

'I am so, so sorry,' Tom said, emphasising every word.

'No, it's fine. I'm not saying it for sympathy, just saying how it was.'

'I can't get past the fact that Rosemary knew and didn't keep in touch to find out if you needed anything.'

'I wouldn't have taken a thing from her anyway. Honestly, Tom, I never want to see that woman again. I know I should learn from your grandad's estrangement with his two sisters, but this is different. That was a misunderstanding that caused two people who loved each other to fall out. My mother loves no one but herself and your father. I'm losing nothing. There's no relationship to save. The reality is that you can't make someone love you if they don't. I think Bonnie Raitt said that,' she joked. 'But it's true. I came to terms with that a long time ago.'

'So you don't want to see her while she's here?' he asked.

Chrissie shook her head. 'I really don't. It's not out of anger, or rage, it's out of pure indifference. She means nothing to me any more. I just don't want her disinterest in me to touch my life or to touch Ben. I'm absolutely positive she doesn't even know he exists, because she would have been sure that I wouldn't have gone ahead with the pregnancy. I'm happy to keep it that way. She doesn't deserve to know him.' There was a ferocity in her voice, but she didn't care. If Tom didn't agree with how she felt, that was fine. She didn't need his approval. This was who she was now, this was how she felt, and he could accept her or not. She wasn't going to change or dilute her feelings for him.

'I don't think my father will have any interest in a grandson, either. But I hope you think I deserve to be part of his life?' he asked, alarmed.

'I do,' she softened. 'And I'm sorry, I know I sound harsh, but that's how it is. I'm not bitter and twisted, I promise. Just a little battle scarred.'

'I get that,' he said, and she knew he meant it. The way he looked at her told her that he was sincere. 'Is it okay if I buy him twelve years of Christmas presents, though?'

'Absolutely not,' Chrissie replied, her stomach flipping, realising there were going to be so many firsts. Ben's first Christmas with his dad in his life.

There was a pause as they tried to recalibrate, to take the conversation back to a lighter place. Tom spoke first and managed it perfectly. 'So, your first date in twelve years and you had to pick Davie Bailey. That's bad luck right there.'

'It sure is,' she laughed. 'Although, he's lucky he escaped with his bits intact. Val and Josie wanted to come with me to vet him – they even walked me to the restaurant door – and if they'd heard any of the smarmy presumptuous bollocks that he was spouting, they'd have slayed him.'

'Shame they didn't. How long were you there with him?'

'About twenty minutes. Did I mention earlier that before I walked out I tipped ice on to his crotch? That's round about the time that a bloke I went out with in high school pitched up and decked him.'

Tom was laughing hard now. 'You tipped ice on his crotch? Oh, that's brilliant.'

'He can send me his dry cleaning bill,' she said. 'I've no idea how anyone can fall for that nonsense. Or maybe I'm just woefully out of touch with how to date these days.'

'It must work for some, because, believe me, he has an endless stream of affairs and one-night stands, but nothing ever lasts for long. It's all just ego fuelled nonsense.'

'Well, he won't be fuelling his ego anywhere near me,' Chrissie retorted, with an overtone of sass.

Their laughter eventually drifted into silence, and after a long pause it was Tom who spoke first again.

'Do you think...' he stopped, and Chrissie had a premonition of what he was about to say. It was the heartbreak in his voice, and the combination of fear and hope on his gorgeous face. It was exactly the expression that Ben had when he was asking for something that he really wanted, but was scared that she would say no. 'Do you think that we could...? That we...' he stopped, thought, came back stronger. 'Do you think that we could try to make things work with us again?'

Her mind went blank, as all her senses raced to deal with the collision of emotions that were firing along every nerve in her body.

Could they work?

Could they at least try?

The biggest part of her wanted to say yes – it really did. But losing him last time almost broke her. They were adults now. Different people. And she was so much wiser.

She'd forgiven him for leaving, but she wasn't sure she could forget. She'd loved him then, but would she love him again now? Until she knew that for certain, she wasn't sure it was a risk she was willing to take.

Thirty-four

Tom

It was a loud beep that woke him and his head sprang up, his eyes immediately darting to the monitor beside George's bed. Nothing was flashing, no alerts activated. Heart thudding, his gaze went to his grandfather's face, his hand to his grandfather's chest. George was warm. His chest was very slowly rising and falling. It took a moment for the relief to replace the anxiety that was coursing through him. George was okay. He was still with them.

Tom smiled, his grin widening when he turned his head to the side to see Chrissie curled up in the chair he'd slept in many times before. Someone must have come in during the night and put a blanket over her and she looked perfectly peaceful. He watched her sleep, unable to believe she was actually there. He hadn't dreamt the whole thing. It had happened. Chrissie was there. He had a son. A rush of adrenalin cursed through him. He had a son.

Another beep, and this time he realised it was coming from his phone. He stood up, stretched out his legs and fished his mobile out of the pocket of his jacket, which was hanging on a hook on the back of the door. He checked the time on the screen first: 6 a.m. He'd only been asleep for an hour.

They'd talked long into the night, covered the years, ironed out all the misunderstandings. They both knew now exactly where they were and that was right back at the beginning, with a fresh slate, and a wonderful son to bring up together. Even as the words had come out of his mouth, asking her if they could be more than friends and co-parents, he'd known it was a mistake. It was too soon. He'd put her on the spot and she'd declined to answer.

Watching her now, he had the same thought that he'd had last night. He could wait. As long as she and Ben were in his life, he could wait until he'd rebuilt her trust, until she knew that no matter what happened he'd be there for her.

It was the very least she deserved.

His gaze went to the phone screen again, to the source of the beep – a text from a number he didn't recognise.

Hey there, this is Shauna.

Of course. He'd given her his number and asked her to text in the morning.

He read on.

386

Did you sleep? I hope George has had a restful night and all is well. I know this makes me sound like I'm insatiably needy, but we are heading to the airport shortly. Would it be okay to stop by the hospital to say goodbye? We would be bringing a bribe of bagels and coffee. Please know that we won't be offended at all if this is a bad time or if you'd rather we didn't come. It was more than enough to meet you all yesterday and to know that I have family. It means the world to me.

Tom felt his jaws ache as he smiled. Amongst the tears and the difficult conversations last night, there had been so much laughter. His face hurt from the sharp increase in movement. So far, he was loving this dramatic increase in the size of his family.

He texted back.

That would be great. Look forward to bagels. Chrissie still here too. Xx

Great! Will bring breakfast x2. Thank you. Be there around 7 a.m. Xx

An image of Flora popped into his mind. She was quite a woman. He had a feeling she was going to be a lovely person to have in his life and he was looking forward to filling her in on the situation with Chrissie and Ben. He couldn't wait to tell the whole world.

He was only sorry George hadn't got that chance to spend time with Flora. Whatever happened between them was obviously water under a very ancient bridge.

Flora had come to make amends and he was sure George would have been willing to do that, too.

There was movement in the chair as Chrissie woke, stretched first, then opened her eyes and murmured a sleepy 'Good morning,' before reaching over and taking George's hand. God, she was beautiful. Only an hour's sleep in a chair, after a traumatic and emotional night, and he still thought she was the most gorgeous sight he'd ever seen. One that he could never, ever tire of looking at.

'Good morning, Mr Butler. I hope we didn't cause you a restless night with all our chatting,' she said softly, before speaking to Tom. 'Did I hear a phone beep?'

'Yes, it was Shauna, my cousin that we met last night. Still feels really weird saying that. They're going to stop by on the way to the airport to say goodbye.'

'I'm so glad she found you,' Chrissie said. 'Be nice for you to have more family now.'

'Nothing can beat the new member of my family that you introduced me to last night.'

'I keep thinking about how happy you made him,' Chrissie said. 'There's a part of me that feels so guilty for not finding you, for not making sure you were a part of his life before now, but I thought...' she paused, struggling to say it.

'You thought I didn't want him. Or you.'

Her nod was slow and sad. It was true.

'I'm so sorry,' he said again.

'You don't need to keep apologising,' she assured him and he knew she meant it. 'There was fault on my part, too. Hindsight. Nothing we can do to change it now.'

'I know,' he said. 'I just want us to be okay.'

'We are okay,' she promised, reaching for his hand and holding it, reassuring him.

Another beep on his phone, and he barely glanced at it, assuming it would be from Shauna again. It wasn't.

'It's from my dad,' he said. 'That can't be good.'

Chrissie didn't say a word.

Tom opened it and read it aloud. 'Any change?'

No "good morning". No civility. No apology that they left last night, or thanks for letting them stay in his home. Nothing.

'Christ, he is such an arse. Sometimes I really can't believe I'm related to him. You know, I'm pretty sure he only came back because he wants to ensure he gets the proceeds from George's estate.'

Chrissie looked puzzled. 'But why would they need the money? I thought they were loaded?'

Tom had asked himself the same question many times since Norry had turned up, and always came back to the same answer. 'They are. None of it makes any sense. My dad didn't bother to come back for his mother's funeral, yet he's turned up now. Let's face it, they were never close. I always felt so bad for Grandad. He tried so hard, but my dad could just never bring himself to care about anyone but himself.'

'Well he married the right person then. Definite compatibility there. My mum was no stranger to splashing out on the finer things in life after she married your dad. She loved all that. One day we were struggling to pay the rent, and the next she was decked out in head to toe Gucci. I hate speaking badly of anyone, but…'

'Grandad wouldn't mind. It was his greatest sadness, but he knew exactly what my dad was like. Said he reminded him of his own father and that wasn't a good thing.'

Chrissie leaned forward and took George's hand again. 'I'm sorry to hear all this, Mr Butler. I just want you to know that history isn't repeating itself. Your great-grandson, Ben, well, he's a lovely kid. He's kind and he doesn't have a malicious bone in his body. I wish you could spend time with him, I really do. I know you'd love him. He keeps his room much tidier than Tom ever did.'

'Hey! Don't malign me in front of my grandfather,' Tom joked. 'In his eyes I'm perfect. Isn't that right, Grandad?'

Laughing, Tom tossed the phone on the bedside unit without replying to Norry. Instead, he got up, opened the cupboard at the side of George's bed and took out a hairbrush and a facecloth. He ran the cloth under the tap, and then gently washed George's face as he did every morning. The nursing assistants had offered to do it for him, but it felt right that he should do it. George had been a very private man in life; Tom didn't want to take that from him now.

He patted George's face dry, then stroked his cheek. He didn't need shaving today. It had only been done yesterday and there was no growth as yet. Tom definitely thought it was slowing down. When George had come into hospital four weeks ago, he'd shaved every morning. Now it was only necessary every few days. He tried not to think about what that meant. He dropped the cloth back into the sink, then picked up the brush and ran it through George's hair.

'You take such good care of him,' Chrissie said quietly.

'He took such good care of me,' Tom replied simply.

Chrissie, still holding George's hand, was quiet for a moment before she asked, 'Do you want to be here alone with George? I don't want you to think I'm intruding. I would completely understand.'

He stopped, heart suddenly thudding once again. 'Do you want to go? Do you need to be home for Ben?'

She grinned. 'You obviously have no idea of the weekend routine of the teenage species. He won't be out of his bed until around eleven and even then, he'll drag his duvet down to the sofa, and he'll hide under it with a book or the TV for another hour. Val always has him on a Saturday because I'm usually at work, so she gives him until somewhere around noon, then her husband Don coerces him into doing something involving fresh air and exercise. He pretends to resist, but he loves it really. Today they were planning to go for a bike ride – Don is trying to get fitter – and then they'd bought tickets to see some superhero movie this afternoon. He'll want to see you, though.'

'Maybe I could stop by for a minute when I drop you home, then come over tonight for an hour or two?' he suggested, trying not to be pushy. The truth he never wanted to let Ben out of his sight ever again.

'Ben would love that.'

He really hoped that she would be happy about it, too.

'Do you have to go to work today?' he asked, hoping beyond hope that she didn't.

'No,' she said. 'Jen gave me the day off because of my big date last night. Didn't quite work out how we'd anticipated, did it?'

He managed to muffle his loud sigh of relief in a yawn. She didn't have to go. He didn't have to say goodbye.

'Don didn't know about that though, so he'd already gone ahead and bought the tickets for the cinema,' she explained.

'Then would it be okay if you stayed here with me for a while longer? I usually pop home for a shower and change my clothes, but I was going to leave it until later if that's okay?'

He didn't want to leave, he realised. George was here. Chrissie was here. There was nowhere else he'd rather be, apart from hanging out with his twelve year old son, but he wasn't out of bed yet.

There was a knock at the door, then it opened and Shauna, Flora and Lulu came in. There were hugs and kisses all round, before Shauna held up a bag of bagels and Lulu distributed the four cups of coffee that were precariously balanced on a cardboard cup holder. Flora, however, pulled a flask out of her bag.

'Please, Mrs McGinty, take this seat,' Chrissie said, standing up to let the older woman sit down.

'Thank you, pet. And Tom, thank you so much for letting me come here today. I was going to come this afternoon, but, well, truth is, I didn't sleep a wink last night. I just wanted to be back here with George. I don't want to miss a minute more with him because...'

Emotion blocked her words and she didn't finish the sentence. Instead, after a pause, she turned to George.

'Good morning, George. Don't be rolling your eyes under there. I told you already that I'm sentimental in my old age.'

The other four were all perched at the far side of the room now, leaning against the window ledge with their coffees.

'Thank you for delivering the luggage to my dad and his wife last night,' Tom said.

'No problem at all,' Shauna chirped, and he wouldn't have noticed anything untoward if he hadn't switched his glance to her friend Lulu at the very moment she gave Shauna a meaningful glance.

'Okay, I'm not usually great at picking up subliminal messages, but I'm sensing something here. Am I wrong?' Tom probed.

'Lulu!' Shauna rebuked her, then switched back to Tom. 'I'm sorry. Her feelings are always written all over her face. You've no idea how much trouble that's got us into over the course of our lives. My gran, Annie, used to say...'

Lulu butted in, 'I believe her exact terminology was that I'd be "shite at poker".'

Flora chuckled. 'Did you hear that, George? Doesn't that just sound like our Annie?'

Chrissie took up the conversation. 'So, go on then, confess all. What did Norry and Rosemary do to cause that look from Poker Face?' she teased Lulu.

Shauna looked like the ground could swallow her up. 'I'm sure it was just a misunderstanding and—'

Lulu butted in again. 'They were rude to Flora and practically accused us of being fraudsters that were after George's money.'

'Lulu!' Shauna chided her again. 'You can't say things like that. I've just met my family and they're going to take out a restraining order if you carry on.'

'I promise it's fine,' Tom said. 'It actually makes it much easier to explain. My father, well, let's just say he and I are not close. Nor was he close to my grandad. George and I hadn't seen him for twelve years until he came back yesterday. To be honest, I wish he hadn't bothered turning up at all.'

'That's a bit of a relief to hear you say that actually, because Lulu is right, they were so rude. Especially to Flora.'

'Nothing I couldn't handle, pet,' Flora piped in from over at the other side of the bed.

Tom carried on. 'And the woman with him, my stepmother...' he glanced at Chrissie, 'let's just say they deserve each other.'

'Oh, thank God you feel that way,' Shauna said. 'Because she was downright abrasive.'

'She was a complete cow,' Lulu confirmed. 'Have you met her?' she asked Chrissie.

'Indeed I have,' Chrissie replied casually. 'She's my mother.'

Thirty-five

Shauna

'Oh sweet Jesus,' Shauna blurted out. 'I'm so sorry. I didn't realise that you were related to her. I thought that...' She gave up and went with, 'I am so confused right now.' She rounded on Lulu. 'They are going to ban us from the whole of Scotland and it'll be your fault.'

Lulu gave her customary shrug and Shauna felt the knot of mortification grow in her gut. She'd just totally embarrassed that poor woman and there was no way of taking it back. She glared at Lulu. It was definitely time to trade her in for a friend with some concept of tact.

'No, no, it's fine,' Chrissie assured her. 'I'm not offended. In fact, I'd probably have avoided you at all costs if you'd come here gushing about how sweet my mother was.'

'But...' Shauna's eyes darted from Tom to Chrissie, back to Tom, clearly trying to work out the dynamics. 'Okay, you're going to have to explain this to me because I'm not following all the family ties.'

Chrissie laughed. 'We definitely don't have a conventional family tree. Tom and I dated when we were teenagers. We lived next door to each other. Our parents had an affair, and ended up marrying, then moved to Australia.'

Shauna was fairly sure she had a grasp of it now. Sort of. 'And now you're...?'

'Now we're friends,' Chrissie answered.

'Ah, okay. That's nice that you keep in touch. What age is your son?' she said to Chrissie, trying to win her over with charm and interest so that her new cousin would not delete her from his contacts list the minute she stepped on the plane.

'Our son...' Chrissie said, smiling as she gestured to Tom. 'He's twelve.'

Shauna was astonished. Clearly she didn't have a grasp of it after all.

'We're definitely coming back here. I love it,' Lulu interjected, revelling in the intrigue.

'Perhaps we can bring Ben down to London to meet you all,' Chrissie suggested.

Shauna noticed that Tom beamed when Chrissie said that. There was definitely more to this story. She couldn't wait to hear about it.

'That would be great. My daughter Beth would love it. She's eight, but she thinks she's at least twelve, so they'd get on well.' She thought some more about what Chrissie and Tom had said about their parents. 'It's nice that your parents came back to be with your father when he's ill though. Especially given their circumstances,' she offered, trying to take the middle ground, desperate not to rock the boat again. Only... Tom and Chrissie were staring at her again, like she'd just said something significant.

'What circumstances?' Chrissie asked, with definite meaning.

'Nothing. I just...' Oh, bollocks. Bollocks. Bollocks. Why did she feel like she'd put her foot in it again? 'We were in the same lift as them yesterday, before we were formally introduced...' Lulu began, ignoring Shauna's panicked glare. 'And they were arguing with each other because your dad said they didn't have the money for a hotel. Your mum,' Lulu said, to Chrissie now, 'made it clear she wasn't happy about being here.'

Shauna slapped her hand to her forehead, despairing that Lulu was stirring things up by being woefully indiscreet.

'What?' Lulu said, her face a picture of innocence. 'They were rude to Flora and you know Annie would have wiped the floor with that woman.'

'She's right,' Shauna conceded, just as an alarm pinged on her phone. 'That's our cue to get to the airport. Which is just as well, because it means Lulu can't defame anyone else in your family,' Shauna quipped. 'Please keep in touch,' she said. 'I'm coming back up next week or the week after to see Flora. I've left it open because I know she wants to be here as much as possible. You know I'll be thinking about you all.' She put the coffee cup in the bin, and hugged Tom and Chrissie, before crossing to Flora. 'Aunt Flora, Lulu and I have to go now.'

Flora stood up and hugged them tightly in turn. 'Thank you so much for coming here, for giving me back George, for giving me all of this. You'll never know how much this has meant to me. You haven't even left and I'm so looking forward to seeing you again.'

While Lulu was saying her goodbyes, Shauna leant down and kissed her uncle on the forehead. 'Goodbye, Uncle George, I'm so thankful I got to meet you,' she whispered. 'Please say hello to my gran when you see her. Tell her how much I miss her. I think you two are going to have a great time.'

With another hug for Flora, and another wave for Chrissie and Tom, they slipped out of the door.

In the lift, Shauna exhaled, feeling her lungs deflate.

'This has been, without a doubt, the craziest, most unexpected twenty-four hours of my life,' she announced truthfully. 'And I say that as someone who has been your friend for over thirty years and put up with a whole load of crazy and unexpected.'

'Good point,' Lulu concurred.

Shauna softened and put her arm around Lulu's shoulders. 'Thank you for coming. It wouldn't have been the same without you. You know how much I love you.'

'I do,' Lulu chirped. 'But I'm very aware I just slipped down the pecking order under Flora. Don't worry, I can live with it.'

The doors slid open and Shauna talked as they walked. 'I'm so grateful we found her. I think I loved her on sight. Annie will either be spitting furiously at me for consorting with her former foe or over the moon that we've met.'

'I'm pretty sure she'll be loving it,' Lulu said, as they reached the taxi, where John was waiting for them. He'd clocked off at midnight last night and then insisted on coming back this morning to pick them up at the hotel. 'I'll just take you to the hospital and the airport and I'll get back for a wee kip afterwards,' he'd insisted. Shauna was pretty sure he just wanted to see how it all worked out and get the latest developments, but she would be eternally grateful to him for taking such good care of them.

The roads were quiet, so they made it to Glasgow Airport in under fifteen minutes. Shauna and Lulu hugged him at the drop off point.

'We can't thank you enough,' Shauna said. 'You've been fantastic.'

'Aye, that's the effect I have on women,' he joked. 'If the real Lulu had met me back in the day, I'd have swept her off her feet.' He pulled their bags out of the boot. 'Now, remember to give me a shout when you come back. And I've given your Aunt Flora my number, so she can call on me any time.'

'You're lovely, you know that?'

'Don't tell anyone. I've got a hard man image to maintain. Right, off you go then.' He sat until just before they turned out of the car park and gave them one last wave.

The queue for security held them up for twenty minutes or so, but they still made it through in time to do a dash around the shops for some extra stocking fillers for Beth and then stop for a coffee. They found an empty table in the corner of the café.

Shauna opened her phone to view another text from Beth. She was standing between a large Goofy and Pluto and the three of them were giving a thumbs up to the camera. She showed the picture to Lulu.

'Bugger. I think I'm losing the "favourite aunt" status. Justin Bieber is definitely going to have to up his security because I think he's my last hope of reclaiming her.'

Shauna laughed, then yawned, suddenly exhausted. They'd spent an hour at Flora's last night, then they'd headed back to the hotel, where they'd been too wired from the events of the day to sleep. They'd ended up sitting up, dissecting the day, until after 4 a.m. Shauna had been stunned when Flora had called her at 6 a.m. to ask them to pick her up on the way to the hospital.

'Are you sure, Aunt Flora? You must be exhausted. You've had so little sleep. Don't you want to wait and go over later?' she'd asked.

'Shauna, dear, the two men I love most in the world are both lying in a building miles away from me. What's the point of me sitting in this house alone when I can be with them? I'll sit with George until visiting hours on Arthur's ward, then I'll go back over to George until evening visiting. That poor boy Tom looks exhausted and he's been handling everything on his own. If I can help him, then I'd like to be there. I've got a lot to make up for,' she'd insisted.

Shauna had capitulated and picked her up. In truth, she was delighted to get to spend as much time with Flora as possible.

'Seems bizarre now to think that we only landed here twenty-four hours ago with nothing but two letters to help us find my family. Now we know Flora and George, and Tom and Chrissie.'

'And the other two, but I don't think we'll be sending them postcards,' Lulu interjected.

'Nope, think we'll settle for the nice ones. I'm so glad we came, but I just wish we'd done it sooner, while George was still okay. I'd love to have talked to him and heard all his stories. I don't want to be morbid, but let's come back for George's funeral. I'd like to be there,' Shauna said.

'Me too,' Lulu agreed. 'For Flora, and for Annie, too.' Lulu stirred her coffee with her finger. 'Has it helped?'

'What do you mean?'

Lulu sighed. 'Shauna, since you lost Colm, it's like you've been immersed in a well of sadness. You put on a happy face for Beth, and for us, but you've been treading water, barely existing,' she said, with uncharacteristic insight and tenderness.

Shauna thought for a moment. 'I think I've just been drifting, feeling disconnected. Annie was always my anchor, that older woman I needed in my life to go to, to ask for advice, to share things with. After she was gone I realised how much I missed having that person there, someone who had been there, done it all, and could steer me through things. When Colm died, the hole I'd fallen into just got even deeper. You were all brilliant, and I love you for every single thing you've done to support me. But I would have leaned on Annie too when I lost Colm and she would have been the person who got me through that because she'd been widowed herself. I know that I've got you, and Beth, but I've just felt such a void in losing them both. It was like I was the only person left in my family and I just felt I didn't belong to anyone. I've no idea how things will turn out with Flora, but I feel so much better that I'll have her there, that I know her. I know it sounds crazy, but I'm choosing to believe that Annie orchestrated this whole thing to give me the rest of the people I need in my life.'

'I don't think it was Annie,' Lulu said.

'Why not?'

'Because there would have been line dancing involved if she was behind it.'

Two suits at a nearby table looked on disapprovingly as Shauna and Lulu had an outburst of hilarity.

'You're absolutely right,' Shauna chucked, before going on. 'It's weird, but I was dreading Christmas before I came here. It's hard without Colm and I try to stay cheery the whole time for Beth, but inside...'

'I know,' Lulu said, taking her hand.

'But now I feel like we can have things to look forward to. We'll have Christmas in Richmond as always this year, but maybe next year we can all come up here and celebrate with the Scottish side of the family.'

'Why wait?'

'What?'

'Fuck it, why wait? We can speak to Rosie when we get back, but all we were going to do was hang out at my house for three days of Quality Street and competitive board games. Why don't we just come back up here instead? It can be our new thing.'

'Yes! Oh bugger, Lu, you're brilliant. You sure you don't mind?'

'Nope! As long as we can stay for Hogmanay too. I'm so down with men in kilts.'

'Yes, yes, fecking yes!'

The two blokes glanced over again, appalled that she might be doing a Meg Ryan.

'I'll find us a house near Flora, I don't even care what it costs. We can fly back tomorrow or the next day.' Excitement was raising Shauna's volume with every word. 'I'll get it all sorted as soon as we touch down.' She reached over and spontaneously hugged Lulu, much to her mock disgust.

'That's our gate up,' Shauna said, as she caught sight of the board overhead.

They both rose, and as Lulu was passing the table of disapproval, she gave them a wink. 'You know, you two really need to laugh more.'

On the plane, they settled into their seats. Shauna stared out of the window, at her gran's home town, and felt such a pull of belonging that she knew, with absolutely no doubt at all, that Annie was there with her.

'Thanks, Gran,' she whispered. 'And goodbye Glasgow. It's been a blast. I'll be back before you know I'm gone.'

Thirty-six

George

It was the clacking sound that woke me. It took me a minute to pinpoint it, but eventually I recognised it from the far away days of my childhood. Knitting needles. Flora was sitting next to me, no doubt working furiously on her latest creation. My mother used to do the same, every day of her life, before my dad came home from work. He couldn't be doing with the noise of it, so she put it away the minute he crossed the threshold. I'd always found the rhythm of it comforting, relaxing, and that is the effect it is having on me now.

'My mother knitted all her days,' Flora is saying, just as Chrissie tells them she's nipping out to get more tea for everyone.

'Tell me about her,' Tom replies, and Flora begins to talk of my ma, of our childhood, of the woman that raised us, for good and for bad.

Tom asks questions, but mostly he listens to tales that I remember so well.

She is telling them about my da's ferocious temper, when I hear the door open and I assume it's Chrissie returning.

But no.

'He's still here then?' says the voice, and don't think I miss the exasperation in his tone. Norry. And I know he's talking about me. What an arse, as our Annie would have said.

'Seriously, dad? That's what you come in with?' That's Tom, and he doesn't sound a bit pleased. The tension in the room is palpable and my nerve endings absorb it all.

'Good timing,' Flora says, trying to be breezy about it. 'I was just going to nip downstairs and drop in some things for my Arthur. Bye, George – I'm off to share all this excitement with the other man in my life now, but I'll be back later.'

She was always the diplomatic one, our Flora, but I didn't miss her overtone of distaste. I hear her footsteps fade and the door close behind her.

'You didn't return my text,' Norry says, all het up. 'So I figured he'd gone. I've come right over here, not even had a bit of breakfast yet, and it's been a waste of time.'

'Told you it would be,' Rosemary moans.

'A waste of time? Are you kidding me?' Tom snaps, and I can hear that he is seething. 'Nothing about being here is a waste of time. Here is the only place you should even think about being right now.'

'Just sitting here, waiting? I don't think so,' says Rosemary.

At that the door opens again. 'I could only get coff—' Chrissie. And she's suddenly stopped speaking. There is a pause before she starts again. 'Hello Rosemary. Norry. Tom, I'm just going to reverse right back out of this door. Let me know when they've left.' I smile inside at the gumption in her voice and words. Good on her.

'What kind of way is that to greet your mother?' Norry chides her. 'After not having the decency to keep in touch with her all these years?'

'After everything I did for you,' Rosemary adds, petulance ripping out of her.

'Don't you ever...' Tom begins.

Chrissie speaks over him though. Good on the lass. 'It's okay, Tom,' she says calmly, before the direction of her voice changes. 'Norry, don't you dare reprimand or criticise me. Not that it matters, because please know that I care not a single toss about what you and this woman think of me. And, Mother, after everything you did for me? You're not worth my time, and I owe you no explanation, but here's what I'll give you. When I was eighteen years old and I told you I was pregnant, you cut me off. Here's what happened next. I had a beautiful boy, I had a happy life, and now Tom and I are finally – with absolutely no thanks to your devious, back-stabbing behaviour – going to bring him up together. I know now what a mother is, and you are far from fulfilling the criteria. So don't speak to me, don't lecture me, don't try to rewrite history, for you are nothing to me and my son, and that will never change.'

'You f—' Norry begins.

There is a shuffle – my Tom getting to his feet I think. Dear God, I want to open my eyes and see this.

'Say it, Dad. Go on, say it. Because I can't tell you how much I want you to give me an excuse to knock you out. And truthfully, I think Grandad would approve.'

Aye, I would, son.

There is a pause. Norry must have backed down. Bullies always do.

'Let me lay this out for you,' Tom says. 'I hoped you were coming back here to make your peace and pay your respects to Grandad. If that's true, Chrissie and I will leave for now and let you have a few hours with him today. But somehow I don't think that's the case here. I think you've come back to make sure you benefit from Grandad's estate. Let me tell you right now, there isn't one. Nothing. Grandad signed everything over to me many years ago and now that will all go to my son. I won't be taking a penny of it and neither will you.'

'That's not bloody right! I'll be getting a lawyer...' Norry is spitting his words out and I bet his face is purple. Bloody serves him right.

'Please do. He'll tell you there's not a thing you can change, because everything was done properly and so

409

long ago that there's no way to challenge it. But you feel free, if you want to waste your money on legal bills – or don't you have any money left?'

Tom has gone right to the crux of it.

'That's it, isn't it? You've blown it all.'

'There was an investment that went wrong, and well...'

Rosemary pipes in, all spit and arrogance. 'You don't need to explain yourself to him, Norry. George's money should be yours and we'll be fighting for it.'

Go on, Tom – don't you dare let her away with that.

'You go right ahead, Rosemary,' Tom tells her. 'As I said, you'll be wasting your time. As for now, though, you don't belong here. Whether my dad stays to see Grandad's final hours or not, you're not welcome. You never cared for Grandad, and you never cared for Chrissie. More than that, your actions cost me twelve years of not knowing I had a son, of leaving Chrissie alone to raise him. Get out of this room and don't you dare come back, because I never, ever want to see your miserable face again.'

'Are you going to let him speak to me like that?' she wails, outraged, to her husband.

'Bugger this. Let's get out of here,' Norry spits.

'Dad, if you leave, don't come back, because then I'll know you only came for what you could get and not for Grandad.'

That's it, Tom, you tell him, son.

More movement and then Norry's voice, moving away.

'Don't think for a second you'll get it all,' he challenges again. 'Call me when this is done.'

'So now I know,' Tom says, and I can hear the sadness overlaying the anger in his voice. 'Don't bother going back to my flat for your things, I'll have a friend bring them to the downstairs lobby of the building. You're a disgusting specimen of a man and you're no longer any father to me.'

'Fuck it,' Norry says. 'You were always your mother's son anyway.'

'And I've never been more glad of it.'

The door opens again, and then their footsteps tell me they are gone.

That's where we are now. Right now. Just Tom, Chrissie and me.

'I just need to make a quick call,' Tom is saying. 'I'll get Zoe to nip to my flat and take their stuff down. They won't have unpacked in such a short time. I know it's pathetic, but I don't want them going back to my house and going through my things.'

'Zoe, your ex as of yesterday?' That seems to amuse her.

'Yeah, I know, sounds crazy, but we were friends for years before we were more, and she'll do this for me. She lives just around the corner and she's a good person.

She'll understand. I may have to get her an incredible Christmas present though.'

He leaves the room to make his call and I feel Chrissie sit back down in the big chair to my right, then her hand takes mine.

'I don't know if you can hear me, Mr Butler, but if you can, then I just want you to know that I will look after Tom. Both Ben and I will make sure he's happy, I promise. Ben will adore him and I... well, I love him, too. Although, I'm guessing if you've been listening to all this you'll know that already.'

With just those words, the lass wipes away the shame I've been feeling about how I've treated her and it's replaced with peace and gratitude.

A few minutes later Tom comes back into the room, and as he relays his phone conversation to Chrissie, I realise something.

It's selfish of me, I know, but I'm not ready to go yet.

Only a few hours ago, I told my Betty to come for me, and now I'm hoping she'll leave me as I am for a little while longer.

Flora will be back shortly and she'll be returning tomorrow, and every day after that. There is so much I want to hear about her life and the decades that have gone by. I know my Betty won't mind.

The boy, Ben... I've only just met him and I can't bear the thought of causing him sadness by leaving just yet. I'd like to know him better. Like I said, he sounds just like our Tom did when he was that age, and Tom reckons he looks just like him. Imagine that.

There's no point wishing for the things that cannot be. I can't recover from this. I can't have a reprieve that will allow me to spend time with the youngster and build a relationship with him. Or that will allow me to sit with Flora, in our dotage, swapping stories of our lives and making up for the time that was lost. Knowing that I will be with Betty and Annie again gives me so much happiness and I will gladly take that journey when the time comes. However, the last few hours have given me something to live a little longer for.

I've lost track of time, but I think it will be Christmas Day soon, maybe three or four days away.

I do hope with all my heart that I can wait a while, that I can hear a little more, that I can feel their hands touching mine through a few more days and nights.

So Betty, my love, my darling. I am longing to be with you with every fibre of my heart. And Annie, you never were one for patience. But I ask you both, to please, please wait for just one more Christmas so that I can come to you with more to tell of the loved ones we've left behind.

Tom is back in the room, and Chrissie is speaking to him now. 'I've never been prouder of you,' she is saying, with a tenderness that could make me weep.

'I was about to say the same thing,' Tom replies. God, he still loves this lass. I can hear it clear as day. 'It all needed to be said, for George, for me, and for you and Ben. I didn't stick by you once before, that won't happen again. Not ever. No matter how things turn out for us.'

I'm beyond proud of the man that boy has become. Far better than me and a thousand times the character of his father.

There's another silence and I wish I could see their faces, read their thoughts.

'I've been thinking about what you said earlier,' Chrissie tells him and I try to think, to go back, but the days and nights are blending together and I'm not sure what she means. Damn this failing body and mind.

'About us, about our future together,' she goes on, and I'm grateful for the clarity.

'I know I shouldn't have said it,' Tom tells her. 'We'll talk about that again when you're ready.'

There's movement, and I feel Tom sitting down next to her, in the other chair to my right.

'I'm ready now,' she tells him. 'I love you. Always. Only you.'

Another sound. A kiss.

I feel my fading heart swell inside my chest and I know now that when I go, today, tomorrow, or the next day, I'll go a happy man.

A few moments later I feel Tom's hand on mine again.

'Grandad, I hope you heard all that,' he says, and I hear his voice choke with emotion.

414

It takes everything I've got, but one last time, just for a second, I manage to open my eyes and smile.

Epilogue

January 7th, 2019

The kitchen in George's house was as busy as it had ever been. The funeral had been a celebration of life and many tears had been shed, but now, hours later, there was only laughter and tales of great days gone by and talk of more to come.

At the table, Flora sat with Arthur beside her in a wheelchair, next to Shauna and Lulu. They were chatting to Tom's friend, Zoe, who had come back to the house with the family at Tom's request. She would be taking over from Davie as Tom's partner in the firm, now that Davie had decided his future lay in New York. At least the dating scene there would be more forgiving of his ways.

Val and her husband Don, and Josie and Liv, were over by the breakfast bar, still chatting about the incredible twist of fate that had brought two very different strands of their lives together. Josie had finally met Tom and adored him on sight, although she had informed him he would be on a probation period until she decided whether he was good enough for Chrissie and Ben. He'd promised he was up to the task.

Ben and Beth were sitting next to each other on the kitchen worktop, both huddled over a game they were playing together on the new iPads they'd both got for Christmas. Beth's was a gift from her mother, and came with a bejazzled Justin Beiber case from Auntie Lulu, while Ben's was his first ever gift from his father.

The two kids had met on Christmas Eve. Shauna and Beth, Lulu and her husband, Dan, and Rosie and her boyfriend, Jude, had touched down at Glasgow Airport and gone to a beautiful old four bedroom cottage they'd managed to rent for the week thanks to a last minute cancellation. Shauna and Lulu had spent a couple of hours at the hospital that night, then they'd all met at George Square, to drink in the wonderful spectacle of the Christmas lights and decorations. They'd loved it all, and Shauna was grateful that she was able to join Flora, Tom and Chrissie at George's bedside when he drew his last breath.

Norry and Rosemary were not present. They'd returned to Australia on the same day that Tom had challenged them in the hospital. They hadn't been seen or heard from since and they weren't missed.

Still dressed in funereal black, Tom and Chrissie were standing by the back door, the one he'd run in and out of since he was a toddler. On Chrissie's wrist was a bangle, the one that Tom had bought her when they first fell in love all those years ago. On the inside were the words, "*Chrissie, I love you now and always. T xx*"

Turns out that was true.

Tom put down his glass, but his other hand still held on to the love of his life. He cleared his throat. 'Everyone, I'd just like to say thank you to you all for being here. Since my grandad died on Boxing Day, I have missed him every minute of every day, but I know that he will be looking down on us right now.

'I still find it hard to believe that so much has changed in the last three weeks. Back then, George and I had each other, but we thought we were the last of our family. I know how thrilled he will be to see that isn't the case. Ben, he would have loved you and he'd be so proud that you are his great-grandson.

'I will carry him with me always, just as Shauna has Annie. And Flora, you now have us all.

'George was the wisest, kindest, most caring man I have ever known. He was funny, he was strong, and always tried his very best to do the right thing. He was a man of decency and a man of honour. He wasn't perfect, but then none of us are. However, he taught me what it means to care for and protect the people you love and I hope I can repay him by doing the same with the family we are now.

'I love you all and thank you for being here today as we said goodbye to him.'

He lifted his glass.

'To George Thomas Butler, may he rest in as much peace as my gran, Betty, and his sister, Annie, are willing to give him.'

When the rousing cheer was over and the conversations reignited, Tom leant down so that only Chrissie could hear his words.

'George told me to sell this house when I was ready, but I've decided to keep it and rent it out, so one day Ben can decide what he wants to do with it.'

'Are you sure? Would your grandad be okay with that?'

Tom looked over at his son, then back to the only woman he had ever loved. His family. He was making plans for their future, taking care of the people who mattered. And he knew that George Thomas Butler would definitely have approved.

Acknowledgement

It continues to be an absolute joy to work with the fabulous, inspiring and infinitely supportive Caroline Ridding, and the awesome team at Aria. Thank you for all you do.

Endless gratitude to Jan and Lyndsay, who are always on hand with laughs and cakes that they assure me are calorie-free.

And to Liz, Gillian and Gemma, who are family, but also three of my favourite people.

Finally, as always, buckets of love to my guys, J, C & B who made me approximately 2364 cups of tea in the making of the book. Gents, it must be time to put the kettle on…

Love,
Shari xx

HELLO FROM ARIA

We hope you enjoyed this book! Let us know, we'd love to hear from you.

We are Aria, a dynamic digital-first fiction imprint from award-winning independent publishers Head of Zeus. At heart, we're avid readers committed to publishing exactly the kind of books we love to read — from romance and sagas to crime, thrillers and historical adventures. Visit us online and discover a community of like-minded fiction fans!

We're also on the look out for tomorrow's superstar authors. So, if you're a budding writer looking for a publisher, we'd love to hear from you. You can submit your book online at ariafiction.com/we-want-read-your-book

You can find us at:
Email: aria@headofzeus.com
Website: www.ariafiction.com
Submissions: www.ariafiction.com/we-want-read-your-book
Facebook: @ariafiction
Twitter: @Aria_Fiction
Instagram: @ariafiction